Praise for *Blink of an Eye*

"William Cohen's finest work yet . . . riveting, chilling, and an all-too-real premise. From its engrossing start to his extraordinary climax, this is one book where the pages seem to turn themselves."

—Richard North Patterson,
New York Times bestselling author of
In the Name of Honor

"Cohen's book, which gains a lot presumably from the first-hand knowledge of Secretary Cohen, allows you to start off the New Year not with a whimper but a bang."
—*All Things Considered* (NPR)

"Former secretary of defense William S. Cohen has published this, his second novel, and struck terrifying gold. *Blink of an Eye* compellingly presents a nightmare nuclear scenario that has kept national security professionals and senior political leadership awake nights since September 11, 2001. . . . Cohen brings to his novel the intimate knowledge of a longtime Washington insider and veteran of countless high-level meetings, negotiations, and political crises."—*The American Spectator*

"There is something of the Ayn Rand in Mr. Cohen."
—*The Wall Street Journal*

"A riveting, intense story told by a man who understands this potential threat better than anyone else in America! Guaranteed to make you think twice about just how safe we are!"   —Gen. Hugh Shelton, U.S. Army (Ret.),
14th chairman, Joint Chiefs of Staff,
and author of *Without Hesitation*

Forge Books By William S. Cohen

Dragon Fire
Blink of an Eye

BLINK
OF AN
EYE

WILLIAM S. COHEN

A TOM DOHERTY ASSOCIATES BOOK | NEW YORK

This is a work of fiction. All of the characters, organizations, and events portrayed in this novel are either products of the author's imagination or are used fictitiously.

BLINK OF AN EYE

A Forge Book
Published by Tom Doherty Associates, LLC
175 Fifth Avenue
New York, NY 10010

www.tor-forge.com

Forge® is a registered trademark of Tom Doherty Associates, LLC.

ISBN 978-0-7653-6608-5

First Edition: November 2011
First Mass Market Edition: November 2012

Printed in the United States of America

0 9 8 7 6 5 4 3 2 1

To Velvet
Smooth, beautiful, and dangerous

Historians report that in 1914, with most of the world already plunged in war, Prince Bülow, the former German chancellor, said to the then Chancellor Bethmann-Hollweg: "How did it all happen?" And Bethmann-Hollweg replied, "Ah, if only one knew!"

If this planet is ever ravaged by nuclear war . . . if the survivors of that devastation can then endure the fire, poison, chaos, and catastrophe, I do not want one of those survivors to ask another, "How did it all happen?" and to receive the incredible reply, "Ah, if only one knew!"

PRESIDENT JOHN F. KENNEDY,
UNIVERSITY OF MAINE, OCTOBER 19, 1963

JUNE

Ned Winslow, Google News Network's best-known correspondent, stood at the edge of a dusty parade ground in his familiar pose—white shirt, sleeves rolled up, hair mussed, one hand clutching a microphone, the other one pointing. Viewers were used to seeing him grimly pointing toward the wreckage produced by another suicide bombing. But today he was smiling and pointing to arrays of soldiers, Americans in ranks on one side, Iraqis lined up on the other side. Between them was a tall pole with an American flag snapping in the breeze.

The camera swung away from Winslow to the flagpole. The American flag came briskly down to the waiting hands of two American soldiers. Two Iraqi soldiers stepped forward to raise their flag as GNN SPECIAL REPORT: GOODBYE, IRAQ ran across the bottom of the screen.

"Yes, the last of the troops are going. As you know, the combat troops left little more than a year ago, leaving behind fifty thousand soldiers who were designated as noncombat and given "advisory and assistance" missions. These are those soldiers, hauling down the flag, handing Iraq over to the Iraqis."

. . .

Among the millions of screens showing GNN's "Good-
bye, Iraq" coverage was a large screen on a wall in the
library of a mansion on a hill that rose from the Con-
necticut shore of Long Island Sound. The owner of the
mansion watched from the depth of a gray leather chair.
He was alone in the room.

"Yes, goodbye," he whispered. "Goodbye to America."
He walked to a long mahogany table that served as his
desk, opened the drawer, and reached for a cell phone. He
hesitated for a moment, put down the phone, and resumed
looking at the screen.

Live appeared on the upper right of the screen. The view
changed to a seascape of docks, small boats, and landing
craft.

Winslow now stood in one of the landing craft. "Within
minutes of the flag-raising ceremony earlier today," he
said, "American troops here in Basra began boarding
landing craft like this one. Now all the ceremonies are
over and we are bringing you the final act. They have
handed over responsibility to the Iraqi Army and we are
on our way out."

The camera panned to the grinning soldiers surrounding Winslow. They wore their usual camouflage combat
uniforms and caps instead of helmets. They did not carry
weapons or backpacks. Piled around the craft were duf-
fel bags bearing soldiers' stenciled names.

"We're leaving via the port of Basra and heading for
the USS *Elkton,* an amphibious transport," Winslow said
as the camera aimed toward the gray silhouette of a ship,
about half a mile offshore.

Winslow's British accent sometimes strayed toward
donnish. But he always leavened it with a sardonic air that

reached out to his audience, as if urging them to connive with him in telling the story. He had the confident look of a correspondent who knows he is trusted.

"In her enormous hold, the *Elkton* can accommodate a fleet of amphibious vessels like this one, along with about four hundred troops—a small percentage of the thousands of U.S. combat troops leaving Iraq. Others have been flying out of Kuwait in transport planes or leaving by sea, as we are—in the last wave. The boats around us are U.S. landing craft like this one and local port lighters, slim little boats carrying supplies to the *Elkton*.

"Welcome to Goodbye Day," Winslow continued. "Yes, it's Goodbye Day for U.S. forces in Iraq. A personal note. I was here—here in Basra—for the start, in March 2003, when it all began." A few moments of taped battle scenes appeared behind Winslow, fading as he said, "And now, on this momentous day, I am here again."

The landing craft was close to the *Elkton* when the camera suddenly shifted from Winslow, drawn to the image of a boat that was pulling away from the others, its frothy wake spreading into a broad V.

Winslow kept speaking: "In this ship, and in many more, the last American soldiers are leaving this war-torn land that the United States invaded in March 2003. And today—" Noticing the speeding boat, Winslow turned his head and interrupted himself. "That boat . . . What's happening?"

The camera focused on the speeding boat, now within one hundred yards of the *Elkton*. The camera switched to a telescopic lens that zoomed down on the boat. A new image filled the screen: a green-hulled boat, a bearded man, black-hooded, crouched over the steering wheel in the bow; another man at the stern, clutching a weapon.

"Jesus!" Winslow, off-camera, exclaimed. "He's got an RPG! Looks like he's aiming it at us!" A billow of smoke erupted from the rocket launcher.

In a blurring whirl, the image of the boat vanished from the screen. The horizon tilted, as the helmsman sharply swung the landing craft away from the speeding boat. "Get it!" Winslow yelled at the cameraman. "Get the boat!"

The camera turned back to the boat, which was alongside the *Elkton*. In the image, the ship's gray hull loomed large. The boat veered, striking the hull, near the *Elkton*'s bow.

On camera, the roar of an explosion. A cloud of smoke. A jagged hole in the hull. The sea rushing in. Bodies in blue shirts and dungarees bobbing in the sea.

In the Connecticut mansion, the man stood and picked up the phone again, his eyes never leaving the screen.

"They will pay for this," he said aloud. He punched a number, waited a moment, and spoke rapidly, his voice gruff and angry.

He lived amid one of the great private art collections in America. The paintings in the library, his favorite room, reflected his eclectic taste: On one wall, a Jean-Baptiste-Camille Corot, his colors merging sea and sunset and hinting at the impressionists to come. On another wall, a tranquil seated nude by Henri Matisse, known not so much for its soft beauty as for its price at a Sotheby's auction: $41 million, topping the bid of the Museum of Modern Art.

The library's south wall was a window on the Sound, framing an ever-changing view of sea and sky—"the greatest art in this room," he inevitably said to his rare visitor. At the moment, the clouds were darkening.

. . .

On screen, the camera was focused on the *Elkton*. Sailors jumped into the sea to recover the dead and wounded. Helmeted, shouting men appeared along the deck, waving weapons.

Winslow's landing craft swung around, as did all the other boats and landing craft. "We're heading back to shore," Winslow said "The RPG missed us. We're all okay." The camera swept around the craft, showing the soldiers' faces as they tried to take in what they had just seen.

Winslow hated disseminating to the world the sight of America's soldiers at their most vulnerable and desperate moments, but he had no choice. He was a professional journalist, one of the very best in the business, and for him, there were no holidays from tragedy or history. As he and his crew headed back toward shore, he continued to describe the attack and the desperate effort being made by those aboard the *Elkton* to save their comrades and their ship.

Suddenly, the on-screen image changed. The unfamiliar face of a young, frazzled-looking woman appeared at a newsroom desk. GNN REPORT: TERROR AT SEA scrolled across the bottom of the screen, as it would for many days to come. "GNN has just learned that the suicide boat that struck the *Elkton* is of Iranian origin," the woman said, her voice quivering. "It's a kind of boat called a Bladerunner. The original, British-built Bladerunner has a top speed of sixty-five knots per hour and can carry one or two Russian-made supertorpedoes." She looked down at the sheet of paper in her hand. "The source of this information is said to be highly reliable."

2

President Blake Oxley was seated at the table in the conference room of Air Force One, thirty-five thousand feet over Missouri when his chief of staff, Ray Quinlan, opened the door and shouted, "Put on the television!"

Oxley looked up from a lined yellow pad, picked up a remote, and aimed it at the wall in front of him. One of the screens lighted up, but all that appeared were wavy white lines. He switched to other channels and saw the same image.

He turned to Quinlan. "What the hell is going on?" he said. Quinlan was a large, curly-haired man, whose height and width made him look rectangular. He wore a maroon-and-gold Boston College sweatshirt, maroon sweatpants, and sneakers of an indeterminate color. Big as he was, he moved as swiftly and smoothly as a dancer.

Oxley's press secretary, Stephanie Griffith, appeared next to Quinlan at the open door of the conference room, the central space of the presidential suite. The table dominated the rectangular room. Curtained portholes ran along one wall. On the three other walls were rectangular screens.

"Iraq," she said. "Attack on a ship. One of our ships."

A Secret Service agent shouldered his way past them and stood between them and the President. "We have temporarily lost some communications, Mr. President," the agent said. "The pilot ordered electronic countermeasures. We have a tech figuring a way to clear for television signals." The agent closed the door and stood before it.

The phone console next to Oxley rang and a light lit in the row of direct-line buttons. Next to each small light was a title. This one was FALCONE, for the national security advisor, Sean Falcone. "Well, something's working," Oxley said, picking up the phone and motioning for Quinlan and Griffith to take chairs at the table. "It's Falcone."

"Mr. President, when can we expect you back?" Falcone asked, his voice sounding as if he were in the back of a cave.

"Sean, what the hell is going on?"

"An attack. You haven't seen GNN?"

"We've got some kind of blackout." He clicked the remote on and off as he spoke.

The phone rang again. Another light, this one CJCS, for Chairman of the Joint Chiefs of Staff, General Gabriel Wilkinson.

Oxley turned and pointed to the console in front of Quinlan. "It's Wilkinson. Take it. Tell him I'm talking to Falcone.

"Gabe is on another phone, Sean," Oxley said into the phone. "What's happening?"

"A suicide bomber—two, it looks like—hit one of our ships in Basra. Many sailors killed. We think twenty-one. We're in contact with the ship through Central Command. It's not in danger of sinking."

"Jesus! What else do we know?"

"Not much. About all we have is what was on GNN. They filmed the explosion. And they aired a report that it was the Iranians. You've seen it?"

"Sean, I'm completely in the fucking dark. Jesus!"

Oxley looked up at the agent. "Tell the pilot to turn off that goddamn electronics thing."

"I'm sorry, Mr. President," the agent said. "Defense of the aircraft. For jamming hostile radar. It's part of DEF-CON Three."

"Who ordered DEFCON Three?"

"The Secretary of Defense, sir, on recommendation of General Wilkinson."

Oxley pointed to Quinlan. "Tell Gabe I just ordered us back to DEFCON Four." He pointed to the agent. "And you tell the pilot Air Force One is now at DEFCON Four." The agent left.

"I'll meet you at Andrews, Mr. President," Falcone said. "Shouldn't take two hours."

Quinlan, after speaking briefly to Wilkinson, hit another button, put his hand over the mouthpiece, and listened in to the Falcone call. He began looking at Oxley and shaking his head.

Oxley looked toward Quinlan, nodded, and continued talking to Falcone: "This is a big fund-raiser, Sean. It's Dallas-big."

"I realize that, Mr. President. But I am sure the appearance of politics as usual—"

"Let me do some thinking and call you back, Sean," Oxley said, hanging up and aiming the remote at the screen again where, after a moment, Ned Winslow appeared. He was back on shore, standing by an armored personnel carrier. Behind him, two helicopters were heading out to sea.

"—to pick up the wounded. There's understandable confusion here," the reporter was saying. "The U.S. troops we saw leaving are reassembling. Iraqi soldiers are no-where to be seen."

Winslow pointed to landing craft whose ramps had lowered. Soldiers were streaming down the ramps, splashing through the surf, and forming lines to trucks, where arms, helmets, and armor vests were being passed out. As each soldier was armed, he joined a force that was forming a cordon around the Basra waterfront. More personnel carriers were rolling in.

"We can't turn around," Quinlan said, eyes on the screen.

"I know that, Ray. I know that," Oxley said, his eyes also on the screen. "I assume you mean leaving Iraq."

"I mean Dallas, Mr. President, and I know damn well you mean that, too."

Oxley looked toward Griffith. "Steph. Tell the comm guys in back that I need them to pump in a replay of GNN on one of the screens here. They'll figure a way. It's got to be all over the Internet."

Griffith stood. She was a tall, red-haired woman who looked perpetually beleaguered. "It's a zoo out there, Mr. President," she said. "They're screaming for information."

"Tell them I'm in constant touch with Falcone and Wilkinson."

"We're not going back to Washington?"

"Next stop, Dallas, Steph. But don't tell 'em yet. Get back here in ten minutes. And bring in Barry. We're going to need some quick speechwriting."

The room was still. Oxley and Quinlan, their heads close, did not speak for a moment. Then Oxley said, "Tell me one thing, Ray. I'm the President. I've got—what?—sixteen intelligence agencies. How come I don't know a goddamn thing that GNN doesn't know?"

In the stillness, the phone flashed again, indicating a call relayed from the White House but not through the red-phone lines.

"Senator Stanfield, Mr. President," the White House communication officer said.

Oxley signaled Quinlan to listen in on the phone in front of him.

"Mark? How good of you to call. What can I do for you?"

"About the *Elkton,* Mr. President."

"Yes?"

"I believe that the nation—"

The phone line went dead.

"What the hell's going on? I thought they had it fixed," Oxley said, looking to Quinlan, who was already on his feet and heading for the door.

"I'm on it," Quinlan said, heading for his small cubicle next to the conference room. Using a red-phone line to the White House, he learned only that line was available. He tried to reach Stanfield but someone in his Senate office told Quinlan that the senator was on the road and not immediately reachable. Quinlan thought for a moment— only a moment—about leaving a message explaining the phone cutoff. But what was the point? Whatever that gasbag Stanfield wanted to say would not help Oxley prepare for Dallas.

3

Sean Falcone got up from his desk and stood by a tall window. Sheets of rain blurred his view. *Summer's started. Already heat and rain. Heat and rain. And tourists. Don't forget the tourists,* Falcone thought, the view reflecting his soggy mood. Then he was lifted by a sudden memory of

Boston summer, when the days were full of baseball and prayers for the Red Sox.

The phone rang, and he turned away from the window, catching a quick glance at himself. *Still got a chin,* he thought, *No wattles yet. The 4:30 A.M. daily workouts are killers, but they help.*

But looks were deceiving. Outwardly, he still appeared strong and vigorous. At just under six feet tall and a trim one hundred and ninety pounds, he looked as if he could still go a few rounds with someone twenty years younger. But fatigue seemed to be his constant companion these days. The long trips, once so easy to bounce back from, were draining. He needed more rest, but rest didn't go with his job description.

Just another few months to go, he told himself, *and I'll get back to a more normal life.* But the realist within him laughed at the absurdity of what he was thinking. It was a joke. He had never known anything close to being normal. In fact, he didn't have a clue to the definition of the word.

Somewhere—maybe it was by William F. Buckley—he had read, "Industry is the enemy of melancholy." Maybe that was it. The reason he kept putting in eighteen-hour days, inhaling ten to twelve cups of coffee just to stay alert and keep an edge. He didn't want to deal with the downtime. There was too much melancholy in his blood. . . .

Falcone went back to his desk and sat down just as the phone rang. He picked up the handset and before he could say "Hello," he heard: "Goddamn it, Sean. The Man just knocked it up to DEFCON Four."

Gabe Wilkinson sounded as if his usual slow burn was speeding up. "The commands will think we don't know what we're doing."

"Well, Gabe—"

"I know what you're going to say. In fact, a lot of the time we *do* know what we're doing."

"Cool down, Gabe. I'm on your side on this. What's the latest?"

"The latest is this DEFCON thing. I know he's commander-in-chief. But there's a convention coming up and he's about to be renominated. When that happens, he's a presidential candidate in a tough race. Screwing around with our alert status looks a little like political stuff. There's a lot of running around here and other places. The *Elkton* attack triggered dozens of false terrorist reports."

"As usual, Gabe. The bloggersphere is steaming with crazy reports. A couple of airliners made emergency landings after passengers claimed they were seeing suspicious activity. And I just got a Secret Service report of an actionable death threat in Dallas. Cops there yanked the guy in. But there's no way the President is going to call it off, Gabe."

"Dallas? What the hell is he doing in Dallas?"

"It's a big fund-raiser in a big state, Gabe."

"Quinlan should make him turn around. But he won't. I don't trust that son of a bitch Quinlan, especially about anything that's military. "

"We're trying to work the DEFCON switch into his Dallas speech, Gabe. Calm reaction to a crisis. That's the message."

"Thanks for the message."

"The President will be back here by early evening. He wants a Principals Meeting in the Situation Room around ten. I was just about to call you."

"I'll bet you were."

"Gabe, you're always first on my list."

"Bullshit. Here's what I really called you for." Wilkinson's voice changed to its normal cool tempo. "The *Elkton* is still afloat. Those sailors did a helluva good job bailing her out. Casualties still twenty-one KIA. We think they recovered most of the remains. Some are just scraps enough for DNA. Sixteen wounded, three seriously. Choppers got them all to our military hospital in Baghdad. Thank God we didn't close that down yet.

"We poured in a lot of force protection: choppers, strike forces. We're packing the waterfront with everything we can find. Two destroyers are peeling out of the Persian Gulf task force and heading for Basra. The city is tight as a drum."

"Where was the force protection when the bad guys hit the ship?" Falcone sighed.

"We got word from State that we were not to provide full force protection because State wanted a 'peaceful image.' Don't get me started, Sean. Shades of the USS *Cole*. I hope the fucking Secretary of State will be able to make it to the Principals Meeting. He's the son of a bitch to ask."

"I know."

"That whole goddamn Goodbye Day bullshit was Bloom's idea. He said that, as secretary of state, *he* was going to run it, not the military. Can't believe that President Oxley signed off on that."

"It happened pretty fast, Gabe," Falcone said, shaking his head. "I didn't get much notice."

"No choppers. No big show of force protection. Bloom wanted it all to look good, like we were leaving the country in competent civilian hands. All PR. And, from what I hear, he gave GNN an exclusive. So, goddamn it, there they were with the cameras when the bad guys arrived."

"There's hell to pay, Gabe. The Iraqis insisted they had all the force protection that was needed and for us to stay out of it. We've got to find out what happened. And find out fast."

"There's a bunch of FBI and CIA people leaving Andrews in about an hour. I've got a Marine colonel with them who'll be reporting directly to me. And I've been trying to track that GNN report about the Iranians being to blame. We've got nothing on that."

"And I just talked to the CIA," Falcone said, trying to keep his voice from sounding weary. "Nobody over there can confirm GNN. Where in hell did GNN get that? We're trying to get some dope on that Bladerunner that GNN mentioned. But tell me about what's happening with the ship."

Falcone was looking at one of the screens on the wall nearest his desk. The screen showed a close-up of the hole torn in the *Elkton*'s hull. GNN REPORT: TERROR AT SEA kept running across the bottom of the screen. He assumed that Wilkinson was looking at the same image.

"There's a heavy-lift ship and tugs on the way from Dubai. As I understand the operation, the heavy-lift ship will fill her ballast tanks to submerge her deck. Then the tugs will maneuver the *Elkton* to position her over the heavy-lift ship, which will then empty her tanks so that her deck slowly rises until the *Elkton* sits on blocks on the deck. Then she gets carried to a U.S. shipyard. With an escort of the destroyers."

"And the dead?"

"Remains get . . . get field-prepared in Baghdad and flown to Dover for . . . for preparation for burial."

"Get me an estimated time of arrival at Dover. I'm going to want you and the President there."

"Well, it's Navy. So Ken and, I guess, all the Joint Chiefs will be there. I've got to get back to work."

"So do I. See you tonight," Falcone said, hanging up, and wondering how many minutes he had until the next phone call.

4

Falcone, who had a reputation for telling the truth, felt a wince of conscience after Wilkinson left. In Falcone's code, the omission of an important fact was tantamount to a lie, so it was damn close to a lie to withhold information from Wilkinson. Falcone realized that if he had admitted knowing about Goodbye Day twenty-four hours before word was passed to the general and Secretary of Defense George Kane, Wilkinson would have lumped him and William Bloom together. And Falcone did not want that to happen. His delicate relationship with Wilkinson depended on the chairman of the Joint Chiefs seeing himself as an ally with Falcone and a bureaucratic foe of Secretary of State Bloom.

Falcone was remembering when he first heard about Goodbye Day. President Oxley had been talking to him about the pullout from Iraq. "I don't want any more analyses, Sean," Oxley had said. "God knows I have enough of them. I want pure Falcone."

And that was what Falcone had given him. Falcone had been against what he called a stupid, meaningless war. "It was insane to go into Iraq in the first place," he had said. "We disbanded the military, broke up the leading political party, and became an army of occupation rather than set up a provisional government. We didn't know what we were doing. But it would be even more stupid to pull out all the troops now, without knowing what we're doing.

"Sure, the American people are tired of the war. Thousands dead. Tens of thousands wounded. But pulling every soldier out could leave our embassy people in real danger. It's the largest embassy we have in the world. One hundred and four acres. Big as Vatican City. We need to have a reserve force to handle contingencies."

"Sean, the Iraqi government wants us out."

"You mean Prime Minister Chalabi? That's just saying that Iran wants us out. He's their mouthpiece," Falcone said with disgust.

"It's not just Chalabi. The American people want us out. So, we're getting out."

Oxley had told him about Bloom's plan to publicize the final withdrawal with Goodbye Day images. Falcone had urged Oxley to scrap the idea. "A pullout, slow and quiet? Okay, Mr. President," Falcone had said. "But withdrawal should be an offstage process. It's no occasion for a television event."

"Sorry, Sean. I've already committed to Bloom on this. It might even be a model for Afghanistan. Not tomorrow, of course, or even next year, but one day."

"Jesus, Mr. President!" Falcone had exclaimed, leaning forward and pounding his fist on the President's desk, directly above the panel bearing a carving of the Presidential Great Seal. The eagle in the seal faced toward the thirteen arrows of war in its left talon instead of the olive branch in its right talon, as in the official Great Seal.

"Sorry for the emotion," he hastily added, staring at the seal. He leaned back and said, "You know what I think about your decision to stay there for another four years. We don't need that kind of force, not with those numbers. . . ."

"I don't get you, Sean. First, you want me to keep our soldiers in Iraq when everyone is telling us to get out. Then you want to get out of Afghanistan when our military says we need to stay."

"I'm not saying pull everyone out. Just that we need to cut the numbers way down. Give our kids a break. When you think about Afghanistan, sir, I suggest that you also think about that British soldier in Rudyard Kipling's poem. Iraq is a country. Afghanistan is a wild, ancient land where foreign soldiers wind up dead."

"You recited that poem to me a long time ago, Sean."

"Well, a couple of verses. But, with all due respect, here's the stanza to remember:

When you're wounded and left on Afghanistan's
   plains,
And the women come out to cut up what remains,
Jest roll to your rifle and blow out your brains
An' go to your Gawd like a soldier."

"Thanks for the lesson, Sean. But, getting back to Iraq, Goodbye Day stands."

Lessons. Sometimes Falcone wondered what lesson he had learned that got him to this office looking at that telephone and waiting for it to ring.

He had walked away from the Senate and from public service more than a decade ago. He had grown weary of it all, the superficial greeting of people he knew he would never see again, his hand stretched out for campaign contributions. It was the worst part of political life, the constant search for more and more money to feed the giant media outlets that had become the lifeblood of persuading the public that you stood for truth, justice, and the American way.

He had grown sick of it. The arteries of our democratic system so clogged with special-interest groups and their lobbyists. They can hit a button and suddenly flood Congress with five thousand letters overnight. Or fifty thousand e-mails. Or checks. People writing big checks with the expectation that there was something you were going to give them in return. How about just good governance? Sure. Get real. How about a vote for my company, my union, my industry, my save-the-polar-bears charity?

After two terms in the Senate, he had had enough. Let someone else carry the torch. Someone who was hungry for the job. Someone, hopefully, who wanted to do good for the country, and not just feed off the fleeting adoration granted to those who carried the title of United States Senator.

Yet here he was, back in the middle of it all. And just what good was he doing? Giving advice that Oxley pretended to listen to and then ignored? We were sending our kids right into the heart of hell. Not once, but two, three, even five times. And for what? Prevent Al Qaeda from slipping back from Pakistan to set up safe havens? Tame the warlords and Taliban? Drag a fourteenth-century country into the twenty-first? Many had tried and all had failed.

That's what Kipling was saying. Afghanistan was a goddamn graveyard. Don't send your boys to die there . . . *Or have them come back,* Falcone mused, *without limbs and with nightmares that never go away.*

Falcone knew what battle did to soldiers. What fighting ghosts was like. In the stillness of night, even now, when he lay in bed and stared at the ceiling, he could still hear the sounds of war, the screams of the dying. He could still feel the bloated leeches emerge almost from inside his skin, sucking his life blood away before he could flick them off. . . . Guilt sometimes seized his mind, calling him back to those minutes when he had failed to see how close the VC were. . . . He had lost count of the times he had gone over the terrain and failed to notice the signs that were there to see. If only he had talked with the villagers, if only he had listened, respected their customs and fears. If only he had seen the right things, had done the right things. . . . He could still. . . .

The phone rang again, breaking Falcone's dark mood. The label said PRESIDENT, but Falcone knew it would be Ray Quinlan.

"Sean, listen."

What the hell else do you expect me to do? Falcone thought. When Quinlan was agitated, which was most of the time, his voice had an undertone of snarl. And he certainly was agitated.

"We're about to land. The President will try not to do any talking on the tarmac. I'm shoving him right into the limo. And I told him not to say anything to the traveling press. But as soon as he gets to the rally, he's going to get hit with this thing. So I've gotta know the latest."

Falcone told him what he had been told by Wilkinson and asked about the change in DEFCON.

"DEFCON? I don't know any of that military shit, Sean. I'm in a hurry. See you later."

Quinlan hung up before Sean could ask for a copy of the

President's planned remarks. And, as usual, no time for goodbye. *Well, maybe working with an arrogant bastard like Quinlan isn't worth it. But did I really have any choice once the President called, asking me to help my country one more time? Maybe for the last time?*

For a few moments, Falcone fell into a reverie again. When he retired from the Senate, he decided to practice law. Not the run-of-the-mill type of Washington lawyering, billing fat-wallet clients in eight-minute increments of his time. No, he wanted something more, something different. And he was a man used to getting what he wanted.

He was granted a full partnership with DLA Piper, the largest law firm in the world, with forty offices spanning the globe. He made a seven-figure salary, not counting his annual bonus, which was ample by anyone's standards. And the only thing the firm asked for this princely sum was his advice on national security and global affairs. He was worth it. After all, he was regarded as a war hero, a man who had endured extreme torture as a prisoner of war in the notorious Hanoi Hilton in North Vietnam. He never liked the notion that he was considered a hero. *For what?* he used to muse publicly. *Getting captured?*

But, looking back on those years as a prisoner, he often thought about that dark cell, not as an ordeal but as a strange sanctuary. His cell was where he found and nurtured the discovery that he had an ability to sort things out, to look through events and see their causes, to search through complex situations for shards of simplicity.

In that cell, to keep himself from going mad, he had tried to channel his mind. He would conjure up visions—of city centers, of skyscrapers—and then he would build them, brick by brick, or block by block, the evolving images becoming clearer as his ability to concentrate improved. Sometimes, he felt that he could step into his creations, walk around, and spend time in an alternate world. He had never told anyone about this Zen-like life in the cell. But he often told himself that when he finally emerged from his cell, he was not the man who had entered.

The phone rang.

"This is Anna, Sean. I would like to see you as soon as possible."

Anna Dabrowski, the deputy national security advisor, was extremely polite and always followed the rules. Every time he heard her soft, tentative voice, Falcone remembered for an instant how difficult it had been to get her to call him Sean, and how, during their first awkward meeting a couple of months ago, she had called him "Mr. Falcon," "Senator Falcon," and "Mr. Advisor." And he remembered how embarrassed they both were when he informed her that his name was pronounced *Shawn Fal-cone-e. "My first name doesn't sound like it looks. And my last name has three syllables. Anna, blame my name on having an Irish mother and an Italian father."*

He realized at that first meeting that she hadn't been born when he was in Vietnam, was probably in high school when he was in the Senate, and was studying Arabic at the American University in Beirut when he went to DLA Piper. She had blushed—actually blushed—when she tried to explain that she had frequently *read* his name but had never actually *heard* it.

"Anna, come on in," he said on the phone. She stepped across the hall from her small office and entered his. She never entered without a preliminary phone call. As usual, she wore a dark suit over a white blouse, a fluffy collar her only touch of femininity. Her blond hair was gathered in what he assumed was the only bun in the White House. She wore rimless glasses in a silvery frame. She had once told him that she had an aunt back in Chicago who would not respond to a letter unless it was addressed to *Miss* Eva Dabrowski because without *Miss,* her name looked like it belonged to a careless woman.

In a moment, the door opened and she stood there self-consciously, as if she had never entered his office before. He motioned her to a seat.

"That's all right. I just wanted to tell you something."

"What?"

She pointed toward the array of television screens. "Take a look at GNN."

Falcone hit a button and, on the small screen of the small set near his desk, came the handsome, square-jawed face of Senator Mark Stanfield of Texas, who was being touted by commentators as the most likely candidate to oppose President Oxley. National conventions had yet to be held, but an Oxley versus Stanfield presidential race seemed almost certain.

Stanfield's message was simple: By running for a second term, Oxley was putting the nation on the road to tyranny while also losing the war on terror. Stanfield was calling for a party platform that was little more than his campaign slogan: "Bring Back America."

Stanfield was leaning forward in a chair on his campaign bus. A rural roadside was streaming past the window behind him. "I'll say again. He was well aware that he was rejecting advice from the Joint Chiefs of Staff. Urgent military advice."

"Let's get this straight, Senator," the GNN interviewer said. "What exactly happened? What's so important about the DEFCON order?"

Falcone hit another button to record the interview. He motioned to Dabrowski. "Sit down, Anna." She chose a chair next to Falcone's desk, and he was pleased to see that she was not sitting on the edge of her seat.

"Let me put it this way, Frank," Stanfield said. "DEFCON is the thermometer of our armed forces. It's the thermometer that shows the level of alert that is needed at any given moment. You're a general or an admiral—or a colonel or a commander—and you look at the DEFCON and you know how dangerous the world looks to your theater commander. DEFCON Five? Nothing dangerous is happening. DEFCON Four? Just keep your eyes open, buddy. DEFCON Three? Well, suddenly you realize that something may be up. You don't know what it is. But you *do* know about the terror attack on the *Elkton*. And you wonder, Are we next? What's happening? You get all your guys and gals at the ready.

"And then, *about ten minutes later,* you get a new temperature reading. It's DEFCON Four again. You don't know why. Well, *I* know why. *The President overruled the Joint Chiefs. That's why.*"

A small screen opened on the lower left of the screen, with the underline PRESIDENT ARRIVES IN DALLAS.

"Thank you, Senator," the GNN correspondent said hastily. "We're about to switch to Dallas, where—"

"There's one more thing, Frank. But I hesitate—"

"Only have a moment, Senator."

"Well, I wasn't going to mention this. But when I attempted to call the President about the *Elkton,* he . . . he hung up on me."

"That son of a bitch!" Falcone exclaimed, hitting the mute button on the remote. As a shampoo ad appeared on the silent screen, he looked across his desk to Anna and began speaking rapidly.

"Tell Hawk I want everything there is to know about DEFCONs. Tell him I want all the classified material boiled out of a short memo that can be used by the President. I need it in fifteen minutes. Also, put someone in touch with Air Force One and tell them I want— immediately—a classified time line on the DEFCON messages. Have someone else call Kane's office and get a SecDef classified time line. DEFCON orders are supposed to come through him. Keep the queries separate and secret from each source. I have a hunch the two time lines won't agree."

Kane was George Kane, a former Ohio congressman who had been chairman of the House Armed Services Committee. Trusted and knowledgeable about the ways of the Pentagon, he had been the first cabinet member selected by Oxley. Hawk was Marine Lieutenant Colonel Jeffrey Hawkins, military aide to the National Security Council.

Falcone knew that Anna had trouble being the thirty-two-year-old boss of a Marine light colonel, but Hawk, a chain-of-command man on a star-destined career path, had no such trouble. Falcone trusted Hawk, probably more than any other military officer he had met on this job. Certainly more than Wilkinson, who played a complex game.

"Between you and me, Anna, I figure that Wilkinson, or someone on his staff, set a new speed record for leaking to Stanfield."

"Mice play around when they don't smell the cat,"

"Another proverb from your Aunt Eva?"

"Yes," Dabrowski replied, with a smile that instantly lightened Falcone's mood.

"I'm taking a short walk on the grounds, Anna," he said. "Until I get back, you're in charge of the world."

5

When Falcone took the job, he assumed that his little world, the National Security Council, would be concerned only with aiding the President on strategic issues: war and peace, nuclear proliferation, keeping the Middle East from blowing up. But day after day, despite his efforts at managing the NSC and herding the government's countless agencies toward some kind of unified direction, he found himself bogged down by domestic issues that were knitted into foreign issues. DEFCON. Dallas. Stanfield.

The rain had stopped as suddenly as it had begun. Falcone left his office to wend his way out onto the West Wing colonnade and walk briskly along the South Lawn, a Secret Service agent a few steps behind.

You can never be alone around here, he thought. *And you never get much time to just think. Let us review. Why an attack in Iraq when we were finally getting the hell out? Well, why anything? Start with Osama bin Laden, a Saudi Arabian exile, now thankfully dead, his ass part of the Pacific. He launched a sneak attack on America, knocking down the twin Trade Towers in New York and ripping a gigantic hole in the Pentagon. This act of terrorism was met with a vigorous military response against terrorist strongholds in Afghanistan. Then, Iraq.*

The price tag for the decision to invade and then occupy

a country had drained the U.S. treasury of a trillion dollars. And add Afghanistan and it looks like we're heading for the two-trillion-dollar mark today, Goodbye Day.

But bad as that was, Falcone couldn't let it go: *We were making a big mistake pulling everyone out. Iraq couldn't handle the security yet. The hit on the* Elkton *was proof of that. The Iranians are still messing in the sandbox, the Saudis are backing the Sunnis, the Iraqi government doesn't know how to govern.*

And there's that knitting, that crazy pattern. A dollar spent here winds up somewhere else. Where does the U.S. economy end and the global economy begin?

The masters of the universe who put our economy into a nosedive weren't global. They're as American as the Stock Exchange bell. And those brilliant financial wizards who answer the bell like Pavlov's dogs have only one loyalty—to the god of greed. They pedaled "securitized assets," credit default swaps, collateralized debt obligations, and other exotic financial instruments that no one understood but all were desperate to invest in or acquire. It was one of the greatest frauds ever perpetrated, one that nearly brought the global financial system to its knees.

Everyone had to pay for the crimes except the people who committed them. . . . Well, at least our esteemed secretary of state, William Bloom, can't be blamed. Wealthy as hell, smart as hell. He's not a master of the universe. He's the master of the knowledge world. He knew when to make deals in China, when to put some money into obscure startups like Facebook. Good guy, great mind. But Goodbye Day was not one of his better ideas. . . .

The thought of Goodbye Day pulled Falcone back to today, back to his job.

. . .

When President Blake Oxley had asked Falcone to serve his administration, it wasn't the first time. After Oxley's stunning upset victory, in a private conversation the President-elect had asked Falcone to serve as his secretary of state. But when Ray Quinlan and other campaign strategists discovered what Oxley had proposed, they strenuously objected. Falcone had done nothing to deserve such an honor, they argued. He had sat on the sidelines during the campaign.

"Christ, he didn't even contribute to your campaign," Quinlan said (or at least that's what one of Quinlan's many enemies told Falcone, quoting the Quinlan remarks). "So he's a war hero. So fucking what? You're going to reward him with the plum job in your administration? What about the people who paid their dues? The ones who put everything on the line for you? Just what signal does that send if—no, *when*—you run for reelection?"

Oxley did not know about a Falcone-Quinlan feud that went back to Falcone's Senate days when, as chairman of the Senate Select Committee on Intelligence, he had stripped Quinlan, one of the committee staffers, of his Top Secret clearance for letting a lobbyist, who was also a girlfriend, see classified documents so she could impress her Brazilian client.

The rise and fall of the Falcone nomination had been tightly held. The media assumption was that Oxley's first choice was William Bloom, former chairman of the board of the Council on Foreign Relations. He was also a major contributor to the campaign, Quinlan's basic requirement for the job. Philip Dake, the *Washington Post*'s star reporter, wrote, in profile of Bloom, "He was an immensely wealthy self-made man who had a résumé that had earned him a right to be considered on the basis of his ability."

Bloom, the grandson of Russian immigrants, worked his way through Yale, made Phi Beta Kappa, and went on, with a full scholarship, to earn an MBA from Harvard Business School. He liked learning languages, adding Mandarin to French and Spanish. He and two other Harvard graduates formed a small company that introduced information technology to stock trading. He bought out his partners, joined the vanguard of American businessmen who discovered China, and made his first billion. A short stint as a vice president of Goldman Sachs convinced him to keep his own company privately held.

As a globe-trotting apostle of the knowledge industry, he had met heads of state, served for a time as the long-distance, de facto finance minister to two developing countries, and was renowned at the Council on Foreign Relations as a man who gathered his own facts in travels to trouble spots. *Fortune* estimated his personal wealth to be $14 billion.

Bloom and Oxley had been at Harvard at the same time but hardly knew each other. Drawing from that slight connection, Oxley sought him out and got the first of what would be many sizeable contributions. When Oxley nominated Bloom, he called him the smartest and best-qualified secretary of state since Thomas Jefferson.

Then, meekly, Oxley went back to Falcone. "What about national security advisor? It's not State, but still, you'd be in the White House, with me on virtually every decision. . . ." Left unsaid was that Falcone would serve as a kind of stand-in for a frequently traveling secretary of state.

Falcone had declined. "I'm not going to compete with America's new Thomas Jefferson," he had said. *National security advisor? Nice title,* he thought, *but a staffer's job, and, despite the lofty title, a mere presidential aide. After being a United States senator? No thanks. . . .*

That was before his longtime friend, Admiral Mike Ryan, suffered a massive heart attack while playing tennis and died on his way to Georgetown University Hospital. Oxley was in trouble. He needed a replacement for Ryan immediately, someone who could command the respect of the prima donnas on Capitol Hill and secure support for the President's promise to pull out of Iraq and Afghanistan . . . to cope with a resurgent Russia and China's ambitions for a blue-water navy. Falcone couldn't refuse. Not this time.

Quinlan again had resisted, had even sniffed around for opposition to Falcone on Capitol Hill. News about that had got back to Falcone, too. When he was making up his mind about taking the advisor job, he knew that he was on Quinlan's permanent enemies list. But coolly looking at the political and personal algebra of the appointment, he decided that Quinlan, as chief of staff, would mostly be concerned with domestic issues and the President's image. To give Quinlan some credit, he had been staying out of Falcone's territory. *He knows,* Falcone thought, *that there aren't many campaign donors in the places where I have to operate.*

The sound of an airliner, on approach to Reagan National Airport, entered his mind. *September 11, 2001.*

Anyone who was in Washington that morning possessed unforgettable moments that came back at unexpected times. You remember hearing it on the radio as you drove to work. Or on the Metro as bits of news passed through the crowded car. Or someone running into your office or your cubicle and saying that something had happened in New York. A Tower hit. Then the second Tower. And then . . .

Falcone was being driven to an appointment in Virginia. The car was on the Whitehurst Freeway, parallel to the Potomac River, about to cross the Key Bridge. Then nothing was moving. He was listening to the radio, envisioning what others were seeing on television. He heard a plane, flying low. He craned to look up. In an instant, he heard a dull explosion, muted, like a clap of distant thunder. He looked out the window and saw, across the river, the thick black smoke coiling up from the Pentagon. . . .

Now he hurried back across the lawn to the colonnade. *My job is about an attack on a U.S. ship, not DEFCONs and Stanfield. And my job is serving the President.*

At his desk, he ordered what they still called a red-phone call to the presidential limousine heading for the Dallas Convention Center.

Quinlan answered. But, when Falcone said, "Give me the President," Quinlan, sensitive to political voice tones, did not say a word and handed the phone to Oxley.

"Mr. President, I'm e-mailing to your comm officer five hundred words on what we know about the *Elkton*. The press will demand more. But it's all we have. We have absolutely no knowledge of the possible Iranian connection that GNN reported. Repeat: no knowledge. Be prepared for questions about DEFCONs. Just say, as commander-in-chief you had to override Secretary Kane's DEFCON decision because you needed all the information you could get—and that had to transcend any remote danger to Air

Force One. I'll also be e-mailing Stephanie a briefing paper on DEFCON that will have enough to hold off her friends in the press."

"Good, Sean, good. I've cut down my speech to a quick 'Howdy, partners,' and I'll do a fast turnaround. Meet me at Andrews."

"Right, Mr. President. I've set up the Principals Meeting for ten o'clock. Goodbye."

"Yeah. Goodbye. Well, it's Goodbye Day, isn't it?"

6

George William Parker stepped out of the front door of the brick house on East Capitol Street and took down the American flag that flapped on a brass pole jutting out from a bracket above the door. He folded the flag until only a triangular blue field of stars was visible. Then he stood for a moment on the wrought-iron landing, his gaze sweeping the street in both directions. *The fools are gone,* he said to himself.

Moths darted around the lights flanking the front door. A siren grew fainter and the jingle of an ice-cream truck grew louder. *Capitol Hill,* Parker thought. *Killers and kids, muggings and Good Humor, Congress and . . . what? So many thoughts ended in questions these days.* Parker ran his right hand through his close-cropped white hair as if to wipe away his errant thoughts. He must concentrate on the briefing.

Parker wore a white shirt, sleeves neatly rolled up, and sharply creased khaki slacks. His laced brown shoes were freshly shined. Anyone wise to the sights of Washington would assume him to be a retired military officer. As *Time* once said of him, he was "every inch the modern Army general: tall, slim, weathered face, eyes with that thousand-yard stare of remembered combat."

Two weeks before, a photo of the house had been splashed across the front page of the *Washington Post,* along with a photo of Parker, his face a mask of controlled outrage. Over the story, headlined "The House of The Brethren," was the byline of Philip Dake, not only the *Post*'s reportorial star but also the chief investigative reporter. "In the shadow of the Capitol," Dake wrote, "is a house that is more than a house. It is a religious edifice, according to District of Columbia records, and, as such, is exempt from D.C. property taxes. The small brick house, at 201 East Capitol Street Southeast, is owned by The Brethren of the Covenant of Jesus, a religious sect with extraordinary political connections. It does not resemble a church, it does not have a congregation or a pastor, and it does not open its door to worshippers who are not members of The Brethren.

"In this seemingly holy place, politicians and power brokers study the Bible and give each other spiritual advice, calling themselves 'leaders led by God.' Here, some also have slept with their mistresses, played high-stakes poker, and established agendas for the Far Right." He went on to depict the house as a lair for religious zealots determined to put America on the path to Christian governance.

Dake only vaguely described past events at the house. He did not connect any specific incident to the present-day occupants: Parker and two congressmen. All three, Dake wrote, were members of The Brethren, as was one of the frequent visitors to the house: Senator Mark Stanfield of Texas, "who is the likely candidate to run against President Blake Oxley in this year's election campaign."

The article was a typical Dake creation. He hinted at much more than he reported, leaving his subjects worrying about what he might reveal in future articles or in one of his bestselling books.

Senator Stanfield declined to comment, but Parker did. "This house," he said, "is a spiritual resting place, where we warriors for Jesus can find refuge from the chaos of official Washington." Asked whether The Brethren was a Christian religion, he replied, "We believe in a covenant of Jesus. It was known originally only by the initiates of early Christianity and is a revelation direct from Jesus."

Parker refused to tell what the covenant proclaimed, saying that he, like all Brethren, "kept the covenant in my heart and not on my tongue." But Dake reported that the secret theology of The Brethren centered on Armageddon, the biblical prophecy that foresees the end of the world in an apocalyptic battle between good and evil. Dake noted that 59 percent of Americans say they believe in the coming battle of Armageddon.

Dake traced the history of the house back more than a decade, during the administration of President Eric Hollendale. "Clayton Skillings, Hollendale's chief of staff, lived for a time in the house," Dake wrote. "He was said to have allowed Senator Joshua Stock to use the house during trysts with the senator's girlfriend. Stock, accused of allegedly spying for Israel, later was the victim of a bizarre, videotaped murder that became one of Washington's most notorious homicide cases."

Dake had been hounding Parker for nearly a year, ever since Parker had abruptly retired from the Army.

"Much of his career had been in the Delta Force," Dake wrote. "Although Delta once was the most publicized of all U.S. Special Forces, very little is publicly known about Parker's black operations, either as a participant or a leader. But his missions were well known among those military officers and civilian officials privy to information about the U.S. Special Operations Command, which has overall authority over the special forces of the Army, Navy, Marines, and Air Force.

"Parker had been given command of the USSOC and had moved from the Pentagon to Special Forces headquarters at MacDill Air Force Base in Tampa, Florida. He had been there less than a month when, in a letter to the Army Chief of Staff, he had resigned. Neither he nor Army spokespersons would reveal the reasons for the abrupt resignation. The letter of resignation is classified as Top Secret, apparently because of the allusions Parker made to 'black ops' that he had led.

"Special Forces insiders compared Parker to such legendary generals as Douglas MacArthur and George Patton, both of whom were renowned for their courage and arrogance. Unlike them, however, Parker commanded not battlefields but the back alleys of the war on terror.

"Parker's resignation had been reportedly demanded by President Oxley because of Parker's remarks during a CBS *60 Minutes* profile. Parker had said that he and his Special Forces troops were 'modern Crusaders, fighting and dying for Christ and country, just as the original Crusaders who marched against the Muslims in what is still the Holy Land, where Jesus Christ was born and murdered.'

"Parker has moved from the headquarters of the U.S.

Special Operations Command to the Washington head-quarters of The Brethren of the Covenant of Jesus. Although his new post is legally a religious site, it remains as secret and mysterious as his previous command. He was a warrior there, and is a warrior here, but in another cause."

The day after Dake's article was published, the two members of Congress moved out of the house and into a residential hotel. For days afterward, curious strangers appeared on East Capitol Street and cars slowed down as they passed the house.

The story did not produce much of a reaction, but Parker knew that Dake was still sniffing around. And there were others who might be out there, spying, plotting. Parker assumed that among the pedestrians and motorists were intelligence agents. Perhaps Americans working for the CIA, perhaps Israelis working for the Mossad. And he included them among the fools who had been gawking on East Capitol Street.

Parker entered the house, carrying the folded flag and placing it on a chiffonier near the front door. He rolled down his sleeves, buttoned his collar, added a tightly knotted red tie, and put on a summer-weight blue blazer that was hanging on a hook on the chiffonier. As he checked himself in the mirror, he heard the distinct ringtone of a cell phone used by only one caller. For a moment he had the feeling that he was being watched so closely that some-one knew he had just entered the house.

Parker pulled a smartphone from a holster on his belt. The phone did not have a keyboard or number pad and could not make outgoing calls. On a narrow screen appeared a six-digit number, which changed every twenty seconds.

Parker spoke the numbers—"four, nine, six, two, eight, zero"—into the phone. He knew that the caller's phone would show the same six numbers, satisfying him that he had reached the customized cell phone. Two minuscule screens on the phone showed green, signaling that the phone's voice analyzer had confirmed the identities of both the caller and the person who had answered the phone. On that phone, Parker, who was called Amos, was under instructions to refer to the caller only as Isaiah.

A scrambler made the caller's voice sound as if a robot were forming each word: "You have seen the news. Iran. I *know* it is Iran. GNN knows it is Iran. Our spineless government knows it is Iran. But Oxley will not admit it. Did you hear him, talking to those whores in Dallas?"

"He says there is no proof about Iran," Parker said to the robotic voice. He always wondered how his voice and Isaiah's voice sounded on the Isaiah phone. Parker also wondered what Isaiah looked like. They had never met.

"And Oxley lies." After a short pause and what sounded like a sharp intake of breath, the voice added, "No proof? Are you doubting my knowledge?"

"No, no, Isaiah. I . . . I was only quoting Oxley."

Another pause. Then, "Never believe him. Never!"

Parker desperately wanted to change the subject. "What shall we do?" he asked. "Is it time?"

"Yes, it is time. Instruct your men to begin preparations."

"Good," Parker said. "When will you and I meet?"

"A meeting is not necessary. Particularly now, in the blaze of that *Washington Post* article by that imbecile Dake. He is ignorant. But he thinks he knows so much."

"Why now, I wondered? Why did the *Post* go after us right now?"

"Perhaps, Amos, Oxley's people suspect that we are moving toward an action phase. There has been some amateurish surveillance, some wiretaps easily found—the stuff of warnings, not threats. They are probing, using many tools. But I feel that it's not the Oxley administration that has taken an interest in us. Whoever it is, Dake is one of their tools and does not know it."

"That would seem to add urgency to Operation Cyrus," Parker said.

"Not to worry, Amos, not to worry. You must follow the schedule we agreed on. The die has been cast."

"Very well," Parker said, worry trickling into his voice.

"Not to worry. Look at your numbers, Amos."

The call ended, as usual, without a goodbye.

Parker looked at the numbers on the phone screen: 56 10 11. He did not need to go to a Bible. Long before, he had memorized chapter 56 of Isaiah. He mentally ran through the first nine verses until 10–11 came to his mind:

His watchmen are blind: they are all ignorant, they are all dumb dogs, they cannot bark; sleeping, lying down, loving to slumber. Yea, they are greedy dogs which can never have enough, and they are shepherds that cannot understand: they all look to their own way, every one for his gain, from his quarter.

7

Getting ready to head for Andrews and meet with President Oxley, Falcone picked up a red-and-white binder labeled EYES ONLY. As he did, he glanced at the appointment calendar on his desk. Months before, he had met with the heads of the major U.S. intelligence agencies at the National Counterterrorism Center in suburban Virginia. The center was in the same Tyson's office building as the CIA's Counterterrorism Center and the Pentagon's Joint Intelligence Task Force on Counterterrorism. Falcone learned more about intel bureaucracy than Al Qaeda: The three centers obviously operated independently from each other.

The National Counterterrorism Center was a hive of pulsating wall-size screens and people hunched over small-size screens. Each day about six thousand reports came into the Center from satellites, drones, phone taps, bugged buildings, monitored cellphones, surveillance cameras, and some human beings. A similar avalanche of data buried the other centers every day.

We listen. We watch. But what do we hear? What do we see? Falcone had thought as he looked up at one of the giant plasma screens. In streaks of red it showed the ever-changing location of every plane approaching the United States.

At the end of the meeting, he had been given a National Counterterrorism Center calendar. At first glance, it looked like a typical appointment calendar, with each day set off in a box big enough to jot down notes. But on this apocalyptic calendar, the boxes contained not only the date but also anniversaries—from January 1 ("Serial explosions in Guwahati kill five and injure 67") to December 31 ("Right-wing extremist Binyamin Kahane and wife killed in ambush by Intifada Martyrs").

A few of the boxes contained only the date; there was no parenthesized horror to commemorate. To Falcone, those days seemed ominous because he could not believe that a day went by without some act of terror somewhere by someone. *We just didn't know about them.*

Falcone kept the calendar on his desk to read the reminders. Today had begun with an attack on a U.S. warship. The long day would end with a meeting of people who had many questions and no answers. Today, he saw, was an anniversary: a suicide car bomber in Algeria killed forty-three people. Al Qaeda was blamed.

Terrorism. It was a world that Falcone lived in, a world that Oxley knew about only through Falcone. But what world did Oxley live in?

Falcone thought Oxley had the potential to be a great president, but there was something . . . something indefinable that was missing. He had a beautiful wife and twin teenage girls whom the American people adored. He was smart as hell and possessed a self-confidence that, on more than one occasion, slipped into a chin-elevated display of arrogance. He didn't suffer fools gladly—an admirable trait—but the problem was that he thought just about everyone else was a fool. He was the smartest kid in the world's biggest classroom and he couldn't resist letting everyone know it. What was missing was the ability to touch people's hearts. Say something and not only make them believe it, but feel that it was real. . . .

Maybe that's what accounted for his slip in the polls. Yes, unemployment was bad, but there were signs that things were turning around. No doubt it happens to all presidents once they get into office and have to govern, make decisions. But the magic that Oxley was able to weave when he first took office was gone. The soaring oratory that he was able to sprinkle like angel dust had fallen from the eyes of all but his most ardent supporters.

It was odd. Falcone knew that Oxley liked being president, but he really didn't like the game of politics. Not like Ronald Reagan or Bill Clinton. Oh sure, he liked the power but not the process of making the wheels of government turn.

Oxley was a big-picture man and disdained having to meet with members of Congress. Well, Falcone could hardly fault him for that, given some of those who had recently been elected. Didn't matter whether they liberals or conservatives; they all liked to shout at the top of their lungs that they held the keys to the kingdom of wisdom and prosperity.

Most of the people around Oxley were solid and principled; maybe a little on the unimaginative side. Oxley did his best to give them the impression that he cared about their opinions, and during meetings he would solicit the views even of those who had no real decision-making responsibilities. It was a charade, of course. Oxley made up his own mind, and once he made a decision, he was not open to changing it.

Then there was Ray Quinlan. Falcone couldn't figure out why Oxley let Quinlan get anywhere near him. Ray was a foul-mouthed hothead who liked to bully people. He snapped off provocative one-liners, believing members of the press would think they reflected a quick and agile mind, one worthy of getting greater exposure on the Sunday talk shows. It worked. He had become a regular on *Meet the Press*. But it was just a matter of time before Quinlan would do something thoroughly stupid. And Oxley would pay the price for it. . . .

Well, only a few months to go until the election. Then, whatever happened, Falcone was going to walk away. This job was his last act of public service.

At 8:22 P.M., Air Force One touched down at Joint Base Andrews, as the place was now officially called in deference to Navy–Air Force comity. One of the black SUVs pulled out of the motorcade lined up nearby and stopped alongside just as the stairway rolled up to an opening door and President Oxley appeared. At the bottom of the stairs he gave a jaunty salute to the duty commander at Andrews and, followed by Quinlan, headed for the SUV. Other passengers filed out and scattered, reporters to a shuttle bus, a few White House staffers to the motorcade vehicles.

"No limo?" he asked Falcone, who was seated on the left side of the wide rear seat.

"Secret Service rules," Falcone said "I think the agents believe we're still at DEFCON Three." He looked squarely at Quinlan, who waited for the President to enter and then slid in. He leaned forward to nod to Falcone across Oxley but did not speak. Falcone had been informed about three new death threats the Secret Service took seriously. But Falcone did not mention them.

"Thanks for that brief on the *Elkton* and the advice on the DEFCON business," Oxley said as the car started to move. "I saw a tape of Stanfield on GNN. NBC picked up a squib of that, topping with me using the DEFCON explanation you gave me. I think it all went off okay. Right, Ray?"

"You looked presidential. Stanfield looked like an ass-hole getting his GNN minutes," Quinlan said.

Quinlan was right. Oxley had started looking presidential in the last year or so. He was tall and slim, still looking young but starting to gray prematurely. He loped across a room like the athlete he had been. His deep voice had a lyrical quality. His rhetoric could still madden his foes, who claimed that his words were mere fluff. His election campaign in various ways had revolved around that issue: Was Oxley, as they said in Texas, all hat and no cattle? Or, was he the leader who finally got the combat troops out of Iraq? The wizard who started moving the nation out of an economic crisis?

Oxley's projected cool inspired critics in the media and in Stanfield's camp to claim that the cool was a mask that concealed a cold-blooded ruthlessness. "He could throw his mother under a moving truck if it served his interest," an anonymous congressman said in a *Washington Post* profile by Philip Dake.

"What's on the agenda?" Oxley asked, looking at his watch. "Ten o'clock, right?"

"Right. I think the best thing is to just lay out what we know—which isn't much. And there are the inevitable call-ins and Middle East videos with people claiming responsibility. The CIA hasn't come up with any information about who did it."

"That's sure no surprise," Oxley said. "I'm thinking about announcing the formation of a commission to investigate the attack."

"I don't think a commission is a good idea," Falcone said.

"Why not?" Quinlan asked, swiftly changing the conversation between Oxley and Falcone to an exchange between himself and Falcone.

Falcone ignored Quinlan and leaned toward the President. "You'll get all the pundits and bloggers on you for taking the standard nonaction Washington move. A commission, I think, sounds old and lame."

"You have a better idea?" Oxley asked sharply, ignoring Quinlan, who looked as if he was about to speak.

"Not better, Mr. President. Just different," Falcone diplomatically replied. "I'm suggesting that you get Vice President Cunningham to use his considerable persuasive powers as a former Speaker of the House to shift the spotlight from the White House to Congress.

"Well, that sounds promising," Oxley said. "How do you propose to do that?"

Falcone tried never to start off an idea with the preface *During my time in the Senate*. He consistently used his experience as a senator as the basis for his political counsel. But he knew that no one, especially someone as cocky and self-assured as Oxley, wanted to listen to advice based on another politician's experience. Advice was supposed to come as if from an oracle.

"The Vice President goes to his successor as Speaker and convinces him to appoint an investigative committee; then he goes to the Senate Majority Leader and asks her to do the same thing. And then—"

"*Two* committees?" Oxley interrupted. "Sounds like double trouble."

"No. Congress doesn't like playing doubles. What will happen in reality—and the Vice President will know how to push this—is that the two investigations will quickly merge, and what will result is a joint committee consisting of House and Senate members of both parties—with someone suggested by the Vice President as chairman. *Our* chairman."

"And it gets that nice label, bipartisan," Oxley said. "I like it." He turned toward Quinlan and asked, "What's your feeling?"

"It's true that commissions are usually bullshit," Quinlan replied. "We may have a better chance with a joint committee. And I do think that Cunningham can handle it. I can give him some good, useful names, and we can make sure that most of the Senate members of the committee will not be running for reelection in the fall. That would mean maybe some televised hearings—but no committee report until after the election."

"So much for the commission," Oxley said. "I'll talk to Cunningham. Set up a meeting tomorrow, Ray. But are we sure there's nothing that's going to make us look bad in congressional testimony?"

"Well, there's that report on GNN claiming that Iran did it," Quinlan said. "What about it, Sean?"

"Absolutely no proof and plenty of doubt," Falcone said. "The CIA says it's highly unlikely that Iran was in on it. All the doubts will be in the PDB, I'm sure," Falcone said, referring to the President's Daily Brief, the nation's most secret document, which assembles the Intelligence Community's most sensitive analysis involving key national security issues and concerns of the President. It is given only to the President, the Vice President, and a very select group of cabinet-level officials designated by the President.

The PDB was prepared in the Office of the Director of National Intelligence and was usually delivered in person by the director himself, Charles Huntington, better known as Chuck. He had joined the CIA out of college and served in the Clandestine Service, specializing as a core collector, the innocuous name for the CIA officers who gathered intelligence from agents in dangerous places. Some of his work became known to members of the Senate Select Committee on Intelligence, and when Oxley had nominated him, his confirmation was assured. As director of National Intelligence, Huntington oversaw the sixteen agencies that made up what was known as the Intelligence Community.

"So what's on the Principals Meeting agenda?" Quinlan asked.

"Get everybody on the same page, Ray," Falcone replied.

"Including William Bloom, our revered secretary of state? Mr. Goodbye Day?"

Falcone thought of his two DEFCON time lines. The one from the Office of Secretary of Defense George Kane showed that General Wilkinson had called Secretary Kane once, suggesting the one-notch rise of DEFCON and getting Kane's acceptance. The time line from Air Force One showed two calls from Wilkinson, one presumably to instruct the pilot to go to DEFCON Three and a second call—that one to Quinlan. Falcone imagined Wilkinson and Quinlan had teamed up to swiftly build a culpability case that would incriminate Bloom and the State Department rather than Wilkinson and the Department of Defense.

Falcone filed away what he had learned, treating it like

a deposit in a bank, saving the information but not knowing how it would be spent. His job was to put things together, not to make decisions or make policy. But he could push and pull, advise and react. He served the President, and sometimes he had to do that in ways that the President did not need to know about.

When the motorcade reached the White House, Oxley headed for the Residence, Falcone and Quinlan for the West Wing.

Back in his office down the hall from the Oval Office, Falcone unlocked a drawer in his desk, dictated a memo-to-self about the backseat conversation into a small digital recorder, returned it to the drawer, locked it, and pocketed the key. He called Anna Dabrowski to tell her that the President was back and the Principals Meeting was on. She and her assistant put out the call to the Principals, who already were on alert for the meeting. Although Dabrowski usually attended such meetings, Falcone said "good night" to her, knowing that, according to West Wing ritual, you did not go home until your boss said those two words. "Good night," she repeated.

At twenty minutes to ten, Falcone left his office and walked down a short flight of stairs to the ground floor of the West Wing. He turned right and entered a foyer guarded by a Marine. By tradition, members of the cabinet did not have to show their photo identification badges to enter the Situation Room. Falcone, a powerful presidential aide but not a cabinet member, was neither fish nor fowl ("neither fish nor flesh," as Anna's aunt Eva put it).

Falcone was inevitably treated as a cabinet member at this checkpoint, since he ran the NSC, and the NSC ran the Situation Room. But Marine guards did not let any-one, including Falcone and cabinet officers, pass without placing cell phones in a lead-lined box on a table that stood next to the Marine guard.

Falcone placed his smartphone in the box. The Marine saluted, opened the door, and stood aside for Falcone to enter a narrow hall that linked a suite of separate rooms: a video conference room where the President and his advi-sors spoke to, listened to, and saw the facial expressions of battlefield commanders; the ultra-secure President's Briefing Room, ready for the commander-in-chief when he wanted a meeting place less populated than the Situa-tion Room; the Watch Center, and finally the Situation Room itself, officially known as "the intelligence manage-ment center."

Fifteen minutes early for the Principals Meeting, Fal-cone stopped in at the Watch Center, where he chatted with one of his handpicked duty officers who manned the center twenty-four hours a day. Three others—a Navy lieutenant commander, a CIA analyst, and an Army major—were working at computer terminals connected to Intelink-TS, part of the Joint Worldwide Intelligence Communications System.

On Intelink-TS, the White House and other high-level consumers got the closest-held secrets, such as the latest chatter from intercepts of Al Qaeda communications and photos from drones flying over Pakistan. Intell-TS was tightly administered, much like the State Department's Net-Centric Diplomacy, the worldwide computer system that had been illegally downloaded on an Army computer to provide WikiLeaks with more than 250,000 U.S. em-bassy cables.

The Watch Center also received contributions from

the National Counterterrorism Center, the Defense Intelligence Agency, the FBI Counterterrorism Division, the Department of Homeland Security, and any of the thirty-five Joint Terrorism Task Forces in American cities that hopped out of the hierarchy and found a way to make a report on their own.

In a few hours, the gleanings from the Watch Center would be distilled into the Morning Book, prepared for the President, the Vice President, Falcone, and senior White House staffers chosen by the President and Ray Quinlan. Besides that, the President would be handed the President's Daily Brief.

Falcone's thoughts went back to the National Counterterrorism Center. He wondered how many secrets rolling through that mill were not rolling into the Watch Center or appearing on the very special, very secret documents that would be read by President Oxley.

Walking into the Situation Room, Falcone, as usual, found himself to be the first to arrive. It was, after all, his turf, and at both cabinet meetings lacking the President, and at meetings when assistants and specialists of the NSC Secretariat gathered over routine crises, he took the head chair at the long, gleaming table with its large leather chairs, six to a side. On the walls of the long room were six large plasma screens controlled by communications specialists under Falcone's direction. And in lesser, but comfortable, chairs arrayed along the walls were deputies, assistants, and aides, the people Falcone liked to think of as the ever-changing supporting cast to the stars in the big chairs.

President Oxley would, of course, take the head chair and the Principals would take seats according to the pecking order he had established. Falcone walked around the table, satisfied that each seat had before it a bottle of water and glass, next to a yellow legal pad and a coveted ballpoint pen labeled WHITE HOUSE.

Over the objection of computer zealots, Falcone had barred all electronic devices—except for the heavily encrypted iPad or smartphone that President Oxley sometimes decided to bring. As Falcone told anyone who complained, "Every word in this room is recorded and every minute is captured by highly visible cameras. Those words and images are for the President and no one else. If he wants to share them, that's his business."

Vice President Maxwell J. Cunningham came in and took the seat at the left of Oxley's chair. "Evenin', Sean," he drawled. Cunningham was a pudgy former Alabama congressman and ex-Speaker whose amiable exterior cloaked a tough politician who kept score for Oxley on friends and foes on the Hill.

"Thanks for getting here early," Falcone said. "I wanted to warn you that you'll be getting a call from Ray Quinlan." He told Cunningham about the idea for a joint committee and added, "I've got a name for you: Gregory Nolan. He's on the House Judiciary Committee."

Nolan, a member of the House from Minnesota, had filed an impeachment resolution months before, declaring that President Oxley had violated his oath of office by signing a U.S.–Russia treaty that banned the use of weapons in space. Most newspapers mentioned the resolution in a short story on an inside page. Television pundits dismissed Nolan as a publicity-seeking fool who had pulled off a meaningless political stunt. Political bloggers called him a whackjob. The only Nolan photograph that newspaper editors thought appropriate was one showing the mustachioed congressman playing bingo with constituents.

The chairman of the House Judiciary Committee did not allow a hearing on Nolan's resolution, effectively consigning it to legislative limbo.

"Nolan filed another impeachment resolution today," Falcone said. "This time he's saying that the President had abdicated his responsibilities as commander-in-chief by failing to prevent the attack on the *Elkton*. Now, if the Speaker were to appoint Nolan to . . ."

Cunningham pondered Falcone's suggestion for a moment. Then he lightly punched Falcone on the arm, and, laughing, said, "You clever ole son of a bitch! Put him on the committee and shut him up. I'm on it."

"Thanks, Max." Falcone knew that anything he said to Cunningham would never leak.

"You are very welcome, Sean. Quite a day. What's the latest?"

"I'm saving my important disclosure till the rest of the gang gets here," Falcone said. "But I'll let you in on a secret."

"What's that?"

"We don't know shit."

"In other words, it's not that different from Army days," Cunningham said. He and Falcone were the only military veterans among the Principals. Cunningham had been awarded the Distinguished Service Cross for wiping out a Vietcong machine-gun nest while bleeding from three bullet wounds in his shoulders and chest. He sometimes said that all he had to do to get elected was show his scars.

8

At the West Wing entrance, black SUVs lined up to drop off the rest of the Principals, who silently made their way to the Situation Room. Falcone nodded to each one: Secretary of State Bloom, looking a bit pale, accompanied by Deputy Secretary Marilyn Hotchkiss, a slim, regal woman; Secretary of Defense George Kane and General Gabe Wilkinson; Director of National Intelligence Chuck Huntington, with three tired-looking deputies; Sam Stone, director of the Central Intelligence Agency, with the head of the CIA Clandestine Service; and Secretary of Homeland Security Penny Walker, who ruled over more than 180,000 people in twenty-two agencies but who walked into the Situation Room alone.

Falcone notified the Residence that the Principals had assembled. Eight minutes later, President Oxley entered and took the chair at the head of the table. Ray Quinlan, who had followed Oxley into the room, slid into the chair at the end of the room so that he was in the President's direct line of sight.

Tiny red lights lit up alongside the camera lens that poked from the walls at each end of the room, and a rectangular black indicator light appeared: MIC ON, warning everyone in the room that their words were being recorded.

"First of all," the President said, "this meeting was called to find out what happened. I want to know that before I try to find out why we let it happen. So I am starting with Chuck. Who did it, Chuck?"

Chuck Huntington turned to one of the men seated behind him. The deputy handed Huntington a paper. He stared at it for a moment, as if he were trying to translate it. He made a slight sound, as if clearing a throat that did not need clearing, and said, "It is our best belief at this time that the *Elkton* was attacked by two indigenous individuals who may or not be associated with Al Qaeda. This is, of course, a preliminary finding."

"Any connection with Iran?"

"Not to our knowledge, Mr. President."

"What about the GNN report?"

"We have no reason to believe or disbelieve it, Mr. President."

"Sam? What does the CIA think?"

Sam Stone, a hard-eyed man, said, "We think it's a red herring, a phony, Mr. President."

"Based on what?" Huntington cut in before the President could speak. Stone ignored him.

"We simply analyzed the GNN tape, Mr. President. Obviously, the correspondent on the scene, Ned Winslow, did not have a chance to get any information beyond what he had witnessed. The information claiming Iranian involvement was reported by a news reader in a GNN studio in Washington."

"And?"

"We asked NSA for whatever intercepts they picked up during the twelve minutes from the time the *Elkton* was struck to the time the news reader said, 'the suicide boat that struck the *Elkton* is of Iranian origin.' "

At the mention of the NSA, Secretary of Defense Kane and General Wilkinson simultaneous looked across the table at Stone. The National Security Administration, the powerful eavesdropping agency whose budget far exceeded the CIA's, was seemingly independent but officially under the Department of Defense. If Stone queried the NSA without going through proper channels, he and the CIA had strayed off-turf.

"*Iran* is, of course, one of NSA's watchwords in several languages," Stone continued. "Of the millions of intercepts picked up in those twelve minutes, *Iran* was picked up, in English, four hundred and thirty-six times. When the landline phone numbers of GNN's Washington's news bureau were applied to the NSA *Iran* collection in that time frame, analysts came up with nine hits. And one stood out."

"Coming from where?" the President asked.

"An anonymous smartphone with no known Iranian connection," Stone responded. "The NSA is very conscious of this particular smartphone, which seems to be unique and untraceable and is a target of an NSA special team. But NSA says any further information on that is so sensitive that we can only be told that the origin of the call is apparently domestic. But obviously someone at GNN accepted the call as authentic and was familiar with it as a source. Because of privacy rules, NSA could not identify the person who accepted the call and directed the information to the news reader.

"The information about the Bladerunner was relatively accurate. But our preliminary analysis of the GNN film indicates that the boat was a Bladerunner knockoff, a type that is showing up in a lot of places around the Persian Gulf, and not just Iran. We believe that the caller was a provocateur, someone who was trying to put blame on Iran for purposes unknown."

"So, from an intelligence viewpoint, we don't know a goddamn thing," Oxley said. "I believe that sums it up."

Oxley turned toward Secretary of State Bloom. "Now, Bill, let's hear how Goodbye Day came about."

. . .

On the day after Falcone and Cunningham talked about the appointment of Gregory Nolan to the committee investigating the attack on the *Elkton,* General Parker was in his study reading the latest classified report he had received from his principal contact in the Pentagon, Army Brigadier General Richard Castleton, military advisor to the Deputy Secretary of Defense. The report, prepared by U.S. Naval Intelligence, described the Iranian Navy's recent acquisition of a new kind of missile boat, a catamaran that the report called China Cat because the craft had been built and sold by China.

As Parker turned a page and began reading—"Faster and with a lower radar cross-section than boats with conventional hulls"—the phone in the holster on his belt quivered. He pulled out the phone and spoke the six numbers that appeared on a narrow screen and waited until two tiny screens showed green, signaling that the phone had accepted him and was ready to scramble the conversation.

"I have just learned," the robotic voice began, "that Falcone has made a clever move. He has arranged for our friend Nolan to be on the committee designed to whitewash the *Elkton* attack."

Parker was used to hearing "learned" from Isaiah. His ability to ferret information highly impressed the general, even though Parker's many covert missions had taught him not to be surprised by dark national-security secrets hidden behind the facade of official information.

"Through an intermediary I learned of Nolan's appointment," the voice continued. "Nolan is a very helpful fellow. He will have an even more helpful role in the near future, when he will gain national recognition. I want you to be informed, though I know you disdain politics. Nolan will be valuable. There will be a minority report, telling the truth. Yes, the truth."

"And Stanfield will be able to use it," Parker said.

There was a metallic laugh. "You are learning about the dirty game of politics, Amos. You are learning."

AUGUST

9

On a night graced by the full moon, Falcone stepped out onto the broad terrace of his Pennsylvania Avenue penthouse, swishing around the ice in a glass of Grey Goose vodka. He shed his coat jacket and tossed it on one of two tufted chairs that, in calmer days, he had lounged in during nights like this. In the serenity of those days and nights, he could clear his mind of thoughts for DLA Piper. He gave himself some time for thinking about his own life, a chance for reverie. He rarely had such a chance anymore.

But tonight had come in the midst of calm for Falcone. His job description did not include strategizing presidential itineraries or poring over polls to determine how much time President Oxley should spend in Michigan or whether first-time voters in Iowa were leaning toward him. So Falcone was able to view with some detachment the events leading up to the national convention and the renomination of Blake Oxley.

The party's problem, as Falcone understood it, had been to somehow make the convention exciting. Ray Quinlan easily switched roles from chief of staff to behind-the-scenes campaign director. All that Falcone knew from his aloof perch in Washington was what he saw on television, and that was not much. The networks all treated the convention in Kansas City as a routine event that did not warrant what once was called gavel-to-gavel coverage.

The only excitement had centered on Vice President Max Cunningham. His renomination had been challenged by a Pennsylvania billionaire trying to buy her way into national politics. But Cunningham had called in enough congressional chits to squash her so hard that her name had not even been brought to the floor.

Oxley's acceptance speech was cautious, its muted theme "an economy that lifts every family." The speech was more a look back at his accomplishments in restoration of America's competence and credibility than a look ahead into an uncertain world. One of his accomplishments had been the withdrawal of U.S. forces from Iraq, but to mention that would conjure up images of the *Elkton*. Oxley's unusually limp rhetoric passed over foreign entanglements; he used the phrase "here at home" nine times and only briefly spoke of the war on terror.

Quinlan's polls and focus groups had shown a lessening interest in external menaces and a burgeoning interest in jobs and house prices. If Quinlan's campaign theme were printed on a bumper sticker, it would say, OXLEY, KEEPING AMERICA'S PROMISE. In fact, the blue-and-white bumper stickers merely said OXLEY.

The Joint House-Senate Investigative Committee on the *Elkton* attack had been working for weeks, organizing and digging through a mountain of intelligence reports. The committee made its televised debut in the week following the convention. The highlight of the hearings was the arrival of an Iraqi informant, who was ushered into the hearing room by two Capitol police officers. Like the thin, hunched-over man they escorted, the officers had on bulletproof vests.

The informant, wearing a black balaclava-style mask, sat at a table next to an interpreter. Each question was repeated to the informant, who reacted with gestures and a whispery string of words, which the interpreter pondered and then translated. The process was numbing and slow. What all the words and pauses amounted to was this: The raiders were Iraqis—Al Qaeda suicide bombers "celebrating the departure of the occupiers."

The witness was identified as an Iraqi Army officer who had infiltrated an Al Qaeda cell in Baghdad. He emphasized that the terrorists known as Al Qaeda in Iraq had no connection with terrorists in Iran.

As director of the CIA, Sam Stone theoretically had no more of a role in a presidential campaign than Falcone did. But it had been Stone's case officers in Iraq who had found the whispering witness and presented him to the White House. Falcone, suspicious of the Iraqi, wanted a more solid source.

Falcone had flown to Pakistan and traded some good intelligence about India to Muhammad Bashir Ispahani, director of Pakistan's Inter-Services-Intelligence (ISI). Ispahani believed that Falcone was being bureaucratically bold, usurping what was supposed to be the work of the CIA. Falcone, in fact, had secretly cleared his visit with Stone, an old hand at trading intelligence.

Ispahani's risk had been a genuine one, for he could have lost a high-level agent in order to give Falcone rock-hard assurance that Iran had nothing to do with the attack on the *Elkton*. Each attempt to communicate with the agent, a ranking officer in Iran's Revolutionary Guards

Corps put him in deadly peril and risked the exposure of the agent's ISI control officer, who was under diplomatic cover in Pakistan's Embassy in Tehran.

"Our asset, to use your CIA vocabulary, provided the control officer with what we accept as dependable evidence," Ispahani told Falcone, handing him the transcript of a cell-phone call from an Al Qaeda agent under ISI surveillance in Tehran to an Al Qaeda operative in Baghdad.

"The Tehran caller," Ispahani continued, "clearly is censuring his colleague in Baghdad for letting—and here I quote—'local fools stage an incident that serves no revolutionary objective.' Clearly, Iran was not involved."

Like most possessors of solid intelligence, Falcone decided it was too good to reveal, and so the President had to remain silent about the source. Falcone told Stone a substitute bit of evidence was needed. And Stone's officers in Iraq found the Iraqi officer in time for his dramatic appearance before the Joint Committee. It was his testimony, rather than the cell-phone transcript, that became the Oxley administration's publicly revealed foundation for confidently denying Iran had not been involved in the *Elkton* attack.

The Joint Committee, as Falcone and Cunningham had expected, was in no hurry to complete its investigation. The committee members would not be able to file a final report until after the election in November. Word was slipped to Falcone that there were tentative drafts of both majority and minority reports being prepared. Off the record, Falcone was told that most members had concluded that, based on the evidence to date, they were convinced that local suicide bombers, not Iranians, had attacked the *Elkton*. But there were several vocal members who, without any persuasive evidence, in a minority report, put the blame on Iran. A copy of this report was leaked to Stanfield.

Stanfield, a week prior to his party's convention, got two days of publicity out of revealing the report, which added a new flair to his standard "Remember the *Elkton*" speeches. He did not explain how he had obtained the report. But political commentators suggested that the leaker was the author of the minority report, Representative Gregory Nolan of Minnesota.

A Nolan spokeswoman denied that he had leaked the report to Stanfield. The pundits were quick to point out that Nolan could have handed the report off to someone who then had given it to Stanfield, and so the spokeswoman was not strictly lying. Nolan's filing of impeachment resolutions had gained him a small share of attention by the media, and the speculation about the leak added to his notoriety. The bingo image, however, was replaced by more dignified photos and video moments of Nolan in committee, looking grim behind his nameplate.

Despite Stanfield's best efforts to exploit the leaked report, Falcone believed that Oxley had put the *Elkton* issue behind him well in time before the reelection campaign's final sprint. Falcone raised his glass to the moon and sipped a toast to his success. He prided himself on knowing how to play the media game: when to leak, when to punish, when to complain about coverage, in private or in public. But skilled and experienced as he was, he could never predict the life span of a piece of news.

There was an ordinary kind of short-lived news: born one day (CALL GIRL NAMES SENATOR) and still alive for a short while, sustained by a second- or even a third-day angle (SENATOR RESIGNS IN CALL GIRL SCANDAL). The story then drifted off to the world of forgotten news.

And then there was the kind of serious, multi-angled piece of news like the attack on the *Elkton*. Falcone had not been able to find a way to control its life span, but there was no doubting that the *Elkton* was no longer news. The *Elkton* was merely a new artifact in the endless war on terror, a war that spawned distant battlefields for an army of young men and women who lived lives paced not by the moon or by the seasons but by rotations and deployments.

There had been *Elkton* moments, but only when those moments produced images for television: the President and the Joint Chiefs solemn at Dover when the bodies were slowly carried past; the strange sight of the wounded *Elkton* carried high and dry on the deck of the heavy-lift ship as it sailed to a Virginia shipyard; the televised tears in the eyes of Representative Nolan as he listened to the testimony of a sailor telling of his attempt to save a buddy who had died in his arms.

That particular *Elkton* moment, however, endured.

10

Senator Mark Stanfield, Texas-tall and telegenic, with gray hair cut almost a tad too fashionably just above the collar of his Turnbull & Asser monogrammed shirts, exuded the confidence of a man never afflicted with self-doubt. He offered no pretensions to intellectual gravitas. The country was fed up with cerebral politicians who spent their time apologizing for America's power and greatness. Men of action, and surely he was one of them, had little time for introspection.

Stanfield had been barnstorming the country for months as the presumed candidate, and had won the majority of primaries, as all the pundits had expected. His nomination at the national convention in New Orleans would be a coronation and would be far more telegenic than the convention that had nominated Oxley. New Orleans provided more music, more stomping, and more excitement than Kansas City had.

The stage managers of the convention had decided to get Stanfield and his running mate nominated on the same night, shortening the convention to two days and presumably winning votes by lessening the interruption of the networks' regular schedules. Because Stanfield had little serious opposition, the only suspense was generated by his selection of a vice president.

The first day and night of the convention was devoted to speeches by party stalwarts and celebrities who had ventured into politics in the waning years of their careers. One of them was a country singer who introduced a documentary on the rise of Stanfield: rodeo star riding bareback and one-handed. Texas Ranger hauling a perp into a courthouse. Lieutenant Governor presiding over the Texas Senate. And finally, U.S. senator in helmet and body armor climbing out of an armored personnel carrier in Afghanistan.

Speculation about Stanfield's running mate had narrowed down to a retired admiral with scant name recognition and the former CEO of an aerospace company who was equally unknown. Each of the candidates had a small base of supporters and brought no discernible political assistance to the Stanfield campaign.

When the convention resumed on the second day, most delegates were on the streets or in the bars of New Orleans. The formal schedule, which started the prime-time television coverage, began with the routine nomination of Stanfield, an event that produced cheers and cascading balloons.

Next came a prelude to the vice presidential nominations. Each of the two candidates was allowed to have two supporters make five-minute speeches prior to nomination.

But between the moment when the first speaker finished and the moment before the next speaker strode on stage, an image suddenly appeared on the giant screen behind the podium: Representative Gregory Nolan weeping as he listens to the testimony of a grieving young sailor.

Dozens of signs—"Remember the *Elkton*!"—sprouted from the sea of delegates, many of whom started shouting the same three words.

Nolan, looking startled, rose from his seat in the Minnesota delegation. Dozens of supporters, surging in from a nearby aisle, formed a phalanx in front of Nolan and shouldered their way toward the stage. As the leaders of the group neared the stairs to the stage, the convention chairman at the podium pounded his gavel in vain.

At the stairs, bedecked with a red-white-and-blue mass of bunting, supporters stepped aside. The chairman looked down, shrugged with a smile, and lowered his gavel.

The chairman motioned toward the stairs and up came Nolan, a lean man in a blue shirt, no tie, with sleeves rolled up to the elbows. When he reached the podium, he ran his right hand through his close-cut gray hair. As television cameras zoomed in, the tattoo of a Celtic cross could be seen on his right forearm.

"This has surprised me as much as it has surprised you," he said, a smile spreading across his sweaty face. "I came here to vote for the one man who can save this nation . . . not to have you all vote for me. Before I can—"

A chant began to sweep through the convention hall: "No-lan," "No-lan," "No-lan." Nolan turned toward the chairman, who had reappeared on the podium. Behind them still loomed the huge image of Nolan and the sailor.

The chairman started to bang the gavel again. The cheering and chanting slowly ebbed. The chairman pointed toward the Texas delegation. Cameras showed Mark Stanfield standing. He wore a white Stetson, a dark blue suit, a white shirt, and his trademark red string tie. Someone handed him a microphone. "Mr. Chairman," he said, "I move that Greg Nolan, a great congressman and a great American, be nominated by acclamation."

All the delegates were on their feet, cheering. The chant—"No-lan," "No-lan," "No-lan"—began again.

"The chair accepts the motion," the chairman said. He could hardly be heard about the roar. "Two-thirds of the delegates having voted in the affirmative," he continued, "the motion is adopted."

Nolan's acceptance speech was hardly more than a thank-you. He spoke a few words about God and country. Then, scrapping the schedule and confusing television commentators, he asked Stanfield to come to the podium.

Stanfield hurried to the stairs, took them two at a time, and strode to Nolan's side. He shook Nolan's hand and grasped his right shoulder. As the two candidates raised their arms in victory, the screen behind them faded, replaced by a rippling American flag. Nolan walked off and

Stanfield went to the center of the stage. The hall darkened, the crowd calmed, and Stanfield stood in a spotlight. He doffed his Stetson, held it at his side with his left hand, and began to speak in a deepening drawl.

"I launch a crusade tonight, a crusade against those who hide behind the shield of their religion as they attack us and our way of life. I use the word crusade because I know that the word enflames our foes. It is a word that our timidity has erased from our vocabulary. I say crusade, crusade, crusade—in loving memory of those brave knights, who marched with a cross emblazoned on their armor to free the Holy Land.

"Those warriors, those crusaders, must be our model as we take up their task in our time. I want to lead a crusade against fear, a crusade that will wipe out our enemies once and for all, a crusade that will use our military strength—not slick, soft words—to transform the land that had been holy into a land that is holy once more because it is blessed by freedom.

"We live in a time of great peril, a time made even more perilous by an administration that cringes in fear, unwilling to take up the sword against the enemy who threatens our existence and the existence of Israel, the nation that preserves the heart of the Holy Land against all foes.

"I pledge"—he placed his right hand over his heart—"I pledge to restore pride and power to our nation. I pledge this in the name of God—and in the name of Jesus Christ.

"No longer will this great nation have a trembling leader, a leader who would not seek out, would not hunt down and punish those killers in Iran—the evil men who ordered their minions to kill brave American sailors.

"I pledge that on my watch America will be America, Americans will be Americans, enemies will be enemies. On my watch there will be retribution and not appeasement, righteous anger and not sniveling apology, the glory of victory and not the shame of defeat. . . ."

11

As Stanfield neared the end of his speech and was saying, "Let us now pray together," Falcone grabbed the remote. "That's enough for me," he said. Stanfield vanished from the television screen on a wall in the room that served as Falcone's library.

"Why turn him off?" Philip Dake asked. "What about 'Know your enemy'?"

"I already know enough about that son of a bitch," Falcone said. "I suppose you can remember the whole quote."

"Well, the gist of it: 'If you know your enemies and know yourself, you can win a hundred battles. If you only know yourself, but not your opponent, you may win or may lose.' "

"And," Falcone said, 'if you know neither yourself nor your enemy, you will always be in danger.' Sun Tzu, *The Art of War*."

"Well done," Dake said. "That calls for another glass of my wine."

Falcone reached across the low table between their chairs and picked up a bottle of Chardonnay. "So, you come over here and give me a bottle of Virginia wine—

good wine, but Virginia wine—and you expect I'll let you in on some NSC secrets."

"Right. Start disclosing. And, by the way, I got that wine for free. I own a piece of the winery."

For the book he was writing about Oxley's presidency, Dake had been conducting on-the-run interviews with Falcone—a few minutes in Falcone's office, a quick lunch in the White House Mess. Finally, Falcone had approved a long, formal interview in his West Wing office. It had been a relatively quiet day, mostly because of the political season, which effectively shut down Congress and focused most of the West Wing on Oxley's domestic agenda. As Falcone was leaving his office, on an offhand impulse, he called Dake and invited him to drop by his apartment later and watch the convention.

Dake eagerly accepted the invitation. Judging an informal costume would be right for a post-business-day interview, he donned a light jacket, a blue shirt without a tie, and dark gray slacks and drove into Washington from his home in nearby McLean, Virginia. As he often did when he was anticipating an encounter with a source, he began imagining the paragraphs the encounter would produce. *Falcone, watching the nomination of Senator Stanfield, turned to me and said . . .*

"It's the mention of Jesus Christ that most interested me," Dake said. "Every politician knows that you can safely say 'God,' but 'Jesus Christ' cuts out a lot of people. Muslims, Jews, Unitarians, Buddhists, Shintoists, agnostics, and atheists, to name a few million. And what about saying 'crusade'? That went out of the political vocabulary a long time ago."

"Well, maybe the Muslim haters will like it, and Stanfield's base will like it, just like they'll like 'Holy Land,' "

Falcone said. "The way he used the words, the Holy Land was certainly not a land for Muslims."

"How much do you know about Stanfield and Nolan?" Dake asked, abruptly returning to the convention.

"And so the interview continues," Falcone said wearily.

"Sorry, Senator," Dake said, using the title Falcone preferred over the impossibly awkward *Mr. Advisor.* "If you want to stop the interview, fine. We can just be social."

Surveying his refrigerator, Falcone said, "I don't have much here. I can order pizza. It'll be here in twenty minutes."

"No thanks, Senator," Dake said, patting his stomach. "I'm trying to lose a little."

"How about some scrambled eggs?"

"Eggs will be fine."

Dake's offer to "just be social" was a familiar gambit. He never took notes during an interview, giving his subject the notion that they were merely engaged in a bit of informal conversation. *Not to worry. Just between us two friends.* But he was reputed to have an infallible memory. He could quote verbatim every word spoken in an interview.

Dake's use of *Senator* puzzled Falcone. "It's always been 'Sean' for you, Phil," Falcone said. "Why the sudden formality?"

"I guess it's a reverence for power."

"No, seriously. Why the reverence?"

"I don't really know . . . Sean. *Senator* just came out. I think I suddenly thought, *Power.* Suddenly felt it wasn't like the old days when you were in the Senate. . . . Maybe it was what we just saw at the convention. Maybe it's because I spent some time today in your office, especially when I had to step out because suddenly you were plunged into something secret, something powerful. I guess it dawned on me that you're helping to run the world."

Falcone grudgingly accepted, but officially hated, Dake's talent for ferreting out and then disclosing classified information. Each secret Dake revealed meant that someone who had been trusted had violated that trust. One incident had particularly infuriated Falcone when he was a senator. Dake had disclosed a plan by the Sultan of Oman to support an assassination plot against a dangerous terrorist. Dake revealed that the CIA had provided the sultan with intelligence information that helped assure the operation's success.

As chairman of the Senate Select Committee on Intelligence, Falcone knew about the CIA's involvement in the plot. He called Dake to chastise him for publishing a story that made the sultan, a friend of the United States, a potential target of assassination.

"Maybe the sultan should have thought longer about the consequences before he gave in to the crazies at the Agency," Dake had said. When Falcone thought about that remark, he realized that Dake had willingly made himself an accomplice of CIA officers who were, like the sultan, fighting rival forces.

No one ever knew how much Dake actually had uncovered about operations he had exposed. He had a favorite technique: He would write only part of a major story and then wait for the calls to come in. Some callers confirmed what Dake knew and added new pieces of information. Others contradicted his story and unintentionally opened up new avenues for Dake to explore. All the while, he acted as if he were stumbling along in desperate need of assistance in order to get the story straight.

. . .

For all of the years that Falcone had known Dake, he was not really close to him. There was always a level of distance and unease about their relationship. Dake was friendly enough to Falcone, but Dake's only loyalty was to his craft. He was a political big-game hunter who tracked his prey with a relentless intelligence that left his quarry no exit from the kill zone.

Too many of Falcone's colleagues had mistaken Dake's easy manner and charm for a subtle offer of reciprocity, a you-take-care-of-me-and-I'll-take-care-of-you deal. They thought that if they cooperated and gave Dake the information he was after—or the information they thought he could use—that would buy them protection against becoming one of Dake's future victims.

They learned the hard way that Dake was not in the protection business. He gave nothing in return for information. No reward. No safety.

So why, Falcone asked himself, did he ever talk with Dake? Why invite him over to his apartment to watch a three-ring political circus? Dake was doing a book about President Oxley. So, why not run for the nearest exit? Let Dake go to some other staffer—Falcone reluctantly thought of himself as a staffer, someone of high visibility but still below cabinet level. Let someone else try to convince Dake that Oxley had everything under control, that the country was in great hands. . . .

Falcone wasn't looking to secure "favorable treatment"—two words that didn't exist in Dake's dictionary. Responsible journalism, like everything else in the country, was in a state of decline. The airwaves and print media were saturated with so much raw sewage that passed for news that it was almost impossible to know the difference between fact and fiction. He wanted Dake to get right the story about Oxley's presidency. And no one was in a better position than Falcone to set the record straight. At least that's how he rationalized why Dake was sitting in his living room. . . .

Falcone took four eggs, a stick of butter, and a bottle of milk out of the refrigerator and pointed to a loaf of bread and a toaster on a counter. Dake interpreted the gesture as an order to make toast.

"Nobody runs the world," Falcone said. "But a lot of idiots think they can. And don't worry about social meetings. I'll let you know when you can quote me. And you can quote me on 'idiots.' You can make it 'pompous idiots' if you want."

In what seemed like one move, Falcone grabbed a pan from a rack over the stove, turned on a burner, dabbed butter on the pan, cracked the four eggs into a bowl, whipped in a little milk, and emptied the bowl into the pan. As he shook on salt and ground on pepper, he said, "How much do *you* know about Stanfield and Nolan?"

"Well, they have something in common."

"Jesus Christ?"

"And The Brethren of the Covenant of Jesus."

"So they are *both* Brethren?" Falcone asked. "I knew about Stanfield, from that *Post* piece you wrote. But Nolan? That's surprising, real surprising. What else do you know about The Brethren?"

"Not much."

"I don't mean the kind of double-sourced information you'd write for the *Post* or your books. I mean, in your gut."

The toast popped, Falcone put plates and silverware on the counter, and served out the eggs. The two men sat next to each other on swiveling stools. As Dake talked about what he had written about the house on East Capitol Street and General Parker, he wrote an imaginary color paragraph: *The interview continued in Falcone's gleaming kitchen . . .*

"I think the key to Stanfield is General Parker," Dake went on. "He's been in the back alleys, in the places where ordinary people have never been, places that Americans don't even want to know about. He did all that Stanfield wishes that he could have done if he had donned a uniform. It's like Stanfield saw Parker as a source of heroism, the kind of God-directed warrior that Stanfield could never be.

"Parker volunteered for the Delta Force right after he was commissioned, and he never left that secret world. He was in the Delta mission to rescue our hostages in Iran. He was in the Granada operation, the Panama invasion. He was a leader of the first Special Forces that went into Afghanistan after nine-eleven. He got involved in some nasty stuff that left a lot of drug lords dead in Colombia. He was badly wounded in the botched battle in Mogadishu—and that's where the conversion came."

"What conversion? Born again?" Falcone asked. They had finished off the wine. Falcone left the stool to make coffee.

"Born again in fire. He took a chest wound in Mogadishu. The medic on the evac chopper thought he was dying. But he recovered. And he called it a miracle, a *real* miracle. He told people that God had put him in the Delta Force and kept him alive for some special mission. A psychiatrist recommended that he be transferred to the regular army because—get this—he was too religious for Delta Force. But one of his superiors was even more religious than Parker. He became an inspiration. And the idea of a holy mission—a crusade—appealed to a lot of officers in the Special Operations Command."

"And that's the gospel that Stanfield picked up?" Falcone asked. He took down mugs. "Sugar? Milk?"

"Black."

"Me, too."

"Thanks," Dake said, holding up his mug, which bore the logo of *Meet the Press.* "I think that when you try to figure the connection between Parker and Stanfield and their connection with The Brethren, you get into supposition, speculation. Or you have to do some heavy snooping. The Brethren is a tough bunch to crack. But I'll tell you what my gut says. What we just saw at that convention is scary. A political coup by The Brethren."

"So that Praetorian guard that we saw muscle Nolan onto the stage . . . that was The Brethren?"

"Looks that way to me," Dake said. "There's a brownshirt tinge to those guys. There's a fascist strain that runs through them. And 'fascist' is not a word I use lightly. It's a bolt out of the blue, the way they've crashed into national politics."

"A surprise to most people," Falcone said. "But not to Ray Quinlan. He was incensed that Nolan got on the *Elkton* committee after two impeachment resolutions."

"The resolutions wound up quickly as no-news. They're absolutely forgotten."

"Right. And so was the impeachment resolution introduced against Nixon at the beginning of Watergate. Sure, it got nowhere at the time. But it was there, and its mere existence started making Nixon's supporters take a closer look at him."

"There's no comparison between where Nixon was and the way Oxley—"

"That's not the way Ray Quinlan sees it," Falcone interrupted. "Quinlan has a lot of reasons to be pissed off at me. And I handed him another one when I suggested putting Nolan on the *Elkton* investigation committee. Quinlan thinks that I catapulted Nolan onto the national stage. And don't quote me."

"*Your* suggestion?"

"Right. I thought I could bottle him up in the committee, and that if he went off the reservation, he would look like an idiot and make his impeachment efforts look like the work of an idiot. I turned out to be the idiot. Again, no quote. And here's another quote that didn't come from me: Quinlan predicted days ago that Nolan would get the vice presidential nomination. Get that quote from him."

"Amazing! What led him to predict that?"

"Again, get that from him. I don't know what he'll tell you. But—again, don't quote me—I think he got some information from the President."

"And the President got it from the Intelligence Community?"

"I didn't say that," Falcone said, buttering a piece of toast and handing it to Dake.

"Thanks," Dake said. "Well, from what I've heard, The Brethren has been an intelligence target for some time."

"You know that would be illegal, Phil. The Brethren is legitimately—well, legally—a religion. So the FBI can't snoop around. And it's domestic. So the CIA can't touch it, either."

"I didn't say *American* intelligence."

Dake waited for a response. There was none.

"It's the intelligence service that we dare not speak its name," Dake continued. "The Mossad. Supposedly it's doing the snooping. Israel wonders about The Brethren. And after tonight, Israel will be wondering even more. Sure, the Brethren members support Israel—and they'd be gleeful if Israel bombed Iran's nuke facilities."

To Dake's experienced eyes, Falcone had begun looking uncomfortable. It was time for Dake to pivot the interview from asking questions to giving answers, moving Falcone back to his cooperative mood. Dake had tossed his jacket over a stool. He reached for the jacket and fished a thick envelope from an inner pocket.

"I brought this along because I thought you might like to see it. It's some notes and some noodling I've been doing for a book. It started out to be a book on The Brethren, and then I started getting information on Parker. I brought it along because I knew you'd want to know about The Brethren—and the Israeli interest."

"Funny you happened to have this in your pocket," Falcone said, smiling. He did not reach for the envelope from Dake's outstretched hand. "If I take this, what am I supposed to do with it?"

"Call it a gift. Just unwrap it and decide whether you want to keep it."

"As you undoubtedly know, I have had some complicated relationships with Israel—and one Israeli especially."

"I remember. The Israeli connection to Senator Stock. When he was murdered—"

"No need to go into that," Falcone interrupted. "What I want to do is ask you a question. I think I know you well enough to know that you won't lie to me."

"What's the question?" Dake asked, putting the envelope on the counter.

"Did an Israeli ask you to give me the information in that envelope?"

"No."

"Did you get this from an Israeli?"

"You know I can't give you or anybody else my sources, Sean."

"Well, let me ask you another question. Were you surprised by Nolan's nomination?"

"I was surprised about as much as Quinlan would have been."

"Interesting answer," Falcone said. He was remembering his visit to Dake's home years before, when Dake was helping Falcone solve the murder of Joshua Stock and clear his name. Dake, Falcone remembered, had given himself the code name Music Man.

Dake lived in his multi-tiered home in McLean, complete with what a friend once called his Book Factory on the third floor and his Music Room on the second floor. The Music Room's centerpiece was his Steinway grand piano. Scattered around the room were cabinets containing his collections of recordings and sheet music. He was a nearly professional amateur who once had coaxed the conductor of the National Symphony Orchestra to allow him to play a concerto during a concert that featured Yo-Yo Ma. But while Dake loved classical music, he could just as easily slip into ragtime or R&B. Occasionally, he performed in a trio at Blues Alley in Georgetown, Washington's premier jazz club.

During that memorable visit to Dake's home, Falcone had seen two assistants typing away at computers and filing thick folders into dozens of filing cabinets that lined the walls. Dake had a passion for finding information where nobody else even thought to look for it.

No one had ever successfully challenged him on any substantial fact, but his conclusions and accusations created controversies—and made his books into bestsellers. In a book describing the administration that preceded Oxley's, for example, Dake accused a high-ranking Pentagon official of getting kickbacks from defense contractors. When the official went to court to get an order that he give up his source, Dake refused and spent a month in prison for contempt of court. An appeals court freed him, upholding Dake's right to keep a promise of confidentiality to his sources.

"Okay, Phil. I'll take your gift," Falcone said, reaching for the envelope.

12

A few minutes after Dake left, Falcone went into the locked room that served as his office, opened the envelope, and took out several pages folded in thirds. At the top right-hand corner of each page was BRETHNOTES, followed by the page number. Glancing through the pages, Falcone saw the scrawled marginal notes, cross-outs, and written-in words of a work in progress. The editing had been done on the original printout pages; Dake had given Falcone copied pages.

The numbering of the pages began with *18* and ended with *26*. For some reason, Dake had handed over an excerpt from notes that went on for an unknown number of pages.

Falcone saw that Dake showed his old-school preference for typewriters by choosing Courier for his computer

font. As Falcone deduced the style, Dake used regular
Courier type for what were probable paragraphs for the
narrative text and boldfaced type for notes, some marked
TK for "to come," indicating something that he was still
working on. The handwritten scrawls mostly improved
sentences and did not change the thrust of the narrative.
So Falcone mostly disregarded the scrawls and concentrated on the typescript.

Possible lead-off: One day in 1932, prospec-
tive Democratic presidential candidate Frank-
lin D. Roosevelt was having lunch with
Rexford Tugwell, a member of the advisors
Roosevelt called his "Brain Trust." Lunch was
interrupted by a phone call from Louisiana
Governor Huey Long, a populist who preached
a radical share-the-wealth campaign.

After hanging up, Roosevelt told Tugwell
that Long was the second-most dangerous
man in America. "Who is the most dangerous?"
Tugwell asked. Roosevelt answered, "Douglas
MacArthur," the Army chief of staff.

Roosevelt had not needed to elaborate.
With social unrest rising during the Great
Depression, some Wall Street bankers plotted
a coup that would be triggered by disgrun-
tled veterans and eyed MacArthur as a potential front man. The idea had worked in Italy,
where veterans had helped to put a dictator
in power, and would soon be copied in Germany.

MacArthur had shown his contempt for civil
authority by going beyond President Hoover's

orders to peacefully expel the "Bonus Army," the thousands of veterans who had come to Washington to petition for a promised payment to be given for service in World War I. MacArthur used tear gas and bayonets against the veterans and torched their camps.

The bankers never managed to organize their coup, and MacArthur retired from the U.S. Army in 1937. He went off to the Philippines to become field marshal of an embryonic army.

Now imagine President Oxley lunching with, say, his chief of staff, Ray Quinlan. The lunch is interrupted by a call from, say, Senator Mark Stanfield. If Oxley turned to Quinlan and said Stanfield was the second-most dangerous man in America and Quinlan asked him who was the most dangerous, a good contender would be General George William Parker, U.S. Army (Ret.).

But, instead of exiling himself somewhere after he was asked to resign, General Parker stayed in Washington, took command of a fundamentalist Christian sect, recruited Stanfield and other powerful men as members, and decided to use his talents as a secretive Special Ops warrior to lead what he calls a crusade to transform America.

Falcone was surprised to see that Dake was planning to start a book about The Brethren with an anecdote that implied that Parker was the power behind Stanfield. The

proposed opening of the Brethren book went far beyond
what Dake had said about Parker in his *Post* piece on "The
House of The Brethren." Looking back on the evening's
conversation and scanning the pages that Dake had given
him, Falcone realized that since writing the *Post* piece,
Dake had developed some extraordinarily good sources.

On one page, Falcone read:

```
[find place to work in:]  ". . . had under-
gone sexual and physical abuse as child. . . .
secrecy became his method of survival. Pro-
fessional secrecy helped cloud loathed memo-
ries. Intensive violence became a pathway
for bottled-up hatred and other emotions
that could be relieved by danger and combat.
Not legally insane but not normal. Fantasies
(see "miracle" discussion) may interfere with
Special Ops missions."  [CS13/2nd]
```

CS—confidential source—was an abbreviation well
known to anyone who had been exposed to CIA documents. The information may have come from an Army
psychiatrist, maybe at Walter Reed Army Medical Center, where Parker probably would have been treated and
examined after being wounded in Mogadishu. **13** was
probably the number Dake had given to the source, and,
as Falcone remembered, Dake numbered his sources in
the order he found them. So **CS13** was the thirteenth
source. The identity of **CS13** and all the other **CS** people
would forever remain in one of those locked filing cabinets or in some encrypted computer file.

/2nd initially puzzled Falcone. Then he remembered a

remark from Dake about how he had handled leaks from Senator Falcone's intelligence committee. Dake had said that he gave more credence to an original source than a secondary source, "especially when the second source was just giving me something he had got—or maybe filched—from an original source."

So **CS13** was the possessor of the information that had been given to Dake by **2nd,** who had not been assigned a number. Falcone inferred from this that the notation was more a reminder that Dake had been given the information and had not got it directly from an interview. Another memory came to Falcone: a package of documents found outside his Senate office door; the documents were genuine; the whistleblower was never identified. *Would that qualify for /2nd under Dake's rules? Probably not. He insists that although he uses anonymous sources, he always knows who he is dealing with and never takes anything from anyone who wanted to be anonymous when giving Dake information.*

On the next page was a paragraph labeled **Miracle** and **13/2nd** was again the **CS.** Now that Falcone assumed the **13** was someone who had access to medical and psychiatric records, he decided that the paragraph looked like a digest of an interview between a psychiatrist and a patient. This was the source of Dake's mention of Parker's belief in his divinely inspired destiny in Special Ops.

The longest passage seemed to be potential text:

```
When the air campaign that launched the
Gulf War began in January 1991, Parker was
commanding a small Special Air Ops unit at-
tached to a squadron of aircraft called Com-
bat Talons, huge Hercules C-130s especially
```

outfitted for black missions. Talon pilots were a breed apart. They flew low at night—any nights, clear or stormy. "We never thought about weather," a Talon pilot recalled. "All we thought about was the mission. Get our guys into tough places—and then get them out. We called it a high-speed aerial delivery system." **[CS15]**

On a Talon mission, a man who was to be lifted out of enemy territory inflated a helium balloon that lofted a nylon line a hundred and forty feet in the air. At the other end of the line was a harness that the man donned, awaiting the Talon. The plane lined up on the balloon, extended a pickup hook from its nose, and snagged the line. A crewman winched the man aboard through the open rear cargo door.

Parker, then a first lieutenant, volunteered to be dropped into what surveillance photos had identified as an immense minefield about ten miles from Baghdad. He was told that the mines were supposed to explode only under the weight of a tank. So theoretically a man would not detonate one. He was given thirty minutes to land, install a bomb-homing device, and then be extracted.

The bomb was the BLU-82B, better known as the Daisy Cutter. It detonated a mixture of ammonium nitrate and aluminum and was then the world's most powerful nonnuclear bomb. It weighed 15,000 pounds and was to be dropped by parachute from a Hercules that would follow the extraction aircraft. The bomb was designed to set off mines within a radius of about one thousand feet. Then those mines would detonate more and more mines, clearing the field.

Witnesses of a Daisy Cutter explosion tell of a blinding light and a tremendous shock wave. "You know it's not a nuke," a Talon pilot recalled. "But the thought goes through your mind." [CS15]

Parker, although wounded by a mine that inexpicably exploded, carried out his mission successfully. The Daisy Cutter went off as planned, opening up a path for U.S. tanks, and Parker got the Silver Star. Because the mission was highly classified, it could not be described in the citation for the medal.

The mission established Parker's career as a courageous warrior in the black battles of Special Ops. And the mission changed his life.

Back at the Special Ops base in Saudi Arabia, Parker told another lieutenant that in the desert night, while he was waiting for the Talons, he had had an epiphany.

"I'll never forget those moments with Parker," recalled the lieutenant, who retired as a one-star Air Force general. "We were in his quarters, the day after he came back and had been debriefed. He was very excited. He had a gleam in his eyes, and I suddenly remembered a portrait of John Brown.

Parker took a Bible out of his bedside table and opened it up to a place marked with one of those ribbons that hang out of Bibles.

"I don't know much about the Bible. But I sure remember the name and number. Isaiah thirteen, verses two to four. He held up the Bible, waving it in front of me, and he started talking—talking faster than he usually talked. 'Iraq. It's Babylon. Babylon,' he said. 'I raised the banner.' And he started raving about being chosen to be a vessel of prophecy." **[CS15]**

Isaiah 13: 2–5 is a favorite of fundamentalists who believe that the Bible forecasts events that climax in Armageddon, the apocalyptic battle between good and evil:

2. Raise a banner on a bare hilltop, shout to them; beckon to them to enter the gates of the nobles.

3. I have commanded my holy ones; I have summoned my warriors to carry out my wrath—those who rejoice in my triumph.

4. Listen, a noise on the mountains, like that of a great multitude! Listen, an uproar among the kingdoms, like nations massing together! The LORD Almighty is mustering an army for war.

5. They come from faraway lands, from the ends of the heavens—the LORD and the weapons of his wrath—to destroy the whole country.

That night on the desert, Parker says he

had a sensation, deep in his subconscious self, that he was being miraculously healed of his wound so that he could live and carry out a mission. He believed that he had been chosen for an epochal role in God's plan.

To Parker, the "banner" was the beacon he set up and the "shout" was his radio, which "summoned my warriors," the crews of the Talon and the bomber that dropped the great "weapon of his wrath." He was in an army mustering for war, an army made up of "nations massing together."

In conversations, then and now, Parker even found prophecy in the name of the plane that snatched him. The Law of Talon, an ancient idea of vengeance, says that if you kill my camel, I should kill ten of your camels—or even all of your camels. [CS13]

In Bible study sessions at the House of The Brethren, Parker used his epiphany on the desert as the launching of his own prophecies, defining Iran—not Iraq—as Babylon. (Look at a map of the Babylon Empire of the sixth century BC and you see it encompassed much of both Iraq and Iran. Modern prophets take their choice, depending upon contemporary geopolitics.) [CS13]

One series of Bible sessions was apparently restricted to what appeared to be a Brethren inner circle. Among the men who attended were Senator Mark Stanfield and three members of Congress—Representatives Charles Valeri of New Jersey, Jesse Halloran of Oklahoma, and Gregory Nolan of Minnesota. Nolan gained his two minutes of notoriety by introducing a resolution to impeach President Oxley after the attack on the *Elkton*. The resolution never got out of the House Judiciary Committee.

Another person at the sessions was Norman Miller, the well-known financier who was a major contributor to Stanfield's campaign. Miller owns True North, a private equity firm that has made him fabulously wealthy. True North was one of the few Wall Street enterprises that was neither battered nor wiped out during the economic crisis that struck in 2008. **[CS13/2nd]**

Parker did most of the talking, which first focused on the *Elkton* attack. On the night after he saw the attack on GNN, Parker said, he had had trouble getting to sleep. He dozed off and then awakened in a cold sweat, wisps of a dream or a vision still in his mind: "I was being borne by knights in armor to a cathedral and placed before an altar. I heard the faint echoes of trumpets. I knew that by divine command I had been summoned to lead The Brethren to their destiny, to their crusade. This was my third summons. And I believe it will be my last."
[CS13/2nd]

The first summons, he said, had come in the form of the "miracle" that had brought him back to life after he was wounded at Mogadishu. "My second summons came on a desert night in the Holy Land itself," he went on. He then recounted his epiphany while waiting for the Talon. Next came the summons of his dream.

A fellow officer, Parker said, had attested to the miracle at Mogadishu because he had heard a medic treating Parker say, "He's dying."

The officer, a member of The Brethren, had told Stanfield about Parker. Stanfield then recruited Parker into The Brethren in 2002, when Special Ops was getting more Pentagon attention than ever before. Parker was being groomed for high rank by the few Defense officials and fewer members of Congress who were privy to his secret world of black ops. His sponsors believed that America's future security would be shaped not by conventional warfare but by back-alley Special Forces and their black ops.[CS13]

Biblical study sessions inevitably were more about modern Mideast politics than about God's plan. After Blake Oxley's election, Parker frequently thundered about Oxley's failure to defend the country from Islamic terrorists. The Brethren's agenda, which bonded right-wing voters and evangelical Christians to Israel, was strengthening The Brethren's political clout. But The Brethren's focus on Armageddon was beginning to worry some Israelis. [CS13]

Millions of Americans believe that the Bible can predict the future and that they are living in the End Time. These are not thoughts shared by many Israelis, who prefer looking toward a future that does not include their nation's annihilation. **[CS13]**

During most meetings at the House of The Brethren, participants do not refer to each other by their names. Instead, they use Old Testament names, such as Amos for Parker and Hosea for Miller. The congressmen had New Testament names: Mark for Valeri, Luke for Halloran, and Paul for Nolan. Sometimes, because these names could be real names, participants got confused about what to call each other. **[CS13/2nd]**

Stanfield, who does not trumpet his membership in The Brethren, does not seem to have a biblical name. He rarely attended study sessions. Both he and Parker are known to have expressed fears that their Brethren activities were under surveillance by U.S. or foreign intelligence services. **[CS13/2nd]** (Reliable sources in the U.S. Intelligence Community emphatically deny surveillance of The Brethren, pointing out that there are no legal grounds for making a legitimate religious organization an intelligence target.)

Stanfield, who rarely spoke up at Brethren sessions, seemed to be particularly concerned about the fate of Israel in the End Time. "What of Israel?" he asked. "Won't Israel be destroyed in Armageddon?" **[CS13/2nd]**

"Without Judaism there would be no Christianity," Parker replied. "Israel's holy sites are Christianity's holy sites. We are as one, and it is our destiny to die as one.

"God has known from the beginning of time what would happen in the End Time. He kept that knowledge secret from all who came before us. But now, through biblical prophecy, he is revealing his plan to our generation of the Final Days, revealing to us that we will be the warriors in the terrible battle of Armageddon. I have seen a part of the Covenant that says Armageddon will involve nuclear detonations. That's how specific the plan is." **[CS13/2nd]**

"But Israel?" Stanfield persisted. "What will happen?"

Parker gave another vague answer and then suggested that he and Stanfield meet privately to discuss Stanfield's concerns. Parker changed the subject, shifting back to his denunciation of the Oxley administration's "traitorous failure to stamp out militant Islam, particularly in Iran." **[CS13/2nd]**

Dake had more than hinted that the Mossad had been gathering information on The Brethren, but he had not revealed how he knew. The Dake Donation, as Falcone now thought of the printout, was Dake's way of giving Falcone information: The real message was in the **CS**'s. Falcone did not need these notations about sources in order to read the pages. With a couple of keystrokes Dake could have deleted all the **CS** notations in the copy of the pages that he passed along to Falcone. Why didn't he?

Falcone poured himself a glass of vodka, sat down at the desk in his office, and went back over the pages, focusing on the bracketed **CS** citations. He looked at his watch. Twenty after one.

Half an hour later, Falcone looked up and rubbed his eyes. He had decided that **CS13** was Dake's basic Israeli source, providing background and some observations, probably in a series of interviews. Perhaps **CS13/2nd** was Dake's shorthand for indicating that Confidential Source **13** had provided him with information "secondhand," meaning in some way other than in an interview: supplying quotes from, say, the full or redacted transcript of a phone tap or a room bug. Falcone knew that Dake would never have put quote marks around words unless he was convinced that those words had been spoken.

It did not matter who the source was. What did matter was that intel was coming from a **CS** who apparently had managed to bug the House of The Brethren and perhaps Parker's phone and the phones of other Brethren, perhaps including Stanfield, now a presidential candidate.

Falcone was far from shocked by the probability that Israel had been collecting intelligence in Washington. There was a working relationship between the intelligence services of the two countries. Surveillance of, say, the Washington residence of Saudi Arabia's ambassador would be officially frowned upon but tolerated. But there certainly would not be any toleration of an Israeli wiretap on a U.S. presidential candidate.

Dake's parenthetical remark about an Intelligence Community denial means that Dake had asked somebody knowledgeable in the community about possible foreign surveillance of The Brethren. And that somebody was almost certainly Sam Stone, director of the CIA, whom

Falcone had suspected of being a Dake source ever since the time that Dake broke the story on the sultan's support for the terrorist's assassination and Stone was in the CIA Clandestine Service, operating out of Lebanon.

Falcone believed that a query from Dake would surely produce some interest and inspire a quiet look at Israeli activities in Washington. But nothing like that had appeared in the President's Daily Brief or other ultra-secret reports that Falcone regularly saw.

Falcone decided to keep the Dake Donation in the safe in his apartment rather than take it to his White House office. It would be another deposit in his intel bank account. Like all his deposits, he was not quite sure how he was going to spend it.

OCTOBER

13

By mid-October, Stanfield was inching up in the polls. New television commercials appeared in states where he was showing new strength. But his message was not new. He was sticking to his stale slogan, "Bring Back America!" and his campaign seemed to be based on a promise that he would do whatever needed to be done—and would do it better than Oxley.

Stanfield's running mate, Gregory Nolan, shouted and pounded podiums, surrounded by roaring seas of "Remember the *Elkton*!" signs. The media largely ignored him. One of his biggest television days came when he appeared for the first time without his mustache, inspiring chatter on the talk shows.

Stanfield and his echo chambers in the media relentlessly charged that Oxley had ignored evidence that Iran had ordered the attack on the *Elkton* to disrupt America's withdrawal from Iraq. Stanfield did not offer any evidence of an Iranian connection.

Stanfield was raising enough money to finance a relentless television campaign. Hardly a day passed without a Stanfield or Nolan commercial interrupting popular cable and network shows.

In the most frequently seen commercial, Stanfield stood

before rows of veterans wearing blue-and-gold overseas caps and was ending a speech with "Never Again! Never Again!" Then Stanfield's face gave way to GNN's image of a speeding boat smashing into the *Elkton*. A voice chanted in Farsi. Along the bottom of the screen ran the translation: DEATH TO AMERICA. LONG LIVE ALLAH. LONG LIVE IRAN.

Responding to Stanfield's rise in the polls, President Oxley stepped up his television campaign, which was built around a four-word message: "Oxley, Keeping America's Promise." To match Stanfield's sudden surge of commercials, Oxley had to step up his fund-raising. His campaign managers hastily arranged a four-day swing through what Ray Quinlan called Good News Land: New York, New Jersey, and New England. The major Connecticut fund-raiser was at Stonemill, the ancestral home of the Eriksens, one of America's wealthiest families.

And so came the night when the hostess, Mrs. Harald Eriksen stood, resplendent in a gown of emerald green, on the terrace of Stonemill, making small talk with guests and trying to not look anxious about the first presidential visit to Stonemill. She was waiting for President Oxley, and she was also waiting for her son Rolf.

The party, like all her parties, had begun precisely on time: 6:30, when the sun was low and Long Island Sound was a darkening gray against a black sky. Now it was 7:30, the presidential arrival time estimated by the Secret Service, and Rolf still was not here.

She knew that Rolf, who called himself a libertarian, despised Oxley, and she would not be surprised if Rolf was planning to time his own arrival to coincide with the departure of Oxley. She had a vision of the presidential motorcade and Rolf's Bentley colliding at Stonemill's security gate. *Yes,* she thought. *Rolf will come. He may hate the President but he loves Stonemill.*

Stonemill rose from the Connecticut shore, a monument to the Gilded Age, when men of immense wealth saw castles in their dreams and hired architects to bring forth the dreams. Stonemill was one of the fulfilled dreams—a stone mansion of Romanesque style, with massive walls, decorative quoins, arches, turrets, towers, and oriel windows glowing with light on gala nights like this one. East of Stonemill, within the vast, fenced-in estate, flowed a stretch of the narrow, winding river where a mill's waterwheel once turned. Mrs. Harald Eriksen, better known as Betsy, now stood on one of the mill's grindstones, set in the terrace as giant tiles.

Harald Eriksen's father, Trond Eriksen, had built Stonemill in 1878, reading the architect's plans as easily as he would have read a shipwright's sketches. He was his own contractor, managing a crew of Italian stonemasons, fashionable New York interior decorators, and Norwegian immigrants he had borrowed from the Eriksen Shipbuilding Company in Gloucester, Massachusetts.

Trond had come to America as an orphan in the great wave of Norwegian immigration, when recruiters, sent to Norway by American railroad companies, lured Norwegians to the new state of Minnesota. But, as a biographer wrote, "When Trond Eriksen landed in New York, he turned down the offer of a free railroad ticket to Minnesota. He was a seaman from Bergen, and he wanted to live in a seaport, not in the middle of a wheat field. He made his way to Boston, saw how many Irishmen were looking for jobs there, and traveled on to Gloucester, where he found work in a shipyard. Thus began one of America's great immigration stories. A dozen years later, barely in his thirties, he owned the shipyard, which became the foundation for the Eriksen fortune and the beginning of the myth of the Eriksen Midas touch."

Trond Eriksen's instinct for bigger and better ventures took him beyond the shipyard to finance and international trade, so he shifted operations to New York, America's premier port. His reputation as a solid, honest businessman was enhanced by his backing of the reformers who had overthrown Boss Tweed.

New York society was in the midst of changing the guard. Trond and his Minnesota-born wife, who lived in a fashionable townhouse and saw themselves as good citizens, were deemed nouveau riche by New York's fading society leaders. Unable to view the opera from box seats at the Academy of Music, the Eriksens joined the similarly snubbed Astors, Vanderbilts, and Morgans to build and endow the Metropolitan Opera House.

The Eriksens thus began their dynasty's quiet fame as New York philanthropists and became part of a new class of socially acceptable merchants. Stonemill did not immediately give them entrée to Southport, a citadel maintained by families with colonial ancestors. But society was changing even in Connecticut, and Yankee tastemakers began to realize that there was no sense ignoring money just because it was somewhat new. Besides, a commuter railroad was making Fairfield County towns like Southport attractive for the entrepreneurs earning new money on Wall Street and in the corner offices of New York skyscrapers. Stonemill became accepted as a place that proclaimed wealth, status, and power.

All Eriksen companies were privately held, and privacy was a family hallmark. The immensity of Trond's philanthropy was known only to a small circle of similarly unpublicized donors. Eriksen's public relations managers were hired with the understanding that Trond, his family, his philanthropy, and his financial transactions were not to be publicized.

Trond's only child, Harald, was ten when his father died of a heart attack in his box at the Met. Harald's mother, knowing that Harald, not she, was the ultimate inheritor, turned to trusted managers, most of them of Norwegian ancestry. They ran the Eriksen empire while she, as the titular manager, acted as regent for her son.

Harald continued to live his sheltered boyhood, taught by tutors in a Stonemill tower room that had been turned into a schoolroom. His playmates were the children of Southport's moneyed families. He emerged from Stonemill and from adolescence as a tall, blond, and handsome prince. He was skilled at keeping himself almost anonymous during his years at Yale, from which he graduated summa cum laude.

When Harald came of age, he enthusiastically took up the mission of learning how to run the Eriksen empire, which then consisted of three shipyards and a fleet of merchantmen. He soon took over from the able, cautious managers and resisted their advice to go public. Showing that he inherited his father's shrewdness, he expanded the empire, purchasing oil tankers and giant carriers of liquefied natural gas, along with pipelines, refineries, and offshore oil platforms. He also invested broadly, and within a few years his holdings included forests and oil fields in Alaska, uranium mines in Australia and Canada, three radio stations, and a string of Midwestern newspapers.

Harald's life was centered on the family business, which he ran out of the Fifth Avenue headquarters of Eriksen Inc., where he also had his townhouse. He traveled frequently but usually managed to spend time at Stonemill on weekends. His wife, Ethel, whom he had known since playmate days, learned to live as a society matron with a circle of bridge-playing, tennis-playing friends. As the years passed, no heir or heiress was born, but the idea of adopting a child did not appeal to Harald Eriksen.

When Harald and the twentieth century were turning fifty, his lawyers arranged a quiet divorce with a generous settlement for Ethel, and Harald married the woman who, for several years, had been his secret love. She was Betsy Fleming, a frequent *Vogue* cover girl with dazzling green eyes and red hair.

Betsy was the daughter of a New York City bus driver. A tabloid gossip column claimed that Betsy had met Harald because Mike Fleming, from his driver's seat, had noted Eriksen's brisk morning walks along Fifth Avenue and frequently dropped off his daughter at the right time and place. There was some truth, perhaps, to the story because they did, as a matter of fact, meet one windy day on Fifth Avenue when Harald recovered her flown-away hat. She soon gave up her modeling career and became Harald's mistress.

Mrs. Betsy Eriksen had a miscarriage. Then, to their great joy, Rolf was born. Two months after she and Harald celebrated Rolf's birth, Harald was diagnosed with lung cancer. And the Lombardi Cancer Center in Washington, D.C., became a new beneficiary of Eriksen donations.

Harald, although pleased with how his mother had acted as his regent, decided that Betsy was not adequate to play that role for Rolf. Harald spent the last months of his life at meetings with the nation's leading corporate lawyers and economists. They created a council of well-paid advisors who were to maintain his empire until Rolf came of age.

After Harald Eriksen died and Betsy became the heiress of one of the nation's largest fortunes, she took advice from the council only long enough for her bright, quick mind to learn the basics of Eriksen Inc. She then established herself as the real manager of the empire, finally dissolving the advisory council. She presented termination bonuses to everyone on the council, except Brian Pershing, a young economist. Pershing became her sole advisor, the day-to-day executive manager of the empire. And, in their early years together, he was also her lover.

Rolf, growing up, realized that he would not be allowed to run Eriksen Inc. while his mother was alive. They never discussed the question, but, as he gradually became acquainted with Pershing, he learned the truth and, for a time after he graduated from college, he accepted the idea of being rich and idle.

But in his early thirties, with Pershing's endorsement, Rolf became a company executive with an office, an assistant, and vaguely described duties. He kept aware of the empire's inner workings through his friendship with Pershing, who became his mentor both in business and in the way to live a circumspect but pleasurable New York life.

Pershing was too old for the kind of party scene that Rolf preferred. But Pershing stayed current enough to guide Rolf to discreet escort services that provided beautiful women where and when Rolf desired them. The women rendezvoused with their clients through the middlemen who made the arrangements and identified the clients only by their numerals and particular sexual demands.

Pershing also found Rolf bodyguards who doubled as advance men at parties, establishing that there was no dope on the premises and that everyone in attendance was on Pershing's safe list.

By the time Rolf entered into the family business, Betsy was famous, not only because of the rarity of women CEOs but also because of her philanthropy. She lived a busy double life, managing Eriksen Inc., while also continuing the tradition of Eriksen philanthropy, serving on museum boards and sponsoring charity balls. And, at the age of seventy-two she had kept her svelte figure and was still a lovely, photogenic woman.

As the doyenne of New York society, she received far more publicity than her husband or his father ever did. Her photo appeared frequently in the *New York Times* Sunday Styles section, which gave over a page each week to illustrated moments in the lives of rich New Yorkers who were smiling, dancing, dining, bestowing charitable donations, and giving awards to the talented nonrich.

While Betsy was waiting for the President and Rolf, her guests were talking about her recent $100 million contribution to Lincoln Center in honor of Trond Eriksen, who had not lived to see the center become the home of his beloved Metropolitan Opera. Coincidentally, *Fortune* had just listed her as the second richest woman in America, estimating her fortune at $16.7 billion.

After the Supreme Court ruled, in a bitterly split decision, that corporations could contribute as much as they wanted to political candidates, Betsy made Eriksen Inc. a

major contributor to campaign funds selected by Ray
Quinlan. Those donations led directly to this Stonemill
fund-raiser. An invitation cost $10,000, and hardly any-
one refused an invitation from Betsy.

Now the sun was gone, but the tall bronze lamps that lined
the terrace were giving off flickering light and a steady
heat that warmed the hardy guests who had strolled outside. At 8:10, Brian Pershing, white-haired and graceful in
his flawless tuxedo, slipped onto the terrace and told Betsy
that the Secret Service had notified him that President
Oxley's motorcade would arrive in approximately fifteen
minutes. Pershing also reported that Rolf had just arrived
and would remain in the library during the presidential
visit. Betsy nodded and walked into Stonemill's grand
ballroom.

A reception line was forming under Betsy's direction
and the watchful eye of Ray Quinlan, who stood next to
her, ready to prompt her about the names and attributes of
guests she might not have had on her A-list. On her other
side, given the honor of being the first guest to shake
hands with the President, was Rachel Yeager, who, only
two weeks before, had been appointed Israel's ambassador to the United Nations.

"Welcome back to America," President Oxley said,
shaking her hand. He had been told that Yeager might
make an unconventional surprise appearance. He had also
been given a short briefing paper that noted Yeager's service in the Mossad, Israel's famed intelligence service.

"Thank you, Mr. President. I look forward to my assignment here," she said.

Oxley continued down the line. His "back to America"
remark was a reminder that he knew about her earlier

covert work in Washington. The briefing paper also said that her assignment to the UN inevitably included some spying on the side.

Betsy had known Rachel Yeager for about three years. They had met when Betsy made her first trip to Israel. Rachel, ostensibly a representative of the Israel Ministry of Tourism, was the knowledgeable, witty director of Betsy's small tour group. But Betsy, after spotting the mini-Uzi in Rachel's backpack, believed that she was actually in charge of security. Betsy was half-right; Rachel was also a Mossad intelligence officer.

When Betsy returned from the tour, she made her first contribution to Israel, a relatively small donation to Tel Aviv University. Soon afterward, she got an unexpected call, on her unlisted phone, from Rachel. She said she was in New York on a business trip for the Ministry of Tourism and was calling to invite Betsy to a small dinner party hosted by the Israeli ambassador to the United Nations.

Rachel attended the dinner with Rolf, who was obviously attracted to Rachel, a luminously beautiful woman of uncertain age. Behind her smile, Rolf could see much, much more than he had ever perceived in a woman. Rolf was wise enough to realize that Rachel Yeager was emphatically not his type. But he sensed that she carried valuable knowledge, and he decided that he would try to develop her as a friend.

The smile she gave him was the smile of a Mossad officer who had recruited a dozen highly effective agents so far in her career. At the dinner she had started a kind of courtship, luring him and his mother into a relationship that would provide him with the pleasure of dealing with an attractive woman—and would provide her with entrée to one of America's wealthiest families and to Eriksen Inc., with its global oil and shipping interests.

At the dinner, Rachel introduced Betsy and Rolf not only to Israeli diplomats but also to influential friends of Israel in New York. As Rachel had anticipated back in Israel during the tour, Betsy and Rolf would greatly appreciate an opportunity to join a new circle of philanthropists with Mideast connections.

14

Rolf Eriksen did not like parties at Stonemill. The presence of dozens of chattering people spoiled the illusion of Stonemill's splendid isolation, an illusion that traced back to his tutoring days in the tower. After college, when he began collecting art, he still liked to climb up to the tower room. But the place he cherished most was the library. Now, standing in the library and looking at the starlit blackness of Long Island Sound, he felt the pleasure of isolation and the pleasure of having what he wanted—the art on these walls and on the walls of the gallery that opened off the library.

Members of Stonemill's staff called the library and the gallery Rolfland. The only person allowed to enter Rolfland to clean and maintain it was an elderly maid. And she could enter only if Eriksen was present to press the sequence of numbers that controlled one lock on the library door and then lined up his right eye to a second lock with a device that scanned his retina for a positive identification. A Mayan carving next to the door hid a surveillance camera and a motion detector linked to the computer in Rolf's office.

Eriksen was just a bit over six feet tall and had a fit body that a personal trainer helped him to preserve. Close-cut blond hair edged his high forehead. His tight lips and the sharply sculpted lines of his face gave him a stern look, relieved by eyes as green as his mother's. He wore tightly tailored jeans over black half-boots, a gray turtleneck, and an opened bomber jacket of Italian lambskin leather.

He turned from the window and tossed the jacket on one of the two wooden chairs at the long mahogany table that had served as his father's desk. He sat in the other chair, switched on the computer before him, typed in the password, opened the table's drawer to look at a device about the size of a matchbook, typed in the six numbers he saw, and waited for the computer to start.

Eriksen's computer was shielded so that it did not emit electromagnetic radiation beyond the metal box that enclosed it. The striking of a key in this computer, as in all computers, produced an electronic emission. But each emission in this computer was sealed off from the outside world.

The computer was built to standards developed by the National Security Agency to thwart eavesdropping electronic devices that picked up and reconstructed emanations from keystrokes and video display terminals. The NSA anti-eavesdrop system, called Emsec (for Emissions Security), was highly classified and restricted to key government computers. But Eriksen had been able to obtain the system from a contractor who had installed Emsec computers for the Department of Defense.

Eriksen swiftly scanned several political-news sites, then switched to the STANFIELD FOR PRESIDENT Web page. While he was scrawling down the Stanfield page devoted to his itinerary, a red dot began flashing in the upper right corner of the monitor screen. Frowning, he touched a button next to the keyboard and saw an image of Brian Pershing, waiting at the door. Rolf pressed a button beneath the desk, the two locks snapped open, and he got up to open the door.

In the soundproofed room, Eriksen had not been able to hear the sounds of the party. Now, as he opened the door, for an instant he heard President Oxley speaking as he addressed Betsy and her guests in the smooth, slightly drawled voice he used on such occasions.

"So the son of a bitch is still here," Eriksen said as Pershing entered.

"He'll be gone soon," Pershing said.

"Yeah. Hopefully, he'll be impeached," Eriksen said with a quick smile, to which Pershing responded with a wide grin. Eriksen's face turned stern and he asked, "What's the news?"

Pershing moved his head quickly left and right, as if he was looking for lurking spies. It was an instinctive move that always amused Eriksen. Pershing had a long neck and ears that looked like trophy handles. At Deerfield, after the class read "The Legend of Sleepy Hollow," the skinny, awkward Pershing got the nickname Ichabod, which lasted until he bloodied a couple of noses. He had been self-assured ever since.

"Yes, news," Pershing said pensively, speaking slowly.

"The news is not good. A lot of sniffing around Archway."

"By the SEC?"

"Yes, and the Department of Justice."

"Goddamn. I thought that was all over."

"So did I. But somebody turned on the heat again."

Eriksen motioned Pershing to a chair and returned to his chair at the computer. "What are you doing about it?" he asked, looking at the monitor rather than at Pershing.

"Doing my best to throw them off the scent. I—shall we say?—sponsored a whistleblower at the Cowley Group who is feeding some choice bits to the SEC. Cowley's much bigger than Archway, and that makes them a more attractive SEC target. I think that the Oxley administration is looking for election-year headlines about cracking down on Wall Street."

"You think he's after me or after Archway?"

Pershing leaned forward, elbows on the desk, made a tent of his hands, and stared at the Matisse nude on the opposite wall. "The way I see it," he said, "you and I are sealed off from federal scrutiny. We're invisible. There's a way to do that, and I have done it. Others have also done it. And it works."

"Tell that to Bernie Madoff," Eriksen said, finally turning away from the monitor and looking at Pershing.

"Madoff was a crook. We're not."

"Tell that to Betsy's accountants."

"We've gone over this many times, Rolf. We are sealed off. The SEC and the Justice bloodhounds are wandering around looking at hedge funds, hoping to find a crook. We're not crooks. We don't screw people." He paused and turned toward Eriksen, "Why are you so edgy all of a sudden?"

"I have my reasons," Eriksen said. "Tell me about Archway. Whether it's healthy or not I am going to need some cash. Not money. Cash. One million."

"I'll make the usual arrangements," Pershing said. "But—"

"No buts, Brian. No buts. One million."

Pershing nodded, a frown his only sign of displeasure. Internally, however, he was seething. *He knows damn well that cash is dangerous,* Pershing told himself. *Asking for cash can make a bank clerk pick up a phone and call The Law. So I have to do some more money laundering. Like a goddamn drug dealer. The money's for that asshole religion he's so secret about.*

When the unexplained requests for cash began, Pershing had put a private detective on Eriksen and learned that he was frequently driven to an East Side brownstone that was the little-publicized New York headquarters of The Brethren. Pershing was checking up on Eriksen not so much to protect him as to protect Archway.

Archway was a hedge fund that Pershing had set up several years before, financing it by siphoning off a few million from Betsy Eriksen's holdings and creating a dummy corporation to run it. Pershing had done a couple of dry runs while he was on the council of advisors and saw that his double-game could work. He pictured himself as a genius who skillfully oversaw the maintenance of Betsy's wealth while giving himself a bit of it.

He had begun by finding an employee of a London bank who could delay a multibillion-dollar transaction for an hour or so while money moved from one point on the globe to another. During that hour, the interest on the money was deposited in one of Pershing's Swiss bank accounts and was never missed in a global financial world awash in money measured in billions. The gambit got him his seed money.

While deciding what to do next, he focused his investment skills on mortgage-backed securities. The two sides of his character emerged: his cautious self kept Betsy Eriksen's money away from that risky brand of securities, but his gambler self decided to take a chance for Archway and bet against the subprime mortgage market. He won his bet.

His next move was to draw Rolf into the scheme. Rolf's salary and bonuses from Eriksen Inc. gave him enough walking-around money for a top-tier New York social life. And, like the prince waiting for the queen to pass on, Rolf was well aware that her realm would someday be his. But Pershing knew that the wealthy always wanted more wealth. Rolf certainly did, and he wanted it quickly.

So Pershing, in his avuncular way, told Rolf that they would only be taking a kind of bonus on the money that Pershing's talent had streamed into Betsy's coffers. By partnering with him, Pershing told Rolf, he was merely getting the money that was due to him, a little ahead of time.

As soon as Rolf agreed, Pershing knew that he had a built-in insurance policy. If his detouring of Betsy's money were ever to be discovered, the focus would be on Rolf as an impatient heir, and the lawsuits would mean exposure of a very private man.

Rolf was trying to continue the Eriksen tradition of privacy in the Information Age, when Google, Facebook, Twitter, blogs, and Internet videos made anonymity all but impossible, especially for the heir to one of the nation's largest fortunes. But riches mean power, and Rolf managed to remain out of the pages of the magazines and the videos dedicated to tracking celebrities.

Never being photographed sometimes meant that, now and then, one of his security men had to smash a camera or break into a paparazzo's apartment and trash it. But there always might be someone with a cell-phone camera, and Eriksen hit upon the simplest and easiest tactic: a regular retainer to the editors who decided what celebrity photos were to be published. Thanks to this simple tactic, Eriksen's photograph never appeared in the places where celebrity photos usually appeared.

If an entry in Wikipedia meant the achievement of celebrity status, then being *removed* from Wikipedia meant the demonstration of extraordinary power. Anyone who looked up "Rolf Eriksen" on Wikipedia found, under his name, the words, *This page has been deleted.* Anyone who went to Wikipedia's Deletion Log and asked why the page was removed was cryptically informed that the author of the article on Rolf Eriksen "has requested deletion." This was not exactly true. Rolf Eriksen had made the request, and the author knew that if he had not withdrawn the article, he would never have another word published anywhere.

Intelligence agencies and expensive financial newsletters got scant new information about Eriksen from the Wikipedia entry, which lasted on the Internet for only two days.

Rolf Eriksen was born on July 14, 1962, in New York City. He is the chief operations officer of Eriksen Inc., whose CEO is his mother, Betsy Eriksen. He has been offered membership on a number of boards but has no

other ties to any corporation. His personal wealth—
including the value of his known art collection—is
estimated to be $1 billion.

Eriksen graduated from Choate in 1980 and from
Yale University in 1984 (B.A., economics, summa cum
laude), where he was a member of Skull and Bones and
Phi Beta Kappa. He was an intern at Goldman Sachs in
July 1984, and was offered a permanent position. But he
declined and later assumed his present position at Eriksen Inc.

Little is known of his private life. His photo does not
appear in either the Choate yearbook or in any edition
of the school's weekly newspaper. The only photo in
the Yale yearbook shows him as one of several students
gathered around a library table, heads down studying.
His only known recent photo was taken by a photographer outside the New York headquarters of Eriksen
Inc. One of Eriksen's bodyguards was arrested, but not
charged, for assaulting the photographer and destroying his camera. The photographer managed to salvage
the memory card from the wreckage. The photo was
published in *I See,* a celebrity news magazine, which
Eriksen promptly bought through intermediaries and
shut down.

See Betsy Eriksen.

After a short discussion of Archway's dependable performance, Eriksen shifted to Mark Stanfield's campaign.

"So there's no way you can . . . redact my name?" he
asked.

"No. Your contribution to Stanfield is personal and must
be identified," Pershing replied.

"What about my mother? She puts in millions and she only gets mentioned for a minor contribution."

"A *personal* minor contribution to Oxley. The millions go to his party through her corporate enterprises."

"Then set up a corporation for me," Eriksen said, raising his voice. "And send him a million."

"Very well," Pershing said, his voice chilly. "But I cannot guarantee anonymity."

"No buts, Brian. No buts," Eriksen said, turning back to the computer. He pressed the button to open the door and Pershing left.

15

Twenty minutes after Pershing left, the red dot in the upper right corner of the monitor screen started flashing again. Eriksen punched a button, expecting Pershing's return on some boring matter. But he saw instead the image of Rachel Yeager. He pressed the button snapping open the two door locks and strode rapidly to the door.

"To what do I owe the pleasure?" he asked, nodding toward the chair that Pershing had vacated.

"I looked for you at the reception," Rachel said, sitting down. "But, as I understand it, you don't go to parties, especially those honoring your president."

"So be it. I can see why you went, even though it's unusual for ambassadors to show up at a political event. Very undiplomatic."

"There are times when we have to ignore the rules,"

Rachel said with a slight shrug of her right shoulder, a gesture she had inherited from her father.

"Well, okay. Support for Israel and all that. Sure," Eriksen said. "But why a visit to me? Or am I more charming than I think I am?"

"Yes, you are a charming man, Rolf. But charm is not what brings me here. I came to give you a friendly warning."

Eriksen swiveled his chair to face Rachel directly and asked, "About what?" Thoughts of Archway and the SEC flitted through his mind.

"It's about The Brethren," she said.

"The Brethren?" Eriksen said, relieved.

"Yes. I speak to you as a friend from a country that you and your mother have generously supported. Israel greatly appreciates the way the Eriksens have helped to sustain our country. We also know that you have been giving support to The Brethren, an extremist group that believes in Armageddon."

"What business is it to you—or to your country—who I support?" Eriksen said, a touch of anger in his voice. "As you well know, my support of Israel is simply good business for the oil and shipping ventures of Eriksen Incorporated. It is true that my mother and I also believe strongly in supporting Israel on moral grounds. But I do not appreciate your butting into my religious beliefs."

"Rolf, there are people in Israel who believe that talk about Armageddon is becoming serious. We have watched the fundamentalists in America, and, yes, we have accepted their support in the past, but we believe that their theology has taken a dangerous turn. They want to help bring about Armageddon by encouraging war on Muslims in the Middle East. Obviously, Israel would be destroyed if the biblical Armageddon were to take place."

"I know of no attempt by The Brethren to help God bring about Armageddon," Rolf replied with a quick smile.

"It's not merely The Brethren. It's the matter of Armageddon," Rachel said. "We—well, certain people in Israel—feel that some American fundamentalist Christians, among them Brethren members, are not just praying for Armageddon. They want to speed it up."

"I would think that you were more sophisticated than this, Rachel," Eriksen said. "Brethren are American patriots. Yes, I am a member of The Brethren, and I am sure that your Mossad has a complete membership list. But you are wasting your resources on some patriotic Christians who are concerned about the way our government ignores threats to America's national security. They mean Israel no harm."

Rachel picked up one of the two toy knights on Rolf's table. Attached to the knight's chest armor was the cloth emblem, the red cross of a crusader. She opened the knight's silver visor, shut it, and held up the knight. "Empty," she said. "Empty knights." She looked up and smiled. "I saw one of your Brethren friends upstairs, by the way."

"And who would that be?"

"Norman Miller. Another friend of Israel. Another member of The Brethren," Rachel said, replacing the knight on the table.

"Oh, so your Mossad is sniffing out a conspiracy? You should be keeping an eye on our home-grown Muslim terrorists," Rolf said, smiling again. He stood and walked toward the window, looking into the darkness.

"Have no fear, Rolf. We do keep our eye on Muslim terrorists wherever they are. But Christians like your General Parker can also be dangerous to America—and to Israel."

"Tell me more," Eriksen said, turning away from the window.

"These are dangerous men, Rolf. Their goal is *creating* Armageddon. It's one thing to hope for the end of the world and another thing to plan to make it happen. We have enough existential threats, Rolf, without the added threat of Armageddon."

"I respect you, Rachel, and I respect the quality of the intelligence that you are no doubt gathering. But, believe me, though some of these men may be zealous, they are not dangerous. They love America and they love Israel."

"Ronald Reagan loved Israel, too, Rolf," Rachel said. "But he tied Israel to Armageddon. And, to us, Armageddon means our destruction."

"Reagan and Armageddon? I don't believe—"

"After Reagan learned about the Israeli bombing of the Iraqi nuclear reactor in 1981, he wrote in his diary, 'I swear I believe Armageddon is near.' Look it up. Some Americans have an obsession about the fight between good and evil, about the Middle East being the site of Armageddon. Well, that is their privilege. But their obsession could mean our destruction."

Destruction. *Americans were far, far away from that word*, Rachel thought. *There was the day of nine-eleven and the aftermath and the fear of terrorists. But it was not the same as fear of neighbors that evolved into hatred of neighbors. Or destruction of your people. . . . She could never free herself from the past, from the fragments of the Holocaust that her parents had told her. The death marches, the mass graves, the belching smokestacks of the crematorium. It must have happened. She had seen the tattoos. But surely it could not happen again. Surely . . .*

Eriksen was looking at her strangely, and she realized that she had drifted out of the present for a moment. "Sorry, Rolf," she said. "I had one of those flashbacks that come at unexpected moments." She picked up the knight again, gripping it tightly, focusing on the present.

"Where were you?" Rolf asked, turning from the window and looking at her tense profile, sensing the depth of her reverie.

"A family memory," she said, smiling and shrugging again. "Perhaps brought on by the image of the night sea. When I was a little girl we went to a little town on the Mediterranean on summer holidays." She put down the knight. "But I am not here for memories. It's the future, the future your Brethren are hoping for—and, I think, doing more than hoping."

"Please, Rachel. Don't give any thought to this fairy tale," Eriksen said, returning to his chair alongside Rachel's. He paused, deciding whether to say what was welling up in his mind. He wondered if he was trying to prolong the conversation merely to keep Rachel from leaving.

"The truth, Rachel, is that I think all religion is sick," he said. "The drug of the weak. They look for whatever it is they want and can't have in their empty lives. So they rationalize by suspending rationality itself. An irony, don't you think?"

"Irony aside," she said, "if you are a cynic—and, I assume, an atheist—why are you a member of The Brethren?" She turned to face Eriksen directly, who looked away for a moment and then returned her gaze.

"I believe that religion will doom us all," he said.

"Christians. Muslims. They all believe we need to die now so they can live forever. I feel that I, as a rationalist—a libertarian—can perhaps contribute some prudence, some rationality."

"I think you would do better to leave religion to theologians," Rachel replied and started to rise.

"Hold on, Rachel," he said, reaching to touch the arm of her chair. "Tell me what the Israelis worship. Wealth? Power?"

"*Chaim,* Rolf. Life."

"The good life is the only one worth living, Rachel. You and I agree on that," Eriksen laughed, sweeping a hand in a gesture encompassing the magnificence of Stonemill.

Interesting, Rachel thought. *I spoke about life. He cared only about living well.*

Eriksen reached for the ornate box on his desk, opened it and extracted a Cuban-made Cohiba Esplendido. He twirled the cigar in his fingers and inhaled its aroma. Then, having second thoughts about smoking in Rachel's presence, he returned the cigar to its box.

"The extremists want to take all of this away from us," he said. "For what? An expedited trip to heaven? By killing anyone they call 'infidels,' they achieve martyrdom and live in the hereafter with seventy-two virgins? Remarkable! It's not exactly clear what rewards are extended to female suicide bombers. And gays need not apply."

He stood and again walked to the window, as if he was gathering inspiration from the darkness. "These are the people who want a nuclear bomb!" he exclaimed. "There's no such thing as rationalizing with the irrational. There's no deterrence, no—what was Kissinger's word? Détente? There is no chance for détente, an easing of tensions. The reason the cold war stayed cold was the existence of mutual fear. Neither we nor the Soviets were eager to see millions of our people liquidated. When two countries share the same nightmare, war is unlikely. But when one country's nightmare is the other's dream, well. . . . It's clear, once they get nuclear weapons they'll blackmail us into submission or actually use them. You can't threaten them because they're so eager to die. Somebody has to stop them."

"I will speak bluntly, Rolf. It is not your role to start or stop something that threatens Israel's existence. We, the Israeli government, we get paid to get things to happen or not to happen."

Rachel also wanted to destroy the nuclear weapons in the hands of the Iranians. She felt a dual sense of agreeing and disagreeing with Eriksen. But the "rationality" he cited meant that elimination of these weapons had to be done carefully and with great planning and coordination. That was not the way of The Brethren. They were up to something, and Eriksen was part of it. Rachel and her Israeli superiors did not believe that whatever they planned to do was in Israel's interest. She wanted to draw him out, get some idea of what his Brethren group was planning to do with all the money he had been slipping to them. *Perhaps if I goad him a bit. . . .*

"Still speaking bluntly, Rolf, I find it difficult to separate your admiration for Israel from your pragmatic support of Israel as the only country in the Middle East that shares America's values, the only country that Eriksen Inc. doesn't have to bribe to make a deal."

"All right. I'll speak bluntly, too," Eriksen said. "I certainly do admire Israel. But I don't admire your fanatics.

And I don't believe that most Israelis, with the exception of your ultra-orthodox fringe, are praying for the early arrival of the Messiah."

"They're not as fringe—to use your word—as they used to be. They are gaining significant numbers."

"Well, that is unfortunate, but I think it's safe to say that the majority still prefer to be in the rulers club."

She looked puzzled.

"Seneca, Nero's tutor"—Eriksen said, and again the quick smile—"Seneca said, 'Religion is regarded by the common people as true, by the wise as false, and by the rulers as useful.' Religion is as useful for rulers today as it was in Seneca's day."

"And The Brethren? Where are they?"

"Some are common. None of them yet wise. . . ."

"Just useful?" She was beginning to feel that she was gathering information through this discourse. But she could not yet put it into a context that would help to explain Eriksen and The Brethren. "Rolf, you just said that religion will doom us all, but you are supporting—generously supporting—a religion. As an atheist, why aren't you fighting The Brethren, undermining them?"

"Firstly, it's not prudent to be an atheist. Bad for business," Eriksen said. "Nearly ninety percent of the American people believe in the existence of God, according to Sam Harris, America's leading atheist. He says that atheists are among our most intelligent and literate people. But if they go into politics and reveal their belief, nobody will vote for them. And if they are in business, as I am, they'll be shunned.

"I'm not a fighter, Rachel. I am a manager, a manager of events. I will tell you something I have never told anyone." He leaned closer to her chair, as if his candor had earned him the right to nearness. "I may not believe in The Brethren's peculiar theology, but I do believe in their mission. They want to destroy Iran."

Destroy. The word echoed again in her mind, and for a moment, the memories of horror returned. "Go on," she said softly.

"The men of The Brethren—and, as you probably know, they are all men—hate the Iranians. They aren't afraid to sound the alarms or wake up our sleepwalking diplomats. They want to tell the world just how crazy the mullahs are. Think about it. The mullahs are waiting for the Twelfth Imam to show up. A boy who's been in hiding for the last twelve hundred years! Supposedly, he's to usher in a period of peace and harmony just before Jesus shows up to announce the End of Days. And we're going to let these idiots have a nuclear bomb?"

"And you think The Brethren are going to stop them?"

"No. But The Brethren can help defeat that coward in the White House who thinks we can deal rationally with the irrational. And Mark Stanfield has the guts to confront the mullahs and give them an ultimatum and mean it. None of that bullshit—pardon my French—that Oxley spins about a nuclear Iran being 'unacceptable.' "

"You simplify, Rolf. Dangerously," she said, now feeling the danger that was an aura around him and his words. "In this world 'there are only two tragedies. One is not getting what one wants, and . . .' "

" 'The other,' " Eriksen said, completing Rachel's thought with a broad smile, " 'is getting it.' Oscar Wilde. Good for you, Rachel," Eriksen said, making little attempt to conceal his condecension. "Wilde was an interesting, rather bizzare fellow who was quite insightful. He also said that a pessimist is one 'who when he has the choice of two evils, chooses both.' I rather like that."

"Interesting," Rachel said flatly. She decided that no useful purpose was served in exploring Eriksen's philosophical musings. "I'm afraid I must get back to work." She stood, signaling that she was ready to leave.

Rolf walked to the door, and opened it for her.

"Please remember one thing, Rolf. Israel cannot afford any surprises."

"Goodbye, Rachel," he said, smiling. "I am forewarned."

As soon as he closed the door, Eriksen returned to the table, looked for a moment at the blank computer monitor, and then took a phone out of the desk drawer. He pressed a button that suspended the Emsec shield and spoke the six numbers that appeared on a narrow screen. He waited until two tiny screens showed green, assuring him that the phone had accepted him and was ready to scramble.

"It is time, Amos, to begin the operation," he said.

"Understood, Isaiah. All is moving into place," General Parker said and ended the call. Neither he nor Isaiah liked long conversations.

16

Pat Flanagan popped the trunk on his Honda hybrid and took out two suitcases. He carried them to a spot designated by a REGAL LUGGAGE sign outside Boston's Black Falcon Cruise Terminal. Young men and women wearing *Regal* nylon jackets were walking along the rows of suitcases, checking their clipboards to match cabin numbers to numbers on the bright green luggage tags. Behind the tag-checkers came other *Regal* employees who loaded the suitcases onto carts.

Flanagan got back into the car and, gesturing toward the luggage, turned to his wife, Kathy, and said, "Not like Logan." Ever since Pat and Kathy decided to take the *Regal* cruise, Pat had made a theme out of comparing sea travel with the ordeal of vacation flights that they had begun by threading through the maze of security lines at Boston's Logan International Airport.

"*Travel* and *travail*. That's where the word 'travel' comes from: *travail*," he said, and not for the first time.

Kathy nodded as he started up the car and drove a short distance to a waterfront garage. He parked the car in a long-term space, got out, and moved quickly around to open the passenger door for Kathy, a rare act of chivalry that signaled his resolve to make this trip a second honeymoon.

A shuttle bus took them back to the terminal. They entered the cavernous main room and followed *Regal* signs to a line of passengers, all of them with name cards pinned to their chests. Many of the passengers looked like the Flanagans: gray-haired white men and gray-haired white women in their late fifties and mid-sixties. Nearly all of the women had sizeable bags slung over their shoulders.

The men wore new-looking white sneakers, gray or tan slacks, and tan or gray sports jackets over white or blue shirts open at the neck. The women wore daintier sneakers, slacks in pastel colors, and contrasting or matching jackets over white or ivory blouses. Nearly all the men and some of the women wore green-visored caps bearing the crown-encircled *Regal* logo.

A few of the passengers, scattered through the line,

did not quite fit the stereotypes. Their attire was similar to the stereotypes' attire, though some had been born in other countries. They were not white; their complexion color ranged from dark brown to light. Pat Flanagan, eying them surreptitiously (as he often did in Boston restaurants and subway cars), identified some as blacks, some as Latinos, and two couples as Muslims—that category based on the headscarves that the women preferred over *Regal* caps.

The line moved smoothly toward a pair of metal detectors near a double door that opened to the wharf where the *Regal* was berthed. After passing, two by two, through the detectors and door, passengers walked toward a gangway bearing the inevitable *Regal* logo. Aft of that gangway was a wider one that was used for loading baggage and other cargo.

"No shoes off here and pat downs here," Pat said as the Flanagans went through the door. "And nobody's nosing through your bag."

Pat was about halfway up the passenger gangway when he noticed two Boston police officers on the other gangway, one preceding and the other following two men wearing what seemed to be identical blue blazers and khaki slacks. The four of them were descending against the flow of suitcases and boxes that crewmen were carrying aboard.

One of the men, the taller of the two, stopped and shouted at a crewman going up the gangway carrying luggage as of it was a sack of potatoes. The shorter man tugged at his companion and the officer behind him gave him a push. He angrily resumed his descent.

At the bottom of the gangway, the police officers and the two men paused. One of the officers pointed toward a door bearing a sign, NO ENTRANCE, and the four passed through a door into the terminal.

"What's that all about?" Pat asked when he reached the top of the gangway and was greeted by a ship's officer in a white uniform.

"Sir?"

Pat pointed toward the other gangway. "There was some kind of commotion."

The officer looked to where Pat was pointing. "Loading, sir."

"I can *see* that they're loading. But there were two men. And—"

"I'm sorry, sir. But the line—"

"You're holding up the line, Pat," Kathy said. "Let's go find our cabin."

The Flanagan cabin was on the starboard side of the upper deck, where the six highest-priced cabins were. Above was the bridge deck and below was the main deck, which was ringed with smaller cabins, each with a window. Below the main deck was the lowest deck, low enough to need portholes locked against the sea. Here was the realm of the smallest, cheapest cabins.

The *Regal* did not divide passengers into classes. Unlike mammoth cruise ships whose passengers numbered in the thousands, the *Regal* was a small democracy. There was only one lounge and only one large dining room for the one hundred and forty-six passengers. People chose their tables at each meal and sat at tables for four or six. There was only one assigned table: the Captain's Table, to which certain passengers would be invited each evening.

On the first night out, the six invited passengers included

Pat and Kathy Flanagan, whose luxury cabin earned them the invitation.

Captain Simon Hyldebrand felt far more comfortable on the bridge than he did at the slightly raised table in the center of the dining room. The Flanagans, first to arrive, chose chairs on either side of the captain who, by long experience, knew that the first to appear on the first night would be passengers who would demand the most attention throughout the cruise.

From the forms filled out by his passengers and filed with the purser, the captain had learned that Patrick Michael Flanagan was a fifty-nine-year-old dentist who lived and practiced in the affluent Boston suburb of Newton and was allergic to shellfish; that Kathleen was fifty-seven years old and taught history at a Catholic high school in Boston; that they both took cholesterol-lowering drugs; and that their next-of-kin to be notified in case of emergency was their niece, Kelly, a Boston police officer.

Hyldebrand liked the *Regal*. She was small, handled as easily as a yawl, and had a reasonable number of passengers. To become captain of the *Regal* he had cheerfully deserted a floating resort that carried more than three thousand people. They danced in a ballroom, had a choice of eight restaurants, and strolled closed, air-conditioned decks, hardly realizing that they were at sea.

The *Regal* was a ship, a real ship, and the passengers usually liked it that way, whether on long cruises or short ones like this one, a leisurely seven days down the Atlantic coast. Hyldebrand had just completed a Halifax-to-Boston cruise. Now he began another, with stops at New York, Washington, Charleston, Savannah, and St. Augustine. At each stop, most of his passengers would be whisked away at dockside by buses for all-day tours. Hyldebrand dropped them off each day, picked them up each night, fed them dinner, and put them safely to bed as he sailed *Regal* to the next destination.

"Well, good evening, Mr. and Mrs. Flanagan," Hyldebrand said. He glanced at their pinned-on name tags and added, "or Pat and Kathy, if I may. *Regal* is an informal place." His words had the clipped, nasal rhythm of a Dane who had been taught to speak English by teachers determined that their pupils would not sound like Germans speaking English.

"I look at your uniform," Kathy Flanagan said, "and I know I just can't call you Simon."

"It's Simon for me," Pat Flanagan said, sticking out his right hand and grasping Hyldebrand's in a tight grip.

"Both of you enjoying your first day at sea?"

"So far so good," Flanagan said. "No complaints . . . but a question."

"I hope I can answer," Hyldebrand said.

"It's about the two men leaving the ship under Boston police escort. I say 'leaving.' It looked to me like they were being arrested."

Hyldebrand frowned, poured a California sauvignon blanc into their three glasses, and said, "Yes. They were disembarked. I'm afraid that I cannot discuss it because it involves legal matters." He looked up expectantly, hoping to see his other guests approaching.

"I noticed that they looked . . . well . . . foreign-looking."

"Actually," Hyldebrand replied, "they were Iraqis, but—"

"Iraqis?" Flanagan interrupted. "Iraqi passengers?" The *Elkton* was bombed . . .

"We do not discriminate against anyone who makes reservations to sail on this ship," Hyldebrand sniffed.

Hyldebrand concealed his anger toward *Regal*'s lawyers who had told him little, and then insisted that he not speak of it with passengers. "The *Elkton*," he said smoothly, "was a warship in a war zone. I assure you, Mr. Flanagan, the *Regal* is on peaceful passage."

"Thank you, Captain," Kathy said quickly. "I'm sure Pat is assured."

"Not completely," Pat said, looking across Hyldebrand at Kathy. "I wonder about security. The way the suitcases were handled. Nobody checked them. Did they have any stowed baggage? And—"

"I thought you liked not having to take your shoes off," Kathy shot back, also speaking across the captain.

"Ah," Hyldebrand said, smiling and rising. "Here come our other guests."

After dinner, and after an hour at the bar in the lounge, Pat and Kathy returned to their cabin. He took his smartphone out of the top drawer of his bureau and began fussing with it.

"Supposedly they have wireless on this damn ship," he said.

"Give it to me," Kathy ordered, taking the smartphone from his hand. She punched a couple of buttons and placed it back in his hand.

GOOGLE.COM appeared on the tiny screen. Pat sat on the edge of his bed, typed "S-a-u-d-i-s and nine-eleven" and hit ENTER.

He scrutinized the information for a moment, tapped the phone, and held it up for Kathy to see.

"There it is. In Wikipedia. Look. Fourteen of those

bastards were from Saudi Arabia. How do we know who those guys who were kicked off really were? And what about those Boston cops? What the hell was that about? We'll have to ask Kelly when we get back."

"You're nuts, Pat. Plain nuts. You see terrorists under the bed. And don't bother Kelly with your cops-'n'-robbers stuff."

Still squinting at the screen, he said, "I'm thinking of calling Homeland Security or something."

"Oh, for God's sake, Pat. Put a sock on it. We're supposed to be having fun. And you're just going into your CSI mode."

"Well, maybe when we get back I'll call." He closed the phone and returned it to the drawer. "Okay. From now on, I promise. We'll just have fun."

Early the next morning, Pat Flanagan slipped out of bed, told a drowsy Kathy that he was going to the exercise room, changed out of his pajamas into a blue-and-white sweatsuit, and took his smartphone out of the drawer. As soon as he reached the deck, he hunched behind a stairway, and turned on the smartphone.

Google gave him the Homeland Security Web site. Under SUSPECTED CRIMINAL OR TERROR ACTIVITY, he saw ONLINE REPORT TO FBI TIPS. A cursor hit brought him to a Web page topped by photos of a bald eagle, the Statue of Liberty's torch, and the Capitol. Below the heading *FBI Tips and Public Leads,* he read,

> Please use this Web site to report suspected terrorism or criminal activity. Your information will be reviewed promptly by an FBI special agent or a professional staff member. Due to the high volume of information that we

receive, we are unable to reply to every submission; however, we appreciate the information that you have provided.

The next lines gave him a moment's hesitation:

The information I've provided on this form is correct to the best of my knowledge. I understand that providing false information could subject me to fine, imprisonment, or both. (Title 18, U.S. Code, Section 1001).

But he plunged on, doing his best to type with one hand while holding the smartphone with the other. His dentist hands were skillful enough to keep his typing manageable as he entered his name, address, phone number, and e-mail. Finally, came the line that said, "Please enter your information."

Flanagan thought for a moment and wrote:

As a passenger on cruise ship Regal, I saw two suspicious, Muslim-looking men being taken off the ship by Boston PD. At least four other passengers appear to be of Muslim persuasion. And security on ship is lax.

17

"Well, the heat's off, at least for a while," General Parker said. "That son of a bitch Dake is back to writing suck-up puffs about another pacifist sellout, our dithering president."

Parker sat in a beige armchair next to a beige couch in

the living room at the front of the house. In another beige armchair on the other side of the couch, turned slightly to face Parker, was Albert Morton, founder of Lodestone, one of the countless think tanks that supplied the Pentagon with a steady stream of responses to RFPs, the requests for proposals that fueled Washington's consulting industry.

"Anything new? The committee still holding up the report on the *Elkton*?" Morton asked, knowing the attack still festered like a boil inside Parker.

"There is no question in my mind that Iran is responsible and there is no question that the committee won't say anything official until after the election. That is no secret," Parker said. "But who cares? With Oxley's boys running that committee we knew that it would say nothing about Iran's involvement. But we still got some points by leaking our stuff before the convention. There was no fucking way I was going to let them squash the truth."

"But, General . . . I mean, Amos. Both the Secretary of Defense and the chairman of the Joint Chiefs have said publicly that Iran had not been involved."

"Take a look at the GNN film that has been all over TV and the Internet, the one that Stanfield uses in his commercials. Thank God for that, and I mean, thank God," Parker said. "That so-called mystery boat that nearly sunk the *Elkton* . . . green, two suicide men in it. Right?

"What about it?"

"You were in the Navy. You know as well as I do that the mainstay of the Iranian Navy are fast coastal patrol boats."

"That was an Iranian boat?"

"Absolutely. Our intel guys know it. Oxley has to know it. Twenty-one American soldiers and sailors blown apart.

And we make believe we don't know who did it. Oxley bagged it because he doesn't want to finger Iran and because he's worried about losing the support of the Russians and the Chinese. Those fuckers will sell us out in a nanosecond."

"Well, GNN's been backing off about the origin of the boat," Morton said. "The British company that builds the Bladerunner says whatever Iran has, it's not a Bladerunner. Seems Iran got one through somebody in Egypt a while ago. Then the Iranians copied it and began building them by the dozen and selling them to anybody who would buy them. But, even admitting that, as the Pentagon finally did, that doesn't put Iranians in the boat that attacked the *Elkton*."

"Cover story, a cover-your-ass story," Parker said. "GNN cracked under pressure from Oxley. Probably threatened GNN with an FCC investigation. Stanfield had to fight to get that snip of film for his commercials."

"And the boat?" Morton asked.

"Believe me, I see documents you don't see. That was an Iranian boat, operated by Iranians, and ordered to do what it did by those bastards in Tehran."

"The sanctions—"

"Fuck the sanctions," Parker said, his face reddening with anger. "You know better than most people in this town that the guys in the White House bubble don't have any idea what the hell is going on in the real world. Kane, Bloom, Falcone, the whole crew. *We* know because we live and die in that real world. Look what happened to you."

Morton, like Parker, was a retired officer. His Navy career included command of a nuclear-powered submarine designed to carry SEALs on covert operations under the Special Forces Command. Parker thought of Morton as Jonah, who had also turned down a mission but later distinguished himself.

God had commanded Jonah to go to Nineveh; instead, he headed for Joppa and wound up in the belly of a whale. Morton had refused to land terrorist-hunting SEALs in Somalia because he believed they were not sufficiently backed up and their exit was not well planned.

Morton had stormed into the office of the Secretary of the Navy, who had known no more about what the SEALs were doing than what he knew about the seals in the Washington Zoo. But the secretary did know that Navy officers are not supposed to act the way Morton did, and began the paperwork to have Morton quietly relieved of command.

Morton immediately retired. The mission he had renounced was carried out by another submarine commander, according to rules laid down by the White House, through the National Security Council. The SEALs were captured and all were beheaded. Their next of kin were told they died in a training accident in the sea off Okinawa and their bodies were not recovered.

Morton, like many high-ranking military officers and members of both Houses of Congress, belonged to The Brethren. In the nineteenth century and the early twentieth century, their counterparts would have been Masons, whose rituals and secret handshakes had united them into a fraternity of power.

The Masons had left their mark on Washington—the massive Masonic temple on Sixteenth Street, the inscribed inner stones of the Washington Monument, the cornerstone of the Capitol, dedicated with Masonic rites. But members of The Brethren had not yet made their mark.

Now had come the mission.

. . .

"We're going to make history for The Brethren, Jonah," Parker said. Morton scowled for a moment. It always took Morton a little while to accept Parker's order that real names not be used during their meetings.

Parker glanced at his digital watch. The meeting was to begin in twelve minutes. As usual, Jonah was the first to arrive. If military men learned anything, they learned that punctuality meant arriving early.

The door chime pealed, and Parker went to the door to admit Malachi. His name in the world beyond The Brethren was Ed Hudson. He had been a Navy SEAL assigned to one of Parker's Special Forces units. When Parker went after him for the mission, Hudson was in Morgan City, Louisiana, working as a diver for oil rigs and sometimes helping out in salvages of sunken ships.

Over Hudson's right shoulder Parker could see a low-slung Harley with black, steel-laced wheels. Hudson gave Parker a salute that cut the air between them like a knife, removed his fleece-collared leather jacket, and hung it on a coat rack in the corner of the hall. As usual, Parker noticed, Hudson had not worn a helmet.

Hudson strode to the couch without speaking to Parker or Morton. Parker had learned some time ago that Ed did not talk much and seemed to exist on his own planet of anger. Malachi had been a messenger of Jehovah, who carried the warning of God's justice.

Ed Hudson is certainly a Malachi, Parker thought. For weeks the general had been going over the identities and skills of his men, weighing the choices he had made, remembering the interviews of dozens of Brethren who had answered his appeal for volunteers to serve under him for a mission he could not describe. None of them knew that

Brethren high in the Pentagon had asked contractors for the Defense Intelligence Agency to do covert background investigations of the eight finalists.

Parker had rejected four good men for reasons he could only call intuition. Now, finally, he had his unit, which he called The Five. Under orders from Isaiah, Parker had given code names to himself and the four he commanded. The real names of the candidates and finalists were not on any piece of paper in Parker's possession.

When Parker passed out the biblical code names, he had not particularly linked the names to the men's attributes. But it seemed to him that there had been a divine instruction behind the names that Parker had chosen.

Parker looked at his watch again, and at the sound of a car door slamming, walked to a window and pulled back a curtain. A black Mercedes pulled away and a slim man in jeans and a white sweater over a blue shirt walked rapidly up the metal stairs. Parker opened the door before the visitor's hand reached it.

"As I've told you before," Parker said in his command voice, "I wish you'd drive yourself here. I don't like extra witnesses. And your driver, I believe, is not a citizen."

"Well, General, and good evening to you. Akua, as a matter of fact, was born in the failed state of Ghana. For the past four years he has been a United States citizen. I'm surprised your vetters missed that."

"Good evening, Hosea," Parker said. He stood aside, and Hosea, known in financial circles as Norman Miller, walked past him. Hosea enthusiastically greeted the others as Al and Ed.

"*Names,* goddamnit, Hosea," Parker yelled. Miller ignored him and sat down on the couch. He took his Black-Berry from its holster and flicked through messages.

"And put that goddamn thing away," Parker shouted. "I've told you all before. No cell phones, no electronic gizmos in this house."

Hosea-Miller stuck the BlackBerry in his pocket and audibly sighed. He was not used to taking orders.

Miller was the only person Parker did not initially recruit. Shortly after the others had been selected, Parker received a call from the man he only knew as Isaiah. "You are progressing nicely," Isaiah said after Parker's terse report. "You will need one more man, a man who can handle the quiet transfer of money from, shall we say, here to there? There are payments you will be making, and they can only be paid by someone who knows the ways of handling invisible dollars. You will soon meet him. He will be known as Hosea."

To Parker, Miller was an enigma, a withdrawn, secretive man who was also a well known public figure and the subject of a bestselling biography, *Man of Many Paths*. The book told of the rise of Miller, the son of observant Jews who began a wholesale clothing business in Brooklyn. He had reached the pinnacle of the financial world, but, famous as he was, he had an inner life that neither his biographer nor Parker ever penetrated.

As a young boy, Miller attended yeshiva, distinguishing himself for his brilliant mathematical mind. He graduated from Yale and won a Rhodes Scholarship to Oxford, where he studied comparative religions and philosophy. He then pursued an MBA at the Wharton School of Finance. During the 1980s, he was a boy wonder in the Treasury Department.

His wonder days were stimulating but financially unrewarding, so he decided to form a partnership with three of his friends who had served in the Office of Management and Budget and the Council of Economic Advisors. They established a private equity firm, True North, which became an overnight financial success.

Miller began to enjoy all the trappings of fabulous wealth: A 30,000-square-foot mansion in Potomac, Maryland. Closets containing dozens of Brioni suits, Patek Philippe and Cartier signature watches. A Gulfstream jet to take him to any one of his five homes around the world. A stable of race horses in Kentucky and an annex to his Florida home that housed a score of vintage cars, including a rare 1936 Bugatti Type 57SC Atlantic, valued at $30 million.

Parker never paid much attention to supermarket gossip magazines. So Parker knew little about Miller's past private life when they met at the National Prayer Breakfast, an annual Washington ritual that has been attended by every president since Dwight D. Eisenhower. The breakfast, in the ballroom of a deluxe Washington hotel, draws about 3,500 people, including members of Congress and the cabinet, diplomats, religious leaders, diplomats from many countries, and a who's who of lobbyists, politicians, and other people who come not so much for the prayers as for a chance to show the kind of influential company they keep.

Although Brethren members were well represented, they did not sit as a bloc. Miller sought out Parker at the breakfast. As Parker remembered the meeting, Miller had walked up to him just before the grace, introduced himself, and said, "There is someone you know whom I also know. A person whose name we do not know." Their assigned seats supposedly just happened to be next to each other.

Afterward, they met at the Four Seasons Hotel for coffee, where Miller guardedly mentioned that he was about to become "the treasurer of Operation Cyrus." Miller's use of the code word stunned Parker, who asked him if he knew who Isaiah was. Miller said he did not.

For a moment, Parker wondered if Miller was telling the truth. But Parker had been in many black ops for which he had possessed only need-to-know facts. And often that included not knowing the real names behind the cover names. To Parker, an op was like what Ecclesiastes said of life itself: it "comes without meaning, it departs in darkness, and in darkness its name is shrouded."

A bit of discreet checking by Parker revealed that Miller had been investigated by the SEC but had been allowed to continue to run True North. And, though born and raised as a Jew, he had converted to Christianity and had become a member of The Brethren.

The last to arrive was a balding, overweight, panting man wearing a long, black, oily Australian duster, whose collar bloomed into a cape. He seemed more tangled in the coat than wearing it. "Expected rain," Dr. Michael Schiller said as he tried to hang up the duster, almost knocking over the coat rack in the entrance hall.

When Parker was passing out code names, Schiller had asked for Micah, quoting from the Book of Micah: "And the mountains shall be molten under him, and the valleys shall be cleft, as wax before the fire. . . ."

Schiller is a strange one, Parker thought as the last of The Five dropped himself onto the couch.

Parker knew less about Schiller than any of the others. Schiller was in his mid-sixties and was about to end his career at the Department of Energy to become a vice president at a trade organization called Nuclear Renaissance, devoted to lobbying for more nuclear power plants.

Schiller's wife, who had once worked on Senator Stanfield's staff, had brought Schiller into The Brethren. She was one of the "Helpmates," women who, unable to become members of The Brethren, served members by cooking meals for Brethren meetings and maintaining Brethren houses. Schiller's convictions about The Brethren, it had seemed to Parker, were like those of a non-Catholic husband who agreed to convert to Catholicism just to please his wife. Still, Schiller was following orders and doing what he had promised to do.

Parker, in the process of picking men for his mission, had drawn on his training and experience in interrogation. He believed that he had a divinely bestowed talent not only for detecting deception but also for finding places where motives and excuses hid. He had gone to one of those places while questioning Schiller about his commitment to The Brethren. Now, looking at him on the couch, Parker recalled what Schiller had said.

They had been sitting in this room. Schiller's wife, Margaret, was in the kitchen with another Brethren woman, preparing lunch.

"I can understand your doubts, General," Schiller had said. "I am a physicist, and you think that makes me somehow automatically an atheist. On the very contrary, I do believe in God. I have been slightly, modestly involved in what is the biggest physics experiment in history—the Large Hadron Collider in Switzerland. Not to go into the technical details, we are looking for an elusive subatomic particle called the Higgs boson. But do you know what some of us call it? The God Particle.

"Some physicists—and I am certainly one of them—believe that if we can find and analyze the Higgs boson we might be able to find proof that the universe was *created,* that it came from nowhere, and that the nowhere is God. "

"That's mighty heady for me, Doctor," Parker said. "It's a long way from The Brethren's core belief in the power of Jesus Christ and his Covenant."

"Oh, but it is easy for me to make that leap of faith, General. I see God as the source of all power. I believe in Jesus as I believe in the universes, the galaxies. Oh yes, General, I believe in power. Imagine a God who created atoms and gave them such power. Certainly if God could bring forth *existence*—existence itself!—then surely he could bring forth a son who would personify God's power. Yes. Yes. I believe in Jesus, and I believe, in some strange way, he has brought me here—brought Margaret and me—to The Brethren to do his will."

Ever since he heard those words Parker had trusted Michael Schiller. He, like Norman Miller, had not been a member of the great fraternity of those who had served in the armed forces. Although he was a total civilian and a strange one at that, Parker believed that he would be dedicated to the mission.

"Good evening, Amos," Schiller said softly. *And,* Parker thought, *he knows how to take orders.*

Parker had chosen Amos for his own name because, when he first began planning the mission he had found these words in the Book of Amos: ". . . though they be hid from my sight in the bottom of the sea, thence will I command the serpent, and he shall bite them. . . ."

As usual, Amos began the meeting by bowing his head and reciting the Twenty-seventh Psalm: "The Lord is my light and my salvation; whom shall I fear? The Lord is the strength of my life; of whom shall I be afraid? When the wicked, even mine enemies and my foes, came upon me to eat up my flesh, they stumbled and fell. Though an host should encamp against me, my heart shall not fear: though war should rise against me, in this will I be confident. Amen."

Parker looked up and said, "We are about to follow the light of the Lord. We will now go upstairs." His cold eyes scanned the room. "Do not speak until we enter the skiff," he ordered, using the acronym-derived word for a Sensitive Compartmented Information Facility. The others followed him up the stairs to the second floor.

Two rooms opened off the landing. Parker unlocked the door to the room on the left. The wooden door opened outward, revealing a metal door. There was a numeric keypad where a doorknob would ordinarily be. Parker tapped in six numbers, pushed open the heavy door, and touched a switch. The door quietly closed behind him and the others. Two tracks of ceiling lights went on, as did an unseen air-conditioning unit.

They entered what seemed to be a huge metal box. The floor and unadorned walls all dully reflected the overhead lights. In the center of the room was a metal table, its legs solid aluminum bars and its top a solid aluminum slab. It was designed to prevent the kind of taps that could be slipped into the recesses of conventional furniture. The six chairs around the table were similarly designed. On a metal table in a corner was a bulky computer whose emanations were also shielded.

When all had taken seats around the table, Parker, in his deep voice of command, recited the last words of the Twenty-seventh Psalm. "Wait on the Lord: be of good courage, and he shall strengthen thine heart: wait I say, on the Lord."

A ragged series of "Amen" responded.

Then Parker spoke in that same stern voice. "This will be the last time we will be together for some time," he said. "We will discuss the operation here. I will give you your assignments. And then each of you will go his own way. If you have any need to communicate with me—and such a communication, I warn you, must be *vital*—use the code system I am providing you tonight. The code word for the operation has changed to Godspeed."

18

Falcone reluctantly left his penthouse terrace and walked into his bedroom to pack a suitcase. He picked up the remote and flicked on GNN's ten o'clock news. He was listening but not watching the small screen on the TV near his bed when Stanfield's voice suddenly boomed. Falcone instinctively looked up. Stanfield stood before rows of veterans wearing blue-and-gold overseas caps. *No cap for Stanfield,* Falcone thought. *The son of a bitch is just a veteran of deferments.*

Falcone picked up the remote, spun around, aimed it like a gun, and killed the commercial.

A couple of minutes after he finished packing, a member of his security detail buzzed the apartment. Falcone, carrying his suitcase and a briefcase, went to the foyer and pressed the button to the private penthouse elevator. He entered the elevator, and a camera in the ceiling moved slightly to record his departure. When the elevator door opened, Falcone was met by a man in a dark suit with a wire coiling out of his left ear.

"Good news from Andrews, sir," the agent said. "Clear skies all the way."

" 'Clear skies,' " Falcone said. "That has a nice sound, Sam." The agent, knowing he could not touch the briefcase, took the suitcase, and they descended. Purring outside was the SUV that would take him to Andrews. Behind the SUV was a similar security vehicle as backup.

When Falcone reached Andrews, an Air Force colonel met the SUV and ushered Falcone and his security men into the VIP lounge, where coffee and sandwiches were laid out. The colonel, looking at his watch, quickly excused himself. "Rehearsal time," he said.

"Weisman?" Falcone asked.

The colonel nodded. "Comes in Thursday. We've got five days to check off a list that's a mile long—State Department protocol rules, Israeli Embassy rules, Secret Service, Israeli security, Mossad, the works."

"Give Weisman my regards," Falcone said, smiling. "I'm going to miss his arrival."

Falcone was on his way to Delhi to meet with Atal Mishra, the national security advisor to the Indian prime minister. There had been another attack by the Pakistani Islamist group that had given itself the name Lashkar-e-Taiba, "Army of the Pure." This time the targets were airliners landing at the Mumbai airport.

The terrorists not only failed to bring down any aircraft, but during a fierce firefight they lost more than a dozen men. India's forces had been alerted by India's highly dependable Defence Intelligence Agency, whose agents had learned of the attack a short time before the terrorists struck.

Falcone's principal mission was to plead with Mishra not to start a war with Pakistan. Falcone knew, from U.S. intelligence analyses, that the terrorist attack at the airport had resurrected India's plan, known as Cold Strike, for a surprise attack on Pakistan from several border points. Cold Strike called for moving Indian forces against Pakistan so fast that Pakistan's army would be defeated before the United States or China could try to stop India's assault. Falcone hoped to learn whether Cold Strike was imminent by getting an honest assessment from Mishra.

"Atal, we need to know if you're planning anything . . ."

"You want me to disclose what my country's response will be to this latest savagery by the Pakistanis? Surely, Sean, you can't be serious."

"Deadly serious. Your prime minister promised that any further attacks by LET would not go without retribution."

"True. There will be retribution at a time and place of our choosing. . . . All I can assure is that . . ."

"But you know how fragile things are in Pakistan. And as conflicted as the Paks are, they're still helping us in Afghanistan. . . ."

"Sean, we both know what a duplicitous game they play with you. They help you one day, and the next night they're sleeping with the Taleban. They take your billions and use the money to prepare for war with us."

For the next twenty minutes, Falcone and Mishra bantered back and forth over Pakistan's double game and how the United States failed to appreciate its true friends in the region. They had had this conversation many times before. It was old turf.

Finally, Mishra said, "Tell President Oxley that for the moment at least, the only war that is underway is a propaganda war."

"And the threat of Cold Strike is a part of that propaganda?"

"As I said, for the moment. I cannot say more."

Falcone felt confident that Mishra had sent him the message he was looking for. Unless there were further attacks against India, there would be no military retaliation. The rhetoric would be hot, but there were no imminent plans for an Indian-Pakistan war.

"Atal, I need another favor. . . ."

"Favor? I'm not in that business."

"Sorry. Poor choice of words . . . As you know, Oxley is under political pressure at home over the attack on the *Elkton*. Do you have any information . . ."

"About Iran being involved?"

Falcone nodded. "Senator Stanfield says he has evidence that . . ."

"According to our . . . sources, that story is without merit. Bogus, as you might say."

Falcone owed Mishra. Added to the information from Pakistan's Mohammad Bashir Ispahani, he had absolute assurance of Iran's non-involvement.

The complexity of Falcone's relationship with Mishra— and with Ispahani—was the heart of Falcone's job: getting knowledge on the workings of the world and giving other nations insights into what the United States wanted. The job was international, not domestic. But frequently the world intruded on U.S. politics.

But, as happened with the intelligence from Ispahani, Falcone decided that Mishra's information should not be revealed, except for a few carefully worded lines in the PDB. And so the President had to remain silent in the face of Stanfield's repeated claims of Iranian responsibility. Quinlan wanted a leak, but Falcone worked around him and talked with the President, who told Quinlan that a leak would cost him his job.

Flying home, Falcone felt a great sense of satisfaction that what he was doing mattered, was important, as Philip Dake had reminded him.

Falcone had scheduled a stopover in Afghanistan on the way home. He, Anna Dabrowski, and representatives of Kane, Bloom, and Wilkinson had hammered out an itinerary that would get him to India and Afghanistan in time to be back in Washington for the President's meeting with Israeli Prime Minister Avi Weisman. But there was no way for Falcone to join in the official party at Weisman's arrival, which was to be followed that night by a state dinner, a major Washington social event.

Falcone knew that Anna could certainly handle the dinner and the Israelis. "It will be a grand experience for you," he told her. "Like going to the world's best prom. I'm being a perk dispenser. I'm also going to see to it that Hawk gets invited. He'll be your date."

Now, thinking back about that moment as he sipped some weak Air Force coffee, he smiled, remembering that Anna had blushed.

19

Prime Minister Avi Weisman's motorcade took him directly from Andrews to Blair House, the President's guesthouse for heads of state and other dignitaries, across Pennsylvania Avenue from the White House. Blair House, a yellow masonry building in late federal style, was actually four interconnected townhouses that formed a complex of 110 rooms, an exclusive hotel as well staffed and as well protected as the White House.

Four Israeli security officers sprang out of the lead security van and took up positions around the black awning leading to the Blair House steps. One man pointed to a plaque on the fence near the doorway and said to another officer in Hebrew, "Keep your eyes open." The plaque commemorated the White House policeman who was mortally wounded in 1950 during a gunfight with men attempting to assassinate President Harry Truman, who was living in Blair House while the White House was being renovated.

Weeks of planning usually preceded the visit of a head of state. But there had been little time for planning. Weisman had requested the meeting with Oxley, but there was no diplomatic way to slip him in and out of America. Secretary of State Bloom had asked Oxley to officially designate the trip as a visit of a head of state. Weisman, famously dour and stubborn, had insisted that arrangements be made for him to obtain a maximum number of hours in conference with President Oxley and a minimum number of hours in festivities.

The traditional arrival ceremony for a head of state—the U.S. Marine Band and a parade on the South Lawn—had been eliminated to accommodate Weisman's travel plans. This gave the Israeli and U.S. media an opportunity to claim that Weisman was being snubbed. But a formal state dinner had been accepted by Israeli planners, and this gave the media of the two countries an opportunity to assert that Weisman was being honored. Protocol officials of both countries agreed that the menu and guest list would not be released in advance so that the media would not have a chance to critique the food or the invitees.

The Israeli ambassador to the United States met Weisman in the entrance hall and led him to a stand holding the guestbook, which Weisman signed. Weisman mumbled a few words and the State Department Chief of Protocol led the two men to the room that had been President Truman's office. Weisman eased his bulk into an armchair near the fireplace and said, "Where's Rachel?"

"She's arrived, but—," said a man who had just entered the room.

"Get her," Weisman said.

The man, a bodyguard who had committed the floor plan of Blair House to memory, headed to the Rear Drawing Room, which had been chosen for routine meetings during the prime minister's visit. Serious meetings of Weisman's entourage would be held in a secure chamber at the Israeli Embassy.

In the Rear Drawing Room, a portrait of a stern Daniel Webster hung over the fireplace. Two Israeli women and three Israeli men bustled about, moving chairs and placing a green baize cover on a round table. A State Department Protocol representative hovered over the Israelis, near a seventeenth-century Chinese ornamental screen.

Rachel Yeager had entered the room quietly, almost unseen. She immediately noticed the American woman near the screen. Switches clicked in Rachel's mind: *Protocol could be her CIA cover, although the CIA was barred by U.S. law from engaging in domestic intelligence-gathering. So, not CIA. But that do-not-touch screen could be bugged. The whole house was undoubtedly bugged. The Israeli-U.S. agreement on not spying on each other is a fairy tale. Especially in Washington. And very especially in a federal bed-and-breakfast. Must be polite, not openly suspicious.*

"Worried about bulls in your china shop?" Rachel asked.

"China? Oh, good one," the young woman said, smiling and looking at the screen. She was not quite sure how to handle Rachel Yeager, Israeli's ambassador to the United Nations, possibly Weisman's mistress, and, according to the State Department's Bureau of Intelligence and Research, soon to become Israel's foreign minister.

The American woman reached out her right hand. "Jessica Baldwin, Protocol, Ambassador Yeager. Welcome to Blair House. The screen is one of Blair House's treasures. It was created for a wealthy Chinese family as a gift for Grandma's ninetieth birthday. The front design depicts scenes from Grandma's life."

"I can't blame you for worrying," Rachel said, warmly closing her left hand over the handshake. "Some of these geeks hardly ever look up from their keyboards. We don't let them near anything valuable." She spoke in Hebrew to one of the men.

"I told him to be careful. And no Coke or pizza."

"Thank you, Ambassador," Jessica Baldwin said. "I have a brother like that. He can break something just by looking at it."

Brother. The word immediately became *Moshe* and summoned instant, indelible memories. Moshe, Israel's Olympic hero. She had been a child when he was murdered—one of the Israeli athletes slain in Munich during the 1972 Olympics by terrorists of Fatah, Yasser Arafat's faction of the Palestine Liberation Organization.

Grief had shortened the lives of her father and mother,

who had emerged alive from Holocaust death camps but could not survive the death of Moshe. Her own life became a passage through vengeance to assassination.

Growing up, she was determined to avenge her beloved brother's murder. She hardened her mind and her body, mastered martial arts, and developed her gift for learning languages. By the time she was to begin her two years of obligated service in the Israeli Defense Forces, she was fluent in English, Arabic, French, Spanish, and German.

During her military service she worked as an interpreter for interrogators of Palestinians at border checkpoints manned by Israeli security officials. Her ability to shift easily from one Arabic dialect to another had been noted by Mossad's counterintelligence operatives.

When she was approached by a Mossad recruiter, she feigned surprise. She knew that intelligence services were suspicious of volunteers. So she had confidently waited, knowing that her skills—particularly her language skills—would attract Mossad recruiters, and she would begin her mission of vengeance.

Before she formally entered the Mossad, a psychiatrist interviewed her. When she mentioned the slaying of her brother, the psychiatrist drew out her passionate desire to avenge her brother's murder. He told high-ranking Mossad officials that this brilliant, beautiful young woman was likely to be a great intelligence officer. And even more valuable than her obvious attributes was her thirst for vengeance, which mirrored Israel's own.

Soon after the Olympic murders, Prime Minister Golda Meir and the Israeli Defense Committee secretly approved Operation Wrath of God—the tracking down and killing of the terrorists responsible for the massacre in Munich.

Not every Wrath of God mission was successful. One was badly blown in Norway, where the Israelis killed the wrong man. Five Mossad agents were arrested, convicted, and sentenced to prison; all were released within twenty-two months and deported to Israel.

Rachel's passion for revenge soon put her on the track for the "Killer Angels," the Mossad's elite assassination team. As the years passed, she moved from successful assassin to skilled intelligence officer. She served under various covers in Israel and under diplomatic cover in Israeli embassies and consulates in several countries, carrying out espionage and counterespionage missions that involved faultless tradecraft but not assassinations.

Between assignments, she served in a Mossad group whose officers arranged security for tourist groups. The keepers, as the officers called themselves, also gathered odd bits of intelligence, especially from Americans in small, expensive tours.

Rachel's combined intelligence and diplomatic experience drew her from the ranks of the Mossad to the hierarchy of the Foreign Ministry, where she had been singled out for promotion by Prime Minister Weisman. He said that she was cool in crisis and always answered questions with brutal honesty. But there was speculation that Weisman, a widower with an eye for the ladies, had made her his mistress.

Ranking Foreign Ministry officials convinced Weisman that Rachel was becoming an unnecessary distraction. They successfully urged him to give her a post that would better utilize both her Mossad and diplomatic background work by naming her as the Israeli ambassador to the United Nations.

. . .

Now, standing in this beautiful old room in Blair House, she was in counter-espionage mode. She would have to look up Jessica Baldwin's biography in Mossad files at the embassy. *And,* she thought, *somebody in the CIA has certainly looked me up.* Thinking at that moment about her identity, she wondered what secrets her CIA dossier might contain. There was, for instance, her involvement with Sean Falcone. At this moment, thinking back to those days, they seem to have been in a previous life.

The aide sent to fetch Rachel entered the room and said in Hebrew, "The Big Man wants you."

Weisman's security detail would have the seating plan for the state dinner, she knew. *I wonder where Sean will be sitting. . . .*

They had met—*what? Twelve years ago?*—at a formal dinner, given by the U.S. Secretary of State to honor the Israeli foreign minister. The glittering event, which had drawn the elite of Washington, was in the John Quincy Adams dining room on the eighth floor of the State Department. He was Senator Falcone then, and she was a Mossad officer assigned to meet Falcone and find out about his one-man investigation into the murder of his friend, Senator Joshua Stock. Falcone wrongly suspected that the Mossad had ordered Stock's assassination.

Falcone had requested an invitation to the dinner, making himself a substitute for Stock, who had been scheduled to attend. He suspected that placing a beautiful woman next to a senator was the work of the Mossad, but he had no idea that he was sitting next to a Killer Angel. She introduced herself as a cultural attaché in the Israeli Embassy.

Even the Mossad could not have known that Rachel had

an uncanny resemblance to Falcone's late wife, Karen. She had died, with their only child, in an automobile accident while he was a prisoner in North Vietnam. "I saw her in the shape of your face, your sea-green eyes," he had later told Rachel. "I felt that my mind—or my heart—was playing a cruel trick on me."

Falcone, with the aid of Philip Dake, had learned more about Rachel and her other names—Rachmella Rafiah, Aviva Kamakovich, Esterly Daniloff.

Long afterward, reconstructing what Falcone had learned and not learned, she discovered what Dake had said of the Killer Angels: "They have to be able to kill," Dake had told Falcone. "Not from a distance but up close, with a garrote, a knife, or a gun inches from their victims' faces. They had to be able to hear them plead for mercy, scream for life, weep for their families, and then put a bullet in their brain or slice a razor across their jugular."

Dake had a motto he was fond of repeating—"Nothing is what it appears to be"—and, during those hectic weeks while Falcone, Dake, and Rachel solved Senator Stock's murder, Falcone had taken that motto as his own. But he had fallen in love with Rachel, whatever her past, whatever her lethal deeds.

Their affair had been short, and their time together had mirrored their separate worlds. It was not exactly a bed of roses from the beginning. During their first private dinner at his favorite Italian restaurant, they had argued about American policy in the Middle East. She thought his "even-handed" approach to creating a Palestinian state was naïve at best and contrary to his professed support for Israel. He had questioned whether Israel could continue to be a democracy if it denied the Palestinians a vote equal to their numbers. Sparks flew at that dinner. Later that night, Russian hit men had attacked Falcone in his garage. She had followed his car home and used her martial skills to save his life that night and once again when they were together in Israel. They had made love on an island in Maine, in a Mossad safe house in Tel Aviv, in the King David Hotel in Jerusalem. They had stopped a Russian agent from blowing up Jerusalem's Temple Mount and turning the Middle East into a funeral pyre.

Peril had drawn them together, and mutual trust had evolved into an irresistible attraction. Now those well-remembered weeks were still with her, and she was surprised at how much she was looking forward to seeing Sean again. She had never met—or made love to—anyone like him.

If she had ever let herself think of marriage, he would have been the one. But that could never be. . . .

20

President Oxley and his wife, Priscilla Longden Oxley, met Weisman at the North Portico entrance of the White House. Weisman, looking uncomfortable in a tuxedo, was accompanied by Rachel. She towered over him, stunning in an off-the-shoulder gown whose blue was the blue of the Israeli flag.

They had walked across Pennsylvania Avenue, flanked by Israeli and U.S. bodyguards and under a hovering Black Hawk helicopter. Blair House guests usually arrived in a car instead of walking across Pennsylvania Avenue. Weisman had scoffed at the idea, and officials had tightened the security cordon that stretched for blocks in all directions. Weisman, stopping at the entrance to chat with a female Secret Service agent, was nudged by Rachel, who acted instinctively, knowing he was a stationary target.

Media coverage had been limited to one pool still photographer and one pool television crew. They had only one photo opportunity: inside, at the staircase. As the President and Mrs. Oxley escorted Weisman and Rachel to a small reception, Priscilla Oxley turned to Rachel and said, "I understand that you have been in Washington before. But in our lovely month of October?"

"I have been here many times in many different months," Rachel replied. "But never have I been here on a more beautiful evening. Or during a presidential election campaign."

"There will be no politics tonight," Mrs. Oxley said, smiling. "Well, perhaps a little. There's always politics in the air."

The reception, a gauntlet to run to before the dinner, launched Weisman into a short but intense political scene. He knew that the guests here would be the elite, the powerful, and the influential, all of them given the privilege of thirty minutes of face time in a room with Weisman. He was quickly and politely surrounded by four senators, six representatives, and a lobbyist. Secretary of State Bloom remained out of the scrub, waiting, a champagne flute in his right hand, until Weisman came to him. Rachel nodded to Weisman, and he walked over to Bloom.

She took that moment to scan the room for Sean. She had not seen his name on the guest list, though that might have been an error. She had decided that he certainly would be at the reception.

Marilyn Hotchkiss, Deputy Secretary of State, was drawn as if by gravity to Rachel, who braced for the quick, complex conversation that would now begin. Neither woman was to say anything significant. But Weisman had instructed Rachel never to miss an opportunity to state his main point: Jerusalem could never become a city divided between Israel and the Palestinians. There was also another matter, but that would come up only when Weisman and Oxley had their most private talks.

While Rachel talked to Marilyn Hotchkiss, she could not keep her mind from drifting to thoughts of Sean, who, she now realized, was not present. She chose not to inquire about him. Certainly their past relationship showed up at least in intelligence files. But, she assumed, those were not the kind of files that either Bloom or Hotchkiss would read.

Looking through the briefing books for this trip, she had found that official State Department biographies of Bloom and Hotchkiss showed that they were married and had grown children. She asked the Mossad's chief American case officer for the latest dossier on Falcone.

She started to skim through the basic biographical details, which she well knew, and she was unexpectedly glad to see he was still unmarried. Her skimming stopped when she saw the description of Falcone's years as a prisoner of the Vietcong. She lingered over *inspirational leader of other prisoners* and *beaten and placed in solitary confinement* and *subject refused early release*. The Mossad document, written originally when Falcone was a senator, had been updated. But the basic assessment about his attitude toward Israel had not changed: *While generally pro-Israel, subject cannot be counted on as an unqualified friend. . . .*

. . .

The Air Force Strolling Strings, in formal uniforms, had been playing in the background. In her reverie, she had hardly noticed the music until the ensemble switched from Vivaldi's *Four Seasons* to a medley of songs by George Gershwin, Weisman's favorite American composer. That was the signal for the President and First Lady to lead Weisman and Rachel out of the reception and into the State Dining Room. The Marine Band—"The President's Own"—sounded four ruffles and flourishes when the President appeared, with Rachel on his arm, followed by Weisman and the First Lady. Then, paced by "Hail to the Chief," he led the way into a room radiant with light and splendor.

"Finally," the President whispered to Rachel. "We can forget our troubles. I promise you a peaceful, lovely night."

21

One hundred and twenty guests were seated at dozens of round tables covered in golden linens. Gold-rimmed plates gleamed and goblets sparkled. Arrangements of lilies at each table paid homage to a flower beloved in Israel and mentioned in both the Old and New Testaments. Waiters glided about, pouring California wines. Under one of the golden chandeliers was a table at which Philip Dake was seated.

Dake was flanked by Secretary of Defense Kane and a young woman who was a rapidly rising NBC correspondent. Others at his table included General Gabriel Wilkinson, a movie director escorting an actress, each a recent

Oscar winner; a member of the Israeli Knesset wearing a blue-and-white yarmulke; and Dake's old friend, the conductor of the National Symphony.

The President had decided to give Dake unusual access for his book on the Oxley administration, and the word had gone out. Dake's invitation to the Weisman state dinner was a result, as was the selection of Kane and Wilkinson as Dake's tablemates.

Oxley had sat for several lengthy interviews and he had ordered his staff and cabinet members to cooperate with Dake, over the objections of Ray Quinlan. It was a simple matter of Oxley's trusting Dake and Quinlan's distrusting all journalists. Quinlan, like many politicians and operatives, had been stung by Dake.

In a book about lobbyists, *Peddlers of Power,* Dake had dredged up an incident from Quinlan's early days on Capitol Hill. Quinlan was on the staff of a senator who was censured for his flagrant trading of votes for campaign contributions. Quinlan had no connection with the senator's malfeasance, and in fact resigned just before the censure vote. Dake had barely mentioned Quinlan, but that mention called Quinlan "a young man who thought he was a staffer when he actually was a gofer."

Dake had been developing an anecdote for the book about Oxley's DEFCON change at the time of the *Elkton* attack. When he asked Wilkinson about it, Wilkinson gave Dake enough information to convince him that he could perhaps broaden it into something about Oxley and his relationship with the Pentagon. He needed all the Oxley anecdotes he could get. The book was not going well.

He nodded to Anna Dabrowski, at a nearby table, looking gorgeous in a canary-yellow gown. Seated next to her was a Marine light colonel in dress blues, looking happy to be with a beautiful woman. *If she's here, that probably means Falcone isn't. I wonder why.*

"Where's Falcone?" Dake asked Wilkinson.

"Can't say," Wilkinson replied.

"Can't or won't?"

"Can't."

"Secret trip?"

"Yeah. To keep the bad guys from knowing where he is."

"Anything to do with Iran and the *Elkton*?"

"You know that one, Phil. There's no Iranian involvement."

From Wilkinson's inflections, Dake got the signal that the JCS chairman was giving him the official line but was not comfortable with it. Dake filed it away in his infallible memory.

Just around the time the White House waiters were removing the soup dishes, Falcone's plane was landing at Andrews. Glancing out the window before touchdown, he saw the crescent moon against the dark sky. For a moment he dozed off and saw the crescent in the flag that flew over Pakistan, over Turkey, Algeria . . . the crescent that flew over so many places. . . .

He was still sleepy when he walked down the exit stairway to the tarmac. After a farewell to the plane's crew and routine greetings from the duty officer who met the aircraft, Falcone headed for the SUV that would take him . . . where?

Weary and muddled by jet lag, he hesitated. He could rush to his apartment, jump into a tuxedo, and make the last of the state dinner. And for what? Not for any official business, but truthfully only to see Rachel Yeager.

He had thought of her many times—sudden, unsummoned thoughts of their short time together long ago. He had vaguely kept aware of her, under various names in various CIA analyses of Mossad activities. The latest mention of her was in the National Security Council's recent report on Prime Minister Avi Weisman's selection of her as ambassador to the United Nations. He had been tempted to get word to her that he would like to meet her again. But the Middle East was complicated enough without injecting a high-level romantic liaison into the mix.

It was Israel's fate always to be under attack by her enemies. And he knew it once had been Rachel's job to eliminate some of those enemies wherever they could be found. That meant everywhere, every day. There was no room for love in her world. Now, if he could trust the intel profiles, she was no longer a Killer Angel. But her life was still dedicated to Israel. Her job had changed from eliminating enemies to managing enemy states.

He knew that in the meetings beginning tomorrow he would inevitably see her in their official roles. *Well, we could at least have lunch, maybe at Positano's, where we . . .*

"Excuse me, sir. Do you go home or to your office?"

Falcone looked blankly at the security man.

"Oh? Sorry. Jet lag. Home. Yes, definitely. Home."

22

As Falcone was heading toward his apartment, the *Regal* was nearing the mouth of the Savannah River under that same dark sky pierced by a crescent moon. A small boat, the *Betty B.* with PILOT emblazoned on its hull and cabin roof, pulled alongside. The boat came abreast of a brightly lighted compartment that opened on the port side of the *Regal*'s lowest deck. When boat and ship were on parallel course, the pilot lithely leaped across four feet of water, shook hands with a crewman, and strode to the first of the stairways that would take him up to the bridge.

The *Betty B.* sharply turned away and sped back down the river to the small bay where it had met the *Regal*. The boat headed south and skirted the coastline of Tybee Island, past the flashing black-and-white lighthouse, and tied up at the *Betty B.* wharf. Over the centuries, the island had become a delta peninsula attached to the mainland by marshes. But people still called it an island. Not much changed around Savannah.

Craig Reynolds, the port's chief pilot, had had a long day and was glad his son, Mike, did the leaping now. In about half an hour, after guiding the *Regal* up the curving Savannah River, Mike would get in his pickup at the cruise dock in Savannah Harbor and drive down U.S. 80 to Tybee and the *Betty B.* wharf, the office and home of Reynolds & Son, Pilots. By long tradition along the East Coast, piloting was a family business that endured for generations.

The *Regal* slowly approached the mouth of the river and in a half hour would tie up at Savannah's cruise-ship dock, next to a long, low building festooned with a string of lighted jack-o'-lanterns and a sign, WELCOME MIDNIGHT-ERS. From a speaker in every cabin came the cheery voice of the ship's master of events: "Welcome to beautiful and historic Savannah! Complete with ghosts and goblins! Halloween is still a week away. But here we are, about to enjoy the tricks and treats of the weird but wonderful city made famous by *Midnight in the Garden of Good and Evil.* If you enjoyed the movie or the book, imagine how you'll enjoy the real thing! In exactly half an hour, the buses will be at the dock to whisk you away to a tour of this devilish city and its rollicking nightlife."

Nearly all the passengers were in their cabins dressing for the tour, which would end with a midnight supper and jazz at a historic mansion dating from the eighteenth century. But Pat and Kathy Flanagan had dressed quickly enough to have time for a photo opportunity before heading for the tour buses.

The Flanagans left their upper-deck cabin and walked to an outside stairway that led up to a gridded metal platform at the starboard door of the bridge. Pat posed Kathy on the platform so that the crescent moon was over her right shoulder. Behind her stretched the dimly lit stern of the *Regal,* and beyond that the dark sea. "Perfect," Pat said. "Stay right there—and for God's sake, smile."

Pat crouched on the stairway and aimed his smart-phone. He pressed the button five times, each press of the button transmitting the image to the name on the top of his speed dial: Kelly, the Flanagans' niece in Boston. As he pressed the button for what would be the last image, a brilliant light filled the sky and an enormous wall of water began hurtling toward the *Regal.*

A surge of heat and pressure swept across the ship. In a searing instant, Pat and Kathy were vaporized and their silhouettes were stenciled on the white bridge door. On the port side, Captain Hyldebrand and pilot Mike Reynolds were walking along the deck when suddenly both were gone. They became part of the wall of water, consigned to the sea that they both had served.

The heat and pressure moved on, crushing the *Regal* and drowning the ship, along with two hundred and thirteen other passengers and crew members. The force rushed on toward Savannah, tearing down the graceful Talmadge Memorial Bridge, which soared one hundred and eighty-five feet above the river. The wave, sinking ships and carrying cars and trucks and silvery pieces of the bridge, swept into the city of Savannah, which instantly vanished into the night as all electricity failed. In the sudden darkness, buildings crumbled and a cross-topped church steeple collapsed as if in a requiem to Savannah.

23

U.S. Coast Guard Lieutenant Samuel Tourtellot, piloting his red-and-white helicopter through sudden turbulence about eighteen miles off Savannah, heard a radio message. All he could make out was *huge wave* and *bright*. Then nothing more—no call letters, no carrier signal, not even the click when a radio was switched off. On a pad clipped to his right leg he noted the time: 2113.

An autopilot system had put the helicopter on a search

pattern that resembled the course of a lawnmower: up one long side, across a short side, then down a long side. Tourtellot had set the computerized search pattern when he neared the area where a fishing boat had sent out a distress call. The autopilot system allowed him to look down at the sea without keeping an eye on the controls.

Simultaneous with the loss of the radio signal, the automatic pilot system failed. Tourtellot grabbed the controls and tried to radio his home port, the Coast Guard Air Station in Savannah. His radio was dead.

"The goddamn computer is out," Lieutenant Susan Hancock, the copilot, shouted. The illuminated dials on the dashboard faded to black. The cabin lost all light. They were in darkness flying through darkness.

"We still have power," Tourtellot said. "But I don't know what side of the search box we're on. I don't know which way we're heading."

He took a flashlight out of a rack overhead and aimed it toward a rescue life raft rigged to be dropped into the sea. "There's a compass in the raft survival kit. We'll get to the coast on that," he said. "And then follow the lights to Savannah. Should see them in a minute or so."

A rescue diver in a wet suit, one of the two crewmen, yelled, "Hey, Lieutenant! Blackout! No light back here. Intercom out."

"Here, too, Ross," Tourtellot yelled back. "Not to worry."

Hancock groped around and found the compass. She held the compass on her lap while Tourtellot shone his flashlight on it and saw which way he had to turn to aim the helicopter toward the coast.

Two minutes later, Hancock said, "There aren't any lights. Are you sure we're on the right heading?"

Tourtellot looked at his watch. "By my calculations

we're over the coast." He peered into the darkness ahead. "Blackout. Some kind of local power outage. I'm heading for Hilton Head." He turned sharply north.

"Wait! Jesus Christ!" Hancock said. "Look at that!"

Two thousand feet below them was a circle of flame. Tourtellot dropped down, and tried to understand what he was seeing. "Looks like one of those big gas tanks."

"Sam, the goddamn thing is *floating*." By the light of the flames they could see a vast carpet of water. "And Sam, the bridge. That's where the Talmadge Bridge is supposed to be."

"I'm heading north until we see light or we run out of gas," Tourtellot said. "And then we'll land and find out what the hell is going on."

Tourtellot did not know how much gas he had because he had no dials. They were not merely dark; they were not working. But it was not long before he saw lights along the coast. He dropped low enough to see the lighted outline of Hilton Head, South Carolina. He recognized the shape of Port Royal Sound, and aimed toward the runway lights of Page Field at Parris Island, the vast flat site of the U.S. Marine Recruit Depot.

Even as he spotted the runways, he saw the lights of two Marine helicopters taking off and heading toward him. Tourtellot could imagine their radio calls to him—and the aggressive reaction that his silence would trigger. As he was further imagining that they would treat him as a hostile aircraft, one helicopter suddenly slanted upward and, flying directly over Tourtellot, shined a powerful light and aimed it at a runway. The second helicopter pulled close alongside. The pilot shone a light on Tourtellot and emphatically pointed down. Tourtellot just as emphatically nodded and continued toward the runway.

As the helicopter landed, a dozen or so Marines surrounded it and, hunching over, closed in as soon as its blades began to stop. Tourtellot was the first to step out, followed by Hancock and the two members of the crew.

"Hands in the air, chopper boy," a Marine shouted, aiming an automatic rifle at Tourtellot's head. He did as he was told. Other Marines stepped forward to seize Hancock and the two crewmen.

A captain carrying a carbine shouted, "What the fuck's going on?" He squinted at the name on Tourtellot's helmet and added something that sounded like "Turtle-O."

"All my lights are out. Radio out. This is an emergency landing," Tourtellot said.

"This is a fuckin' unauthorized flight and landing," the Marine said. He led the four Coast Guards to two Humvees, which took them to a nearby one-story brick building.

The Marine captain ushered Tourtellot into the duty officer's small office and closed the door. After hearing Tourtellot's terse report on a blackout and radio failure, the captain put in a call to the Coast Guard Air Station in Savannah over a military communications line. An operator reported, "Unable to make a connection."

The captain made another call, then led Tourtellot out of the office and to a door labeled PROVOST. At the door stood a Marine sergeant wearing a white belt, a .45 in a white holster, and a red-and-yellow MP armband. He opened the door and closed it behind Tourtellot.

Hancock and the two crewmen were seated in metal chairs along one wall. The captain who had brought them in stood next to the chairs. At a desk sat a Marine major, his bald head gleaming under a flickering fluorescent ceiling fixture. The brass nameplate on the desktop said MAJOR WATTS. He turned to the captain and said, "Take the three other interlopers to the Briefing Room for now." As the others filed out of the office, Watts turned to Tourtellot.

"You have made an unauthorized landing at Parris Island," the major said.

"I made an emergency landing at Parris Island," Tourtellot responded.

Major Watts opened a spiral notebook with an olive-drab cover. "Name, rank, serial number, Lieutenant."

"What the hell is this, major? Am I a prisoner of the U.S. Marines?"

"You are a trespasser who has made an unauthorized flight onto a U.S. military installation, Tourtellot. And I am writing an incident report for submission to my commanding officer. Name, rank, serial number."

Tourtellot responded in a calm voice, then, less calmly, added, "Major, I cannot contact my base. My wife and two kids live in Savannah. I want to call them. Major, there is no incident to report *here*. There's some kind of incident in Savannah."

"Name of duty station," the major continued, acting as he had not heard Tourtellot.

"U.S. Coast Guard Air Station, Savannah, which, as I have been telling everybody, is out of contact."

"What were your orders? Where is your flight—"

The door suddenly opened. The surprised MP stood aside and saluted the commanding officer of the Parris Island base, Brigadier General Michael Greene.

The major rose quickly, Tourtellot not quite as quickly.

Greene glared at one man, then the other. "Major," Greene said, "what the hell are you doing?"

"Writing an incident report, sir," the major said, holding up the notebook. "This man just made an unauthorized—"

"This man, Major, is a U.S. Coast Guard officer, not a goddamn terrorist," Greene said, turning toward Tourtellot. "Now, Lieutenant, tell me what happened."

After hearing Tourtellot's account, Greene looked at his watch. "The time is 2209, Lieutenant. You said you heard the words *huge wave* and *bright* at 2113. Still no answer from your base a few minutes ago. We're wasting time."

Greene ordered Watts to take Tourtellot to the Briefing Room, closed the door, sat at Watts's desk, punched several numbers on a classified military line, identified himself, and put in a call to the National Military Command Center in the Pentagon.

A flag officer is always on duty at the NMCC. The call from Greene was taken by Air Force Major General Michael McHugh. Flag officers frequently know each other, at least slightly, because they had met along their similar paths to their admiral or general stars. But the Marine and Air Force paths of Greene and McHugh had not had any mutual milestones. And so neither could assess the other by drawing from an anecdote, or a promotion party, or a poker game at the Naval War College, the National Defense University, or some other installation attended by potential flag officers. A stranger was speaking to a stranger.

"We believe that a severe emergency exists in Savannah, Georgia," Greene told McHugh. "The Coast Guard Air Station at Savannah has lost communication. The report that reached here indicates a tsunami has caused a massive power failure." *Tsunami* inspired in McHugh's mind images of floating cars and fleeing Japanese.

Greene quickly and professionally described what

Tourtellot had reported, including the failure of the helicopter's radio. The call was a model of an efficient military communication. However, both officers realized that they were not dealing with a military matter, and they were not quite comfortable dealing with it. Their unspoken priority was to get the matter off their agendas.

Ever since Hurricane Katrina, no senior military officer or civilian official wanted to be the person who failed to immediately alert the President to a natural disaster. After only a moment's hesitation, McHugh called the White House Situation Room and relayed the report.

Navy Captain Gregory Spencer, the duty officer in the Situation Room Watch Center, answered McHugh's call. "I think the President should be informed," Spencer said. "Meanwhile, get a detailed report from General Greene and put it in the classified net. It sounds like a major disaster. We'll coordinate it all here, General. Not at the NMCC. "

"Very well, Captain," McHugh said, ending the call and, with some relief, getting a fuzzy matter away from his turf, just as General Greene had.

Spencer, well aware of the clout of the Situation Room, had not sounded like a mere Navy captain speaking to a general. Duty in the Situation Room lifted military officers out of the world of the military and into the world of POTUS, the President of the United States. Spencer was working for the President, not for the generals and admirals of the Pentagon.

Spencer ordered one of the other watch officers to contact military installations around Savannah. Two minutes later, the officer reached the officer of the day at Fort Stewart, headquarters of the Third Infantry Division, about forty miles southwest of Savannah, talked to him for a couple of minutes, made three other calls, and then reported to Spencer.

"Stewart reports loss of contact with Hunter Army Airfield in Savannah, sir," the officer said. "They assumed a communications screwup. I tried to reach Hunter. Nothing went through. Also, no response from the Coast Guard Air Station, which is located at Hunter. Verizon Georgia in Atlanta says all its cell-phone sites in Savannah are down. Also landlines. Same from AT&T Georgia. It's a blackout."

"Cause?"

"No one knows, sir. They all just say blackout."

"What do we know about Hunter?"

"It's an Army base, not Air Force, technically part of Stewart, sir. When the Third Infantry deploys, its transport aircraft use Hunter."

"Okay, Dawson. Keep trying to develop information," Spencer said, "I'm going with tsunami."

Spencer knew where the President was, and, thoughts of Katrina and the Japanese tsunami spinning through his mind, he paused only for five seconds before he picked up a telephone handset on his console and hit the President's button.

24

President Oxley, against the plea of his wife, had put his smartphone in his inner breast pocket when he was heading off to greet his dinner guests. He agreed to set it on vibration and assured her that nothing less than World War III would produce a call to him during a state dinner.

When he felt the vibration thumping against his chest, his first inclination was to ignore it. But he knew he could not. Turning to his right, he said to Rachel Yeager, "Excuse me, Ambassador. It's apparently urgent."

Captain Spencer identified himself and spoke unhurriedly. "We have a report of a major power loss centered on Savannah, Georgia, Mr. President. Looks like a tsunami."

Rachel concentrated on her dessert—nectarine sorbet and coconut pecan brownies—and tried not to look as if she were listening to a presidential phone call.

"Anything from Savannah?"

"Negative, sir. No communications whatsoever. The Watch Center here gets no telephone reception, no television or radio transmissions in the area. Electrical blackout."

"Not spreading?"

"No, sir. What we are seeing looks like a regional blackout centered on Savannah. But I've never seen, never heard of, anything this big. At least in the U.S."

"I can't ask the obvious questions here, Captain. I'll be in the Situation Room shortly. Find Falcone, if he's back, and get him there."

At the mention of Falcone's name, Rachel tensed for a moment, but continued to appear happily dining. She glanced down the table to Prime Minister Weisman, who put down his spoon, shrugged, and stuck out his hands, palms upward in his familiar gesture of frustration.

Oxley pocketed the phone and nodded toward a Secret Service agent who was inconspicuously standing at the wall behind the President's table. The agent stepped forward and leaned down to Oxley, who looked up and spoke softly. "Pete, I have to leave immediately to the Sit Room. Please go to Vice President Cunningham—as discreetly as you can—and tell him to get up here to sit in for me and close down the dinner. Then go to Secretary Kane's table and tell him to go to the Sit Room. Go there yourself and tell them to find Penny Walker and get her to the Sit Room."

"Anyone else, Mr. President?"

"No. I don't want a stampede."

"Yes, sir," the agent said before walking away as fast as he could walk without appearing to be running.

Oxley turned back to Rachel and managed a tight smile before saying, "Sorry about this. We seem to have a natural disaster on our hands."

"Oh, I'm sorry to hear that, Mr. President," Rachel said.

Oxley stood, walked past Mrs. Oxley to Weisman, leaned down, and said, "I'm awfully sorry, Avi. Duty calls. Looks like a tsunami off Georgia."

Weisman, who had an imperfect knowledge of American and Russian geography, looked puzzled.

"Why can't the Russians help?"

Oxley looked puzzled in return, and then in a moment, replied. "It's *our* Georgia, Avi."

By now the room was buzzing, drowning out the soft music of the U.S. Marine Band. The leader swung his baton, upping the volume and tempo. Everyone knew that something was happening, but what? Except for Oxley's staff concerned with his security or with national security, the use of cell phones was forbidden at social functions.

Philip Dake kept his eye on the President's table, irritated because he was supposed to know what went on in Washington, and here he was, as ignorant as everyone else. He caught movement in his peripheral vision and saw a Secret Service agent at Vice President Cunningham's table. As Cunningham rose, the agent approached Dake's table.

Dake swiveled around and heard Secretary Kane tell the agent, "On my way."

"What the hell's going on, Gabe?" Dake asked.

"Don't know," Wilkinson said.

Kane rose, made a wide sweep of his right hand and added, "Good night, all."

The correspondent next to Dake was desperate to call NBC News. Sitting at a nearby table was Ned Winslow, GNN's foreign correspondent, who had been recalled from Iraq when the combat troops left and was now the GNN anchorman in Washington. Winslow raised both hands in the air expressing his frustration. Scanning the room, Dake spotted Secretary of State Bloom at one table and Sam Stone, director of the CIA, at another. They were still seated and looking perplexed. Penny Walker, Secretary of Homeland Security, was not at the dinner.

Dake's instant analysis: *Walker rarely socializes; she was probably home enjoying* Dancing with the Stars *or* Monday Night Football. *Bloom still eating his sorbet. So no military or diplomatic crisis. Why Kane? Oxley needs to hold somebody's hand. Chooses Kane, maybe because Falcone is still overseas.*

Dake knew the protocol. No one could leave a room until the President left. But the President was leaving, Kane was leaving, Cunningham was walking toward the head table, and the dinner was not over.

Oxley stood at his place and raised a glass. Everyone stood except Weisman and Rachel as Oxley said, "Mr. Prime Minister—Avi—it is a great honor to have you under this roof, where you and your predecessors have been warmly welcomed since the birth of Israel. I speak for all Americans when I say that we respect your efforts to find a road to peace in the Middle East."

The President lifted his glass, sipped, and then added: "Avi, I now must leave this wonderful event for a few minutes. There is an important matter I must attend to." Oxley pointed toward Max Cunningham, who was almost at the table. "Max will fill in for me. Please go on with the dinner, and get a second helping of sorbet. I won't say, 'good night,' because I'm sure I'll be back in time to enjoy the entertainment."

The President then headed toward the entrance hall. Ray Quinlan, though not summoned, sprung up from a nearby table and hurried to catch up to Oxley.

A trio of violin virtuosos—Joshua Bell, Alexander Kerr, and Itzhak Perlman—had been scheduled to perform after the dessert had been served. But White House protocol staffers, whose job was to maintain decorum and please important guests, reacted spontaneously to an unexpected event they knew nothing about. They smoothly ordered the virtuosos into the room and told them to play.

The three men entered the room together, an aide escorting Perlman in his wheelchair. They bowed to their buzzing audience, raised their hands for silence, then turned and serenaded Weisman with a sparkling performance of Paganini's "Caprice Number 24."

When the music ended, Jessica Baldwin, in a striking green gown, appeared from somewhere, went to the President's table, and, trying almost successfully to be invisible, advised Vice President Cunningham to say good night to Weisman and Rachel and lead them from the room. Baldwin sensed that his departure, with Weisman and Rachel, would have the same party-ending effect as the exit of a president.

But everyone already knew that the party was over. One by one, the tables began to empty. Some people, however, tarried, their faces reflecting their belief that they were pleasantly puzzled and wanted to stay to see the solution of the puzzle. They knew that something extraordinary had happened and that they would be in the favored few that had an incredible story to tell their friends and children: They had been in the most powerful house in the world when Something Happened. When, they wondered, would they learn what it was?

25

When a White House car pulled up to Penny Walker's Georgetown townhouse, she was at a pottery wheel in the basement, wearing a red bandanna, jeans, a gray sweatshirt, and sandals. Surprised to see a presidential aide at the door, she took off her bandanna and asked him to wait while she washed her hands. As they hurried down the stone stairs to the car, the aide told her that all he had heard was that Savannah had been hit by a tsunami.

In the car, she called her chief of staff at his home in Arlington, Virginia. "Frank. Tsunami in Georgia. Apparently hit Savannah head-on. Don't we have some outfit that handles that? Gives warning? Where the hell was the warning?"

Frank Nakamura was rapidly thumbing through a directory in his smartphone. "Here it is. DART. Stands for

Deep-ocean Assessment and Reporting of Tsunamis. We spent six billion—"

"Never mind how much the damn thing cost. I need to know what the damage is—and why no warning. Get to those people. Find some facts, goddamn it. I'm on my way to the Situation Room. You've got the number. Give me what you get. You're point man. This looks like it's our Katrina. I don't want any fuckups."

She next called the duty officer at Homeland Security's headquarters in Northwest Washington. "Get me Admiral Mason."

"Yes, ma'am. The locator log puts him at CGHQ. I'm paging him there."

Admiral David Mason ran the Coast Guard from its waterfront headquarters at Buzzard's Point, a bit of land jutting out of the confluence of the Potomac and Anacostia rivers in the southwest quadrant of Washington.

The Coast Guard—42,000 men and women on active duty, 7,000 civilians, 8,000 Reservists and 34,000 volunteers in the Coast Guard Auxiliary—was the largest component of the assorted federal agencies that Congress had coagulated into Department of Homeland Security after nine-eleven.

Mason was a full admiral, recently appointed by President Oxley to a four-year term as commandant of the Coast Guard and unanimously confirmed by the Senate. Besides reporting to Penny Walker, Mason wore two other hats, as he reminded her only once. As commandant of the Coast Guard, he reported to the President, and, as commander of an armed military force, he reported to the Secretary of Defense.

"And," as he told Penny Walker when they met for the

first time, "because the United States Coast Guard happened to be jammed into the goddamn bureaucratic basket called the Department of Homeland Security, I also report to you, Secretary Walker."

After that encounter, they quickly settled into a solid working relationship. Both were single, and there were occasional discreet dates for dinner at favorite restaurants. Romance hovered but had yet to land.

"Mason here," he said, answering Walker's call on the first ring. "I think I know why you're calling, Penny."

"Savannah; the tsunami," she said.

"Yes," he said. "I know."

"I'm on my way to the Situation Room. Anything new, please call me through the duty officer there."

"I guess you know that, for us, it struck home," he said, his voice oddly strained. She liked his usual voice— the authoritative command, an admiral on the quarterdeck. To her ear, he wasn't sounding his normal self.

"What is it, David?"

"Our Savannah Air Station. It seems to be gone."

"My God! What? I hadn't—"

"No communications. And that cannot be because of an electrical blackout. We have our own power. Switches over automatically. It's out. Completely out."

The car was pulling up to the West Gate.

"We're here. What should I say about the Coast Guard?"

"We had a helicopter up, looking for a fishing boat in trouble. It lost some of its power and wound up at Parris Island. That's all we've got. I'm waiting for more details. With Savannah out, it basically means no air resources for our entire AOR—Area of Responsibility—which extends from Melbourne, Florida, to the North Carolina/South Carolina border."

"Oh, David. Your people there. What do we know about them?"

"Nothing, Penny. Nothing. We know nothing."

26

Falcone was on the terrace, looking out on the night, when he heard the penthouse door buzzer. That meant that a security man had taken the private elevator and was standing politely in the hallway. Still in the khaki slacks and Red Sox sweatshirt he had worn on the plane, Falcone walked to the door and opened it. The security man simply said, "Situation Room."

Twelve minutes later, he was entering the Situation Room. Captain Spencer was standing at one of the six large plasma screens. They were all showing the same image: a black blot rimmed on three sides by expanses of light. "Moments ago we were able to divert a satellite and get this image," he said. "The blackout has spread across the border to South Carolina, almost as far as Charleston and inland to the outskirts of Atlanta."

"Glad you're here, Sean," the President said. Spencer stopped speaking. "It looks like a tsunami."

"I heard a little on the radio in the car," Falcone said. "How much—"

The satellite image froze on the briefer's screen as the communications producers in the Watch Center put a new image on the other five screens: A man in a white shirt without a tie. BULLETIN appeared on the screen. A voiceover from the Watch Center said, "GNN correspondent. GNN headquarters, Atlanta. Two minutes ago."

The GNN man said, "A tsunami apparently has caused great damage in Savannah, Georgia. Governor Morrill, in Atlanta, reports a widespread electric blackout centered on Savannah. Much of the Southern power grid is down. No estimates yet of casualties or damage. President Oxley has been informed. So far, no word from the White House."

Oxley, speaking into a microphone in front of him, talked to the invisible technicians who were operating the audio and visual displays. "Keep taping GNN. But kill the transmissions until I tell you to resume. I want concentration in the room."

He looked around the table. "For the record, I spoke to Governor Morrill on my way from the dinner to here. He knows pretty much nothing more than what you just heard." Oxley nodded toward Spencer. "What else is coming in, Captain?"

"Many inquiries through military channels, Mr. President. We've got an overload of questions. But I don't think we'll have solid answers until dawn."

"Goddamn it," Oxley said, half to himself. He turned to Quinlan. "Ray, get on to the networks and the cables. Tell them I want fifteen minutes"—he looked at his watch, which showed twenty-five minutes after ten—"at eleven. Tell them to announce it pronto. Oval Office and pool camera. Call in Stephanie. She's hovering somewhere around the dinner, handling the social press. Tell her to call that guy on GNN and say the President will be speaking at eleven. I want that 'no word from the White House' stopped."

"I'll get Barry on it right away," Quinlan said. "He can—"

"No. No written speech. There's only time for me to wing it."

As Quinlan rose and hurried toward the door, Oxley turned to Spencer. "Captain, good job so far. Keep it up. I'll want all you have by eleven, organized as best you can and printed out for me to refer to. And I want you standing by with it in the Oval Office."

As everyone in the White House knew, Oxley had an obsession about Katrina. He had read extensively about the federal government's botched response. He kept a close eye on FEMA, and had warned Penny Walker that he would not tolerate anything less than a swift and efficient response to natural disasters.

Oxley nodded toward Walker and said, "Well, Penny, it looks like you're the point man . . . point person. What do you know? What are you doing?"

Walker looked up from the doodles on the yellow pad in front of her. "We're tracking down tsunami data. We had no warning. After the Indian Ocean tsunami in 2004, the U.S. laid out a lot of ocean-based pressure sensors, which were supposed to be the key to forecasting and warning about tsunamis. But forecasting is still tricky.

"What we do know, Mr. President, is that we've almost certainly lost our best resources for response. There's been no communication from the Coast Guard Air Station in Savannah. It had—or has—the biggest fleet of rescue helicopters on the Atlantic coast."

Spencer, still standing by the screen, raised his right hand and leaned forward, like an eager pupil wanting to be recognized.

Oxley nodded toward him, and Penny Walker turned to glare at him.

"Another resource seems to be lost also, Mr. President. The Coast Guard Air Station is located a few miles inland, at an air base with runways long enough for every type of aircraft we have. Silence there, too."

"I was about to point that out, Mr. President," Walker said peevishly.

"Anything else, Penny?"

"No, sir. But I think we should make sure the FAA warns aircraft away from Savannah until we know the state of play there. And I suggest we begin implementing the DOD emergency plan for providing emergency electricity."

"George?" Oxley asked Kane.

"The plan calls for sending the closest carrier, which then hooks up its electric power system to whatever civilian power grid is plausible," Kane replied. "Civil authorities then ration out the electricity."

"Get that going," Oxley said. He pointed toward Spencer and said, "And get the FAA warning out."

"That's in the Department of Transportation," Spencer said, summoning an aide and, lowering his voice, said, "Get in touch with the DOT duty officer. Tell him to find Secretary Laetner, and make it quick. Tell him he needs to order the FAA to ground or divert all the planes in the region."

Kane rose and walked a few steps to a clear plastic bubble that shielded a wall phone, enabling callers to make calls without disturbing a meeting.

"We need to get FEMA on this immediately," Oxley said, nodding toward Penny Walker. "What's happening?"

"There's a basic response and recovery plan that we plug the disaster zone into," she replied. "We're getting ready to move food, water, medicine, and clothing. And we'll be setting up emergency communication and medical care facilities. If we learn that Georgia's first responders are not available, we'll be bringing in their counterparts from South Carolina and Florida."

"Sean, any ideas?" Oxley asked.

"We need to get something more than a satellite image, Mr. President," Falcone said. "I'm sure the Air Force can get a plane up with infrared for night-vision reconnaissance."

"Good idea," Oxley said. "Captain Spencer, get that going."

"Yes, sir," Spencer said, signaling a Navy lieutenant from a seat against the wall.

"Hand it off to Andrews," Spencer told the lieutenant. "Tell them it's on presidential authority. Tell them we may want to patch into the pilot from here." The lieutenant headed for the Watch Center.

"Also, Mr. President," Falcone said, "we're working from very little information. And first information is usually not the best information. I can't understand how a tsunami can cause such an enormous blackout. Georgia's not Indonesia. And there's no report of an earthquake, as there was before the Japanese tsunami."

"It's all we have, Sean," Ray Quinlan said. "The President has to say something—fast. He has to go with tsunami."

27

Few people outside the secret-ridden world of national security have ever heard about the Space Based Infrared Systems program. Extraordinarily expensive even by Pentagon standards, the program was usually referred to simply as SBIRS and pronounced *sib-irs*. A complex, highly secret enterprise, it was designed as a second-generation passive system to detect missile launches and track missiles. The SBIRS detection would then alert land- and sea-based defense systems designed to shoot down the missiles.

SBIRS was finally operating after years of cost overruns and controversial test results. And when Lieutenant Tourtellot picked up the words *huge wave* and *bright* before his radio went out, SBIRS's high- and low-orbiting satellites were functioning. One of them picked up what its managers called an anomaly.

The anomaly that the SBIRS satellites detected was transmitted to the SBIRS Mission Control Station at Buckley Air Force Base, in Aurora, Colorado, a few miles east of Denver. Watch officers interpreted the data as an unknown "heat signature," a nanosecond burst of very high temperature, in the Atlantic Ocean, apparently off the South Carolina coast.

The commanding officer of the Mission Control Station at Buckley alerted the NMCC with a message sent on a secure phone line. The message said that analysts at Buckley could not attribute the high-heat signature to any natural phenomenon.

The National Military Command Center is responsible

for command and control of U.S. nuclear weapons and for detecting nuclear weapons aimed at the United States. Since the collapse of the Soviet Union and the rise of terrorism, the possibility of a ballistic missile attack diminished while the possibility of a terrorist suitcase bomb or dirty bomb escalated. But SBIRS remained active and in constant touch with the NMCC.

Air Force General Mike McHugh sat in a high-backed gray chair, behind a semicircular console that had four small monitors, arrays of buttons, and a telephone handset. Next to McHugh was an aide, Air Force Captain Sharon Leopold, who handled routine incoming and outgoing calls. Elsewhere in the large, two-tiered room were other NMCC staffers at other consoles. From this command center McHugh could instantly reach every U.S. military command in the world and spiral down, if necessary, to an Army patrol in Afghanistan or a U.S. Navy destroyer on pirate patrol off Somalia.

When the anomaly report came in from Buckley, McHugh remembered a flap over a SBIRS nuclear-detection report that had turned out to be a jet aircraft's exhaust. SBIRS had tightened its calibrations after that. But SBIRS had a reputation in the Air Force as a finicky system. There were frequent tests of its components, frequent unscheduled drills of Buckley-NMCC communications, and occasional highly realistic war gaming simulations involving nuclear-weapon detection.

McHugh, particularly wary of SBIRS, asked for more information on the high-heat signal by requesting an immediate Vela analysis.

"My God, what a night!" he said to Leopold. "Now we have another one of those goddamn SBIRS drills. I wonder if the whole thing tonight is some kind of Homeland Security caper."

"What's a Vela analysis?" Leopold asked.

"Back in the 1970s," the general replied, "a satellite picked up a flash of light that the CIA interpreted as a possible nuclear explosion." He went on to describe what he had read in a highly classified briefing book that had been prepared at the time.

The flash had been seen near the Prince Edward Islands, two volcanic bits of land in the subarctic region of the Indian Ocean, about as close to Antarctica as to South Africa, which claimed the islands as part of its territory. The satellite that detected the flash was dedicated to the Vela program ("Vela" coming from the Spanish *velar,* which meant keeping a vigil). Vela satellites monitored Soviet adherence to a treaty that banned the testing of nuclear weapons.

"A nuclear bomb blast produces a signature, a certain kind of flash," McHugh went on. "According to the briefing on the Indian Ocean flash, we never did absolutely pin that one down. Most experts who looked over the image felt it was from a relatively small nuclear explosion. Probably a test set off by Israel or maybe South Africa, or both, acting in cahoots. But it remained an anomaly."

"So now you're asking Buckley for an analysis that will ratchet up the drill," Leopold said, smiling. "And Buckley won't want to do it because it turns out that this is another drill."

"Right. As far as I know, we've never had a Vela analysis except in a drill. A real one would light up every damn light on this console, send alerts all over the government, all over the world."

A few minutes later, one light—SecDef—did flash on the console.

"McHugh here, Mr. Secretary," the general said, picking up the phone.

"Evening, Mike," Kane said. "I'm in the Sit Room. We need to get a carrier moving tonight out of Norfolk. Mission is to go to Savannah and render assistance for what seems to be a massive electrical blackout. Pass this as a POTUS directive to Navy Ops. Guys there have the cookbook recipes on how to do this."

"Yes, sir," McHugh said. "What's up?"

"Looks like a tsunami hit Savannah and knocked out electricity. I'll get comm here to send you the satellite image. It may be pretty bad, and we'd better get disaster-response operations ready for Savannah. I'll be in as soon as the meeting here breaks up. And get somebody to try to find out what happened to the Coast Guard Air Station at Savannah. It's off the air."

Leopold pointed to the console and mouthed "Buckley." McHugh stuck up his left hand like a traffic cop.

"Yes, sir. We'll get right on it."

"Okay, Mike. Signing off."

When Kane hung up, McHugh swiveled toward Leopold.

"What does Buckley say?"

"It confirms your request for a Vela analysis. And it says this is no drill."

"Give me the printout," McHugh said, reaching for the paper that Leopold had just read from. He read,

It is belief here, on quick-time analysis, that the SBIRS detection has the characteristic double flash of a nuclear explosion. We confirm your request for Vela analysis. This is no drill.

McHugh remembered reading that phrase *This is no drill* in a book about the Japanese attack on Pearl Harbor. There had been drills there, too, before December 7. *This is no drill* was part of the Navy's first report on the attack on Pearl Harbor. Now here it is again. *This is no drill*.

"Jesus! Get me CIA ops," McHugh told Leopold. "They're supposed to have nuclear expertise on tap for the analysis. Then find the Secretary and tell him what's going on."

The lights began flashing on. Leopold, unable to raise the Coast Guard Air Station, had requested information from the Third Division at Fort Stewart.

"CIA ops. Rice here. What's up?"

"This is General McHugh, NMCC. We have a report of a possible nuclear explosion."

McHugh described the Buckley report, the Vela request, and then added. "This is no drill."

Rice searched through computer files for instructions about the Vela procedure and told McHugh how to relay the SBIRS data to a CIA nuclear analyst through the secure Intelink intelligence computer network:

"Where did Buckley say the anomaly is?" Rice asked.

"Off the South Carolina coast."

"And this is no drill?"

"Right. I repeat," McHugh said. "This is no drill."

"My God, General! If that's territorial waters and this thing comes up positive, a lot of things have to start happening."

"How long will this take?" McHugh asked. He looked at his watch: 2255.

"Highest possible priority, of course. I'm contacting the nuc guys now. But this is beyond my pay grade. I'm passing this on to the director."

The satellite image from the Situation Room began downloading on a monitor in front of McHugh.

"Jesus!" McHugh exclaimed, leaning forward. He pointed to a monitor in front of Leopold. "Google Savannah."

Leopold brought up Google. A small map appeared at the top of the monitor. She enlarged it.

"The Georgia–South Carolina border is the Savannah River," McHugh said, leaning toward the monitor. "The SBIRS says the heat signature is off the South Carolina coast. We reported a tsunami off Savannah. Jesus! I think they're talking about the same thing. Get me Secretary Kane. Sit Room."

Leopold punched a button on her console. "The Secretary is no longer in the Situation Room, sir," she reported.

"Well, for Christ's sake, get him on his cell phone."

"Sorry, General. He's not answering. The cell phone is out of service until he leaves—"

"Right. We've got to wait until he clears the no-electronics zone. Jesus! What about Wilkinson?"

"General Wilkinson is at the state dinner, sir, and is not answering. His duty officer is—"

"Never mind the goddamn duty officer. Find the Secretary of Defense and get him on a secure line. *Fast.*"

Next to the monitor showing the satellite image was another monitor that now split into three vertical strips: NBC, FOX, and GNN. A quick glance showed McHugh that all three had hastily assembled various experts on tsunamis and were showing clips of the horrendous Japanese tsunami that had swept away towns, carrying off houses, cars, boats, and thousands of people. NBC shifted to a Japanese refugee center, where clusters of families huddled, looking strangely calm. GNN switched to a Google Earth view of Savannah with red lines indicating the possible area of the flooding.

McHugh selected GNN, whose bottom-of-the-screen roll was saying PRESIDENTIAL ADDRESS 11 EST. The tsunami expert had been replaced by a GNN correspondent reporting that all landline and cell phones in the Savannah area were silent. An airliner, which was to have landed at Savannah Airport at 8:54, was missing.

McHugh again looked at his watch: 2358. He turned to Leopold and said softly, "I think this will be our nine-eleven, Sharon. Get me Sean Falcone."

Falcone had left the Situation Room and was in his West Wing office when McHugh's call came through.

"Mike McHugh here, Senator."

"Mike. Good to hear from you." Falcone's phone console showed the call was coming from the NMCC. "Any news on the tsunami?"

McHugh had been an up-and-coming junior officer in the military liaison office to the Senate when Falcone had been a senator. They had struck up a friendship based on mutual trust and a fanatic faith in the Boston Red Sox. McHugh, Falcone knew, was a by-the-book officer and, by calling Falcone, was stepping out of his chain of command.

"Senator, you've got to stop the President from saying anything definite about a tsunami."

"What'?"

"There's some other information, Senator."

McHugh knew that every word he said in the NMCC was almost certainly recorded. And for all he knew Falcone was recording him, too. *Someday I'll have to testify about this,* McHugh suddenly thought. He paused.

"Tell me, Mike."

"SBIRS. You know SBIRS?"

"Sure. I was there for the creation. And it came up in the Senate quite often. Cost overruns, tests—"

"To get to it, sir: SBIRS picked up a high-heat signature and suspects it's nuclear."

"Where? Don't tell me Iran."

"No, Sean. It's off the East Coast, apparently on the Georgia–South Carolina border."

"Are you saying that what hit Savannah may be a nuclear bomb—and not a tsunami?"

"Yes," McHugh said softly.

A moment later, on a small TV in Falcone's office and in a monitor screen on McHugh's console, the President appeared. He was seated behind his desk in the Oval Office. He had quickly changed out of his formal dress and was wearing the standard dark suit, white shirt, and pale-blue tie. He looked properly grim.

"Fellow Americans," he said, "I come before you tonight to tell you that what appears to be a major natural calamity has struck our dearly loved city of Savannah, Georgia. Preliminary information, from satellite images and reports of the Department of Homeland Security, indicate that the disaster resulted from a tsunami."

He could add little to what he had heard in the Situation Room shortly before, but he stressed that the calamity was local "and in no way resembles the enormous catastrophes that struck Japan in 2011 or Indonesia in 2004." He said he had talked to Governor Morrill and assured him the immediate and full resources of the federal government.

"By dawn's light," Oxley concluded, "we will be able to fully assess the damage and begin the recovery from the tsunami. Savannah, help is on the way! Meanwhile, I ask all Americans to join Priscilla and me in prayers for that beautiful, wonderful city. Good night and God bless America."

28

Falcone and McHugh, each staring at his own monitor as the President vanished, did not speak for a few seconds. Then, his firm voice wavering, McHugh asked, "Sean, are you familiar with the flag word 'Pinnacle Nucflash'?"

"I know that a flag word precedes urgent command and control communications. Wait! *Nucflash*? What the—"

"Yes. I'm reading from a document just handed to me. It's called OPREP-3, the NMCC guidelines for operational reports about events involving nuclear weapons. The flag word 'Pinnacle Nucflash' is reserved for messages that refer to quote detonation or possible detonation of a nuclear weapon, which creates a risk of an outbreak of nuclear war. Unquote. One event that mandates a 'Pinnacle Nucflash' message is quote accidental, unauthorized, or unexplained nuclear detonation or possible detonation. Unquote."

"Jesus, Mike. Are you telling me that we—you, NMCC—that you *must* send out an alert about a possible nuclear explosion?"

"If I follow the book, Sean, as NMCC duty officer I must react to the SBIRS report. I am obliged to put out an urgent message with the flag word 'Pinnacle Nucflash.' I have to send it to the Secretary of Defense, to all armed service chiefs, and to all combatant commanders. Each commander can then decide whether to pass it on to subordinate commands. "

"For Christ's sake, Mike. You can't do that. It will leak immediately. Start a panic. We don't know—"

"I *know* we don't know, Sean. But the instructions—"

"Fuck the instructions. I'm ordering you not to send out the message."

"Sorry, Sean. I called you to give you a heads-up. This is not an official communications. You know damn well that you can't give me an order like that."

Falcone knew that McHugh was right. The chain of command was clearly from the President to the Secretary of Defense, then directly to the four-star generals and admirals who were combatant commanders. The national security advisor, officially the assistant to the President for National Security Affairs, was not in the chain. He merely gave advice. This was also true for the Chairman of the Joint Chiefs of Staff, McHugh's boss. The Chairman did not have operational command of U.S. military forces. Falcone and McHugh had to work inside that bureaucratic structure, designed to make sure that the source of military power was in the White House, where the Constitution had put it, rather than in the Pentagon.

"Give me ten minutes, Mike. I'll get you a presidential order."

"Okay. But it has to be the President himself, not someone speaking in his name."

Falcone rarely used his direct line to President Oxley, following Oxley's preference to have communications to him filtered by Ray Quinlan and his staff. When Falcone did make a direct call—as he did now—he knew that Oxley would realize its importance.

President Oxley was still at his desk, wiping off makeup, and the television pool crew was still gathering up equipment, when the URGENT line rang on his telephone console. The sound surprised everyone in the Oval Office, including Oxley.

Oxley picked up the phone and said, "Hold on, Sean." Oxley put his right hand over the mouthpiece. "Everybody out. Quick. Except you, Captain Spencer." He pointed to Spencer, who had been sitting at the edge of the seat on a wooden chair to the right of the presidential desk, outside the television image.

As the room cleared, Oxley said, "Okay, Sean. What's up?"

"Mr. President, I must see you immediately and personally."

"Okay," Oxley said, again putting his hand over the mouthpiece. He spoke directly to Spencer: "Sorry, Captain. Go through that door and stand by." Oxley pointed to a door leading to a small outer office.

"Okay again, Sean. Come on in," Oxley said, hanging up.

Falcone ran down the hall to the Oval Office and bumped into Spencer, who, looking confused, was exiting through the same door. As Falcone closed the door, Spencer sat on one of the three chairs lined up along a wall across from a desk that had no one behind it.

"Pull up a chair, Sean," Oxley said. Falcone suddenly thought that this would be Oxley's last moment of calm for a long, long time.

"It's about Savannah, Mr. President," Falcone said. "It does not seem to be a tsunami. It may be a nuclear bomb."

29

Falcone told President Oxley about the Nucflash message, along with all that was known up to that moment. He paused, awaiting Oxley's response. The President sat still and silent for one long minute. Then he stood and walked to the windows behind his desk. Falcone stood, not so much out of respect but as a witness, or perhaps, he thought, as a sentinel.

Oxley, his back turned to Falcone, said softly, "Pinnacle Nucflash. There's a script for this, isn't there? 'Pinnacle Nucflash.' Yes, I remember those words. In the nuclear briefing I got on the day I was inaugurated."

He turned around and added, "I listened, and while I was listening I remember I prayed—the kind of prayer that just suddenly rises in your mind. And then I thought, *This can't really happen. It can't happen.*"

He returned to the desk and sat down. It was as if no time had passed.

"Yes, sir. There is a kind of script," Falcone said, sitting down again. "It begins with the Nucflash message. I suggest that you put in a call to the NMCC and tell General McHugh to hold off transmitting the message until dawn, when we will be able to see Savannah."

"Or what's left of it," the President added, sighing. "Okay. Dawn it is." He reached for the console, ordered a call to the NMCC, and in a moment was talking to McHugh, who accepted the presidential order with great relief.

"What next, Sean? Off to the Sit Room?"

"First, we need to notify the congressional leadership,"

Falcone replied. "I know you think that's an oxymoron. But we have an obligation to keep them apprised of what we know. I'll handle those calls. Between now and dawn, sir, I respectfully suggest that you go to the Residence and get some rest. Then—"

"Well, I'll try. I promise to try. Next?"

"Dawn on the East Coast will be at six fifty-two. Every network will be on the air by six at the latest. I suggest that you explain the Nucflash so that the American public— and the world—will be prepared for all that will be happening as a result."

"And what will be happening, Sean?"

"A quick list, sir: DEFCON will rise automatically unless you, as commander-in-chief, stop it. And I suggest that you stand back from that. Leave it to Secretary Kane."

"I've got a pile of calls waiting, Sean. Kane is at the top of the list."

"Let me handle him, sir. I'd like to keep a close watching bricf on the Pentagon during this . . . this . . . whatever it is."

The President had a reputation for maintaining total focus under adversity. He looked down at the yellow pad he had been writing on, then looked up and spoke calmly.

"I'll tell you what it is, Sean. It is a mystery, a basketful of questions: What happened? How could it have happened? Is it a natural occurrence, an act of God? Could it be an act of terrorism? If so, who? And how could they pull such a thing off? Why didn't we see it coming? What is the extent of damage? How do we respond? How quickly can we get help there?"

"We can all but eliminate a couple of possibilities," Falcone said. "A ballistic missile would have been picked up by our missile-detection system. Same for a cruise missile. I'm about as sure of that as I can expect to be sure of anything. So, at this point, I have ruled out missiles. Maybe it was a Russian suitcase bomb that went to Iran on the black market. But Iran has to know we would liquidate them in a nanosecond."

"Suitcase bomb?" Oxley asked. "I thought nothing that small existed."

"Back in 1997, the Russian national security advisor claimed that the Russian military had lost track of more than a hundred suitcase-sized nuclear bombs. Our experts say that it's technically possible to build a bomb that could fit in a suitcase. We have no solid intelligence that it has been done by the Russians. But we did develop a nuclear weapon that a soldier could carry in a large backpack. More a steamer trunk than a suitcase.

"And there is something more, sir. Iran. You'll recall that two weeks ago, some U.S. media spread a report that we were planning to bomb Iran's nuclear sites. The report came out of the Middle East, maybe from Iran, maybe from some nutcase in Israel. We knocked it down as absurd, and that seemed to settle it.

"But two days ago, an Iranian official—on Iranian TV, commenting on Prime Minister Weisman's visit to the U.S.—said he was here to plan an attack on Iran. The official said Iran would unleash nuclear explosions in America if Iran is ever attacked with nukes. 'Nuclear explosions' sounds like they're claiming to have got their hands on some fissile material. Now we get a nuclear explosion in Savannah."

"Iran . . . a suspect, right," Oxley said. "And our intelligence on Israel—such as it is—says Weisman came here to ask me for safe passage through Iraqi air space, making us accomplices to Israel's bombing of Iran. So, maybe Iranians got wind of it. Maybe they *did* do it somehow, thinking they were preempting an attack on them by hitting us and then screaming their innocence to the whole world. It's pretty far-fetched, but there'll be some Americans who will want to see us to blame Iran and wipe it off the map, right?"

The question hung in the air.

The President tapped a pencil on the yellow pad. He put the pencil down, carefully squaring it along the top of the pad before he spoke:

"A lot of questions, Sean. I'm the one who is supposed to come up with answers. But it sounds like you're the one who is looking for the answers. And what you seem to be telling me, Sean, is that you want to tuck me in bed while you handle the crisis."

"That is one way to describe the situation, sir. But, if I may add, we are operating literally in the dark. Until dawn, all we will have will be that satellite image, a lot of TV speculation—a lot of wild speculation, I expect—and whatever images we get from the recon flight. I'd like to work through the dark, Mr. President, to get you prepared for the dawn. It's going to be a long day."

"Let's say that I agree, Sean. What do you propose to do while I'm . . . how did you put it . . . resting upstairs?"

"I believe, sir, that it is imperative that you address the American people shortly after dawn. So, number one, I want Ray or Stephanie to set that up with all the networks."

"What the hell am I going to say, Sean? 'Sorry, folks, about the tsunami story'?"

"At five A.M. we'll have a draft of a short address. You'll have enough information to take your audience through what we know now and what, for a short time, we thought had happened."

"Everything?" Oxley asked. "The tsunami that was not there? The Coast Guard helicopter that lost power? The detection of a nuclear flash? Goddamn it, Sean. *Everything* means that we get people on the ground there. I want eyes and ears there. Firsthand information. I want that *now,* Sean."

"Yes, sir. I agree. We'll get people there as soon as we can. But right now we need to figure out what you say to the American people. Sir, we don't know what's down there. We don't know the level of radiation, the number of casualties, the extent of damage."

"Christ, Sean. What *do* we know? I want answers. I want to know who did it."

"We have no answers, sir. And, I am afraid that you will have to say that. You will have to speak a sentence neither you nor any other American will want to hear. You will have to say, 'We do not yet know who is responsible for—' "

"For what, Sean? 'Killing an American city'? Is that the phrase?"

"I suggest, sir, '*trying* to kill.' "

The President stood, as did Falcone.

"I trust you more than I have ever trusted any man," Oxley said, thrusting his right hand forward to seal his decision with a handshake. "Get to work. I'll see you at five."

"There's one more thing, Mr. President."

"Yes?"

"Continuity of government. We can't rule out the possibility of more nuclear explosions. You need to go to Raven Rock or Mount Weather."

Raven Rock and Mount Weather were code names for the hollowed-out, presumably nuclear-proof mountains—described to the public as "undisclosed destinations"—where federal officials could shelter when the continuity of the U.S. government was threatened.

Raven Rock, also code-named The Rock and Site R, was deep inside a Pennsylvanian mountain about six miles from the presidential retreat at Camp David, Maryland. The redoubt, operated by the Department of Defense, had been created during the cold war to provide a site where a government whose leaders had been vaporized—"decapitated," in the term then current—could still manage to function.

Raven Rock, particularly concerned with military continuity, could house a phantom Pentagon in the form of the Alternate National Military Command Center and the Alternate Joint Communications Center.

Mount Weather was one of the names for a large, elaborate bomb shelter burrowed into a Virginia mountain forty-eight miles west of Washington. Select members of Congress had huddled there after nine-eleven and later created the Department of Homeland Security, which now managed the site.

"Absolutely not, Sean. Out of the question."

"The Secret Service will insist."

"Last time I checked, they worked for me."

"Yes, sir, but—"

"No Raven Rock. No Weather Mountain. I stay right here."

"Very well, Mr. President. But until we know what's going on, I don't think it's wise for you and Max to be in the same place."

"I see your point. Max goes to Raven Rock. As things

ease, he can hop over to Camp David. Get the word to him."

"Yes, sir."

"What else, Sean? I have that certain feeling that you have a list."

"Nucflash will generate other events, sir. We need to be prepared for them: Each combat commander will have to raise the DEFCON and take force-protection measures. DEFCON One means the military go to maximum readiness, prepared for an imminent attack. I know that Secretary Kane can keep this under control so it doesn't look like we've blindly decided to go to war—without picking an enemy."

Oxley nodded and gestured for Falcone to go on.

"We'll get countless Internet messages about organizations claiming responsibility. All the claims will have to be examined. The media will be competing with our Intelligence Community to get answers. I want you to get ahead of the game. All through the night we will be working to get information for you when you speak tomorrow morning."

Oxley nodded again.

"I'll give Bill Bloom a predawn briefing. We've got to let our allies know as much—or nearly as much—as we know."

"And make sure that Marilyn Hotchkiss is at his side, Sean. You know how Bloom depends on her for getting the human side of things."

"Yes, sir," Falcone said, convinced that he had a free pass to prepare Oxley for the dawn.

Oxley took a step toward the door leading to the corridor stairway to the Residence. "You can make the chaos of hell look like planning a picnic, Sean," he said. "I'm just damn glad you're with me. Good night, Sean." He stopped and turned. "Don't hesitate to call me—I can't honestly say 'wake me'—if anything new comes to light."

"We are working in the dark, sir," Falcone continued. "But we're sending a recon plane from Andrews. That'll give us our first view. If we get anything extraordinary— such as a clue to who did this—I will not hesitate to call. Try to rest . . . *what unlikely words* . . . Mr. President."

30

Falcone had assumed the recon plane was in the air when he was briefing the President, even though he had been in government long enough to know that he should not as- sume anything. What Falcone did not know was that the urgency surging through the Situation Room had not yet traveled to Joint Base Andrews.

Navy Commander Wayne Davis, the operations duty officer at Andrews, had reacted to the Situation Room request with his usual caution. This was an unscheduled nighttime mission, and it could not be rushed. Davis was forty-four days away from retirement after twenty years in the Navy.

Davis had dealt with many Situation Room calls. Some were just from someone puffed up by Situation Room duty. This time the caller was some Navy lieuten- ant. If he did not say "urgent" (and Davis did not record that he had), then Davis felt that he had the right to pro- ceed unhurriedly: the alerting of a pilot, the briefing, the maintenance check, the fueling, the communications protocol, the filing of the flight plan.

When Davis heard that the President would be on television, he held up the mission so that the pilot would better understand the situation. "Doesn't sound like much more than a major flood with the fancy name tsunami," he said to the pilot he had selected, Air Force Captain Sarah Bernton, who had racked up more hours of night flying than anyone else in the ready squadron.

In the Situation Room, Falcone assembled what he dubbed the Executive Committee—thus escalating the Savannah disaster to the level of the Cuban missile crisis, which had been managed by a secret group of officials known as the ExComm.

Around the table were General Wilkinson; Secretary of Defense Kane; Homeland Security Secretary Walker; Admiral David Mason, commandant of the Coast Guard; Ray Quinlan; Secretary of State Bloom; and, seated next to him, Deputy Secretary of State Marilyn Hotchkiss. Sam Stone, director of the CIA, sat next to Kane. Falcone had chosen Stone over Chuck Huntington, director of National Intelligence, because he wanted only one intelligence chief on the committee, and Falcone believed that Stone was better tuned into counterterrorism than Huntington. In seats along the wall were Falcone's deputies, Anna Dabrowski and Marine Lieutenant Colonel Jeffrey Hawkins, along with Navy Captain Spencer, who was still holding the folder full of notes that he had used to brief President Oxley for the eleven o'clock speech.

Vice President Cunningham would soon appear on a monitor, joining the Executive Committee via a secure videoconference line from Raven Rock.

Quinlan reported that the networks had agreed to a predawn televised address from the Oval Office. The pool camera crew for the eleven o'clock address was, in fact, still on White House grounds, loading their vehicles, when Secret Service agents herded them back in.

"Stephanie," Quinlan continued, "has Barry Ellicott working on a draft of—"

"Tell Stephanie I'll give Barry a briefing at about four thirty A.M.," Falcone said, breaking in. He was thinking and speaking fast. He knew that Barry Ellicott was the President's favorite speechwriter. But to Ellicott, all issues were political issues, and Falcone was already planning how he would channel his thoughts on the crisis. "The problem . . . and this will be a continuing problem . . . is what we decide to tell and what we decide not to—"

A light lit on the console in front of Falcone. The caller ID said ANDREWS. "The recon," he said, then pointed to Captain Spencer. "Get ready for images."

Falcone picked up the headset and heard, "Commander Davis here. Joint Base Andrews duty officer. Reporting the recon mission is about to start."

"About to start?" Falcone exclaimed. "What the fuck is going on?" Others at the table exchanged surprised looks.

"What is going on, Mr. Falcone, is the beginning of a mission. That is what I am reporting."

Falcone looked at his watch. Twenty minutes after eleven. "Hold on, Commander," Falcone said, turning to the people around the table. "Sorry. We don't have the information I had anticipated. Please remain nearby. We will reassemble as soon as I get the recon."

Anna Dabrowski quickly arranged for National Security Council staffers to set up cots in the cubicles around the Situation Room. She had the White House Mess call in reinforcements for its usual overnight crew. Marines and Secret Service agents donated toilet articles and sweatsuits for anyone who wanted them.

As everyone was leaving the room, Falcone switched back to Commander Davis at Andrews. Trying to keep his voice even, he said, "This is an urgent, high-priority mission, Commander. It should have started more than an hour ago."

"I have no indica—"

Falcone interrupted to ask, "Are you SCI-cleared?"

"Yes . . . sir."

"This is SCI, authorized by the President. Code name is Stonewall. All paperwork about this flight is to be classified SCI. When the pilot returns, a White House vehicle will be waiting to take him to the Situation Room. All understood?"

"Yes, sir," Davis replied. He thought of SCI as Top Secret on steroids. A mission labeled SCI—Sensitive Compartmentalized Information—did not come along that often. SCI was not officially higher than Top Secret, but the SCI designation sharply restricted the dissemination of information only to people who possessed SCI clearance for the mission. "The pilot is Air Force Captain Sarah Bernton, sir."

"Patch me into the pilot," Falcone said.

"She's on the runway. Patching her is rather—"

"Patch me to the goddamn pilot!"

"Air Force Captain Sarah Bernton, sir," the pilot responded when Falcone identified himself. She was at the controls of an A-10 Warthog, a close-air-support aircraft known for its

ability to fly slow and low. The A-10's official Air Force
name was Thunderbolt. But everyone who knew it called it
the Warthog, a nickname inspired by its homely, unaero-
dynamic look: Two jet engines jutted from its double tail
and hung over the fuselage like a pair of misplaced bulg-
ing eyes. The cockpit, inside a large bubble canopy, was
forward of the wings, looking oddly misplaced but giving
the pilot a wide view of the terrain below.

Ordinarily, the A-10 did not have a night vision-imaging
system. But the Air Force had recently ordered a squadron
of the A-10s to be retrofitted with LANTIRN (Low Altitude Navigation and Targeting Infrared for Night) for
special missions in Afghanistan. The aircraft in which
Captain Bernton was seated was an A-10 that now had this
capability.

"Are you cleared for SCI, Bernton?"

"No, sir."

"You are now, for this mission. The SCI name is Stonewall. I assume you are familiar with the use of the scrambler band."

"Yes, sir."

"Switch to that band." Falcone heard a click.

"Done so, sir." Bernton's voice became robotic.

"You are plugged directly into Summit, the White
House Situation Room," Falcone said in a similarly robotic voice. "This is a matter of extreme national security.
Your transmissions and my responses will be automatically recorded and classified SCI. You know the deal: This
mission must not be disclosed to anyone. Understood?"

"Yes, sir."

"Stonewall, there is a serious possibility that you may
be exposed to dangerous levels of radioactivity." Falcone

hesitated for a moment. "You can decline this mission. I am asking if you are willing to volunteer."

"Yes, sir. I am," Bernton instantly replied.

"Thank you, Sarah. Okay. When you return, you'll be checked for exposure. And you'll be given every necessary medical treatment."

"Yes, sir."

"Now, the mission. You have infrared photographing capability?"

"Affirmative, sir."

"Your target area, as you probably know from Commander Davis, is Savannah, Georgia."

"Yes, sir. We heard the President."

"Good. You will photograph as much of the target area as possible. And you will describe what you see when, flying toward Savannah, you observe a blacked-out area. I want you to indicate the northern perimeter of the blackout area, do a recon flight over Savannah, then fly southward to determine the southern perimeter of the blackout. Clear?"

"Yes, sir. May I punch perimeter coordinates into my navigation log?"

"Affirmative. Then, before arrival back at Andrews, relay your log and photos to Summit and then erase the log and infrared photos. Understood?"

"Sir, I cannot erase the log or photos."

"Very well. I will arrange for the aircraft to be impounded at Andrews until I send technicians to remove your photographic and navigation systems."

"Yes, sir."

"ETA?"

"I estimate ninety-six minutes, sir."

"Can't go faster?"

"I'll push the Warthog as hard as I can, sir. But I've got to figure fuel consumption for a round trip."

"Okay, Stonewall . . . Sarah. Good luck."

The Warthog sped down the runway, rose, and headed south through the sky of the crescent moon.

31

When the first transmission came in from Bernton, Falcone was hunched over a cup of coffee and a yellow legal pad in the Situation Room Watch Center, which he had designated as the temporary headquarters for Stonewall operations.

"This is Stonewall," Bernton said. Her strangely dehumanized voice momentarily confused Falcone.

"I am passing over the northern perimeter at slowest possible speed," she continued. "Navigation map display shows me along the Savannah River, entering Georgia from South Carolina approximately at a wildlife refuge near Port Wentworth at the crossing of Interstate 95 and Georgia Highway 21. Port Wentworth is dark. To the west is Savannah/Hilton Head International Airport, showing lights. Wait! Also flames. Flames near an east-west runway. Appears to be aircraft fire."

As Falcone talked to Bernton, he scribbled a note and handed it off to Hawkins. *Check FAA. Report plane down Savannah airport.*

"Very well, Stonewall. Stay slow. As you approach Hutchinson Island, head—"

"Reporting aircraft on fire. Appears to be a commercial airliner and—"

"Ignore the fire, Stonewall. Continue southward to Hutchinson Island, north of downtown Savannah, where the Back River breaks off from the Savannah River."

"Over Hutchinson. It's dark. All dark."

"Okay, Stonewall. Now head west. You will be crossing Savannah and heading toward the U.S. Coast Guard Air Station, which is at the northern end of the Hunter Army Airfield."

A minute later, Stonewall transmitted, "Oh my God! All blacked out. Gleaming water. Map shows a city but I see nothing. Oh my God!"

"Steady, Stonewall."

"I am over central Savannah. I see nothing. Except flames. Flames along what looks like waterfront. Flames lighting up floating debris."

"Keep photographing, Stonewall, and look for the southern perimeter."

"This is so awful. All these people." Her voice trailed off.

"Get hold of yourself, Stonewall," Falcone said. "You're our only eyes right now."

"Coast Guard station dark. Hunter Army Airfield is dark," she said, her voice strengthening. "Some lights showing along U.S. Highway 17 near Richmond Hill. Some lights to the west at site designated as Fort Stewart Military Reservation. Beyond, southwest along U.S. Highway 95, I am seeing some lights."

"Good work, Stonewall. Now head southeast from Hunter," Falcone said, his eyes on a monitor showing a map of the Savannah area. "Tell me when you see lights again."

"Lights begin just north of Montgomery. I am on a line heading northeast toward Wilmington Island. Getting a few lights. Looks spotty. But my map shows wetlands with few towns or population clusters."

"Got it, Stonewall. Now, head toward Tybee Island."

"Darkness, Summit. Darkness. Darkness. A few lights at southern edge of Tybee."

"Okay, Stonewall. Head home. A vehicle at Andrews will take you to Summit."

As Bernton was reporting, her information was being gathered and infrared images were being tagged at a nearby console by an analyst sent to the Situation Room by the National Geospatial-Intelligence Agency. The identification badge on a chain around his neck bore the name James Annaheim. He had never been to the White House before, but he knew that his highly regarded products had been there many times.

The NGA, which operated under the Department of Defense, was a relative newcomer to the Intelligence Community. A descendant of the old Army Map Service, the NGA analyzed satellite images, battlefield overviews, geographical data, and whatever resources it needed to produce geospatial intelligence packets, usually for the CIA, including the CIA officers who produced the President's Daily Brief. The packets supplied coordinates and imagery for CIA operatives directing missile-bearing drones to Al Qaeda targets in Afghanistan, Pakistan, and other troubled spots.

"The burning aircraft seen by Stonewall was probably the Acme Airlines flight due tonight at Savannah International at 8:54 and reported missing on GNN," Annaheim said after consulting an aviation database. "The aircraft is—was—an Airbus A319. Its passenger capacity is one hundred and twenty-five." He tagged the image POSSIBLE FLIGHT 342.

NGA's myriad databases included one that contained information about every major bridge in the world. The analyst was able to zoom into one of Stonewall's infrared images—a huge pile of wreckage along the Savannah River—and identify a length of twisted cable and piece of steel as coming from the main southern pier of the Talmadge Memorial Bridge.

"That's a confirmation on the bridge, sir. Totally destroyed," Annaheim said, tagging the image and adding the information to one of the new Stonewall databases he was creating to document the disaster. Two minutes later, he copied another section of an image, consulted one of the NGA's marine databases, and told Falcone, "There is an identifiable ship, sir. Or a slice of it, in shallow water. It is—was—a cruise ship, the *Regal,* registered in—"

"How many passengers?" Falcone interrupted.

"Full complement, two hundred and fifteen passengers and crew," Annaheim replied, looking up from the database file on one of his twin monitors. "But, as to the number actually aboard last night—"

"Never mind that right now," Falcone said. "Just keep mapping the disaster zone."

A CIA analyst, regularly assigned to the Situation Room, was working at a station behind Falcone. He had overheard the exchange. "We might be able to get the *Regal* manifest from Homeland Security," he said, turning around to address the NGA analyst. "They're supposed to keep track of everyone entering the country. I have a source who—"

"But this is a coastal cruise ship," Annaheim said. "Didn't leave the country, and it—"

"For Christ's sake!" Falcone yelled. "Shut up and keep

figuring out what the hell happened to Savannah." In the moment of silence that followed, he said softly, "Sorry. Nerves. Sorry."

Every workstation in the Watch Center had an analyst from an intelligence agency. Analysts were supposed to piece together bits of information and produce what the handbooks called "an integrated view" of whatever issue they had been assigned to. If the information they had was hazy or not quite trustworthy, they hacked away at the ambiguities until they could present to their customers reasonable interpretations of events and equally reasonable suggestions for dealing with those events.

At least, Falcone thought, *that's the way it was supposed to be. But what about now? What about dealing with the unthinkable? A city destroyed.*

The disaster map, based roughly on what places were showing lights, encompassed a darkness that blotted out about three hundred square miles. Falcone, studying the map, thought of Tourtellot's description of what happened to his helicopter's computer.

"Hawk," Falcone called over to his military aide, who was in a nearby cubicle. "Find Tourtellot at Parris Island and talk to him on a secure line. I want to know everything about the way his radio and computer failed. And get that Coast Guard helicopter impounded. We need a high-tech inspection of it."

"EMP?" Hawkins asked. Falcone nodded. Hawkins realized that Tourtellot's experience pointed to an electromagnetic pulse, a product of a nuclear explosion.

The pulse phenomenon was discovered in 1962 during a nuclear weapon test over the Pacific. The rocket-launched weapon exploded two hundred and fifty miles above a coral atoll called Johnston Island. In Hawaii, nearly nine hundred miles away, streetlights went out and telephone networks shut down. Many homeowners reported odd events—such as burglar alarms going off—as the pulse rippled through the islands. Information about the pulse was withheld while the public wondered about what happened.

Falcone had no way of knowing what the pulse had done in its nanoseconds of existence. He had Hawk find a Department of Energy expert on the EMP phenomenon. Most scientific knowledge, the expert said, stemmed from the high-altitude Johnston Island explosion.

"But," the expert said, "laboratory simulations show that a nuclear detonation at any altitude will produce some kind of EMP, depending upon the explosion's energy yield and its interaction with the earth's magnetic field. Whatever this event is, it does not appear to be high-altitude and it apparently produced an EMP with characteristics we don't yet understand. But I'd bet this EMP burned out a lot of power transmission lines and unprotected electrical and electronic equipment like computers."

After hearing Hawkins's report on what he had learned from the DOE expert and Tourtellot, Falcone had no need to guess what had caused the blackout. And the infrared images of the damage, added to the evidence of the pulse, made a nuclear explosion almost certain. But there was no way yet to determine the boundaries of the nuclear explosion, the extent of the blackout caused by the pulse, or the levels of possible radiation.

Falcone called a classified number at the Department of Energy and asked for the NNSA duty officer. Among the responsibilities of the National Nuclear Security Administration was the security of nuclear weapons. NNSA, whose very existence had once been classified, was also the nation's lead responder to any nuclear or radiological incident within the United States or abroad.

"Antonio Gomez, emergency response officer, speaking. Is this in regard to a nuclear weapon?"

Falcone identified himself and said, "This call is SCI."

"Understood," Gomez responded, checking his console to make sure the call was being recorded.

"I have information leading me to believe that a nuclear device has produced an EMP in and around Savannah, Georgia. There is also some evidence of a denotation of a device. Shortly after dawn, on presidential authority, the Secretary of Defense will issue a Nucflash message. Also on presidential authority, I want a NEST sent to Savannah."

"I must notify Secretary Graham," Gomez said, referring to Dr. Harold Graham, a former Princeton physicist who was the Secretary of Energy.

Falcone knew that Graham would not have any day-to-day knowledge of NNSA activities. Nor would he necessarily be aware of its resources, which included helicopters and aircraft containing radiation-detection devices. Bureaucratically, the large and well-funded NNSA was to the Department of Energy what the FBI was to the Department of Justice.

"You can send a memo to Graham later, Gomez. Right now, I want a NEST flying to Savannah."

Gomez paused for a moment, checking an on-screen procedure manual and an NNSA contact database. "I'm calling our NEST ready-response unit," he said.

Little more than a minute later Falcone heard a deep

voice. "Dr. Reuben Lanier, Mr. Falcone. What is the basis for your request?"

Falcone irritably repeated what he had told Gomez.

"Yes, I can understand your concern," Lanier said. "Now that I think of it, we met at one of those NSC war games where a terrorist is supposed to—"

"We need solid information, Lanier," Falcone interrupted, still sounding irritated. "And, goddamn it, we need it as soon as possible."

"All in due time, Mr. Falcone. All in due time, I promise you. Do you have any *direct* evidence of a nuclear device? And, if Savannah is so extensively damaged, where exactly can we insert our team?"

"I have given you all the information we have at this time, Lanier."

"Are you aware, Mr. Falcone, that NEST personnel have been involved in well more than one hundred nuclear threats? And they have responded to, well, at last count, I think, thirty. They have all been hoaxes or false alarms. You can understand my reluctance to—"

"What I understand, Lanier, is that the President of the United States wants NEST in Savannah. And if you refuse to do so, I will personally see to it that you are placed in federal custody under the U.S. antiterrorism law."

"Very well, Mr. Falcone," Lanier said, his tone unchanged. "My databases shows Hunter Army Airfield as the nearest—"

"We believe that Hunter is inoperative. Savannah/Hilton Head International Airport appears to be undamaged. But we have no knowledge of the extent of radiation. That is the most urgent information we need."

"Very well. A NEST group, with hazmat suits, radia-

tion shielding, and detection kits will be ready for transport in approximately ninety minutes, along with—"

"Where are you, Lanier?"

"At Los Alamos National Laboratory in Albuquerque,
New Mexico."

"We'll send an aircraft from the nearest Air Force
base."

"That would be Kirtland," Lanier responded. "We
have an arrangement for instant use of military aircraft.
We drill about that all the time. I've already pushed a
button. I know you said you have given me all the information you have. But you mentioned a disaster map and
infrared images. Please send them right away so we can
begin evaluation."

" Got it. You'll have them immediately," Falcone assured him.

"The NEST personnel will conduct ground surveys
and, after delivering the personnel, the NEST aircraft
will take air samples at various heights. I will call you—in
the Situation Room, I assume—to confirm the takeoff."

"Thank you, Dr. Lanier. I assure you that this is no false
alarm."

Falcone returned to staring at his monitor, watching
Annaheim's preliminary disaster map roll down the
screen. Savannah had been laid out in 1733 as a city consisting of four squares; the city grew along a grid plan,
square by square. Each of Savannah's twenty-four squares
was now a small, leafy gem—Johnson Square with its
sundial, Columbia Square with its fountain, Washington
Square with its old garden. . . .

Annaheim used the squares as a grid in the center of
the map. He superimposed the infrared aerial images as

a transparent layer upon the squares, the heart of the city. Falcone had gone to a friend's wedding in Savannah a few years back. He remembered the vibrant squares now as he looked at the spectral images that showed, in flowing shades of red, the ghost of a vanished city.

32

Just before 4 A.M., Captain Bernton, still in her flight suit, arrived in the Situation Room Watch Center, escorted by two Marines. She was a tall, trim woman. Her black hair framed a tense pale face.

Falcone nodded to a Secret Service agent who had been trained in radiation detection. She ran a dosimeter over Bernton and said, "You're clean, Captain. But as soon as you're through here, a White House vehicle will take you to the National Naval Medical Center for a thorough examination."

"Nice work, Captain," Falcone said, stepping forward to shake Bernton's hand. He had left the monitor and was in the small Watch Center office that he had made his headquarters. Next to his desk was a cot that he had yet to use.

The agent went off to arrange the transportation. Falcone pointed to a cubicle. "There's coffee and sandwiches next door, Captain," he said. "When you're ready, I'd like to debrief."

Bernton stepped into the cubicle, poured coffee into a white mug, picked up a sandwich, and returned to Falcone. He motioned her to a metal chair in front of the desk. He pulled his chair around the desk so that he faced her directly. He held a yellow pad, half of its pages full of his notes. He curled the pages back and wrote BERNTON on a new page.

"Have you ever been to Savannah? I mean, on the ground, walking around?"

"No, sir."

"A beautiful city," Falcone said.

Bernton nodded in response.

"This mission, as I told you, is highly secret."

"It won't be secret for long, sir."

"You're right. At dawn the world will see what you saw in infrared. And at dawn the President will speak." Falcone paused. "Tell me, Captain, in your own words, what you saw."

Her pale face blank, her eyes staring straight ahead, Bernton spoke: "I saw death, sir. I was looking at death. All of those people. . . ."

Falcone could not ask her any questions. He was hearing not robotic sounds but her natural voice: soft, touched with what could be a Maine twang. In those few words she had given him her debrief, the truest, most powerful debriefing he had ever heard.

"You have had a terrible experience, Captain. If you want, take a rest here. He took a fresh yellow pad out of a desk drawer. "Write down anything you want. Again, please take a rest. I want you here until after the President speaks. Then you'll be taken to the medical center."

"Very well, sir," she said, leaning forward, her hair spreading across the yellow pad as she rested her head on a page that would remain blank.

Falcone, carrying two mugs of coffee, returned to the monitor. Annaheim, his fingers moving swiftly over the keys, was still working on the map, adding new details he had extracted from the infrared images. Falcone handed him a mug.

"Anything to add from Captain Bernton, sir?" Annaheim asked

"Death, Annaheim. Just death."

"Sir?"

"Did you read *Midnight in the Garden of Good and Evil*?"

"No, sir. But I saw the movie," Annaheim said. He touched three keys. "Is this what you mean?"

On the monitor came the two-ply image, made into what looked like three dimensions by Annaheim's manipulations. The map showed a large tract of land near the eastern city limits. Upon the map was part of an image, which Annaheim enlarged and tagged BONAVENTURE CEMETERY. Uprooted live oaks and coffins floated in shallow water beneath the infrared scrim.

"It said in the book that midnight was a special time," Falcone said, half to himself. "As long as it lasted, there was good magic and after that was the time for evil magic."

33

At 5 A.M., the Executive Committee members filed into the Situation Room and took their places at the table. "Ex-Comm will come to order," Falcone said, and the MIC ON indicator lights appeared.

Quinlan and Wilkinson, who, like Falcone, were history buffs, exchanged glances when they heard Falcone's shorthand version of "Executive Committee."

All rose as the President entered at 5:05. Like everyone else in the room, he looked as if he had not slept, but he had showered, shaved, and changed. His tie was a blue so dark that it was almost black. He was followed into the room by Attorney General Roberta Williams and J. B. Patterson, director of the FBI.

Patterson, every inch the stolid, sharp-eyed FBI agent, had been known as J. B. ever since his girlfriend, a drama major at Notre Dame, noted that his initials (for James Benjamin) were the name of her favorite play, *J. B.* by Archibald MacLeish. When Patterson joined the FBI, J. Edgar Hoover insisted on a first-name-plus-initial identification, which Patterson retained until he became the director and could order exactly what to put on his nameplate and business cards. Patterson told the story many times, always noting that the girlfriend became his wife.

As the newcomers entered, Patterson, in an awkward moment, stepped back to allow Williams to precede him. But she motioned for him to go ahead, looking faintly bemused by Patterson's misplaced chivalry. They usually got along well, though Patterson, white and Mississippi-born, sometimes overly demonstrated his approval of a black boss who also happened to be a woman.

"Two more for . . . ExComm," Oxley said. Falcone realized that Oxley had heard the word while he lingered at the entrance to the Situation Room, perhaps to take a few moments to gather his thoughts. The slightly sardonic way that Oxley had said "ExComm" gave Falcone a message, as did Oxley's surprise appointment of Williams and Patterson: either Oxley wanted to add heft to the group or he wanted to establish his authority and rein in his national security advisor a bit.

Fair enough either way, Falcone thought. *It's Oxley's call, not mine.*

The President took his seat and nodded toward Roberta Williams. "I've added Roberta because I want to make damn sure when we react to . . . to whatever this is . . . we stay legal. As for J. B."—Oxley pointed to Patterson—"I want the FBI here from the beginning." He looked down the table at Sam Stone. "Along with the CIA." Oxley turned to Falcone. "Okay, Sean. What have we got?"

Falcone signaled for Annaheim's disaster map to be shown on all the wall screens. There was a sudden silence, punctuated by gasps and, from someone, a quiet utterance of "Oh my God!"

"There is no doubt that much of Savannah has been devastated," Falcone said. "And there are at least two other collateral disasters. The label REGAL refers to a cruise ship with as many as two hundred and fifteen people aboard. POSSIBLE FLIGHT 342 can carry one hundred and twenty-five people. As you can see, the center of Savannah appears to be destroyed. The damage seems to irregularly extend outward to the east and—"

"What's the population of Savannah?" Oxley asked, his voice barely audible.

Falcone looked down at the fact sheet Annaheim had prepared. "Approximately one hundred and thirty-one thousand, Mr. President," Falcone replied.

"My God!" Oxley exclaimed. "And how many . . . ?"

"We have no way of knowing the casualty count at this time, sir," Falcone replied. He looked down again at the fact sheet, which contained figures that Annaheim had derived from databases on disasters. "We have several estimates, based on the little we know. In a catastrophe of this size, the number of dead—"

"I spoke to Governor Morrill about an hour ago," Oxley

interrupted. "He is still thinking tsunami and is expecting casualties in the thousands."

"Worst case analysis, sir, is twenty thousand, with three thousand the lowest probable—all based on extremely limited data from large-scale disaster casualty experience. We are hampered by the power outage blotting out communications."

"Morrill says Atlanta still has power," Oxley said.

"There is reason to believe that the blackout was caused by an electromagnetic pulse, an EMP, and that—"

"EMP?" General Wilkinson exclaimed. "That means—"

"That *probably* means," Falcone continued, "a nuclear event of some kind."

"Event?" Wilkinson nearly shouted. "Event? Good God, Sean! It's got to be a nuclear explosion, a nuclear weapon."

"We don't know that for sure, Gabe," Falcone said.

"Possibly a nuclear power plant?" Penny Walker asked.

"Not likely. There are two plants in Georgia," Falcone replied. "One is about eighty miles to the west; the other is about one hundred and twenty-five miles south."

"Radiation?" Oxley asked

"Nothing on that yet," Falcone replied. "We've got a NEST—a Nuclear Emergency Support Team—heading to Savannah."

"Where the hell did that goddamn tsunami report come from?" Oxley asked, sounding impatient.

Falcone quickly recounted the events—Tourtellot's pickup of the *huge wave* transmission, the computer failure in Tourtellot's helicopter, the report to the NMCC, the probable nuclear flash seen by a satellite. "Piecing it all together," he continued, "it appears that some kind of a nuclear device exploded off Savannah and created a tsunami-like wave that surged into Savannah, preceded by an EMP that—"

"Device?" J. B. Patterson exclaimed. "You mean a nuclear bomb has been detonated in American waters?"

"Again, we don't know that, J. B. All we do know is that power has been knocked out in and around Savannah. There has been great physical destruction with many, many people dead or injured. There are fires burning out of control, and—"

"Sean, is there any question that this is an act of terrorism?" Patterson asked. "I want an FBI counterterrorism team heading down there right now. And I mean, right now. We are the lead agency for domestic terrorism."

"Slow down, J. B. I don't want anything to happen until I get on the air and talk to the American people," Oxley said.

"Agreed, Mr. President," Patterson said. "But the minute you—"

Ignoring Patterson, Oxley took charge of the meeting. "About an hour ago," he said, "I asked the attorney general to lay out the legal boundaries if the situation in Savannah makes it necessary for me to declare a national emergency. Roberta, if you will."

Roberta Williams had been the captain of the women's basketball team that had twice won the national collegiate championship. She still played one-on-one with any man or woman in Washington who dared. A *New Yorker* profile described her voice as soft but steely. Everyone looked up and listened to that voice when she started to talk.

"For decades," she began, "president after president has declared various emergencies in response to local disasters. But in 2007 came the National Security and Homeland Security Presidential Directive, which trumped all previous directives regarding presidential power. That directive has the effect of a federal law. And, incidentally, it makes no reference whatsoever to Congress.

"Under the Presidential Directive, if President Oxley declares a national emergency, he may, for instance, seize property, including farmers' harvests and any 'agricultural commodities' he chooses. He may also seize and control all transportation and communication, restrict travel, and, of course, declare martial law."

"As you know, Gabe," she continued, turning to General Wilkinson, "in October 2002, the Department of Defense established USNORTHCOM, making the United States a command theater and giving the President an armed force to aid him in the protection of the homeland. Essentially, USNORTHCOM becomes the President's army."

"Tanks in the streets, right, Roberta?" Wilkinson said, shaking his head. "You well know that a very old law—Posse Comitatus—says soldiers cannot be used in civil situations."

"We've come a long way since Congress passed the Posse Comitatus Act in 1878, Gabe. That was in reaction to the use of federal troops by U.S. marshals in southern states. This is a *federal* emergency. I'll send you an up-to-date memo," Williams said. "In a declared national emergency, the President can essentially use the armed forces in any way he sees fit."

She shifted her attention to Penny Walker and said, "Under both the congressional legislation creating the Department of Homeland Security and a specific National Security Presidential Directive regarding a catastrophic emergency, the President is empowered to maintain 'continuity of government.' One of the specific definitions of that kind of emergency is 'extraordinary levels of mass casualties,' which looks like what we are facing. Under that law, the President can assume strong—some may say dictatorial—powers."

When Williams paused, Ray Quinlan blurted out a question: "Can the President postpone or cancel the election?"

Williams leaned forward, her hands outspread on the gleaming tabletop. "That particular question, Ray," she said, a touch of exasperation in her voice, "has been on the Internet paranoid hit parade ever since President George W. Bush signed the Homeland Security Act. There was another flare-up of paranoia in 2007 when he issued the Presidential Directive. There's little doubt in my mind that the directive gives the President the power to postpone the election."

"But is it specifically in the law?" Quinlan persisted.

"I cannot legally respond to that, Ray," Williams replied. "Large portions of the law are classified."

"What?"

"Attached to the law were several documents called 'Annexes.' They are classified in a special way. According to the language in the law, the Annexes shall be 'accorded appropriate handling, consistent with applicable Executive Orders.' And those Executive Orders are classified. It's a maze. Essentially, the President, while dealing with a 'catastrophic emergency,' can do whatever he believes he needs to do to maintain continuity of the federal government."

"Let's get to the structure, Roberta," Oxley said sharply. "We're running out of time."

"Yes, sir," Williams said, leaning back. "The law creates the position of a single national continuity coordinator, responsible for maintaining the operation of the federal government. And the Department of Homeland Security becomes the lead agency for handling the coordinator's decisions. The directive specifies that the assistant to the president for homeland security and counterterrorism is to be the national continuity coordinator. And since that particular assistant to the president post is not filled at the moment, the President may pick anyone."

"I guess that's my cue, Penny," Oxley said. Reaching out to pat Falcone on the back, Oxley added, "You now have another title. Start coordinating."

"Thank you, Mr. President," Falcone said.

Before Falcone could say another word, Oxley stood, signaling his exit and bringing all in the room to their feet. "I'm off to see what Barry and Stephanie are putting in my prompter," he said. "You'll be joining us, Sean?"

"Yes sir. I'll be there very shortly," Falcone said.

Still standing for the departure of the President, Falcone held up his hand and said, "I want everyone in this room—except Penny, Anna, and Hawk—to go to their regular offices and begin carrying on whatever business you'd be doing on any other day. At dawn, America will begin to see the reality of what we have seen through infrared images. At dawn everything will change. There will be panic, rumors, false claims, a media frenzy. But we have to project confidence—and continuity.

"Max"—Falcone looked at the videoconference screen showing the Vice President's ruddy face—"for the next little while, I think you should stay in your 'undisclosed location.' We'll keep you in the loop."

"God be with you, Sean, and with the rest of us," Cunningham said as his image faded away.

"Captain Spencer, you're our early witness. We need you," Falcone continued, pointing toward the Navy officer. "Find a place for a couple hours of sleep and then set up an operations post in the Watch Center. That's going to be your duty station until you're relieved."

Penny Walker stayed at her place as the other Ex-Comm members filed out. Falcone walked around the table, sat next to her, and held her hand.

"Penny, you've got the lead on the biggest catastrophe in American history. I want you here, in the White House, not across town at DHS. Use my office for now. We'll rearrange things so that you'll be right at hand. As you know, we need an incident commander. He or she will be the face of the catastrophe, at the scene, twenty-four-seven. Any ideas?"

Walker stared at the ceiling for a few minutes. "You want someone who is centered—we say that in pottery about the clay on the wheel. Being solid, concentrated, balanced," she said. "And you want a human being who is not a bureaucrat, someone who has commanded, who has the look of authority. I know who you want. Admiral David Mason."

Falcone hesitated before saying, "The commandant of the Coast Guard? I . . . I don't really know him."

"I do. He's the finest man I have ever known. And he is smart, damn smart."

"I'd like to talk to him . . . first."

"Sorry, Sean. You take him on my word or you don't. Right now. I'm not going to call him to come in for an audition."

"Your point is taken, Penny. Call him and get him here. And tell him to bring his sea bag."

34

An hour before dawn, a GNN helicopter took off from Atlanta and headed for Savannah, timing its flight so that it dipped low over the center of the city minutes after the first rays of the sun pierced the blackness. "We are above Savannah. Or what used to be Savannah," said Ned Winslow.

GNN had charted a private jet aircraft to whisk Winslow down to Dallas and then back to Atlanta in order to avoid any flight restrictions imposed along the eastern coast. When the helicopter banked, his profile partially framed an image of dark water, still as a pond, shrouding what lay beneath.

In the growing dawn, shattered buildings emerged, and the curving course of the Savannah River was faintly outlined. "We are looking at total desolation," Winslow continued as the helicopter pivoted over the twin towers of the Cathedral of St. John the Baptist. "Part of the roof is torn away. I can look right down into the nave of the cathedral."

The image shifted, bringing the river into focus. "I can see a pile of cars, jammed together. There is no sign of life. No sign anywhere."

Along the shore, huge gas tanks spilled fires that flowed atop the water. Upriver, the tangled remains of the Talmadge Bridge were partially visible. "I can see what I guess was a ship," Winslow said as the camera zoomed to a torn white hull. "My God! It looks like part of a cruise ship." The camera turned away. "And there's another ship—a freighter, I think—lying on its side like a giant toy."

The helicopter followed the river to the sea and swung over a vast wetland dotted with clusters of wreckage. "It's hard to see where the sea ends and the land begins. It looks as if the tsunami flowed across the marshes and the waters are slowly receding. The damage—the disaster—is immense. There are no lights anywhere. Electric power—"

"I don't want to see any more private helicopters in that airspace. Where the hell is the FAA flight ban? I want a flight-exclusion zone centered on Savannah and radiating out twenty-five miles in all directions. Get on that right away, and—" Falcone was giving Hawkins orders when, on Falcone's Watch Center screen, the GNN image suddenly shrunk to a square in the lower left corner.

The rest of the screen filled with the image of President Oxley in the Oval Office. The image also appeared on screens that had been showing the reporting of all the networks. They were covering the disaster from their Washington studios or from correspondents in Atlanta. No one had wanted to venture into Savannah at night. Only GNN had sent in a helicopter.

Now the site of news had shifted to the Oval Office, and all were covering the same event, a presidential address that promised to be momentous.

"Good morning, my fellow Americans," President Oxley began, his voice strong, his face taut. "Dawn has brought us the reality of the catastrophe in Savannah. Last night, when we had only fragmentary information, I said that a tsunami had struck Savannah. I have now learned that some kind of high-explosive device—possibly a nuclear device—caused this catastrophe.

"During the night, after getting reports of a possible nuclear incident, I ordered a Nuclear Emergency Support Team to enter Savannah to determine whether a nuclear or radiological event had occurred. The team, known as NEST, consists of scientists, technicians, and engineers operating under the United States Department of Energy's National Nuclear Security Administration.

"We expect that the NEST experts will detect some radiation produced by a nuclear device. We believe that the widespread electric power failure, centered on Savannah, may have been due to an electromagnetic pulse produced by the explosion of the nuclear device.

"All the resources of our federal government have been mobilized to deal with this catastrophe. As I speak, a Navy task force including two aircraft carriers and a hospital ship are steaming toward Savannah. The carriers' electrical systems will be connected to the electric grid to provide emergency power while the grid is being restored. Air Force aircraft sent off by the Department of Homeland Security have already landed near Savannah. They carry food, water, medical personnel, portable hospitals, and supplies of pills that lessen the effects of radiation on the body.

"We do not have any casualty figures or any damage estimates. Nor have we found the actual dimensions of the catastrophe. But clearly Savannah has been grievously damaged.

"We, as a nation, must now deal with three vital tasks: We must go to the aid of Savannah and the victims of this catastrophe. We must determine how this catastrophe happened. And, if it happened because of the evil designs of an enemy, we must find and punish that enemy.

"While aid is speeding to Savannah, our intelligence agencies are focused on determining the source of the explosion. Our allies throughout the world are also helping us in many ways.

"At this point, we do not believe that the catastrophe is part of a general attack on the United States. But under long-standing Department of Defense procedures, the report of a nuclear incident produced a global response. All military commands are on full alert. And, as a precaution, the Homeland Security Threat Advisory has risen to Severe, the highest alert.

"A decision to declare a Severe Threat automatically produces, throughout the government, predetermined protective measures. Many of these measures cannot be publicly announced at this time. But I pledge to share with you as much information about the catastrophe and the threat as possible, consistent with the safety of the nation.

"Because of the enormity of this catastrophe, because responding to it is clearly beyond even well-prepared city and state governments, I am declaring a national emergency, under the National Security and Homeland Security Presidential Directive. That directive was created by a previous president as a mechanism to guarantee continuity of government during a catastrophic emergency.

"Acting under that directive, I place the immediate area of the catastrophe under federal management. Further developments may call for a similar decision about other areas.

"The lead federal agency, under the law, is the Department of Homeland Security, which is sending teams to the area. Those teams will work closely with Governor Morrill and local authorities.

"I have named my national security advisor, Sean Falcone, the national continuity coordinator, a post called for in the Presidential Directive. He will be the overall federal administrator. The incident commander, who is on his way to Georgia, is Admiral David Mason, commandant of the Coast Guard. He will be the day-to-day director of operations.

"I have further decided that I will curtail my reelection campaign so that I may concentrate on what has happened—and whatever may happen—in the days to come.

"Vice President Cunningham will not be campaigning. Until we determine the true dimensions of this event, we must be concerned about the continuity of government in the event of a successful attempt on the life of the President.

"Vice President Cunningham is in a location I cannot disclose. Until the threat level is lowered, he will remain there, in constant touch with me, as assurance of presidential succession.

"When we find out the source of this catastrophe, we will provide you with all the intelligence that we can reveal without imperiling methods and sources. During our worldwide investigation, we will demand cooperation from any nation that possesses information that will help us determine the cause of this catastrophe.

"If we determine that this was the launching of an attack on the United States by another nation or by an organization given sanctuary by that nation, the consequences for that nation will be extremely severe.

"Catastrophe has launched us into a new world. We

have never experienced on our soil a calamity of such magnitude. This new world is full of unknowns. It is a place of uncertainties, a place without familiar paths.

"We must do what Americans have always done when facing the unknown: We banish fear, solve the problems, blaze the paths. As a people, we have always turned away from the past and moved into the future with confidence in ourselves and faith in our God. We will do so once more, beginning with this new dawn.

"No matter what the future holds, we are one nation, under God. No matter the crisis, we will honor our pledge of liberty and justice for all.

"And now we must all get to work.

"God bless Savannah and God bless the United States of America."

Army Brigadier General Richard Castleton, military advisor to the Deputy Secretary of Defense, watched the President's address on a monitor in a modest office in the E-Ring of the Pentagon. As soon as the President finished, Castleton locked his office door, unlocked a desk drawer, and removed a metal box with a combination lock. He spun the dial four times, opened the box, and took out a cell phone. He looked at the device that was now buzzing urgently. On a narrow screen appeared a six-digit number, which changed every twenty seconds.

Castleton switched on the cell phone and repeated the six digits he was seeing on the screen. He saw two green lights, heard the sound of a buzzer, waited a moment, then said, "You heard truth. Oxley and his crew have no idea what happened."

"Expected," said the metallic voice of Rolf Eriksen.

"But do we have any idea what went wrong? How in hell could this have happened?"

"At this point, we don't have an answer, sir," Castleton said evenly.

"We can't let them know what we were doing! Do you understand?" Eriksen's voice retained its artificial quality, but was no longer calm.

"Yes, sir. There will be no fingerprints."

Castleton put the smartphone back in the box and into the drawer and then turned to his computer to continue reading the first draft of Secretary Kane's top-secret report to Falcone on the availability of troops for martial-law duty.

35

Falcone entered the Oval Office just as the television crew was leaving. He was not surprised to see that Ray Quinlan was already there, sitting in one of the two straight-back chairs in front of the President's desk.

"Your speech was exactly what the country needed, Mr. President," Falcone said before he sat down. "You let everyone know that there would be information you can reveal and information that it's necessary to withhold. That's an important point."

"'Curtail' was just right about the cutting back on the campaign," Quinlan said. "You indirectly damped down any rumors about cancelling the election. The blogosphere is already filling with that bullshit."

"But wait till Stanfield gets a look at the Executive

Orders on the books," Oxley said. "We're in for a rough ride."

"There's more than Stanfield to worry about, Mr. President," Falcone said. "The crazies are going to be in full battle cry. As you said, there are three tasks. Savannah gets the humanitarian attention. But, for national security, the most important tasks are finding out what happened and deciding what to do about it.

"My instincts give you forty-eight—maybe seventy-two—hours before the mobs are in the streets . . . and, if that happens, you'll have to use those Executive Annexes, which will make you into a dictator."

"I agree with Sean," Quinlan said. "And that doesn't happen very often. You have less than a week to be the hero who will rescue Savannah and find the bad guys. In that time I think you should be the leader, not the candidate. But maybe Max could be out there, your surrogate?"

"No dice on that," Oxley said. "It would look like I'm ducking. Max stays put. As a matter of fact, I gave him a job. I told him to call all the important Southern senators and representatives to assure them that the feds aren't on the march in Dixie. Don't forget, I came close to not carrying Georgia."

"Remember how Stanfield howled when President Bush invoked an Executive Order after that hurricane hit Texas?" Quinlan chortled.

"Roberta mentioned that when she briefed me," Oxley said. "It was an order, going back to Kennedy, that gave the president emergency power over all forms of transportation. FEMA used it to aid the evacuation of Houston by ordering that all lanes of a two-way highway be used for a one-way route out of the city. My God, a simple traffic change."

"Yeah, I remember," Quinlan said, laughing. "Stanfield went after the traffic-rage vote by denouncing FEMA for expanding federal power. But he never said a goddamn word about what had happened, just before, in New Orleans."

"Wait until he goes on Google and looks for ways to attack me," Oxley said. "Take a look at this. Roberta told me about it." He gestured for both men to go around the desk and look at the monitor. Oxley hit the button to call up the Internet, via Explorer. He then called up Google, and across the page came this message:

Under the National Emergency Presidential Declaration, the Department of Defense's Cyber Command and other U.S. Government agencies may routinely intercept and monitor communications on the Internet for purposes including, but not limited to, communications security; defending against cyberterrorism; and for law enforcement and counterintelligence purposes. An Intrusion Detection System is in force, defending against unauthorized users attempting to gain access to vital U.S. Government networks. At any time, the U.S. Government may inspect and seize data stored on this computer.

"My God!" Quinlan swore. "Wait till the loonies on the net get ahold of this! It's a conspiracy theory come to life."

"This particular bit," Oxley said, "comes under a directive that allows the government to seize and control the communication media."

"So screw the First Amendment! Wow! It's a dictator wannabe's wet dream."

"Calm down, Ray," Oxley said, lightly. "I'm not going to order *60 Minutes* off the air."

The mirthful political chatting in the midst of catastrophe bothered Falcone. But he had worked in Washington long enough to know that, rain or shine, peace or war, politics always trumped. He excused himself and headed for the Situation Room as Quinlan was talking about the need for a discreet poll to determine whether Oxley's popularity had gone up or down after his speech.

Falcone, as national continuity coordinator, had staked out a section of the Situation Room Watch Center. Dabrowski and Hawkins occupied two adjacent cubicles. Penny Walker moved into Falcone's West Wing office. Her principal aides took over NSC offices in the nearby Eisenhower Executive Office Building, the imposing nineteenth-century edifice that once held the State, War, and Navy departments.

Falcone had hoped for fifteen minutes on his cot, but Dabrowski and Hawkins were waiting for him when he returned. During the night, he had roughly worked out a division of labor. Walker would handle the catastrophe, while he, Anna, and Hawkins would work on finding out what caused it. He decided to start with the possibility that the source of the explosion was a stolen U.S. warhead.

"I asked a nonproliferation guy at CIA if we'll be able to identify the source of the radiation," Hawkins told Falcone as he eased himself into the chair in front of his monitor and telephone console. "He was very guarded about that. It's very sensitive. He says that the only reliable answer would have to come from a higher pay grade, like Director

Stone or the Secretary of State. And he believes that Los Alamos will have to tap into IAEA data."

"That's almost certainly bullshit," Falcone said. "If possible, I want to keep the international atom people out of this at this time. But let's not ruffle anybody for a while. I've told Lanier we've got to find the origin of the bomb . . . the device . . . whatever the hell it was." He turned to Dabrowski. "Anna, what do you have on the inventory?"

"Secretary Kane doesn't expect results until tomorrow at the latest."

"What the hell is so goddamn difficult about counting how many nuclear weapons and where they are?"

"The DOD reasons are a mile long," Dabrowski replied. "What they amount to is that there is no specific number so that no one can look at the weapons tally and say, 'Oh, one is missing.' There's a climate of deep secrecy. And the weapons are scattered. It's like an attic. Lots of boxes and barrels. And each box or barrel is sealed. Everything is top secret or SCI."

Falcone motioned to the chairs in front of his desk. "Okay, let's try to organize our thinking. We don't know whether we're trying to investigate an act of terror by an organization or a country; an act of evil by some wacko; or some kind of an extraordinary accident. And if it is an accident, was it caused by good people or bad people? We've ruled out some kind of long-range accident from one of the Georgia nuclear power plants, right?"

"Right," Hawkins answered. "We've gotten a lot of DOE nuke experts out of bed, gave them what we know, and they absolutely rule out either of the plants being responsible. NNSA, which not only runs NEST but also keeps track of all transporting of nuclear material, says there was nothing dangerous moving in, through, or out of Georgia for the past year." He hesitated, allowing a signal of doubt to enter his brisk delivery.

"But," he continued, " 'nothing dangerous' struck me as an odd phrase. I poked into NNSA's installations. There's something called SRS."

"Never heard of it," Falcone said.

"Let's hope that's true of the media, too. SRS means Savannah River Site. It's about one hundred and thirty miles north of Savannah."

"What goes on there?"

"NNSA—or at least the NNSA duty officer—says SRS processes tritium, an isotope of hydrogen gas used in nuclear weapons. NNSA's Web site says tritium is a relatively low-risk radioactive source. That's where the 'nothing dangerous' probably comes from.

"But tritium is in nuclear weapons and has to be replenished continually because it decays so quickly. The site recycles tritium from disassembled warheads and introduces new tritium by extracting it from rods irradiated in nuclear reactors. The rods come from an NNSA site in Tennessee. To do what it does, the Savannah River Site has to move a lot of nuclear material around.

"I called back, talked to the duty officer again. Not to worry, he says. It is keeping a careful watch on all this stuff, and that makes it nondangerous."

A nuclear facility called Savannah River Site, Falcone realized, would be a natural target of speculation by any reporter trying to find a possible source of the radiation in Savannah. But, Hawkins told him, luckily few outside NNSA knew anything about the place.

"When things calm down," Hawkins said, "maybe we'll be able to take another look at SRS. But right now, moving forward, I think we should assume it's benign."

"Well, for now at least, that gives us an end point. It looks as if we can eliminate SRS along with the power plants," Falcone said.

"To make an end is to make a beginning," Dabrowski said.

"Aunt Eva?"

"No," she said, smiling for the first time since the first Savannah report came in. "T. S. Eliot."

Falcone, also managing a smile, said, "Okay, Anna. You're up. Stockpile inventory."

"There are three stockpiles," Dabrowski said. "All told, we've got about nine thousand, nine hundred warheads. I have to say *about* because, at any given moment, the count can change. Warheads are being shifted all the time from one stockpile to the other.

"But how do we count the nuclear weapons that *aren't* there? When the cold war ended, the United States had about twenty-three thousand nuclear weapons. There were not only obsolete missile warheads but nuclear oddities, like the SADM, the Special Atomic Demolition Munition, small enough for a soldier to carry in a knapsack and blow up places in the event of a Soviet invasion of Europe."

"What happened to them?" Falcone asked. "They sound like those Russian suitcase bombs."

" 'Accounted for' is the basis for our treaties on nuclear weapons. Theoretically, when both sides started counting nuclear weapons for treaties, both sides dismantled— and accounted for—all the excess warheads, presumably including those suitcases and knapsacks. So, essentially they disappeared as weapons and their fissile material was recycled for use by nuclear power plants or stored away in waste tanks at NNSA sites like Hanford in Washington State.

"Then there are the nuclear weapons on various seafloors. They're in the wrecks of U.S. and Russian submarines or were accidentally dropped from planes, and so forth. The experts I talked to insist that in these cases, 'lost' doesn't mean 'unaccounted for.' Nor are they considered dangerous. So I didn't get into detail about the socalled lost nukes.

"We also must demand accounting from the Russians. That would mean getting assurances from a lot of former and current nuclear warhead sites. About seventy sites, at last count."

"To get a reasonable count fast, I think we should also ignore the storage sites right now and start with the existing stockpiles.

"I've asked for immediate stockpile information from three sources—a lot of people are losing sleep at the CIA, Department of Energy, and the Pentagon. And I drew up recommendations for dealing with each stockpile. If we can get NNSA people to give us their data—with three or four of our people asking questions and verifying the counting—we should be able to see if anything appears to be missing or suspicious. It's all laid out in this."

She handed Falcone a one-page memo:

We must determine immediately if any U.S. nuclear weapons are missing. They are in three categories known as "stockpiles." Here is the status of the stockpiles and recommendations for dealing with them.
<u>Operationally Deployed:</u> Fully operational weapons

mated with delivery systems. Incidentally, there are eight types of nuclear warheads, and most of them have a dozen or so variations. These are combat-ready weapons whose warheads are regularly counted under arms-limitation treaties. <u>Recommendation:</u> No need for an independent count by us. We can assume that alarms would be going off if any warhead in this stockpile is missing. We should give priority to the other two stockpiles.

<u>Active Stockpile:</u> A mixed bag of weapons that are not "operationally deployed," meaning, for instance, ballistic missiles on submarines that are not at sea (which is about two-thirds of their time). In this stockpile are also "spares" for active-duty warheads that are undergoing maintenance. And, at various bases, are warheads that are not officially deployed by treaty definition. These are just as ready-for-use as the weapons in the Operationally Deployed Stockpile, but, because they are not subject to treaty counts, they are scattered and inventoried under varying rules. Remember the B-52 bomber that flew across the central United States carrying six nuclear cruise missiles that had been accidentally attached to the bomber's wing? Those warheads were real. They might not have been "operationally deployed," but each one had the power of as many as ten Hiroshima bombs. There were a half-dozen security breakdowns in that incident alone. And each one could have resulted in the theft of a nuclear missile. <u>Recommendation:</u> We can't assume anything here. We need a rigorous, site-by-site count by the NNSA under our direct surveillance.

<u>Inactive Reserve:</u> These are weapons that are kept intact but not in operational condition. This is an

in-between stage defined in treaties as "undeploy-able." But they should still concern us because these are weapons that only need re-assembly. <u>Recommendation:</u> Get an NNSA expert to go over this category, site-by-site, also under our surveillance.

"We've got a huge job here, Anna," Falcone said, after quickly reading the memo. "Bring in everybody you can from the NSC staff for the counting surveillance. We can't leave this to the NNSA alone." He handed the memo to Hawkins, who read it and nodded.

"And who did you wake up, Hawk?" Falcone asked.

"Proliferation specialists at State and the CIA mostly," Hawkins replied. "Of the nine countries in the Nuclear Club—us, China, Russia, the UK, France, India, Pakistan, Israel, and North Korea—we obviously have to focus on three: a loose nuke in Pakistan or India or North Korea, and a real or rogue use by the North Koreans."

"What about a loose one in the other countries?" Falcone asked.

"Analysts at State and CIA are drawing up a country-by-country intelligence assessment on the likelihood of a foreign source. They say they'll have something for us by around noon."

"Okay," Falcone said. "When we get that, then State, through our ambassadors, needs to contact every country with nuclear weapons and demand that they verify the status of their stockpiles to make sure that nothing is missing or has been stolen. One of our Iraqi contacts can get through and warn Iran. And tell China that they have to lean hard on North Korea to give assurances or face the consequences."

"Which will be?" Hawkins asked.

"God only knows. We're going minute-by-minute. About that high-noon report, who are the analysts writing it?" Falcone asked.

Hawkins looked momentarily perplexed. "I don't know their names, Sean. I worked through our State liaison, Mitsue."

"Tell her I want their names and their job evaluations. I don't want any goddamn contractors on this job. I want feds all the way."

"Right, Sean," Hawkins said. "But, remember that *Washington Post* series on intelligence? Hundreds of companies are putting their employees in the game. More than eight hundred and fifty thousand people—the overwhelming majority of them contractors—have top-secret clearance. I think the best you can hope for is that federal analysts will be the principal contributors, not the only ones."

"Okay," Falcone said wearily. "Let's hope for the best from our many, many helpers. And let's all try for a few minutes of rest and get back here to figure out what happens next."

36

On day one, television networks had little to show about the biggest catastrophe ever to strike the United States. Producers built their continuous coverage around the President's speech and cautious estimates of the death toll. One anchor commentator said, "Thousands had almost certainly died." Another said, "The toll may well be in the tens of thousands."

After Falcone created the aerial exclusion zone, the only disaster videos available were GNN's helicopter images. All networks picked up the GNN report, overriding Ned Winslow's commentary with speculations and theories from pundits and nuclear-weapon experts sitting in studios and expounding on what they knew about nuclear explosions.

Every network produced similar images: Upon Google satellite views of Savannah, the experts placed circles in varying shades of red showing the probable area of destruction from nuclear weapons of varying size.

Everything in television and in newspapers and in countless new blogs was guesswork, for nothing was coming out of the White House, under siege by reporters, and Falcone had buttoned down every other possible federal source with dire warnings about jeopardizing national security. He continued to keep all of the reconnaissance imagery top secret. So no news medium was able to show what had been seen in the Situation Room.

The catastrophe was the strangest ever to challenge the media. Print reporters, along with television commentators and anchors, could not provide eyewitness reports. As in Japan during its nuclear reactor crisis, the exclusion zone kept changing. And fears of radiation poisoning haunted editors and television producers planning live coverage. A little research showed that the intrepid Russian journalist who made the longest immediate film of the Chernobyl disaster died shortly later of radiation poisoning. Because Homeland Security had temporarily closed down all airports, print reporters and television crews headed down U.S. 95, not knowing what was the edge of the danger zone.

Google showed that a little town called Ridgeland, South Carolina, was the highest point between Charleston and Savannah. So Ridgeland became a media center. Motels and restaurants filled. Trailers arrived to house anchormen and anchorwomen. TV camera trucks cruised the area looking for vantage points to position cameras with long-distance lenses aimed in the general direction of Savannah, thirty-six miles to the south.

They were trying to cover a catastrophe that was both invisible and silent. The electromagnetic pulse, which knocked out all radio and television stations, also severely damaged the electric grid centered in Savannah, and silenced the landline phone system. NBC found an electrical engineer who speculated that the blackout could last for a long time because the pulse probably had destroyed countless high-voltage transformers serving the grid.

"They handle enormous amounts of electricity," he said. "But they are very sensitive. A pulse can fuse their copper wiring, ruining them beyond repair. The transformers weigh as much as a hundred tons. They're made in Europe and Asia, and there's about a three-year waiting list for new ones."

Unable to show Savannah and deciding that scenes from the 2011 Japanese nuclear disaster were too static, television news producers drew on grainy, panicky film from the 1986 explosion and meltdown at the Chernobyl nuclear power station. On CBS, while images of sickly children appeared in the background, a George Washington University physicist talked about "Chernobyl's long shadow," quoting a United Nations report that more than

6,000 cases of thyroid cancer were reported in children and adolescents exposed to radiation at the time of the accident.

On GNN, Ned Winslow tried to keep coverage centered on the need for dependable information. "We really have no idea what happened in Savannah," he said. "We must wait for information from people on the ground." He predicted that the incident commander and NEST experts would soon be producing reports. But he lost control of his panel of experts as the giant screen behind them broke into squares, each one showing scenes from an American city.

New York: Mobs fight in Grand Central Station as people seek to flee the city by train because the airports were closed.

Chicago: The Nation of Islam's mosque is in flames. White youths throw bottles and bricks at firefighters. White and black rioters clash in a haze of tear gas. The blaze was kindled by a radio talk show host who claimed that black Muslims possessed nuclear bombs and planned to set them off in every state that had supported the Confederacy.

Detroit: A mob on the suspension bridge to Canada struggles with Canadian Army soldiers manning hastily erected barriers. Shots are fired at the soldiers. They fire back, killing at least eight Americans.

Miami: Six mammoth cruise ships, ordered into port by the Department of Homeland Security, jam the Miami waterfront. Thousands of passengers, unable to get rooms, vandalize luxury hotels. The Red Cross sets up cots and a soup kitchen at the Miami Beach Convention Center.

Los Angeles: A massive traffic jam paralyzes the city. Dozens of fights break out. Hundreds of men, women, and children—many of them in white robes—line up on the Santa Monica Pier, awaiting the end of the world.

Atlanta: In the atrium of City Hall, the mayor addresses members of families with relatives in Savannah. "We know nothing more. We can only pray," he says, his voice nearly drowned out by angry shouts: "Liar! Liar!" and a chanting "Tell us truth! Tell us truth! Tell us truth!" Police officers in riot gear push their way through the crowd, surround the mayor, and escort him into the building. Police stand shoulder-to-shoulder, guarding the doors of City Hall.

As the networks began focusing on cities of choice, the Associated Press in Lebanon transmitted a bulletin, instantly read by television reporters: "In an audio message broadcast on the Arab television network Al Jazeera, Al Qaeda leader Tariq Bhutani claims responsibility for the destruction of Savannah. He warned that other American cities were targets of 'Al Qaeda's many nuclear weapons.' He also vowed that more attacks would be launched. There was no way to confirm the voice was actually that of Bhutani."

Later, Al Jazeera interviewed an Al Qaeda leader who said, "The United States is Islam's known enemy, and we will never expect mercy from them. Nor should they expect mercy from us." Muslim terrorist groups claimed that the Savannah bomb was one of more than a dozen other bombs hidden in U.S. cities. The terrorists warned that if the United States tried to harm any Muslim country in revenge, the bombs would be detonated.

In the realm of bloggers, the two leading explanations for the disaster were government conspiracy and God's wrath. An FBI analysis of the most frantic blogs showed no foreign origin. One blog said that God had destroyed

Savannah because it was "a city of sin and extraordinary evil, full of voodoo, homosexuals, devils, and ghosts." That blogger claimed to be a member of The Brethren. Mindful of Dake's "donation," Falcone put that report aside for later investigation.

Around noon came television's first human connection with Savannah. GNN televised it first, driving all else off the screen. Then, quickly, every network showed it: the image of a blond teenage girl in a yellow Georgia Tech T-shirt. She had aimed her smartphone camera at herself and the black-and-white cat in her lap. She was smiling a strange, trembling smile of survival. Behind her, not quite in focus, was an upside-down, mud-streaked blue car.

The image also appeared on the wall screens in the Situation Room interrupting an ExComm videoconference presided over by Falcone.

"My God," he said, stunned. "Is that real?"

After a moment's silence while participants looked at each other and shrugged, Penny Walker said, "It certainly is. I saw it on Facebook late last night."

"Facebook?" Falcone asked. "What the hell were you doing on Facebook?"

"I was doing my job," Walker shot back. "That image on Facebook is our best lifeline to Savannah right now. And it's already inspired a Savannah Emergency Facebook Committee, like the one that Facebook people all over America started after the Pakistan floods and Japanese earthquakes. They raised millions of dollars and organized a help line for relief workers. We're hoping to develop something like that when we get our teams into Savannah."

"So this girl sent her picture to somebody's Facebook page?"

"She apparently sent it out to all her friends—forty or fifty people—from her Facebook page. And one of them, or perhaps many of them, passed it on to GNN. By some fluke she was near a cell tower that was working. She didn't speak. She only sent the photo. Her message was the photo."

"But the blackout, the EMP?" Falcone asked.

"We've got NSA guys trying to tease out information about the status of that cell tower," Walker said. "The idea is to 'walk back the cat,' as our NSA liaison says, using the tower as a reference point to find out what might still be working in Savannah." Walker turned to Frank Naka-mura, her chief of staff, who was seated along the wall. "Frank, tell us what we know."

Nakamura's expression changed in a moment from the surprised look of a student who had not expected to be called upon to the confident look of a student who had done his homework.

"NSA has been scanning for any communication from the Savannah area. They picked up the photo as soon as she sent it out, tagged with her name," he said. "NSA got her profile and pinpointed her location. She had a 4G—fourth generation—smartphone, which sends very fast burst transmissions. That's probably how she got through.

"NSA thinks her phone found a control channel that could pick up a roaming phone signal and move it to a cell that accepted a connection. NSA says the accepting cell was on Hutchinson Island in the Savannah River, north of downtown Savannah.

"The overturned car, about a quarter of a mile from

where the girl was, probably had been taken by the river during the tsunami-like wave that surged up the river and then receded, with the wetlands absorbing a lot of the water.

"The girl—her name is Victoria Anna Meredith—lives about a mile west of Hutchinson Island. The land there is flat. But she was probably on the second floor of her house, giving her a line-of-sight not available at ground level. From all those bits of data, NSA was able to get some idea of one boundary in the mapping out of damage areas and the probable extent of EMP penetration. We think—"

"I thought the EMP produced a total blackout," General Wilkinson cut in. "We've been planning our response on that assumption."

"This one is different from what we know about EMPs," Nakamura said. "In the case of the Hutchinson tower, the island itself seems to be blacked out. But NSA's cell-phone experts found the company that owns the tower. It's relatively new and has a self-actuated electric generator, a type that reacts instantly to a power interruption, switching first to batteries and then a diesel generator. Also, the EMP may have been blocked in some peculiar way. There's a high-rise hotel there that may have screened it. But, like so much, we just don't know."

"Thanks, Frank," Walker said, smiling. "Now, Sean, you can see what we were doing on Facebook. We've inserted what we learned into the master disaster map that the NGA people have been putting together."

Smiling ruefully, Falcone said, "Thanks, Penny and Frank. Good work." Taking her reference to the disaster map as a cue, he signaled the communications staff to bring it up on screen. Across the top of the map were the words TOP SECRET/SCI.

"A secret map," Quinlan said scowling at the image. "Christ, Sean. When are we going to have anything to say? We're getting clobbered for holding back. The White House media guys are all but carrying pitchforks and torches. All the media has to work with is the President's speech. So that puts the focus in one place: *here*. They want to know what the NEST guys found. And they want casualty numbers. How many bodies? That's all the bastards say, 'How many bodies?'"

Quinlan, Falcone, Secretary Walker, Attorney General Williams, CIA Director Stone, and General Wilkinson were the only ExComm members at the table; Max Cunningham was there as a Raven Rock talking head on their video consoles. Marilyn Hotchkiss attended via a hookup from the State Department videoconferencing system; she and Bloom were handling international offers of assistance and assessing the silences from several other countries. The rest of the ExComm members, frantically working in their own offices, were available if Falcone wanted to press for their attendance in person or on video. He had a feeling that Quinlan would never miss a meeting because he felt obliged to keep watch on Falcone. Or perhaps he was watching on Oxley's orders.

"I'm due for a NEST report by noon today," Falcone said, turning to Quinlan. "On the basis of that, I'll decide whether Penny and I should hold a press conference. I'm assuming, Ray, that we're going to have a two-track media approach: Deciding what we say publicly and what we keep our mouths shut about."

"Amen to that," Wilkinson said. "Let's keep a lid on as best we can until we get things set up—I'm talking, of course, about the military response."

"I can ride with that, Gabe," Williams said. "And, Sean,

I hope we don't have to declare martial law—not out loud anyway. Gabe's got an old Army Civil Disturbance Plan in some filing cabinet. It goes back decades and was used in the Los Angeles riots in 1992. Using troops to aid civilian authority is as American as apple pie and those awful words 'martial law' haven't been used for a very long time."

Marilyn Hotchkiss, an old hand at videoconferencing, saw a moment to speak up without sounding as if she were interrupting. "There have been some early reactions," she said. "Prime Minister Weisman has advised us that he has put the Israeli Defense Forces on full alert. Also, NATO has invoked Article Five of the NATO Treaty, which essentially says that an attack on one is an attack on all."

"Sure," Quinlan said, bending forward toward the image of Hotchkiss on the videoconference monitor. "They're all Americans now. They'll all be with us until we decide to bomb the hell out of whoever did this. But just ask them then, 'Who'll be with us for the attack?' and they'll all sound like a bunch of wigged barristers in a British court, insisting that we satisfy a burden of proof. We don't need them. They'll just complicate any response we may want to make."

Hotchkiss ignored Quinlan, as she usually did on the rare occasions when they met. She continued, "We have a cable from the Swiss Embassy in Tehran sending us a message from Iran denying any responsibility for what has happened and offering their full support in finding and punishing the perpetrators."

"What did you expect?" Quinlan said with an artificial laugh. "A confession and an invitation to send them an ICBM?"

After a slight hesitation, she went on. "There's also a

blog claiming to be from the Army of the Guardians of the Islamic Revolution saying that they planned and orchestrated this—just as they did for the hit on Khobar Towers back in 1996. There is no proof that they did it then or now."

Stone looked up. He had been writing on a pad, tearing off pages, and pivoting in his chair to hand the pages to a man who sat along the wall looking like a bored patient in a dentist's waiting room. He was the head of the CIA's Analysis Division, and sometimes he wrote on the pages and returned them to Stone. It was as if they were at another meeting. But Stone was back at ExComm the moment he heard Hotchkiss make what sounded like an intelligence reference.

"We've got more or less the same thing, Marilyn," he said, without looking at her image. "All bullshit. The fact is that we just don't have anything real on this yet. And, Sean, thanks to you, I guess, I'm getting courtesy calls from NSA. They haven't heard anything worthwhile. No proof."

"How the hell can you be talking about proof?" Quinlan exclaimed. "You think when we find out who did this we'll read them a Miranda warning and give them a trial before a jury of their peers? You all heard what the President said: 'Our response will be extremely severe.' *That's fucking French* for nuclear retaliation. That's the reality. Stick a few nukes up the ass of the mullahs in Iran."

"It's not that easy, Ray," Falcone said wearily, beginning to show signs of sleep loss. "How could Iran have done this? And why? Iran may have the intent. Sure. Maybe they'd like to blow a lot of us up, maybe wipe Israel off the map—but there is no chance of that right now or in the near future. Intentions are one thing; capabilities, another. If we're talking capabilities, it could just as well have been the Russians or the Chinese."

"Then they just declared World War III and they're going to pay!"

"Jesus!" Falcone said in exasperation. "I'm not saying the Russians or Chinese were involved . . . Just that we don't know anything yet. Assume that it wasn't state-sponsored, but a rogue operation? You still want to—"

"I'm saying we've got to stop talking like lawyers. About needing proof. The President can't just remain calm on this. He's got to show some passion. Tell the American people that he's going to avenge the deaths of thousands of our citizens who have been just turned into ash heaps."

"By attacking whom?" Falcone persisted.

"It doesn't matter, Sean. The American people are going to want blood . . . anyone's. Send a message to the Muslims. Carpet-bomb the hell out of Medina and tell them that Mecca is next!"

"Oh, that's just great. Now you want to start a religious war. Another Crusade."

"Hello! What do you think's been going on anyway? You can't print a cartoon about Mohammed without getting a goddamn fatwa in your mailbox saying they're going to slice and dice you and your family into little pieces. We take a shot at Medina and they'll get the message. We're not going to take their bullshit about Mohammed any longer."

"Ray, you're close to being certifiable," Falcone said. "Someone hits Savannah and you want to attack Saudi Arabia, an ally who hates the Iranian mullahs as much as we do."

"I shouldn't have to remind you of all people that fifteen of the nineteen terrorists who attacked us on nine-eleven were Saudis. Those bastards have been preaching the most virulent brand of Wahhabism for years . . . absolute hatred for the West. Time to tell them that their fried chickens are coming home to roost."

Falcone's neck thickened and his face turned crimson, a sign that the string had run out on his patience. He was not a man you wanted you make mad. "I'm wasting my breath on you. . . . You should be working for Stanfield and Nolan. You're talking as nutty as they do."

"Well, if the Iranians didn't do it, maybe it was the gift of a friend," Quinlan said, rising from his chair, half turning away from Falcone.

"Are you suggesting the Israelis?"

"Why not? What better way to get us to eliminate their enemy?"

"With that logic, you might just as well accuse them of delivering the bomb!"

"From your lips, not mine," Quinlan said, turning back toward Falcone and stabbing an index finger at him. "Was it a matter of mere coincidence that the Israeli prime minister was in town when it happened?"

"So now you're telling us that the Israelis were in fact behind this. You are one sick son of—"

"No. Only that they stand to benefit if we decide to attack Iran. And they sure got out of town fast."

"I thought all the Jew-bashing bastards were cleaned out after Nixon. Man, now you sound like a shill for the Iranian mullahs."

The angry dialogue produced an embarrassed silence. Everyone knew of the feuding between Falcone and Quinlan but rarely did it break out into the open.

"That's it, Sean. For me, the meeting's adjourned," Quinlan said, heading for the door.

Penny Walker broke the silence. "Well, let's get back to Savannah."

37

After studying the infrared images and disaster map that Falcone had transmitted to him, Lanier decided to make his headquarters at Fort Stewart. It was farther than Lanier preferred—about forty miles southwest of Savannah. But it was safely beyond the western edge of the apparent disaster zone. And, as the largest Army installation east of the Mississippi River, Stewart would provide him and the NNSA with security and access to unlimited military resources.

Before taking a helicopter from Albuquerque to Kirtland, Lanier called Stewart, using NNSA protocols that the intelligence officer recognized. Fort Stewart was already reacting to the Nucflash message, and Lanier could sense the tension in the officer's voice.

The officer told him that electrical power had been restored at Stewart's Hunter Army Airfield. Electricians discovered that a computer controlling the self-actuated electric generator had been destroyed, "as if by a lightning strike," the officer said. They replaced the computer and the generator went on line.

The aircraft that Lanier would be sending to Georgia were given special Nucflash designations and cleared for landing at Hunter. Lanier was pleased that he did not have to waste time by landing at the Savannah/Hilton Head Airport. He was also pleased to have obtained Army information that trumped Falcone's. Given the choice, he would usually rather deal with a military officer than a civilian official, a realization that often surprised him.

Lanier liked the anonymity of the Hunter base, which was operated not by the Air Force but by the Army. He had frequently flown to Hunter for unannounced visits to a NNSA nuclear reservation, known simply as the SRS, for Savannah River Site.

Lanier had often made surprise inspections of the site because he was concerned about the possibility that a minor incident at the SRS could be magnified by the media. Now, with *Savannah* synonymous with *nuclear disaster,* he made a last-minute secure call to the director of the SRS.

"You're the second paranoid caller so far today," the director told him. He recounted the conversation with Hawkins, then added, "Obviously, Rube, they don't know what this is about. Who the hell did this?"

"Well, Bert, at least it's not us," Lanier said lightly. But he felt a flash of anger when he realized that Falcone's search for perpetrators had apparently begun with the NNSA.

Lanier's title—Energy Senior Official of an emergency response—did not sound like much. But he issued orders under the mantle of the National Nuclear Security Administration. As director of the NNSA's Office of Emergency Operations and field manager of NEST, his power reflected the covert clout of the NNSA.

The Department of Defense's Nucflash message, which had alerted every Department of Defense facility in the world, had also galvanized the nuclear side of the Department of Energy, whose NNSA controls and guards U.S. nuclear weapons. By the time the President authorized the Nucflash alert, Lanier was already gathering his NEST group and assuming control of the NNSA response.

NEST was part of the NNSA's Office of Emergency Operations. For decades, NEST—America's "Nuclear Bomb Squad"—had been highly visible and well publicized. NEST was an arm of the nearly invisible NNSA. Besides designing and making nuclear weapons, the NNSA watched over U.S. nuclear reactors and the handling of radioactive waste, and, through its system of National Laboratories, sponsored more scientific research than any other federal agency.

As secretary of the Department of Energy, Dr. Harold Graham gave close scrutiny to the NNSA, but his interest reflected his career as a nuclear physicist who had been more concerned with getting rid of nuclear weapons than with building them. Lanier's Office of Emergency Operations, by demonstrating the mortal danger of nuclear weapons, emphasized the need to get rid of them. But, as a man of action and a seeker of results, Graham had little patience for NEST's participation in countless tabletop games and expensive exercises. When Lanier got the call from Falcone, Graham was at a nuclear disarmament conference in London. Essentially, this put Lanier in charge of NNSA's response to the catastrophe in Georgia.

Lanier and the three NEST operatives he had chosen were sitting in the Ready Room at Kirtland, waiting to board F-16B Falcon fighter jets. Each NEST member would fly as a passenger in a two-seat Falcon. The second seats in two additional F-16Bs were already jammed with the team's hazmat suits, radiation-detection devices, and communications equipment.

Elsewhere on the base, forklifts were bringing pallets stacked with wooden and aluminum boxes of equipment to the gaping aft cargo hold of an Air Force C-17 Globemaster. At the same time, the aircraft's load chief was briefing the first wave of the NNSA response team: forty-five other NEST members, the advance group from the Office of Emergency Operations, twenty-six people from the Aerial Measuring System, and the entire Nuclear/Radiation Advisory Team. Lanier had also reached into the NNSA's Office of Electricity to find a team of experts on large-scale electric power outages. And, after thinking about a nuclear explosion without a clear provenance, he added four experts from the Nevada National Security Site, which had long been named the Nevada National Test Site. N2N2, as the site was known, had shifted its emphasis from testing nuclear weapons to conducting highly secret experiments aimed at thwarting terrorists.

As the Globemaster's aft door quietly closed, six Falcons roared down a runway, formed into a V high above, and headed for Georgia.

38

Aboard a jet fighter travelling at 1,300 miles per hour, Lanier thought of the many times he had flown to a drill or to a false alarm. Now he was flying toward reality. Only once in his career—more than a decade ago—had he entered reality with NEST. He rarely talked about it.

He had been in a full-scale exercise involving more

than five hundred engineers, doctors, technicians, CIA, and nuclear experts who ranged from bomb designers to NEST bomb disposers. Also involved, but mostly out of sight, were Rangers from a U.S. Special Operations Command unit and Navy SEALs.

More than sixty aircraft full of equipment and supplies flew in and out of a remote Royal Air Force base in the Cotswolds, headquarters of the highly realistic exercise. As usual, the exercise involved the finding and disabling of a nuclear device planted by terrorists. Lanier, a connoisseur of exercise code names, wondered who picked this one: Jackal Cave.

The exercise was still going on when participants learned that real terrorists had struck in America. The coincidence of a terrorist exercise occurring during a terrorist attack merely added to the long list of improbabilities that people like Lanier had lived through in their responses to nuclear alarms.

Lanier had had a physics professor at Stanford who turned discursive one day and said that every coincidence led to inevitability. "Coincidences," he said, "were one of the many ways we try to understand fate. We live our lives between moments of fate and moments of chance. And at memorable junctions, we come upon events we call coincidences."

The professor's remark was one of the thoughts that had spun through Lanier's mind on that September day when, while Lanier was acting in an imaginary catastrophe in England, a real catastrophe had struck America. Jackal Cave ended abruptly, and Lanier was given a real mission.

The White House had to know, without producing further panic, if a dirty bomb was part of the terrorist attack. Lanier and his NEST group were put on one of the few aircraft allowed to fly that day. When they landed in New York, Lanier was told to report to the officials directing rescue operations at the Twin Towers.

NEST operatives were like volunteer firemen. They had other jobs at the NNSA, but when the alarm went off, they became part of the NEST response, a unit that could mobilize as many as sixty men and women. At the heart of NEST were the searchers. They had been trained to risk their lives as inconspicuously as possible, looking like ordinary people walking around streets or down the halls of buildings, carrying attaché cases that contained radiation detection devices and transmitters that would send telltale beeps to ear buds that led to what looked like iPods. The beeps would focus NEST on the possible bomb. And if it were real, next would come the disarming and the disposal, which brought in the other members of the team and the ultimate purpose for the team's existence.

And so Lanier and his team went to work at Ground Zero. As far as anyone working at the Twin Towers knew, they were some FEMA guys flown in from Washington to search for unseen fires smoldering under the rubble. When the NEST squad was done and made a classified report to the NNSA, their superiors knew that no nuclear material had been used in the attack.

This time, Lanier thought, *we go in knowing that something did happen . . . Something nuclear.*

39

"Welcome, Rube," said Major General Frank Wethersfield, commanding general of Fort Stewart, as Lanier led the other NEST members from the runway to the operations center at Hunter Army Airfield. A second van pulled up and two soldiers began unloading the hazmat suits and equipment.

Wethersfield, who wore a sharply creased camouflage uniform and combat boots, shook Lanier's hand. The broad-shouldered general towered over Lanier, a man so thin, short, and bent that he appeared to be frail. But his grip was surprisingly strong, and a closer look showed him to be wiry rather than frail. Behind his wire-rim glasses were bright, piercing blue eyes. He and his companions wore khaki slacks and blue windbreakers with LOS ALAMOS NATIONAL LABORATORY embroidered on the left front.

Lanier introduced Wethersfield to the other members of the smallest Nuclear Emergency Support Team he had ever assembled: Russ Belcher, an authority on radiation poisoning; Fred Malcomson, a physicist specializing in nuclear-weapon design; and Liz Dalton, an expert on identifying the origin of nuclear radiation.

They all entered the operations center while Lanier and Wethersfield lingered on the outside steps.

"I guess you know we're getting ready to go in ourselves," Wethersfield told Lanier. "As soon as we hear from FEMA. We have two brigades—about six thousand men and women. We're on full wartime alert. The whole goddamn fort's in lockdown, waiting for what happens next."

"It's pretty surrealistic, isn't it?" Lanier said, with a trace of the accent he had when he entered the prestigious Bronx High School of Science. From there he had gone to MIT, then to Stanford—and, twenty-one years ago, to Los Alamos. "I've spent most of my work life doing drills. I've been like a fireman who has jumped on the fire truck a thousand times but has never seen a fire."

Wethersfield nodded. "The Army's a lot different," he said. "We don't need exercises. We've got the real thing. Most of my men are Iraq or Afghanistan vets. They all know they can be shot at and maybe die. Now they've got a mission where they might get cancer. They didn't go into the Army to get fucking cancer. I can't send them in and sit on my ass back in Stewart. I'm going, too."

He suddenly paused. Then he asked softly, "Who the fuck did this, Rube? Who the fuck did this?"

Lanier looked up at the general and said, "I don't know, Frank. All I know is I'm supposed to help find that out."

Wethersfield and Lanier entered the operations center together and walked into a room where members of the general's staff had assembled. "Dr. Lanier, head of the Nuclear Emergency Support Team," Wethersfield said by way of introduction to officers who had already been briefed about the arrival of NEST. He nodded to a colonel who stood before a wall map holding a pointer.

"Good morning, Dr. Lanier. We are here," the colonel said, aiming a laser beam at a gray area marked HUNTER ARMY AIRFIELD, east of a much larger gray area marked FORT STEWART RESERVATION. "We have sent out recon patrols as far as here." The red dot moved eastward on the map to a line indicating the boundary between Hunter and the U.S. Coast Guard Air Station.

"A Coast Guard station that far inland?" Lanier interrupted, a scowl reflecting his puzzlement.

"Yes, Doctor. It's only nineteen kilometers from the sea and is—was—a safe spot from coastal flooding," the colonel replied. "Well, here we detected traces of radiation and pulled back the patrols. We believe there are casualties at the Coast Guard station." He turned to Lanier.

Lanier stepped up and looked at the map for a full minute. The Savannah River, flowing farther east, curved sharply, forming what looked like an outline of a cup. He imagined a wall of water rushing up the river to the top of the curve, then spilling out, as if from the cup. The curve would divert the flood, pouring the wall of water out of the cup and into the city.

Turning away from the map, Lanier said to the colonel, "I'd like to see the recon reports and the report of the electricians who got your electric power back. It might give us some clues about the power of the EMP. And we're going to lay out a preliminary radiation zone based on whatever information we can get. What the White House needs most right now are radiation readings. That's what NEST is going to get."

A few minutes later, Lanier and the other three NEST members in their yellow hazmat suits and black boots awkwardly stomped out of the building. They would not pull on their wide-visored hoods and respirator backpacks until they were about to enter a probable radiation area.

Clipped to the right sleeve of each suit was a direct-reading dosimeter that showed accumulated exposure.

The device, the size and shape of a fountain pen, contained a thermometer-like indicator set at zero. As X-rays or gamma rays struck the dosimeter, the display moved up in proportion to the radiation exposure. Lanier knew that the hazmat suits would shield him and the others from an injurious exposure. But he wanted everyone to be alerted to danger, and, in case of a suit failure, alerted to a possible overdose.

Wethersfield accompanied the team outside. "We've got two Strykers and volunteer crews, ready to roll," he said, pointing to a pair of eight-wheeled vehicles nearly nine feet high. "They're stripped of weapons and we ramped up their communications to your specs." Lanier had asked Wethersfield to set up a direct line from the Strykers, through Fort Stewart's command center, to Falcone in the Situation Room.

Each Stryker had a driver and a vehicle commander. The commander of the lead Stryker stepped forward, introduced himself to Lanier, and gave him and the others a quick tour. When the vehicle was sealed, the crew looked at the world through periscopes. The commander could leave his seat and stand on a platform that allowed him to open a hatch and stand half exposed. The two NEST passengers would ride in a rear compartment that could be opened so that they could enter and leave.

A camera attached to the periscope in Lanier's Stryker streamed images into his laptop, then to the Situation Room through the Fort Stewart communications center. The two vehicles were also linked by radio, as were the four NEST members. They had microphones and earplugs built into their hoods so that they could talk to each other. Lanier could also patch in to Stewart and thus to Falcone.

The Stryker crewmen were wearing CBRN suits, camouflaged military versions of hazmats, designed to be quickly donned over uniforms in combat. Once called NBC suits for protection against nuclear, chemical, and biological threats, they got a fourth initial when dirty bombs became a new possible hazard. The soldiers had not yet put on their hoods and breathing masks.

The two Strykers rumbled off, Lanier's in the lead. After looking at the map, he had decided to aim toward what he thought of as "the cup." He laid out a route that took them to the Coast Guard Air Station at the northern end of Hunter, then right to the Truman Parkway, which ran along the southern end of Savannah's historic district, ending at the river. From there the Strykers would explore the center of the city.

At the air station, the NEST members got their first view of destruction. Lanier ordered the Strykers to stop and told everyone to put on their full hazmat suits. The Stryker commander climbed onto the platform and opened the hatch, then stepped aside to allow Lanier to stand in the hatchway. Lanier told the commander to turn on the Webcam that would stream video into Lanier's laptop, which transmitted the video into the Stewart-Situation Room net.

"Stewart. This is Lanier. Put me through to Summit," he began.

"Falcone here."

"We are looking at the Coast Guard Air Station to the east of Hunter. I am sending a Webcam video stream with a GPS locator to augment my observations. About one hundred meters ahead are the remains of a large building, apparently a hangar. About twenty meters to the left of the ruins are the scattered wrecks of six helicopters. They seem to have been along a heliport flight line. There are muddy high-water lines along the standing wall of the building. The high-water lines look to be five to ten meters above the ground.

"I see five bodies, in what look like flight suits. They are lying facedown, several meters apart.

"My dosimeter"—he looked down at his right sleeve— "shows a background radiation level that is about the dose limit for nuclear industry employees and uranium miners. You'll get details and much more after the emergency response team. But for now I am not seeing any dangerous radiation here, at this point. I emphasize *here*."

"Can we say that publicly?" Falcone asked.

"I suggest you hold off until we can get some solid data to back up this first very preliminary report. I've got a Globemaster full of experts and equipment coming into Hunter today."

"Okay. But I'll tell the President, Admiral Mason, and Penny Walker, Homeland Security."

"What about my boss?"

"Secretary Graham is on his way back to Washington. When he gets here I'll brief him. But all—I stress *all*—of your reports and *all* that comes out of NNSA efforts down there must come to me. I'll then dole it out to Admiral Mason, the incident commander, and to Secretary Walker. Homeland Security is the lead agency, *not* DOE."

"So you're the big boss. Okay. And we've got a new bureaucracy setup. Okay. But please keep what I'm telling you tightly held." Lanier paused. "There's something else."

"What?"

"I'm sticking my neck out. Use your discretion about

telling the President or your other advisees. What I am thinking right now . . . the picture I get right now . . . is a wall of water coming up the Savannah River to a big curve—you'll see it on the map—and then flowing westward, smashing into the city and into the Coast Guard Station, but not as far west as Hunter Airfield, and then withdrawing, back to the river, across marshes, then back to the sea. That movement is the basis for the tsunami illusion. And it means we are probably looking at a water explosion rather than an air burst."

"I'm looking at the disaster map and seeing what you mean about the tsunami. And the idea of a water explosion," Falcone said.

"Okay. Now we'll be leaving the Strykers. We'll do a fast walk-around survey here at the station. And then we'll head into the city. I'm signing off."

Lanier and Liz Dalton, their hazmat hoods up, their respirators pulsing, got out of the Stryker and walked to the first body. The dead man looked to be in the mid-forties, his close-cropped black hair touched with gray. Lanier and Dalton had worked side by side at the Twin Towers. Now they were among bodies again.

They looked at one another through their visors for a moment. Then Lanier ran the wand of a radiation-particle detector along the flight suit that encased the body. "Count is far below lethal level," he said into his lavalier microphone. Liz nodded. The detector's transmitter sent Lanier's words and the detector reading, along with the time, date, and GPS location, to Lanier's laptop in the Stryker. The computer was programmed to begin the creation of a disaster-area radiation database.

Dalton walked to the ruins of the hangar. She ran her detector along the standing wall, and then took a scraper and plastic bag from her tool belt, and scratched at the bits of mud that speckled the wall. "We've got higher counts here in the mud," she said into her microphone.

"Got enough for analysis?" Lanier asked.

"Barely. If I can get higher—"

Lanier spoke to the lead Stryker, asking its commander to bring it alongside the hangar wall. When it came close enough for Dalton to climb onto it, she stretched from the top of the vehicle so that she could run her scraper near the top of the high-water mark.

"Little hotter here," she said, transmitting her reading. She climbed down and joined Lanier, walking as fast as she could in her bulky suit.

The other Stryker dropped off Belcher and Malcomson, who ran their radiation-detection wands over the other bodies. At Lanier's order, they did not touch the bodies. He was determined to focus on making a rough map of the radiation left behind when the wall of water withdrew.

The two Strykers continued to the eastern end of the Hunter reservation and then went off in separate directions, taking two of the highways that surrounded the center of Savannah. Slow-moving cars and pickup trucks, bumper-to-bumper, were moving north on Route 516 as Lanier's Stryker entered the line of traffic, then made its way along the shoulder of the highway.

Lanier spoke into his microphone. "Lanier to Falcone. There's an exodus out of the city. Highways clogging. You'll need to get troops here to handle the traffic and personnel to provide security for food, water, and distribution of potassium iodide tablets by DHS. We should try to keep people in the city until they are examined and given the tablets."

"Okay," Falcone said from the Watch Center. "We're

relaying this to DHS and Admiral Mason, who is steaming toward the Savannah River. What is the radiation level?"

"Looks to be averaging at about sixty millirems."

"Translation, please."

"About what you'd be getting walking around on the high plateau around Denver. We're all going to learn a lot about ionizing radiation, Mr. Falcone."

"What can I tell the President? What can he say publicly?"

"I'm in the middle of the answer to that. We're following a procedure that will give you solid information. We need a few more hours."

"I need information *now,*" Falcone said.

"Okay. You can say that a preliminary survey indicates a relatively light radiation dose but heavy destruction. NEST is preparing a detailed study of the impact area. That's all for now," Lanier said, signing off.

For the next three hours, the Strykers passed along the edges of the devastated city center, veering occasionally into side streets in a random pattern that Lanier was improvising. Every two hundred meters, one NEST member stepped out of the open back of the Stryker, wiped a piece of debris with a small, circular piece of cloth, and recited its serial number into a helmet microphone.

The serial number, along with a GPS location and a time stamp, went to a laptop and then into a backup hard drive at Fort Stewart. The wipes were placed in a lead-shielded container. Data from this collection of wipes would lay the grid for the radiation survey.

Lanier tried to focus on his prime mission. But he could not to ignore the dead and dying that he knew were beneath the ruins he was passing. His Stryker rolled toward a small mall: dry cleaner, Wendy's, pet store, Chinese restaurant, pharmacy. It looked intact.

But, as he got closer, he saw that the mall was a shell. Its roof had been torn off and the interiors had been blown through the windows and into the parking lot. The cars, smashed together and lying on their sides, were splattered with the flotsam of the mall. Lanier ordered the Stryker to stop.

For a moment Lanier did not understand what he saw. And then he realized that he was looking at parts—of men, of women, of children, of dogs, of clothes, of bottles, of boxes, of chairs, of tables. Nothing was whole. Even the cars, torn and buried in horror, did not look like cars. The Stryker commander did not need an order to move on. Neither Lanier nor the others spoke.

But, when his Stryker neared the river and he saw a small wooden church smashed open, its steeple gone, he switched on his microphone and said, "Falcone. We've got to get first-response teams in here right away. Volunteers for shifts no longer than five hours. They'll need dosimeters and their shift must be followed by mandatory decontamination and ten hours off. I take responsibility. There are people here who are trapped. I don't want them to die."

40

The Globemaster carrying Lanier's NNSA group and their equipment had landed by the time Lanier and his crew returned to Hunter. They crawled out of the Strykers, loaded their hazmat suits into red decontamination bags, and got into Army staff cars. Lanier rode with Colonel Paul Mann, Wethersfield's adjutant, to an empty Fort Stewart barracks, where one of Lanier's Los Alamos deputies was supervising the setting up of a laboratory and an incident operations center.

The landscape flashing past the car looked to Lanier like a small town: shopping mall, restaurants, a movie theater, bowling alley, museum, chapel, neighborhoods with kids' playgrounds. The cars stopped in front of the three-story brick barracks, which had been vacant, held in reserve for occupancy by potential troop surges.

They walked up the front stairs, entered a wide foyer, and turned to the left into the barracks orderly room. Lanier's communications director, Debra Knowlton, was removing equipment from an aluminum box.

Lanier introduced the colonel to Knowlton, a short, sturdy woman whose blond bangs curtained her frown.

"I've seen your rules, Colonel," she said, pointing to a document behind glass in a black frame hanging on the door. "I'm afraid I've got to break a couple."

"What?"

"That one in particular." She touched the glass at a line saying, *Soldiers will only use one appliance cord per extension. Cords will not run under rugs or across doorways where they may be walked on.*

"Our regulations specifically—"

"I think we'll need a couple of the fort's electricians, Colonel," Lanier, sensing a potential argument, interrupted. "The Globemaster delivered our own standby generators. But we'd like help from the local talent—like those guys who ended the blackout."

Mann nodded and excused himself, saying that he would send a captain from his staff to be Lanier's liaison to the Army. *If I could deal with the Taliban,* he thought as he left, *I certainly will be able to handle these people.*

Lanier stood at the table where Knowlton was installing gear, put his laptop on the table, and described the circuit he had temporarily arranged to transmit the Stryker preliminary survey.

"And now you want all the secure transmissions to what's his name?—Falcone?—shifted to here?" She made a sweeping gesture taking in the room.

"Right," Lanier said. "This will be NEST headquarters until further notice. We also need a hotline to the guy who is the incident commander, Admiral David Mason."

"Where is he?"

"Last I heard he was on a Coast Guard cutter heading for the Savannah River," Lanier said.

"This is looking like a damn complicated exercise."

"It's not an exercise, Debra. This is the real thing."

"Honest? I thought it was looking pretty damn realistic. Wow! So it's real! Okay, I'll get the details from Falcone's people on how to keep in touch with Mason."

The *Trumbull,* a new U.S. Coast Guard cutter on antidrug patrol off Virginia, had just stopped a ship and seized 11,000 kilos of cocaine when her captain received an urgent message from Coast Guard headquarters: another cutter was on the way to take over the patrol because the *Trumbull* had a new mission.

An hour after Lanier told Falcone about the probable radiation level in Savannah, Admiral Mason boarded a Coast Guard helicopter and was flown out to the *Trumbull,* along with a White House communications video cameraman and two National Security Agency technicians ordered to Savannah by Quinlan.

Mason had been around Washington long enough to know that the ubiquitous cameraman came with the incident commander job. As what Falcone called "the face of the catastrophe," Mason realized that he had been given the role of White House face, the person who gave the world the idea that the Oxley administration was responding to the disaster. The NSA technicians, who had been briefed on *Trumbull* electronic capabilities, went straight to the command and control center.

Mason met with the captain in his quarterdeck office, dismissed the video cameraman, and laid out all he knew. Mason, who was only a high-ranking passenger, could not tell the captain what to do. The captain of a ship cannot be told to hazard his ship, especially for public relations purposes. But, as commandant of the U.S. Coast Guard, Mason knew all there was to know about the *Trumbull,* which was officially called a national security cutter. She had an underwater sonar array designed to scan for such potential underwater hazards as mines and swimming suicide bombers.

While the *Trumbull* steamed toward the mouth of the Savannah River at twenty-five knots, Mason convinced the captain that the river held no danger. The *Trumbull*'s sonar could be used to detect debris as the ship ascended the Savannah River. As for radiation, Mason pointed to the fact that the ship was equipped to defend itself against chemical, biological, or radiological attack by locking out a dangerous atmosphere.

Finally, there was the question of the safety of the *Trumbull*'s crew of nearly one hundred men and women. The captain agreed that Mason could address the crew over the ship's intercom system. And Mason agreed that the video cameraman could cover the address.

The chief boatswain's mate hit the intercom system button and piped the two notes that sounded throughout the ships, signaling, "All hands!" The captain of the *Trumbull* introduced Mason by his two titles—commandant of the Coast Guard and the presidentially appointed incident commander.

"Fellow Coast Guard men and women," Mason began. "We are sailing toward dangerous waters. Savannah has been severely damaged by what appears to some kind of nuclear device. Our air station seems to have been hard-hit, probably destroyed. President Oxley has asked me to go to the scene, and I have chosen to go there aboard your ship.

"My job is to maintain a connection between the people of the disaster area and the rest of the American people. This I will do aboard the *Trumbull* until such time that I can establish a site ashore.

"You all undoubtedly are concerned about radiation. The Department of Energy's experts on nuclear weapons have entered the disaster area and report a relatively light radiation aftereffect. Because we have radiation-detection gear aboard, we'll be able to make our own measurements and react accordingly.

"We plan to moor at a point in the Savannah River outside the disaster area. I can assure you that none of you will be put in an area where there is a radiation hazard.

"Finally, I want to assure you that I am a passenger aboard the *Trumbull*. Your captain is still your captain. Some of you may be assigned to duties aiding me in my role as incident commander. I am sure we'll work together in the grand tradition of our motto, *Semper Paratus*. I take it as a good omen that many years ago the lyrics to our *Semper Paratus* march were written by Captain Francis

Van Boskerck in the cabin of a cutter docked in Savannah. As he wrote and as we proudly sing, " 'We're always ready for the call.' "

The boatswain piped, "Carry On," and the video cameraman rushed to the *Trumbull*'s control and command center, which had established a direct channel to the White House communications office. He streamed Mason's speech, preceded by a Coast Guard cameraman's view of Mason's helicopter arrival. Within an hour, the finished product—Mason, sternly confident, and the *Trumbull,* "ready for the call"—was being broadcast again and again on TV channels throughout the world.

White House press secretary Stephanie Griffith followed through with a conference call to television news producers. "Admiral Mason," she told them "will issue progress reports twice a day on the Department of Homeland Security's response and recovery operations. The reports will be streamed to all of you." Off the record, she said that Admiral Mason was working on making arrangements to allow accredited correspondents to enter the disaster area. The producers, with great relief and anticipation, realized that the Savannah news blackout was over.

41

The *Trumbull* moored at Port Wentworth off Hutchinson Island, north of downtown Savannah. By then, Fort Stewart's troops under Major General Wethersfield were rolling into Savannah. Medical units set up inflatable structures for combat hospitals with their own electric generators. Military police aided Savannah police officers who had begun untangling traffic jams. Strykers and military ambulances carried Army and local emergency medical aides to sites where Army reconnaissance patrols had found survivors.

Penny Walker arrived at Savannah International Airport with the first contingent of the Department of Homeland Security's FEMA responders: emergency medical volunteers equipped for search and rescue. Other workers headed into the disaster area in commandeered airport buses to set up rows of large white tents for centers where food, water, and radiation-resistance pills were distributed. Electrical engineers began searching for functioning transformers and ways to restore electrical power. They also laid out a network for connection with the electrical systems of two aircraft carriers arriving at Tybee Island, near the mouth of the Savannah River. Still at sea and heading for Port Wentworth was a Navy hospital ship.

Walker had hoped to see Admiral Mason, but they were only able to talk on a secure and official communication network. Both agreed that a meeting would not justify use of scarce resources. She made her temporary headquarters at the airport, which also became the assembly area for the growing corps of FEMA workers.

Falcone had handed over to Walker and Mason the on-the-scene humanitarian needs of Savannah. They would respond to the President and Ray Quinlan, who wanted real-time information, especially casualty estimates and assessments of radiation effects. Quinlan, never forgetting that the President was running for reelection, had his own political demands, such as a presidential visit to

Savannah. That decision would have to come from Savannah, not from Falcone in Washington.

Mason was handling the disaster, and Quinlan was handling Mason. In President Oxley's name, Quinlan directed General Wethersfield to assign a squad of infantrymen to the mission of finding Victoria Anna Meredith and getting her to the *Trumbull* so that Mason would have a surprise human-interest story for one of his briefings. Quinlan assigned the NSA technicians to the task of establishing a press center in a dockside warehouse near the *Trumbull*.

Although the official "organizational design document" showed Falcone in the top box of a neatly laid out hierarchy of boxes, a realistic version of the design document would show new little boxes quickly sprouting in many places. The Army . . . Homeland Security . . . Mason and his Coast Guard cutter . . . Lanier and his NEST . . . Quinlan and his presidential campaign—each was running its own Savannah operation.

Falcone saw the reality in a way different from all the other forces responding to the Savannah disaster. He saw a war. There were dead and wounded. There were U.S. military forces moving on land and sea. There was DEFCON One. It all added up to war. *But who is the enemy? And who will help me find the enemy?*

The answer to his last question was Lanier.

Falcone called Lanier from the Situation Room soon after Lanier arrived at the Fort Stewart barracks.

"Dr. Lanier, this is Falcone. A most urgent call."

"Well, for 'urgent' let's dispense with 'Doctor.' Call me Rube."

"Okay, Rube. This is Sean," Falcone said. He felt that the swift shift to informality somehow gave them a sudden new confidence in each other. "I realize that Savannah needs all the help we can give its people. But I want to stress that there's nothing more important than finding out who did this. Who is our enemy? A lot depends on that, as you can imagine."

"Accusation. Retaliation. What can happen then is almost beyond imagination," Lanier said. "Let me give you a quick rundown on what we're doing right now about what we call attribution—and what you rightly call our enemy. Dr. Liz Dalton is the nation's leading expert on attribution. If anyone can get you the answer, it's Liz.

"Even as we speak, Liz is in a portable laboratory here assaying scrapes from radioactive bits of debris. I doubt if she will have much trouble determining the samples' composition, including isotopes—the nuclear configurations of the atoms in the samples.

"That's step number one. After she gets what might be called the fingerprint of the nuclear device, she needs to identify the fingerprint. And that's where the job gets really tough. She then has to turn to information from outside our laboratory."

"Is there anything we can do about getting that information?"

"Negative. Even on the most secure phone in the world I wouldn't want to go into details. But let me say that we have—what Liz has right here—is essentially a nuclear fingerprint database, based on material plucked out of the air and from land and sea for many years."

"Sounds as if we'll get the identity pretty soon."

"Don't hold your breath," Lanier said. "There's a lot of

intel involved. Ambiguity abounds. We've done a lot of drills on attribution. This is the first time we've had to deal with a real nuclear event."

"Okay. We'll stand by. And we're lucky to have you, Rube. Goodbye."

42

Falcone left the Situation Room and returned to his desk. Now that Penny and her staff were in Savannah, he had his office back. But the disaster had turned him into a commuter shuttling between the claustrophobic tensions of the Situation Room and his office. His desk was stacked with reports, which had been flying in like meteors.

One glance showed that Mae Prentice had put the most important reports on the top. *Thank God for Mae,* Falcone thought. The indispensable Mae called herself his secretary, despite the White House personnel director's insistence that she was officially the national security advisor's office manager.

The information that the reports contained was fragmentary, and almost all of it was bad. NATO's Article V— an armed attack against any member would be considered an attack against them all—was welcome. The Europeans were "all Americans now," as the French had proclaimed after the nine-eleven attacks. *Nice to have friends in a time of trouble,* Falcone thought. But he knew that the support of NATO nations could potentially be trouble for President Oxley.

I'm looking at a gift horse in the mouth and I don't

like what I'm seeing. They'll expect us to take collective action. Sure, there's security in numbers. But that means twenty-eight nations will have to agree on a plan of action. If one objected, no action could be taken by the organization. And if the U.S. decided to go it alone. . . .

Falcone cleared with the President an order to the White House switchboard to direct all incoming calls from foreign dignitaries to his office for the next three hours. Ostensibly, this would give Oxley time to rest and reflect on the crucial choices before him. But Falcone really feared that pledges of support from other nations could be a trap that Oxley would find hard to escape. Even a mere thank-you-for-your-concern could be interpreted by the caller as an implicit agreement that Oxley would consult before making a decision.

Falcone himself would be tied down in the Oval Office monitoring the calls so he could rebut anyone trying to make such a claim. This would take him away from his job of coordinating everything. He began making a list of calls that he would have Oxley review later.

As expected, Presidents Wang Xi Chang of China and Vladimir Khorkovsky of Russia publicly declared their horror over what had happened and pledged support for the American people in their time of tragedy and need. Simultaneously, as Falcone expected, they called for restraint until all of the facts could be established because a rush to judgment could produce a world calamity.

Stall. Delay. Defer. Anything to stop Oxley from making a unilateral decision. It was wise of them to do so, but coincidentally, Wang Xi Chang and Vladimir Khorkovsky were also the leaders who had direct ties to all of the suspects: North Korea, Pakistan, and Iran.

Countries would release an avalanche of documentation

that shifted blame to someone else. Each country would strive to create a record showing that its leaders had done everything to prevent this catastrophe. Like it or not, Falcone was the point man, and if he discreetly questioned motives or claims, he would be taking all the arrows in the chest for the President.

The best of the scant good news was a report from Admiral Mason that he had set up an information campaign, using leaflets, vehicles with loudspeakers, and door-to-door calls by soldiers, members of Georgia National Guard units, and local volunteers. The town criers, as he called his crew, had mostly succeeded in getting people to remain calm.

Given food and water and assured that Savannah was healing, most people agreed to stay in their homes until they received word of the all-clear. Electrical power had been restored in some neighborhoods. Two local radio stations had resumed broadcasting and local television stations were expected to be back on the air in less than a week.

FEMA took over Skidaway Island State Park, on the coast south of Savannah, and set up a refugee camp of tents and trailers. FEMA chose two golf courses as burial sites, one for mass burials and the other for transformation into a new cemetery with individual graves for identified victims. The work of identifying and burying the dead was supervised by specialists from the Army Central Identification Laboratory in Hawaii and the mortuary facility at Dover Air Force Base in Delaware. Interfaith ceremonies preceded mass burials. At Falcone's insistence, an imam from the Islamic Center of Savannah took part in the ceremonies.

Elsewhere in the country, there had been violent incidents. But surprisingly, the panic had started to subside and now there were only isolated reports of people still trying to flee their cities.

Falcone knew, however, most Americans were waiting for their president to make a decision. To take action. To find the bastards who did this. Rage was building. The people would not wait much longer. At any moment they could be taking to the streets in mass protest. And Senator Stanfield was ready to make sure of it.

"I can understand how someone could slip an ounce of explosives into their shoe or their underwear," a GNN pundit had said in the inevitable analysis after the President's speech. "But a nuclear bomb? Our government had been guilty of a dereliction of duty. Someone's head has to roll."

The first head, Falcone believed, would be the President's—unless he acted fast. *But if Oxley unleashed the dogs of war, not knowing who was responsible, where would it stop? A holy war between Christians and Muslims?*

Blood lust. The trouble with satisfying a blood lust is that it's never satisfied.

The phone rang. Falcone had given Mae a list of people who could break through his telephone blockade. Every one of them could be calling in bad news. He took a deep breath before picking up the phone.

"Vice President Cunningham, Sean," Mae said in her stern telephone voice. "He's here." Falcone felt his stomach tighten. If Max needed to talk face-to-face, it meant really bad news.

"Got to talk," Cunningham said as he entered. He eased himself onto the amber settee that was a couple of steps from Falcone's desk. Above the settee was a Winslow

Homer seascape titled *The Gathering Storm*. Cunningham pointed to it and said, "How appropriate."

"You look bushed, Max," Falcone said, taking the chair
in front of the settee. Cunningham nodded. He had his
usual rumpled look: striped tie askew, brown suit coat
limply hanging open, exposing a wrinkled blue shirt.
Black socks peeked out between the cuffs of his brown
trousers and his brown loafers.

"I think I lost some weight at the goddamn Rock,"
Cunningham said wearily, knowing he had not had time
to drop an ounce. "It's a goddamn prison. Did me good, I
suppose. Losing weight, I mean. But age is creeping up,
Sean. Creeping up."

He straightened up and ran a hand through his bushy
white hair. "Something's up in the House, Sean. You know
those 'Presidential Annexes' that the attorney general told
us about? Somebody started a rumor that the President
was going to begin using them like a dictator and would
make the Carolinas, Georgia, and Florida into a Federal
Security Zone under martial law."

"That's crazy," Falcone exclaimed. "Things in Savannah are going better than we could possibly expect. There's
no reason—"

"Reason isn't around much in the Congress these
days, Sean. Stanfield and his people are pounding drums.
There's impeachment in the air."

"Oh, come on, Max. That imbecile Nolan files impeachment resolutions—saying what? The President pushed a
U.S.–Russia space treaty or he was somehow responsible
for the attack on the *Elkton*. So what? Jeb Duffy never let
them out of committee."

"Jeb Duffy may be the chairman of the House Judiciary

Committee," Cunningham said. "But he's not Speaker of the House."

"Meaning what?"

Cunningham leaned forward and lowered his voice. "Meaning," he said, "I think Stanfield has convinced Jack Gill to allow a new resolution to go directly to the floor of the House."

"Max, with all due respect, you're out of your fucking mind," Falcone said, suddenly standing, as if ready to pace the room. "You *made* Jack Gill the Speaker. He's one of us, a supporter of Oxley since Day One."

"Sit down, Sean, and listen to me. Jack is from Georgia and full of anger over what happened in Savannah. Stanfield and Nolan have been working on him. And so have some others. It's feeling like a goddamn conspiracy. Some of our own people in the House are smelling blood and hedging their bets by dealing with Stanfield and Nolan because they could win. Sean, face it. Oxley can go down. "

Falcone sat down at the edge of the chair, as if ready to spring up again. "Okay," he said, "so another impeachment resolution gets filed. We control the House. It's all campaign theater."

"It's more than that, Sean. Much worse than that. My predecessor in the House told me what it was like back then when they were smelling Nixon's blood. An impeachment resolution had been filed against Nixon over his order to bomb Cambodia. It got nowhere. It *was* theater—but it put the idea of impeachment in the air, and the idea was hovering there when the House Judiciary Committee voted to issue articles of impeachment over Watergate. Then Nixon knew it was over: He was forced to choose resignation or an impeachment trial."

"Again, all due respect, Max, but you're stretching. Oxley is not Nixon. Savannah is not Watergate. Terrorism is not Vietnam. Our side controls the Judiciary Committee and—"

Cunningham awkwardly squirmed his way out of the settee and stood. So did Falcone. "The House has always been somewhat of a mess," Cunningham said. "When I was Speaker, there were so many quarrels and dumb ideas that it was always a wonder we ever got anything done."

He placed his hands on Falcone's shoulders. "Sean, we worked in different worlds. Your Senate used to be clubby. Now it's no different from the House. These days it's hard to tell them apart. It takes a miracle to get anything done in either chamber. But in some crazy way, the Savannah attack was that miracle—and what is getting done is impeachment."

Falcone reached up, grasped Cunningham's right hand, and shook it. "Thanks for the information, Max. You know more about politics than I'll ever learn. What should I do?"

"You can start by watching C-SPAN tonight," Cunningham said. "The leadership has decided to reconvene. And I've heard that Stanfield is about to announce that he will be making a major speech. He's keeping it secret. When we hear what he has to say, then we'll know what to do."

Fear and rumors were sweeping across Capitol Hill. Anonymous bomb threats had been phoned in to the Capitol Police. Bomb-sniffing dogs appeared in the hallways of the Capitol and the House and Senate office buildings. Capitol police officers, in SWAT gear and carrying automatic weapons, stood at every entrance. The underground Capitol Visitors Center was evacuated and closed. But members of Congress did not want to be seen hiding out and shirking their responsibilities. Most had suspended their campaigns and returned to Washington. They wanted to been seen in action, particularly because President Oxley had remained in town.

Around five o'clock, newspaper editors, TV producers, and TV pundits began orchestrating the evening news cycle. At 5:15, in time for six o'clock news shows, congressional leaders announced that both houses were reconvening. And Stanfield's campaign manager called a press conference to announce that Stanfield would "speak to America" from the floor of the Senate at 8 P.M. that night.

43

General George William Parker had been awake almost every moment since the news broke about the disaster in Savannah. He had sat before the television set in what he called his den on the first floor of the brick house on East Capitol Street. He had not gone to bed. He had not even lowered the flag at the sunsets that had passed. He had sat here thinking of the past, trying not to think of the present.

He frequently pulled his special smartphone from the holster on his belt and stared at the narrow screen with its ever-changing six-digit number. As he stared at the screen, he prayed that Isaiah would call. There was no way that Parker could call Isaiah. The phone had no keys. He could only verbally repeat the six digits that appeared on the screen when receiving a call from Isaiah.

Lying on the small table next to his chair was his own cell phone, delivered to him months before by a Brethren messenger who told him he had been sent by Isaiah. He had, on Isaiah's orders, given the number only to the others in the op. He understood the vital need for dependable communications on an operation. *Botched communications had doomed the Delta op to rescue the hostages in Tehran back in . . . when was it? Back in 1980. We landed—and every goddamn thing went wrong. Traitors? Maybe.*

He cleared his mind of that dark memory and went over each step, each order as Operation Cyrus progressed. He had gone over it again and again, and still had not discovered what had gone wrong.

Isaiah had called shortly after Oxley, *that asshole Oxley,* said that the destruction of Savannah had been caused by a nuclear device. "You will receive instructions, Amos," Isaiah had said. "I am working very hard to assemble Plan B, a plan that will provide an explanation. Sit tight. Go about your daily life. Make no calls."

He had obeyed. But the calls had come to him. *Radio silence, that used to be the rule.* He had given strict orders that no one was to call him on his phone except in an emergency *during the operation.* That was the key part of the order.

As soon as the operation was over, he was to destroy the cell phone. He was also to destroy it if the operation were aborted. *Abort! Abort! At Desert One.* He had wanted to fight that order. *We could have got them out. Medals all around.* But he did not have enough rank to do more than feel rage and shame. He had made a pledge to himself: *I will never abort Operation Cyrus. Never.*

Miller—Hosea—was the first to call. *Calm. I guess big money keeps you calm. Said he hadn't signed up for this. But he'll keep his mouth shut.*

Schiller—Micah—called next. *Scared out of his mind. Muttering, making no sense. He could break.*

I'll never hear from Jonah or Malachi. Nobody will.

The phone in his hand suddenly quivered. He read the six numbers that appeared on the narrow screen, repeated them, and waited until two tiny screens showed green. The phone had accepted him. Scrambling would begin.

"Thank you for your patience," said the robotic voice. "We are ready with Plan B. Your instructions will arrive shortly."

"What shall—"

"Please, Amos. Do not speak. Silence is golden at this time." The call ended.

Three hours later, Norman Miller rang Parker's doorbell. Parker cautiously opened the door, which was held by a chain lock. "Your name, please," Parker asked. His appearance—unshaven, shirt with what looked like an egg stain, bedroom slippers—surprised Miller.

"I am Hosea," Miller said impatiently. He wore a black topcoat, open to reveal his perfectly tailored blue suit, blue shirt, and pale blue tie.

Parker slipped the chain and fully opened the door. It was a ritual familiar to both men, used when Miller brought a black briefcase filled with hundred-dollar bills. Once inside, Miller stood in the hallway and made no move to enter any farther.

"I am to hand this to you," Miller said, passing the briefcase to Parker. "And, Amos, this is my final move for this operation. We meet for the last time."

"Don't be so sure, Hosea," Parker said. "I command this operation, and I say when it is over."

"Well, you better say it's over because it certainly is," Miller said, turning smartly, walking to the door, and closing it behind him. As he rounded the corner, with the Capitol looming in front of him, a black Mercedes pulled up. He nodded and got in.

The briefcase did not contain stacks of hundred-dollar bills. Inside were two plain brown envelopes and a cell phone. AMOS was carefully lettered in black on one; CONFIDENTIAL was similarly lettered on the other.

Parker went back to the den and opened the AMOS envelope, which contained a single piece of paper containing handwritten instructions:

> *Call this number—202-555-6942—using the enclosed cell phone. The person who answers will direct you to a Washington office where you will be met by the person for whom the sealed confidential envelope is intended. You will recognize each other. Merely tell the recipient that you wish him to have the contents of the envelope. Destroy the phone by smashing it with a hammer. Tonight, drop the pieces in two or more sewer openings.*
>
> *Operation Cyrus is ended. Isaiah.*

44

After ushering Max Cunningham out, Falcone went to his desk. In a few minutes, on the screen of his small television set, he saw a red-and-yellow BREAKING NEWS logo that GNN had just inserted to announce Stanfield's forthcoming speech.

He turned away from the screen and started going through a list of telephone calls, all marked urgent. There was also a red folder with the usual white diagonal stripes indicating Top Secret. Inside he found a note from Sam Stone on his DIRECTOR CENTRAL INTELLIGENCE AGENCY letterhead and an official White House photograph of President Oxley shaking hands with Rachel Yeager. A caption on the back of the photograph identified her and the time and place.

He assumed that the photograph was a contribution from the Secret Service to the CIA, which was strictly prohibited by law from conducting intelligence in the United States. But the Secret Service could gather domestic intelligence and pass it on to the CIA or any other agency in the Intelligence Community.

The note from Stone read, "Enclosed is a decrypted NSA intercept of a cable from Ambassador Yeager's UN office (code name Velvet) to Mossad HQ. Routing is not indicated, but Mossad officers under UN cover usually send routine messages in low-grade encryption. Interesting. Thought you'd like to see it. Note ref to Brethren."

Falcone scanned the cable:

MET WITH MIDAS, GAVE WARNING RE BRETHREN. THEIR PLANS STILL UNKNOWN. VELVET.

Falcone did find the terse message even more interesting than Stone had thought: It confirmed Falcone's suspicion, based on the pages that Dake had given him, that Israel was concerned about The Brethren.

Next, Falcone looked over the list of telephone-call names—Graham, Kane, Huntington, Stone, Walker, Mason, Cunningham, Dake, Yeager—and called Anna Dabrowski. She entered in a moment and, as usual, stood until he motioned her to a chair. Anticipating the summons, she had a copy of the list clipped to the green loose-leaf notebook she always carried.

"I know what Graham wants," Falcone said, looking up from the list. "I've been talking to his man Lanier, and Graham is curious. It's a matter of my violating bureaucratic Department of Energy protocol by not going through Graham. Please call him and just say that I was talking to Lanier while acting as national continuity coordinator. And leave it at that."

He paused over the next name, then said, "On to Kane. We have to pay high heed to cabinet members. Hand him off to Hawk to find out what's on the Pentagon's mind and say I'll call him as soon as I'm through with what the President wants me to do.

"Huntington and Stone. Hmmm. Probably have the same thing to say: no new information but many leads. Tell Stone, thanks for the note. I'll tell you about it later. Tell both of them that I want memos on the latest leads on responsibility for the bomb. That'll keep the intel shops busy.

"What's left?" Falcone asked, looking down at the list. "Walker, Mason, Cunningham, Dake, Yeager. You call Walker and tell Hawk to call Mason. Tell them that I'm working on urgent matters and want to hear from them: I want each one to send me each morning, through secure channels, a one-page report on conditions. That should hold them."

"Okay. And Vice President Cunningham?"

"I just talked to him in person. He's celebrating getting out of The Rock. I want him to call a couple of heads of state in the President's name. I'll give you the names."

"That leaves Phil Dake and Ambassador Yeager," Dabrowski said. "She's not just a callback. She requested a meeting. Said it was urgent. Of course, they *all* say it's urgent."

"Tell Dake I'll call him as soon as I can. That won't satisfy him, but it will slow down his next call. As for Rach . . . Ambassador Yeager . . . I'll get Mae to call her at the Israeli Embassy and—"

"She's at the Hay-Adams. Room 311. Here's her cellphone number," Dabrowski said, handing Falcone a slip of paper.

"You took her call?"

"She called me directly. I guess the Mossad knows the name and number of everybody in the White House. We exchanged pleasantries, and, since she was . . . is . . . an ambassador—"

"Okay. I'll call her," Falcone said, deciding that Anna, who knew everything, had slightly hesitated because she knew about the romantic interlude between Falcone and the diplomat who now called herself Rachel Yeager. As soon as Anna left, Falcone dialed the number. *Velvet. Intriguing code name.*

She answered immediately, and the sound of her voice kindled a swirl of memories. She had been a beautiful woman, a lover, and a merciless executioner. Their days had been few but unforgettable.

"Your voice is as lovely as I remember it," Falcone said.

"In some ways, I suppose, we have not changed. Except for our jobs."

"And it's the job that made you call Anna Dabrowski when you were looking for me, wasn't it? But you weren't looking for Sean Falcone; you were looking for the President's national security advisor. Correct?"

"Your assistant is very bright. And so warmly human," Rachel said. He remembered her maddening practice of not answering direct questions. "She's not a bureaucrat. I liked her instantly."

"You always were a good judge of people."

"Including judging you, Sean. You were . . . well, you are honest and open. And I must see you as soon as possible, urgently."

"I would like to meet you at the Hay-Adams's grand old bar. I can be there in five minutes. But—"

"But this is business. Urgent business."

"Right. We'll postpone the bar. You'll be met at the West Wing entrance, given your badge, and escorted to my office."

"It's absolutely secure?"

"As secure as the Israeli Embassy. I thought I'd find you *there*."

"Two ambassadors don't fit there very well. Clashing egos, clashing interests. Besides, I like to keep people guessing. See you shortly."

He was standing outside his door, trying not to look unprofessionally anxious, when he saw her striding down the short hallway from the entrance, a Secret Service agent walking behind her. She wore a blue-and-white knitted scarf loosely tied and a black pants suit, its jacket buttoned over a dark blue blouse. She moved with the grace and confidence he remembered.

He was tempted to embrace her, but the temptation faded away when he looked into her face and saw an ambassador on an urgent mission. His memories of their past had endured and were quickening his heart. Now, seeing her, he knew that she had put away her memories and felt no need to bring them forth.

He showed her to one of the two chairs in front of his

desk and took the other one. Across from each other, their eyes met for a moment. Her sea-green eyes were part of her psychological disguise, he remembered, for her eyes always looked innocent and unaware.

"I'm sorry for what's happened, Sean. It's horrible. We've been terrified for so long that such a thing could happen to us. . . . Now you . . ."

"Everyone's nightmare," he said. "Everyone's."

"I don't want to intrude. Not at a time like this . . . I had hoped to see you at the state dinner—"

"I was coming off a long trip and I—"

"At first I thought you might be avoiding me. . . ."

"Hardly. Actually, I wanted to congratulate you on your . . . new line of work. Quite a shift in responsibilities for you. I mean, at the UN."

"Times change. Jobs, too."

"You're right," Falcone said. "But I never thought of you as the diplomatic type."

"I must admit," Rachel said, smiling, "that I have a lot to learn when it comes to diplomacy."

"There are rumors that you're in line to become Israel's next foreign minister."

"The thought strikes fear in the hearts of some. Maybe one day. Not now. . . . Sean, let me ask you. Do you have any leads on how this happened or who?"

"Nothing yet. Lots of speculation, no facts," Falcone said, pausing to decide whether to say more, then adding, "I was hoping you might be able to help."

"If I had to guess," she said without hesitation, "it would be Iran."

"Guess? Really? Never thought the Mossad was in the guessing game."

"I'm no longer Mossad."

"But you still have access to . . . Look, let's not play games about this. What makes you say Iran?"

"Motive. Capability . . ."

"Capability? Our intel people insist that the mullahs were at least a year away—possibly two to three years away—from making a nuclear bomb. The Cerberus computer worm worked," Falcone said.

He was referring to a destructive computer program that nearly everyone assumed U.S. and Israeli technicians had developed to sabotage Iranian nuclear centrifuges. The complex devices were used to produce enriched uranium for weapons. The Cerberus worm was introduced into the computers that controlled the speeds of the spinning centrifuges. Falcone had seen a PDB reporting that about 20 percent of the Iranian centrifuges had spun out of control and destroyed themselves. "Even your former director of Mossad publicly declared that Iran had been set back several years."

"Sean, do you really think Mossad would declare such a thing if it was true? Please. It was disinformation. To buy time, to reduce Iran's anxiety about the immediacy of any plans we might have to attack them. Allow them to think they had more time to take defensive measures. . . .

"Prime Minister Weisman had intended to tell your president that the Iranians crossed the threshold months ago. Cerberus had not changed that fact. We believe that your CIA and others doubt our estimates and say we fabricate intelligence to serve our own ends."

"We are not talking fabrication," Falcone said, allowing an irritated tone in his voice. "We were convinced that Iran couldn't move that fast. And isn't it true that some Iranian nuclear engineers have died mysteriously?"

Rachel unknotted her scarf and said, "Perhaps because we're closer, we see things more clearly. Measure speed differently."

"Or perhaps you want us to run a little faster for you. . . ."

"We gave you hard evidence, but your president insisted—personally to Prime Minister Weisman and then publicly at a press conference—that sanctions were working, and he let it go at that."

"Well, he certainly couldn't mention Cerberus."

She carefully reknotted her scarf, as if that task had to be accomplished before she could respond.

"No, he couldn't," she finally said. "I must say I was greatly relieved to see it did not show up in the WikiLeaks. Those leaks greatly concerned us, Sean. And then we see Cerberus revealed in the *New York Times*."

"Well, we don't have a monopoly on leaks. Remember when the whole world got to see a video of a Mossad hit squad assigned to kill Al-Mabhouh in Dubai?"

"Nothing can be served by you and me having a leaking contest."

"But the fact is that very few secrets can be kept secret anywhere these days," Falcone said. "Especially assassinations of Hamas leaders. Everyone who can use the Internet knows that you tried to kill Al-Mabhouh once before and failed. Tough on the Mossad's reputation."

Rachel shrugged with a flair that Falcone fondly remembered at that moment. Usually shrugs like that were followed by silence, her shield of feigned indifference.

"So, to get back to here and now," Falcone said, "was Prime Minister Weisman going to ask President Oxley to attack Iran?"

"No. Of course, he would have liked to ask America to destroy Iran's potential weapons. After all, you have the power to do so. But no. He was going to request that if Israel decided to act, America would guarantee that our pilots would have safe passage over Iraq and Saudi Arabia."

Falcone stood, and shifting his gaze toward the tranquility outside his window, said, "So we—the United States—would be complicit?"

"No. You'd be able to publically condemn us . . . just as you did when we took out Saddam's nuclear plant. Then you could join hands with your Saudi pals and what remains of your Arab friends in the Gulf and thank us privately."

"You're not being very diplomatic. . . ."

"As I said, I have a lot to learn about diplomacy. For now, I prefer just telling the truth." Rachel walked toward the windows to a world globe mounted on a mahogany stand. She stabbed a finger at Iran and said, "Here is where it all begins. We can talk forever about whether Iran got the bombs six months ago or will get the bomb in six years.

"The point is that Iran *wants* the bomb. It has done and will do whatever is necessary to get it. And a bomb there really means a bomb here." She moved her finger through the Middle East, giving the globe a slight movement. "If Iran gets the bomb, Iran becomes the godfather for those who do not have it."

Falcone walked to where she stood, her scent stirring a memory. He placed a finger on her hand, moving it back to Iran. "So, I suppose, in your scenario, your enemy is the enemy of the entire Middle East and beyond. Iran must be the villain beyond redemption and we must be the heroes—the crusaders—who defeat the villain."

She grasped his hand for a moment, let go, walked back to the chair, and sat down without speaking.

Falcone, still standing, said, "New subject. Why Savannah? Why would Iran decide to attack the United States by attacking a minor port?"

"I can think of two reasons, Sean. First, your main ports are relatively well guarded and defended. Second, Savannah is a major port for sending supplies to Afghanistan. It's an old idea: attack the supply train. The Iranian leaders can be fanatic or even crazy. But they're not stupid. Hasn't your intelligence come up with those answers?"

Before Falcone could respond, Rachel continued, "Or Saudi intelligence? Can you tell your Saudi friends that you want some intelligence help?"

"You must know that Saudi Arabia does not listen to us—especially since the whole Middle East erupted. And neither does Pakistan. I'm sure you know about the Saudis' nuclear-weapon deal with Pakistan."

"Yes," she said. "Pakistan has sent Ghauri-II long-range missiles to the Saudis. They are in silos at the Sulayyil Missile Base."

"And the Pakistani bombs?" Falcone asked.

"Oh, we are playing the do-you-know-what-I-know game? Yes, we understand that the Saudis have flown two transport planes with civilian markings to Pakistan's Kamra Airbase. When and if the Saudis decide they want nuclear bombs, Pakistan will load two of its bombs onto the transports, which will carry the bombs to Saudi Arabia. Correct?"

"Correct," Falcone said. "We call it the cash-and-carry deal. The easiest way to get a bomb is to buy it."

"So you believe that this little sideline deal"—another

shrug—"would be carried out if Iran is attacked? And so that influences your hesitancy to attack?"

"Yes, among other hesitations. And while unlikely, there is always the possibility that Pakistan could be tempted to take advantage of a Middle East crisis to lash out at India. The Ghauri-II's range has been extended. It can strike targets deep within India. Yes, we consider consequences. And does Israel?"

"Muslim rage? Hezbollah rockets? Hamas suicide bombers? Of course."

"All that—and worse—for a year's delay in their program?"

"When every day is a stay of execution, a year is a lifetime."

"So, what will you do now that it is America that must react to an actual bomb?"

"Wait . . . To see what your president will do now. We wouldn't want to compromise his decision . . . or mission."

"And that's why Weisman left you here? An agent in place? Five minutes from the White House?"

"Please, Sean. He felt—and I felt—that I might be of help. A direct line from what I believe is *still* the best intelligence service in the Middle East."

"Whatever help you can give will be greatly appreciated, I assure you."

"Thank you, Sean. But what's wrong? You sound like a man who has something else to say."

"Oxley's under a lot of pressure to act," Falcone replied, hesitating before deciding to add, "and a lot of it is generated by some of your friends on the Hill."

"Indeed, we have many friends in your Congress. We're

a small country surrounded by those who hate us. We take our friends wherever we find them."

"But not all of your friends are your friends. Not your real ones."

Their dialogue had been swift, each statement ricocheting off each response. Now there was a pause. Falcone surmised that Rachel suspected he knew more than was saying. He thought of the photograph in the receiving line. *She looked radiantly beautiful,* he thought, then drew back to his job. *But—what about the warning? The Brethren. The Israelis—the Mossad—was feeding the same line to Dake.*

Falcone thought for a moment about mentioning Dake's information and its probable source. Instead, he turned lawyerly. Resuming his seat to begin the deposition, he said, "Let me ask you something. A hypothetical. What if the Iranians saw that you were preparing to attack their country—"

"Believe me, they would not see it coming—"

"But assuming they did. That your disinformation campaign had not worked—and then decided to strike first?"

"They would not have time. We would eliminate them before they could fire a missile. And, just in case, thanks to you, we have the Arrow defense system that can knock down their Shahab missiles."

"But what if they were able to do something else with a bomb: smuggle one . . . just one . . . into an American city, and leave no fingerprints?"

"They could never be sure that President Oxley would not discover their perfidy and order their destruction."

"I thought you were convinced that Oxley would never act."

"True. But not after an American city was destroyed."

"But what if they assumed—and they weave their strategies as fine and complicated as their art—that Oxley would not strike back? Not before Russia and China step in and demand that the UN Security Council prevent any response. They urge restraint and then use the forum as a reason to call for immediate reductions in nuclear weapons, and a nuclear-free Middle East."

"Sean, an interesting hypothetical. Not terribly reasonable, but interesting. Fortunately, I don't live in a world of fantasy. My world is very real."

"You're right. It's hypothetical, perhaps fantasy, to assume that the Mossad was right about Iran having a nuclear bomb or that the Iranians had anything to do with Savannah."

"Sean, as I said, I'm not skilled quite yet as a diplomat, but speaking to you as a friend, I think President Oxley has no choice. It would have been better if he had acted before Iran got close to making the bomb. But it's not too late to prevent another one from going off—somewhere."

Falcone did not immediately respond. He again thought of Dake and the information that most likely came from Mossad wiretaps and bugs. He was wondering whether to brace her about The Brethren and their own fantasy world of Armageddon . . . when his phone rang.

He knew that Mae would hold all calls when he was meeting with a ranking visitor. Visibly annoyed, he picked up the phone and curtly answered, "Falcone."

"Hawk here. Anna said for me to find out what Secretary Kane wanted. Said he wants to talk with you about the legal status of the Fort Stewart troops; he's getting queries from members of Congress, especially Southern members, telling him it's undeclared martial law down there. I was just leaving his office when the President called. Said he wants to view war plans. Iran war plans. Thought I'd give you a heads-up."

"Got it. Thanks," Falcone said, hanging up. As usual, Mae instinctively knew when to trump Falcone's no-calls orders. He turned to Rachel. "Sorry. Reminder I've got a meeting coming up. We'll have to continue—"

The presidential phone rang.

"You're a busy man, Sean," Rachel said. "We'll talk." She rose, walked to the door, and hesitated long enough to hear Falcone answer the phone: "Yes, Mr. President. Thank you." He hung up.

"Something going on?" Rachel asked, right hand on the doorknob.

"Routine meeting," Falcone replied.

"Like the one we just had?"

"Yeah. It will be full of hypotheticals," Falcone said. Then, trying to sound casual, he added, "By the way, the President enjoyed meeting you."

"We didn't get much of a chance to talk. He had to rush away and—"

"Not at the state dinner. I was talking about that fund-raiser in Connecticut. He was quite surprised to see a diplomat there."

He hoped that he would jolt her, but all she said was, "I like to surprise people. He is a very charming man."

Ice in her veins, Falcone thought. *But what else would I expect from a professional assassin?*

"It was great seeing you again, Rachel. I appreciated the geography lesson, but Iran attacking the United States still doesn't make any sense."

"You asked for my opinion. I simply gave it. And by

the way, how much of what's going on in the world today makes any sense?"

He stood in his doorway and watched Rachel and her White House escort walk down the hall. Then he called the President back.

"Mr. President, I'm sorry I couldn't speak," he said. "I had someone in my office. About the meeting. I strongly suggest that you hold back until this evening." He told Oxley about Cunningham's visit and Stanfield's scheduled speech.

"Okay, Sean," Oxley said. "Let's aim for nine thirty."

"Fine, Mr. President. See you at nine thirty."

"Right," Oxley said, a hint of hesitation in his voice. Then he added, "Sean, have you read *Brothers*? The book about the Kennedys?"

"No, sir. Heard of it, haven't read it."

"I'll send it over. Take a look at the pages I marked."

As soon as the President hung up, Falcone called Dabrowski. "Anna, you know everything. What do you know about a book about the Kennedys, titled *Brothers*?"

"I'm bringing it up on Google. The author is David Talbot. Started Web magazine *Salon*. Here's a review on Amazon. It looks at JFK's assassination and Bobby's fears of a conspiracy. There's also a look at JFK and the military— Cuban missile crisis, Bay of Pigs."

"The President has read it and is passing it to me. Why would he be reading it?"

"Maybe our president is interested in how another president dealt with the military in a crisis. Maybe that's it."

"Maybe, Anna. Thanks."

As Falcone was hanging up, Mae Prentice entered and handed him a manila envelope containing the book. Falcone opened it and flipped to a cluster of yellow stickers marking pages about the missile crisis. Falcone felt a shiver go down his spine, for the book recounted how Kennedy had kept a key civilian adviser, Ted Sorensen, out of a crucial meeting with military leaders "to avoid provoking the Pentagon chiefs." President Oxley was doing the opposite, inviting Falcone into the upcoming war-plans meeting perhaps because he *wanted* to provoke General Wilkinson.

Underlined was Sorensen's recollection of how Kennedy burst out of the meeting, hot under the collar and he pointed at the meeting and he said, 'They all want war.' Another underline: he knew time was going to run out.

The commander of the Strategic Air Command had, without presidential or secretary of defense authorization, raised SAC's alert status to DEFCON Two. The alert message, incredibly, went out in the clear so that the Soviet Union would know about it. *And here we are very publicly at DEFCON One,* Falcone thought. *Ready for war.*

Now Falcone looked at the book as a coded message from Oxley in anticipation of the war-plans meeting. Other underlined sections referred to General Edwin Walker, a name Falcone recognized. Kennedy's secretary of defense, Robert McNamara, had relieved Walker of his command of an infantry division in Germany for his extreme right-wing activities.

One of Walker's rants implied that President Kennedy was the "anti-Christ." In a bizarre incident never understood by Kennedy assassination analysts, Lee Harvey Oswald had attempted to kill Walker, firing the same rifle that he later used to kill President Kennedy.

Tucked between two flagged pages was a sheet from

a notepad bearing the presidential seal. The paper was folded over twice and sealed with transparent tape. On it was scrawled SEAN—PERSONAL.

From the moment that Falcone held *Brothers* in his hands, he had been trying to figure out why the President had sent him the book. He hoped that the note would help. But all that Oxley had written was, *Me the anti-Christ? Walker = Parker?*

Falcone, who had never discussed Parker with Oxley, was tempted to call the President and asked what inspired his cryptic equation. But Stanfield's speech and the war-plan meeting were enough; no one needed the distraction of Parker. Still, in some unfathomable way, Parker and The Brethren would be hovering over the meeting.

45

Falcone usually kept the small television set in his office tuned to GNN. This was his window on the world, the window where, with frustration and irritation, he so frequently saw that GNN was reporting news ahead of U.S. intelligence agencies. Today, however, he switched to C-SPAN, the only network officially allowed to transmit the televising of debates in the House and Senate chambers.

After the President's speech revealing a nuclear explosion in Savannah, Senator Stanfield had suspended his campaigning and returned to Washington. He had stayed out of the media spotlight until the announcement about his forthcoming speech "to America." Its timing meant that C-SPAN's coverage would stream into the networks and cable outlets exactly when their largest audiences were watching television.

The Senate had convened late and suspended all business so that senator after senator could rise at his or her desk to speak on the disaster in Savannah. The visitors' galleries surrounding the chamber were jammed with Hill staffers. As Falcone watched, the chamber became a cauldron boiling over with fiery speeches.

Most senators demanded vengeance against nameless foes: "We must strike back" or "These murderers must pay." One senator, seized by the wild justice of revenge, demanded immediate retaliation against Muslims in general: "We know these are the spiritual kin of the nine-eleven killers, sent by their Islamist masters to destroy our country."

The speeches were an overture to Stanfield, who now rose from his seat and appeared on Falcone's television screen. He stood silently for a moment, looking around, suddenly the star of an operatic script that had brought him on stage at this moment. He wore a hand-tailored, blue pin-striped suit and a dark purple tie. His gray hair was cut stylishly just above his stiff, white collar. *He looks straight out of* GQ, Falcone thought. *But he is no gentleman. He's dressed up as a suave, courtly Southerner full of grace and affability. But it's all artifice. He's as mean and treacherous as a Texas rattlesnake.*

Falcone still had mixed emotions about the Senate. It had been a great institution, once populated by lions who fought passionately for the big issues of their day. Yet, they still managed to find the courage to put aside narrow self-interest and do what was best for the country. Today, few lions could be found on Capitol Hill. Many who bore the title of "honorable" seemed small-minded and parochial, dedicated principally to maintaining ideological purity. Compromise was unacceptable, and those who indulged in the art were punished at the polls. The center was no longer holding because centrists were treated as traitors to their political parties.

To Falcone's eyes, Stanfield was a perfect example of what was happening in Washington today. Dressed up in his finery, his cosmetic makeup expertly applied to smooth out lines and blemishes, Stanfield looked like a presidential candidate, a man who could lead the nation through troubled times. But Falcone knew that Stanfield was an unscrupulous politician eager to turn a great tragedy into a political opportunity.

"Mr. President," Stanfield began, addressing the Senate's presiding officer in his chair that rose above the Senate chamber. Falcone reached for the TV remote and turned up the volume.

"It is with a heavy heart and profound sadness that I take to the floor tonight," Stanfield began. "I speak to you, my fellow countrymen, not as a presidential candidate, but as a member of this august body. I speak because a terrible thing was allowed to happen to our country. As one who shares the extraordinary responsibility to help ensure the safety, security, and welfare of all Americans, I have an obligation to come to you today to express my rage, my sorrow, and my convictions on what must be done.

"Our nation has suffered an attack that is unprecedented in our history. One of America's great cities has been destroyed by a nuclear bomb. Thousands of our citizens have been slaughtered, turned to ash in the blink of an eye. Thousands more may die from radiation poisoning or be maimed and disfigured for life."

Pausing, he reached into the inner pocket of his suit jacket and took out what looked to be three or four sheets of paper folded in thirds. Falcone instinctively leaned forward. Stanfield, a master of rhetorical stagecraft, slowly unfolded the pages.

Holding up the pages, he said solemnly, "I have in my hand a list of the passengers who boarded the ill-fated *Regal,* the beautiful cruise ship that carried one hundred and forty-six souls on a voyage that ended in the Savannah River when they, along with the sixty-seven members of the *Regal*'s crew, were killed by the detonation of a nuclear bomb."

Again he paused. He lowered his left hand that was holding the pages and placed them on the desktop. Then he picked up one of the pages with his left hand and touched it six times with the index finger of his right hand. The chamber was eerily quiet.

"Six of the passengers had Muslim names," he continued, again pointing at six lines on one of the pages. "Two of them—two Iranians under assumed names. I repeat, two *Iranians* . . . were taken off the ship just prior to its departure from Boston and were allegedly placed in federal custody.

"But it was *too late*." Stanfield's voice rose, then fell. *"Too late,"* he repeated.

Again a pause.

"What I am about to tell you will seem impossible to believe," he said, his voice lowering.

Falcone edged forward on his chair, drawn toward the screen by Stanfield's mesmerizing performance.

"Although those two Iranians were removed from the ship, *their baggage remained on board* when the ship left Boston.

"That's what I said. Their stowed baggage *remained on board.*

"The two Iranians had carried a nuclear bomb aboard the *Regal.* But they had no intention to be on board when the bomb went off. Oh, no. These mass murderers were not suicide bombers. They were part of an ingenious plot, a monstrous conspiracy I am able only to begin to piece together.

"An agent of the Department of Homeland Security, operating under orders from a superior whose name I have not yet been able to learn, called the Boston Police Department and requested that officers be sent to escort two passengers off the *Regal.* The Boston police officers did so, turning them over to federal operatives who said the men were being taken to a federal detention center.

"The *Regal* sailed out of Boston harbor and began its fated voyage, stopping at ports along the eastern seaboard while a nuclear bomb was ticking away in her hold. As the ship sailed up the Savannah River, bound for the cruise-ship dock, she entered a part of the port operated by the U.S. Navy's Military Sealift Command. Ships of that command use a special Savannah dock for loading vital supplies, including armored vehicles and helicopters, needed by our men and women in Afghanistan.

"The bomb went off, not only destroying the *Regal* but also sinking two Sealift Command ships destined for the Pakistan port of Karachi, the starting point for deliveries to our bases in Afghanistan. Thus, a bomb set off in Savannah, Georgia, became not only a terrorist bomb but also a weapon against our forces in Afghanistan—and a warning that Iran can strike us anywhere, anytime.

"More than two hundred passengers and crewmen died on the *Regal,* and thousands more were killed and maimed in Savannah. We mourn them all. But we will never know how many Americans and their allies were killed or wounded because they did not get the supplies destroyed in Savannah by agents showing the long arm of Iran.

"Fellow Americans, what I have just told you was a secret. But I felt obliged to reveal not only this monstrous secret *but the fact that it is all known* to President Oxley.

"Mr. Oxley knew about the bomb and the two Iranians. But he ordered the suppression of that information.

"At first he concocted the tsunami lie. Then, when the detection of nuclear-bomb radiation demolished the tsunami lie, he was forced to admit the existence of a nuclear bomb. But he declined to reveal the evidence showing that the detonation of the bomb was an act of war by Iran."

Those seated in the Senate let out a collective gasp. Pausing once more, Stanfield surveyed the chamber, raising his eyes and turning his head, as if to acknowledge the staffers in the galleries.

Then he twice thumped the top of his desk, the sound echoing through the hushed chamber. "This did not have to happen, Mr. President!" he thundered.

"This would not have happened had we had a man in the White House who deserved to be our commander-in-chief. Instead, we have what can only be called a commander-in-thief . . . a weak, incompetent pretender who has robbed us of our security, our lives, our future—"

The phone on Falcone's desk rang, shattering the silence like a fire bell. It was Ray Quinlan.

"Sean, are you watching Stanfield? Can you believe this shit? We're in DEFCON One and this motherfucker is attacking the President of the United States!"

"Did you really expect anything else from him?" Falcone said, eyes still on the screen. "He's clubbing the President like a baby seal."

"But that shit about the Iranians," Quinlan asked. "Is any of that true?"

"You see the PDBs. There've been plenty of rumors and false reports. But nothing like the Iranian stuff Stanfield is selling. We need to—"

"Find out if it's a fucking leak," Quinlan screamed. "A fucking leak."

"Get back to Stanfield," Falcone said. "He's not through."

Falcone hung up and turned back to the screen.

"Mr. President," Stanfield continued, pausing to fold the sheets of paper and return them to the inner pocket of his suit coat. "It is clear from Mr. Oxley's record—"

Nice touch, Falcone whispered to himself. Oxley was no longer entitled to the title of President.

"—It is a record that Mr. Oxley must stand on. Not with pride but with deep embarrassment and shame. He has allowed the brave men and women who defend our nation in battle to die at the hands of terrorists. The attack on the *Elkton* was a savage act of war. But what did our commander-in-chief do in response? He did not call for a vigorous military attack upon the nation that has sponsored so many acts of terrorism, the nation of Iran. No! He called for the creation of a congressional investigation!

"Everyone could see what Mr. Oxley was doing. Pretending to be a statesman, cerebrally above it all, calling for patience, no rushing to judgment. Mr. President, it was a political ploy. A trick to delay the need for him to be held accountable for his failures.

"And his failure to act only emboldened our enemies. They see his weakness. They can smell his timidity behind all of his rhetorical perfume. He is afraid to act, and because of his cowardice, thousands of our citizens are dead or dying . . . horribly.

"Mr. President, the American people need not be stripped of our armor and be forced to stand naked before our enemies, waiting for another attack, another nuclear bomb while Mr. Oxley delays, defers, and scolds us not to take action before we know the facts.

"We *do* know the facts. We know that Iran has secret nuclear weapons. We know Iran wants to destroy America and Israel, our only ally the Middle East. The Iranians have attacked us because we have a president who is a coward, who worries what the Chinese or the Russians—or what the United Nations—might say if we respond and defend our nation.

"I could go on at length about what Mr. Oxley has allowed to happen to America during his term of office. But we need action and not speeches, *virtute non verbis.* Deeds not words.

"Mr. President, I'm calling for the Senate and House leadership to convene a joint session of Congress, and that *we*—the Congress—do what Mr. Oxley refuses to do: pass a declaration of war against Iran. It is in our power to do so. The Constitution of the United States of America gives us that exclusive power."

Stanfield reached into his desk, took out a pocket copy of the Constitution, and held it aloft.

"And if the President of the United States refuses to serve as our chief executive in our hour of need, he will be in violation of his oath of office to protect and defend us. He should be convicted of impeachable offenses, removed forcibly if need be from the White House, and punished for betraying our great nation."

The door to Falcone's office flew open. Quinlan, red-faced, barged in cursing. "That son of a bitch. This is the worst shit I've ever seen in all of my years in this city. Sean, you need to get up to the Hill, Tell your old friends that Stanfield is insane. They can't do this. Congress has never initiated a declaration of war. Never! They don't have the power to—"

"Ray, it doesn't matter what's happened in the past. I'm not sure our friends on the Hill won't throw us under the bus. They're all running scared. But even if they refuse to call a joint session, it doesn't matter. Stanfield wins either way. If President Oxley doesn't act, he'll lose the election. He'll be judged to have abdicated his obligation to defend America. If he does act . . . well, we may be starting a war against a country that had nothing to do with Savannah."

Quinlan stood next to Falcone's desk and watched Stanfield continue. As if on cue—and Falcone later learned from Cunningham that the lofting of the Constitution had been a cue—a Senate page approached Stanfield's desk and handed him a note. He reached into a side suit coat pocket, removed his black-rimmed glasses, put them on, and read the note.

"My fellow Americans," Stanfield said, holding the note in one hand, his glasses in the other. "I have just learned profound news."

He placed the note on his desk, the glasses in his pocket,

and continued, "As I told you, I am not here as a presidential candidate but as a United States senator gravely concerned with the actions of Mr. Oxley. And my running mate, vice presidential candidate, the Honorable Greg Nolan, is also in Congress, today as a member of the House.

"As I began this speech of revelation in this esteemed chamber, Representative Nolan was introducing a resolution of presidential impeachment onto the floor of the equally esteemed other chamber.

"Representative Nolan's previous impeachment resolutions have been bottled up in the House Judiciary Committee, which my opponent has controlled with a steely grip. But tonight, I have just learned, the Speaker of the House has allowed the impeachment resolution to reach the floor of the House for free and open debate.

"In that debate, you, my fellow Americans, will learn of the lies and crimes of this president, and the process of impeachment will begin.

"May God grant us the strength and wisdom to guide us through this dreadful, but vitally necessary, ordeal. And God bless—"

"Jesus, Sean," Quinlan said. "What happens next? What do we do?"

"This whole fucking think stinks to high heaven, Ray," Falcone said, his face flushed with rage. "Look at the goddamn timing. We're about to talk about war with Iran with an impeachment hanging over the President."

"You're right. I thought the same thing. What happens next in the impeachment? What can we do about that?"

"Well, I assume Stanfield's telling the truth about the resolution," Falcone said, looking at the TV screen. "C-SPAN has switched over to the House. Looks like all hell broke loose."

"A steamroller!" Quinlan exclaimed. "How do we stop it?"

"I have no idea. Stanfield has set it up so that the President either abdicates to Congress—and Congress takes us to war. Or, Congress decides on another path and allows impeachment to continue. To many a member, impeachment might look more attractive.

"Look at the basics: If the House votes in favor of impeachment—it's decided by a simple majority—the House will send the Articles of Impeachment to the Senate. The Senate will conduct a trial of the President to determine whether the President is guilty of the crimes charged in the Articles of Impeachment. If two-thirds of the Senate vote to accept any Article of Impeachment, the President will be removed from office."

"So, Cunningham becomes president."

"Right. And it doesn't stop there."

"Yeah. I can see what you mean. Cunningham would have to be a puppet or get impeached himself."

"By then, Ray, it may be worse. Much worse."

"What do you mean?"

"If Cunningham were to be removed, the military might get spooked. The Joint Chiefs might start to question whether civilian authority can hold things together, particularly if another bomb goes off. The Chiefs may decide to get involved in the 'continuity of government.' Remember, that's our current status."

"I *am* remembering," Quinlan said, a hard tone creeping into the words. "Those presidential directives that we heard about. Oxley could . . . well, take over. Fuck impeachment. Fuck the election."

"Let's not go there, Ray. See you at nine thirty."

46

At Fort Stewart, in the borrowed barracks that Rube Lanier had named Albuquerque South, he and the other three members of the NEST crew had set aside their hazmat suits and the tools they had used as nuclear responders. Now they were back to being scientists and putting their regular expertise to work.

Lanier was a project director at the Albuquerque National Laboratory. His job was to put together and manage groups for specific tasks. He was doing that job now in Albuquerque South but with a new supervisor, Sean Falcone.

Russ Belcher was a radiation-poisoning expert. Now he was at a long table on the second floor of the barracks. Army cots and footlockers had been piled against the walls to make room for the people and equipment of Albuquerque South. Already, data was flowing in from the detection instruments that team members wielded as they moved through the disaster area. Belcher and two other scientists were working at computers devoted to the work of the radiation-detection team.

The Lawrence Livermore National Laboratory sent experts from the National Atmospheric Release Advisory Center. They created a three-dimensional map whose changing, pulsating colors showed the location and density of radioactivity and the plume of particles riding wind currents. Also fed into the map was regional weather data from the U.S. Air Force Global Weather Center and the National Oceanic and Atmospheric Administration.

Every fifteen minutes the Advisory Center circulated

real-time conditions and forecasts, which were so positive that Admiral Mason used them as reassuring illustrations when he started his twice-daily briefings. Somewhere deep in the map's data were the first bits of information that Russ Belcher and the others had transmitted during their NEST sortie in the Strykers.

Fred Malcomson, a physicist who had become a nuclear weapon designer, and Liz Dalton, an authority on nuclear-weapon attribution, worked in another corner of the room, where Army engineers had assembled a deployable field laboratory. It looked like a boxcar that had been shrunk to one-third normal size. Its sliding door was open. Painted on aluminum siding flanking the door was the new radioactive warning symbol: a large black triangle that framed radiating waves, a skull and crossbones, and the figure of a person running away from something so dangerous that you should flee from it.

Malcomson and Dalton, wearing disposable full-body laboratory suits, disposable gloves, and safety glasses, were trying to tease information out of samples of radioactive debris they had found when the Strykers rumbled through the disaster area. More samples flowed into the laboratory when the new radiation-detection team began its surveys.

Using tongs and tweezers, and working behind radiation-resistant glass shields, they moved samples through instruments and chemical baths. On their wrists were dosimeters tracking durations of exposure to iodizing radiation.

Their mission was to determine the origin of the nuclear material that had produced the radiation. On long-term loan to Lanier from Homeland Security's National Technical Nuclear Forensics Center, Malcomson and Dalton had been trying for more than five years to solve a single problem: how to assess blame for a nuclear or radiological attack.

In their brains and computer files was the sum total of what the United States knew about the arcane science of nuclear tracking. They worked continually at finding methods that would trace a radioactive substance back to the device that produced it—and also back to its birthplace in a reactor or enrichment facility somewhere in the world.

Until now, the secret forensics work of Malcomson and Dalton had been based on their analyses of bits of nuclear material presented to them by clandestine collectors from intelligence, military, and law-enforcement agencies. The two scientists had accumulated a collection of nuclear and radiological materials from all over the world, each one bearing a label, such as CHINA, POSSIBLE LOP NOR TEST SITE or KAZAKHSTAN, PROBABLE VVR-K REACTOR. They did not know how the materials had been obtained, and they were not expected to ask, but they did know that someday their radioactive evidence could doom a nuclear nation or nuclear terrorists as certainly as DNA evidence could condemn a murderer.

Malcomson and Dalton knew they needed more time and more data before they could give a solid, trustworthy answer to Lanier. However, Lanier was not to be denied.

They had been working for fourteen hours and had lost count of how many times Lanier had stuck his head into the laboratory and asked, "What have you got?"

"What we've got is fatigue and a serious chance of making careless mistakes," Malcomson said to Lanier as he made still another visit. Malcomson was in his late thirties, plump, with a full black beard. He wore black-rimmed glasses under his safety glasses.

"We need more time, more data, Rube," Dalton said, looking up.

"Well, happy birthday anyway," Lanier said, smiling. He knew everyone's birthday, and much more, because he had access to the National Nuclear Security Administration's highly classified personnel database.

"Thanks for remembering, Rube."

"You're welcome. We can't wait, Liz," Lanier said. "The White House wants attribution. Did you see Senator Stanfield on television?"

"Are you kidding?" Dalton said. "I haven't looked at anything human except you and Fred all day and into the night."

"Stanfield is blaming Iran. Any way you can tie this to Iran?"

"We've based all our studies on samples from every country that has exploded a nuclear weapon, including North Korea. Iran is not in that club—yet. We have some Iranian samples—smears from control rods, samples of radioactive water and metal shavings that I assume some Iranian spy gave to his CIA contact. That's all. None of the material we have on Iran is forensic, meaning suitable for determining attribution of a nuclear explosion. In other words, there is simply no way for us to pin this on Iran."

"Thanks, Liz. That's valuable in a negative way."

"You're welcome, Rube," she said, then paused and added, "but believe it or not, we're working on something that might be positive." She almost forgot she had safety glasses on. She pushed them up, looked up at him, shook her head, and said, "Positive. As if positive is the word for anything that has to do with all this." She swept an arm to encompass the room.

She had turned sixty the day before but looked years younger, even with her shoulder-length white hair, now bundled into a plastic shower cap. She had a lithe body beneath her white lab coat. If she had not been flown out of Albuquerque because of her NEST duties, she would have been running in a marathon there today.

"Yes, Rube, there might be something," Dalton said, lowering her voice. "Come back in an hour or so." Then she returned to the mass spectrometer she had been using.

"Okay, Liz, thanks again. I've got to make a call."

47

The Situation Room's Watch Center had become the Savannah Center, with Falcone as its commander. The White House Mess had turned two of the Sit Room cubicles into a fast-food franchise, and the White House physician's office was running out of stay-awake pills. Hurrying to the potential quiet of his office, Falcone passed several officers of the Secret Service Uniformed Division. They weren't talking, but obviously there had been a rise in death threats.

The disaster had overwhelmed all other issues involving the White House and the Cabinet. But Falcone still had to keep watch over all the perennials in the back of the closet: Japan's obsession about getting our forces out of Okinawa; NATO resolutions that needed to be acknowledged; European Union resolutions that needed to be analyzed from a

U.S. viewpoint; Australia's concern about Chinese taking control of mineral resources.

He had been behind his desk less than ten minutes when his direct-line phone rang. That phone did not go through Mae, and he handed out the number cautiously. Rarely did that ring signal the arrival of good news.

"Lanier here," said the caller, and Falcone thought, *I might as well have stayed in the Sit Room.*

"I hope you have attribution news," Falcone said.

"Sort of. I saw Stanfield putting the blame on Iran, and—"

"And?" *Maybe good news.*

"And, if Iran did do it, we don't have the means to prove it," Lanier said, going on to briefly repeat Liz Dalton's explanation for being unable to get evidence that could accuse or exonerate Iran.

Falcone did not speak, and Lanier, hearing frustration in the silence, decided to inject hope. "But Liz says she's working on something else. I'm haunting her. I'll get you her news pronto."

"Haven't heard that word in a long time," Falcone said. "Thanks, Rube, for giving me something to cling to."

Falcone looked at his watch. Fifteen minutes till the war meeting. He had not been surprised by Oxley's request for the meeting—or, officially, "combat operations processes," which covered targets, time lines, logistics, and the integration of land, air, sea, and cyber assets. He knew that Pentagon war planners must prepare for crises and ways to respond to them.

Rarely was detailed knowledge of war plans necessary beyond the hierarchy of the Department of Defense and the planners themselves. Occasionally, however, Falcone or Secretary of Defense George Kane might know of a policy change that could affect a specific plan and ask for a meeting. Something like that was happening tonight. But, with Stanfield's claim that Iran had ordered the attack now hanging over Oxley—along with the threat of impeachment—this was hardly a routine meeting.

48

General Gabe Wilkinson was the first to arrive at the President's Briefing Room, a secure niche for small meetings within the Situation Room complex. Falcone thought Wilkinson looked surprised.

"Didn't expect to see you here," Wilkinson said. "It's not about the emergency in Savannah, Mr. Continuity of Government."

"But I've got two hats, Gabe. I'm still the President's national security advisor, and if you warriors are going to start a war, I want to at least watch." *But I want Oxley to get a pure military brief,* Falcone thought. He had decided to remain silent to allow Wilkinson and Secretary of Defense Kane to lay out options without interference or comments by him.

"Well, I hope it's a teaching moment for you, Sean," Wilkinson said, smiling. He laid out a large map on the table, then sat down next to Falcone. As an image of the map appeared on large wall screens, Kane entered and greeted Falcone and Wilkinson. Kane also seemed surprised.

Falcone went through a dialogue similar to the one he

had had with Wilkinson. He was beginning to feel not wanted, and he thought about the underlined pages in *Brothers*.

The others filed in: Secretary of State Bloom, Director of National Intelligence Huntington, and Attorney General Williams. At each seat there was a folder that contained such data as possible targets, assets to be deployed, time lines, and anticipated consequences. Bloom, Huntington, and Williams would probably not have much to say. The presentation would come from Kane and Wilkinson; the questions would come from the President.

President Oxley entered the room. Everyone stood. Ray Quinlan followed a few steps behind Oxley and took a seat between Falcone and the President.

Falcone was not surprised that Oxley made no reference to Stanfield's tirade. He merely said, "Gabe and George, thanks for getting this together so quickly."

"Not a problem, Mr. President," Kane said. "We've been working these issues pretty hard for some time now."

"I take it that this is a Conops?" Oxley asked.

"Yes, sir," Wilkinson said. "A concept of operations."

"And how long would it take to make the concept operational?" Oxley asked, obviously surprising Wilkinson, who had thought that the meeting was little more than a briefing. Isolated in the Pentagon, preparing for the meeting, he had not seen Stanfield's Senate performance.

Kane, who had seen Stanfield making the speech, spoke before Wilkinson had a chance to answer. "It's been pretty much ready to go, Mr. President. And now, with Stanfield . . ."

Oxley nodded and Kane continued, "Normally, it would have taken several days or more to spin everything up. But

we've been keeping this plan on the front burner. As soon
as you approve the targets we've selected and we determine a proposed time to launch, we can execute pretty
fast. Our ships, submarines, and aircraft are all in place.
We're already on DEFCON One, the highest alert possible. We're good to go whenever you give us a thumbs-
up, sir."

Oxley studied the map on the table as Wilkinson, following through on Kane's assertion, said, "As you can
see, Mr. President, there are a lot of moving parts involved in all of this."

Oxley shifted his gaze to a memo Kane had handed
him. "Why," he asked, "do you have Venezuela on the list,
George?" Oxley's brow was furrowed with perplexity.

"Just a precaution, Mr. President," Kane said. "Venezuela has been cozying up to Iran lately. Russia has sent
some S-300 missiles down there. As you know, Venezuela has been trying to undermine Colombia and destabi-
lize other parts of Latin America. I'm not suggesting that
we hit Caracas, just that we have to be prepared for every
contingency and make sure that Venezuela doesn't make
any moves in the wake of an attack on Iran."

Looking at the map, with all the icons showing the location of U.S. military assets and the potential targets that
would be hit, Oxley suddenly grasped the scope and
enormity of the war plan. He took a deep breath and sat
back in his chair. He thought of remarking that it would
be a disaster to bomb Venezuela, a country with which the
United States had diplomatic relations. But, determined
not to show any emotional reaction, he simply said, "Continue, Gabe."

"Mr. President," Wilkinson said after a nod from Kane,

"you asked us to provide you with several options. For the purpose of simplicity, I'll call them Light, Medium, and Heavy."

"The Light one being . . ."

"That, sir, would be a bolt-out-of-the-blue attack on Iran's leadership, the IRGC—Iranian Republican Guard Corps—and all fixed missile launching sites. In other words, a decapitating strike. We know pretty much where they are. Even though their leaders are in bunkers at the moment, we can probably take them out. That would give you the opportunity to demand that Iran suspend its nuclear activities, dismantle all nuclear sites and weapons, and allow for international inspectors to enter the country to ensure that your demands are carried out."

"Sort of Pearl Harbor Light," Oxley said. "And if they refuse?"

"Well, sir," Wilkinson said, smiling, "you've got a nuclear sword of Damocles hanging over the heads of their people. That's the upside of this option, sir. It's light and it's fast."

"And the downside?"

Secretary Kane, eager to show that he was intimately involved in every step of the planning, interjected, "The downside, Mr. President, is the likelihood that you might forfeit the option to strike Iran again if they refuse to accept your demands. Russia and China can be expected to denounce the strike."

"And if they did?" Oxley asked.

"They would most likely demand that you cease and desist until the UN Security Council has the opportunity to bring about a peaceful solution," Kane answered.

Falcone resisted the temptation to add his view of what

an attack on Iran would produce. He remained silent as Wilkinson took off from Kane's remark.

"From a military standpoint, sir, I don't think it's probable that either Russia or China would harshly react," Wilkinson said. "But one or the other might declare that a security treaty is in force with Iran and threaten retaliation if you were to proceed. As I said, unlikely, but—"

"So, you are recommending against this option?" Oxley asked.

"No, sir," Wilkinson instantly responded. "My job is to lay out the options to be considered. It's going to be your call, Mr. President. Whichever one *you* think is best."

Oxley was clearly annoyed with the answer—and was even more annoyed that Kane had remained silent, not wanting to disclose his hand.

"Okay, gentlemen," Oxley said, his brisk tone indicating his impatience. "Option Two involves what?"

"Option Two," Wilkinson answered, "is to hit their deeply buried underground weapons-making sites. This would have to involve our Stealth B-2 Bombers, as well as SLBMs—our submarine launched ballistic missiles—and other precision-guided munitions."

"Are you talking about nuclear weapons, General?"

"Yes, sir."

Oxley, his eyes blazing, looked directly at Wilkinson and said, "But if we use nuclear weapons—for the second time in modern history and the only country to do so—then everything I have tried to do to stop the spread of these terrible weapons . . . everything . . . is gone."

He turned to Kane, as if he felt a kinship with someone in civilian clothes, and said, "Even Ronald Reagan wanted to see a world free of the most destructive weapons man has ever invented. If we need any example of what's involved, just take a look at Savannah. And that was a mere pop gun compared to what you want me to unleash."

"I understand, Mr. President," Wilkinson said quietly, as if he were reacting to some misunderstood technical matter. "It's not an easy call. But it's the professional judgment of our analysts that our conventional weapons don't have the firepower to go deep enough underground to get at Iran's bomb-making facilities. As you know, we had recommended that such a capability be—"

"Enough said, General," Oxley snapped. He did not want to be reminded that he had rejected a forty-billion-dollar proposal to build bunker-busting bombs. *Bombs,* Oxley thought, *that would've busted the budget before it busted any bunkers.*

Wilkinson knew he was wading into deep water by raising this issue now, but he wanted to make sure that there would be no finger-pointing at the military leadership if the Iranian targets were not destroyed.

"Mr. President," Wilkinson continued, his voice drained of emotion, "if we only use conventional bombs, the strike is unlikely to be successful. We'll get none of the upside for having taken action and all of the downside: Muslim riots everywhere, attacks on our troops in the region, suicide bombers here at home, et cetera. It won't look good, sir."

Oxley continued to scrutinize the map, asking detailed and probing questions about the diplomatic issues involved if he were to order a strike, conventional or nuclear.

"It's complicated, sir," Kane said, nodding toward Secretary Bloom. "We'll, of course, have to get State involved before any action is taken. At the very last minute we'd have to talk with the Russians and the Chinese—especially the Chinese, to get them to hold back the North Koreans from launching an attack on South Korea. If the North Koreans get spooked and think that we are targeting them, they could reduce much of South Korea to rubble, even some parts of Japan."

"Jesus!" Oxley said softly.

"We'd also have to persuade the Indians and Pakistanis to stand down," Kane continued, as if he had not heard Oxley's exclamation. "Either one might see this as a chance to launch a preemptive nuclear strike against the other."

Kane nodded toward Falcone and said, "Cold Strike. I'm sure you have briefed the President on—"

"Don't worry, George," Oxley said. "The commander-in-chief knows that any day, at any hour, India might pounce on Pakistan. Yes, Sean has briefed me on Cold Strike. He has also briefed me on Pakistan's deal with Saudi Arabia. You know, the cash-and-carry deal."

Roberta Williams looked puzzled. Falcone's briefing about the deal had been on a need-to-know, and he had believed that Williams had no need to know. Instantly sensing that she had been sidelined, she glared at Falcone. He made a mental note to brief her—and to apologize. He did not need her as an enemy.

"Sir?" Wilkinson spoke up. "Saudi Arabia? We believe the Saudis will remain on the sidelines. Of course, we're not a hundred percent sure, but—"

"Well, General, what can we be one hundred percent sure of?"

"Nothing, sir. Nothing is certain in peace or war."

"Mr. President," Kane cut in to end the colloquy. "We are looking at other possible reactions. Perhaps the biggest challenge will be holding back the Israelis. . . ."

"The Israelis?" Oxley asked, looking mildly stunned. "Why would we hold them back? In fact, if any attack is to be made, why shouldn't they do it?"

Falcone shifted in his chair, looking as if he were about to speak. But he thought better of it and let Kane continue.

"Again, it's complicated," Kane said. "First, they don't have the air-to-air refueling capability to go deep into Iranian territory to hit all of the suspect sites. They'll need our help for aerial refueling or they'll need to have clearance to land in Saudi Arabia to refuel."

"The Saudis will allow them on their soil?" Oxley asked, looking more perplexed than he had when the meeting began.

"The Saudis won't object as long as they can publicly deny that it happened," Kane said. "They want someone—anyone—to hit Iran."

"Do you think the Israelis will attack on their own, General?" Oxley asked, wanting to shift from Kane's theorizing to Wilkinson and his warrior viewpoint.

"They'd have to use nuclear weapons to get at the deeply buried sites—that is, if they even know where they are," Wilkinson replied. "And they'll have to hope that neither the Syrians nor the Iranians have Russian S-300 antiaircraft missiles. They also might decide to try to decapitate Iran's leadership and command and control capabilities. Probably also kill tens of thousands of Iranians in the process."

The casual use of *probably* hung in Oxley's mind, but he stayed with the topic, asking, "What if the Russians threaten the Israelis with retaliation? The PDB has some indications that Russia might be willing to sign a mutual defense treaty with the Iranians. Shouldn't we warn the Israelis about this?"

Falcone again was tempted to speak, but he kept silent.

Before Wilkinson could respond, Kane cut in. "From Iran's point of view," he said, "that would be a pretty good trade to make. Israel bombs their nuclear sites and rallies all of the Muslim world against them. Then Russia puts a nuclear umbrella over Iran and threatens to take out Tel Aviv unless Israel surrenders all of its weapons, gives back all of the territory that belongs to the Palestinians and—"

"And basically agrees to commit national suicide," Oxley added.

"Right!" Kane said, sounding like a teacher praising a bright pupil. "Of course, you would be under heavy pressure from Congress to declare a similar treaty arrangement with Israel."

"So we're back to the nuclear, hair-trigger days of MAD," Oxley said. "Or don't you know about Mutual Assured Destruction? Or duck-and-cover? Or air raid shelters?" He could wait no longer to break Falcone's silence. "What's your feeling about Israel, Sean?"

Falcone thought of the conversation with Rachel, and he thought of all the documents he had read in his eternal quest to understand the Middle East. He was glad to have a chance to speak in this room, which had begun to seem like a military garrison.

"Take a look at Iran from Israel's view—a view shared somewhat with Saudi Arabia," Falcone said. "Iran has become Iraq's ally and is building a new eastern front in Iraq against Israel and Jordan. Those two countries see Iran replacing the U.S. as Iraq's Big Brother. Don't forget,

Iran's missiles were already threatening Israel from north and south. Now Iran, by becoming a strong force in Iraq, is threatening from the east.

"To Israel, our exit from Iraq ultimately means that Iran will be able to deploy their missiles—and Hizballah rockets—in the bases we leave behind. And those weapons will be pointing not only at Israel but also at Jordan and Saudi Arabia. There's no doubt that the Saudis would not like Iran to have nuclear weapons."

"But Sean," Oxley said, "if the Saudis somehow help in the bombing and then deny it, won't everyone see through their denial—a denial of helping Israelis kill hundreds, maybe thousands, of Iranians?"

"The Saudi people don't get a vote, sir," Falcone responded. "The king still controls everything. Besides, the Iranians are not Arabs, as they are quick to remind everyone. They're Persians. And the only people the Arabs hate more than the Jews right now are the Persians."

"Then I repeat, why not let the Israelis carry out an attack? Why us?"

Oxley was clearly asking the question of Falcone, but Kane answered, saying, "If the statements we heard tonight in the Senate are even remotely true, we are the aggrieved party and can respond under international law. We can make a better case than Israel ever can."

"For God's sake, George!" Falcone said, leaning forward, across the map, and turning toward Kane. "The Israelis have the *real* case. It's existential, not retaliatory. The Iranian Mullahs have declared on many occasions that they want to wipe Israel off the map. This is game time for them. Not a dress rehearsal.

"Israel is ready to go nuclear from the get-go. And once they start they won't tolerate any restrictions or requests for restraint. This is all or nothing for them. Half measures mean their asses will be hanging out for everyone to shoot at. If they strike, it will be a warning to everyone: Don't ever fuck with Tel Aviv."

Oxley had had enough to digest. He was about to declare an end to the session, but before excusing himself, he turned to Wilkinson and formally said, "General, you have given me a great deal to think about. Thank you for the brief. Just one further question. What is Option Three?"

"Sir, that's to turn out all the lights in Iran."

"You mean total war?"

"Yes, sir."

Oxley stood, forcing the others to their feet. "Thank you, gentleman," he said. "I'll ponder what we've discussed and will want to go over the options with my entire national security team before I make any decision."

Falcone followed Oxley out of the Situation Room and up the stairs to the second level of the White House. As they reached the top of the stairs, Falcone turned to walk down the short corridor and enter his office. But Oxley motioned for Falcone to follow him to the Oval Office. The President was moving at a fast clip and Falcone could tell that steam was about to pop from both ears.

49

As Oxley and Falcone entered the Oval Office, the President erupted. "Just what kind of fool do they think I am? I've about had it with Wilkinson. Kane, too. I should have fired both of them a long time ago." He headed toward the windows and looked out at the darkness.

"I've given DOD just about everything they've asked for, Sean," Oxley said, turning toward his desk. "I agreed to their request for more forces than we should have in Afghanistan, I— Oh, you know all this. I'm raving." He sat down, looking wearier than Falcone had ever seen him.

Oxley had had what could at best be described as a "working relationship" with the military. He had not worn the nation's uniform and he was not intimidated by all those who strutted into the Oval Office wearing a chest full of medals, thinking they could push him around. But he also did not want to make any enemies, knowing his critics would spread the lie that he was antimilitary. That put him at a disadvantage, and Oxley chafed at the reality that he had to cut back and compromise at times when he didn't want to give an inch.

"Wilkinson said he was not there to make any recommendations," Oxley said, mimicking the general's voice. "And decisions, no. Okay, I get that. Those are mine to make. But no recommendation from the chairman of the Joint Chiefs of Staff, the top military advisor to the President?"

"Mr. President," Falcone said, taking the chair in front of the desk, "Wilkinson and Kane did what every department does: force you into a box. They presented you with two absolutely absurd options as straw men to force you into choosing the one they preferred but would not select.

"Light was too light and Heavy meant the total destruction of Iran. So, therefore, Mr. President, you must choose Option Two as the only responsible choice. That's the game."

"Goldilocks lives, Sean. This one's too cold. This one's too hot. Oh, but this one is just right! Well, bullshit," Oxley exploded, pounding the desk with both fists. "The options were all bullshit."

"Mr. President, I agree. But there *is* another option. And that's a decision not to attack Iran or anyone else. At least not before we're certain who did it." He told Oxley about Lanier's call.

Oxley took a few deep breaths and calmed down. "Sorry for the eruption, Sean," he said. "You're right about not acting rashly. But time is running out on me. You heard Stanfield. If I wait much longer, I won't have any options. Events will be controlling me. And Stanfield has become one of those controlling events."

Falcone thought again of *Brothers* and the underlined words: he knew time was going to run out.

Oxley stroked the back of his neck, trying to prolong his effort to calm down, but he felt his rage returning. "Pardon me if I explode again," he said, "but where in hell did Stanfield get that information about the Iranians on the cruise ship? Is there any truth to what that son of a bitch said?"

"I put Anna on it when I went to the Sit Room. We got confirmation that two police officers were sent to the cruise-ship dock on the day the *Regal* left Boston. It was a very small incident, and the Boston PD records don't show anything except the dispatcher's report on sending the officers.

"The report only says they were responding to a quote request unquote, and that quote the suspects were handed over to federal officials unquote. No names, no titles. Anna asked Patterson to order the FBI to talk to the Boston PD, and J. B. jumped at the chance to get into the picture The FBI is still pushing, but—"

"But getting nowhere. Yeah. Heard that before."

"Stanfield was deliberately vague," Falcone continued. "He said that an 'agent of the Department of Homeland Security' ordered the men off the *Regal*. You know how big DHS is. An added complication is that Penny and her staff are all in Savannah. So we're dealing at the moment with the second team."

"Sometimes, Sean, I wonder how we get to know anything."

"Yes, sir. Well, the fact is that an order like the one that Stanfield mentioned could have come from Customs and Border Protection, the Transportation Security Administration, U.S. Immigration and Customs Enforcement, better known as ICE. My bet is on ICE. So, my last report from Anna was she was focusing there."

"Okay, so maybe we get some piece of DHS paper. Then what?"

"We can legitimately send the FBI up to the Hill and ask Stanfield where he got his information. But—"

"Forget it, Sean. Stanfield would yelp that I'm siccing the Gestapo on him. But I do want to know how the hell he got that *Regal* manifest and the information on the Iranian passengers."

"I'll try, sir. I'm supposed to get you answers. And all I seem to get you are questions."

"Damn it, Sean. You're getting me what I want. One hundred percent," Oxley said, adding with a quick smile, "And now I want more."

"What's that, sir?"

"Set up an ExComm videoconference. There isn't time to assemble everyone in the Sit Room."

"When do you want it?"

"As fast as you can put it together. I've got to talk to

them all about Stanfield's claims. Get Hawk and Anna to help round up the usual suspects."

"Yes, sir. We should be able to have it set up in a half hour. Okay?"

"Fine, Sean, fine," Oxley said, sounding, to Falcone's ear, surprisingly detached. "I want you and Ray here with me. Let me know when you've got the rest of them in front of screens."

White House communications wizards, who kept track of the whereabouts of the ExComm members, easily tracked them down and made the technical arrangements that Oxley would credit to Falcone. Twenty-five minutes after he asked for a videoconference, the President had one.

Oxley's face appeared on the scattered screens as he said, "Good evening. It's been a long day, and I don't want to deprive you of any more rest. But I felt that it was imperative that you all know the situation in the wake of Senator Stanfield's speech tonight in the Senate.

"First, let me say that the evidence produced to date that Iran was responsible is circumstantial at best. It is tantamount to the allegation that Saddam Hussein had acquired yellow cake from Niger and was using it to make nuclear bombs. We have no authentication of Senator Stanfield's accusations.

"Yes, Iran hates America and wants to destroy us and Israel. But hope is not capability. The intelligence that we have to date is that Iran is years away from having the ability to construct a functional nuclear weapon. Sean, do you have something to add to this?"

Falcone's haggard face appeared. To the left was a

partial view of the President's face. Farther to the right, unseen at the moment, was Ray Quinlan's face.

"Yes, Mr. President," Falcone said. "I was advised by an intelligence source that the Israeli prime minister was to convey to you during his visit that Mossad had discovered some very disturbing information, namely that—"

The face of Sam Stone appeared. "Information that you didn't think to share with—"

Falcone's face appeared again. He ignored Stone and continued, "Namely that Iran's bomb-making ability is progressing ahead of our predicted timetable. I chose not to share the information with anyone because I wasn't satisfied the information was credible."

"And when was it that you became an intelligence expert?" Stone cut in.

"Enough, Sam," Oxley snapped. "Let Sean finish."

"Thank you, Mr. President," Falcone said. "The claim was that the previous Mossad assessment about Iran's nuclear program was no longer valid, namely that Stuxnet and the other efforts to sabotage Iran's centrifuges were successful. It seems that China, North Korea, or Pakistan—the Israelis don't know which—has covertly provided Iran with new technologies that allowed them to accelerate their program. We have no evidence to validate this claim."

"But why would you assume Mossad was wrong?" Ray Quinlan asked, jutting his face in, his tone angry. "They were the ones who disclosed the covert programs in the first place. They'd have no reason to feed us false information."

"One reason," Falcone said, "might be that the Israeli political cohesion continues to deteriorate and Prime Minister Weisman believes that we are never going to attack

Iran. So he's decided that Israel has the opportunity to strike a major blow now, while Iran is in our crosshairs.

"You know your history, Ray. This could be like 1956, when we were having a presidential election campaign and Israel hooked up with France and the UK to grab the Suez Canal while we were distracted.

"So now we have the same campaign-and-crisis perfect storm. And my source said the prime minister was going to ask our help in providing safe passage for Israeli pilots who are prepared to carry out a strike. If that—"

"To get back to Senator Stanfield," President Oxley interrupted to reclaim control of the meeting, "as you all know, he declared that he has documentary evidence to back up his account about two Iranians planting a nuclear device on the *Regal* cruise ship."

"Jesus," Quinlan murmured, "what a major fuckup." Quinlan could be heard but not seen. The President's face remained on screen until, sensing that Falcone wanted to speak, Oxley shifted, and Falcone was seen saying, "There is no evidence that the two suspects now in custody were acting on behalf of the Iranian government."

"Just a couple of rogues out for a cruise with a bomb in their Tumi luggage?" Quinlan sneered on-screen. "Come on!"

"It's possible," Falcone responded, "that they were on a scouting or spying mission, gathering intelligence on the weakness in our security system and—"

"But why the bomb?" Quinlan persisted. "Why the bomb?"

"We don't know if they were the ones who placed the bomb," Falcone responded. "We don't know if—"

Oxley looked irritated when his face appeared. He cut off Falcone. "Let's assume that they *did* place the bomb and did so under direction of the Iranian government. The question is, What to do?"

Oxley, who had a remarkable ability to control his voice, sounded eerily calm.

"I called this teleconference," he said, "primarily to tell you that congressional leaders have responded to the rage precipitated by Stanfield's speech by agreeing to hold a joint session of Congress. They've invited me to address the members and the American people on what action I plan to take. The Speaker has alerted me that he has polled the members in the House, and they expect me to ask for a declaration of war. Apparently, it's the same feeling in the Senate."

"You don't have to accept the invitation, Mr. President," Attorney General Williams said, her face glowering on screen. "You can address the nation from the Oval Office. It's more dignified. You won't have to deal with a hostile audience. You can—"

"Sorry to interrupt, Roberta, and I appreciate your concern. But the Speaker also said that Congress is prepared to pass a declaration of war pursuant to Article One, Section Eight of the Constitution."

"That's absurd!" Williams exclaimed. "It's outrageous. The United States has declared war only five times in our history and always at the request of the president. Section Eight was intended to prevent our commander-in-chief from taking the nation to war without the consent of the American people. It was not a grant of power to Congress to *force* the commander-in-chief to take us to war. I repeat, it's absurd, unprecedented. They're a bunch of Visigoths!"

"I agree, Roberta. It's unprecedented. But the Visigoths, as you call them, insist that their power is exclusive and that the language in the Constitution is absolute."

"And they can quote Scripture as well if they want to," she said, her rage unchecked. "It doesn't mean they have virtue. They are choosing to ignore the War Powers Act of 1973. That says the president can only send combat troops into battle for sixty days without either a declaration of war by Congress or a congressional mandate. But there is nothing in the act that says what Congress can do if the President refuses to comply with the act."

"Roberta, I can assemble every constitutional scholar in the country to debate the issue. That won't help. This is not a legal issue anymore. It's political. I can refuse to attend the joint session. I can refuse to call for a declaration of war. Congress could pass one without me, and I can refuse to sign or execute.

"Congress could then cite my refusal to take up the shield and sword to defend the nation as an abdication of my responsibility as commander-in-chief. That guarantees a vote to impeach me and remove me from office. We can battle it out in the Supreme Court, but in reality the battle would be long over."

"Yeah," Quinlan said, his face twisted in rage and disgust, "Stanfield blows the bugle, holds up the flag, and gives a rebel yell: 'Follow me.' "

"Right into the jaws of hell," Falcone added.

"Maybe the election is thrown to the court. But he wins in November and we pack our bags," Quinlan said, as the screen shifted from one face to the other.

"I'm afraid that Ray is right," Oxley said, turning to Sean. "At least on the political reality. I'm not saying what I'll decide to do. But I wanted everyone to understand where things stand at the moment. There's much more that we have to do, and not much time. So, let's get back to work. And thank you all."

Oxley pointed his remote control at the large plasma screen before him and clicked it off.

Quinlan walked out of the Oval Office without a word. Falcone moved more slowly, standing up as if he were in a contest with gravity.

"Remember what happened to your predecessor, Sean," Oxley said, with obvious concern. "I don't want you dying on the job. Get at least a couple of hours' sleep. That's an order."

"Yes, sir," Falcone said. He felt his body resisting his orders to stand and walk toward the door.

50

Precisely one hour after he had last talked to Liz Dalton, Lanier opened the sliding door of the laboratory. Before he could speak, Dalton came to the door and said, "We've found a big ambiguity, Rube. Very big," Dalton said. "I was just about to go find you."

She shut down the mass spectrometer she had been using, stood, and touched Malcomson on the shoulder. "Fred, I'm checking out for a few minutes. Hold the fort."

Malcomson nodded without taking his eyes off a computer monitor filled with fluctuating horizontal lines.

"We have to talk, Rube," she said, motioning him toward a door leading to a fire escape.

Lanier followed Dalton and closed the door behind him. Standing on the gridded metal platform, she stared for a moment into the night. The darkened fort looked to her like a village gone to bed. She turned to Lanier and said softly, "So far, I have not put one word of this into a database. I haven't even spoken to Fred about it. I'll give you a verbal report, and you can do what you judge best about it."

After talking with Dalton, Lanier left the barracks, got into an Army staff car assigned to him, and sped through the darkness toward Hunter Airfield. From his cell phone he put in a call to Falcone's direct-call line.

Falcone had switched his cell phone over to the direct line before flopping on a cot that Mae had ordered for an anteroom to his office. She had also installed a microwave, a coffeemaker, and a portable refrigerator stocked with small containers of yogurt and large containers of orange juice. On a table next to the cot, she had laid out an array of bottles containing various vitamins.

He picked up the cell phone from the table and managed to say, "Falcone."

"Rube here. I've got a report. I'll be at Andrews in about forty-five minutes."

"You can send it on the intel computer net," Falcone said, amazed he was able to utter a complete sentence.

"I know. But no thanks. I need to make it verbally. Face-to-face."

"I looked you up," Falcone said, his voice scratchy and irritated. "One of your admirers calls you an eccentric pain in the ass."

"Correct."

"You can't wait until daylight?"

"This is urgent. As urgent as anything I've ever known."

"Okay. Do it your way. There'll be a White House vehicle at Andrews to pick you up."

"Yes. And you'll be in it."

"Come on, Lanier. Stop living up to your reputation."

"I'm not kidding. I'm about to get into the aircraft. This is serious. We have to talk. I am saying this in terms of national security. I am not playing a game. I assure you."

Falcone called Andrews operations and said that an F-16B Falcon with White House priority was in the air from Hunter. He ordered a White House SUV and said he wanted a fast trip to Andrews.

"At two A.M., it's bound to be fast," the motor pool manager said.

Falcone stumbled out of the office, out to the cold night, and into the warmth of the SUV. He instantly fell asleep.

Falcone was sitting in an easy chair at the VIP lounge in Andrews, dozing off with a yellow pad on his lap, when Lanier walked in.

Falcone had seen Lanier's head-and-shoulders photo in his DOE personnel file, but he would know Lanier just from his gait—somehow a mix of strutting and slouching that sent the message that he was a hard man to deal with.

They shook hands and Falcone motioned Lanier to a chair across from him and asked, "What have you got?"

"It's one of ours."

"What?"

"The signature. The composition of the radioactive materials. One of our weapons. Late fifties. Absolutely."

"Jesus Christ! Who got it? Where did they get it?" Falcone asked, suddenly fully awake.

"I don't know 'who' and I don't know 'where.' All I know is what I said: It's one of ours."

"Who else knows?"

"Just two: Liz Dalton and I, with a possible three—a

scientist named Malcomson, who is in the deployable lab with her at Stewart."

"Any chance—any possible chance—that this . . . this information is wrong? I mean, 'deployable lab' and a quick assessment. No chance of a hasty call?"

"Not a chance in the world, Sean. Liz is the best we've got. If she said, 'Pakistan' or 'China,' maybe there would be a doubt because this is not a perfect science. But the analysis is written on the mass spectrograph like it's carved in stone: One of ours."

"What now?" Falcone asked.

"I was about to ask the same thing," Lanier said. He stood. "This is where NEST ends. Liz will write a tech report. Then it's all intel and FBI."

"Keep that report tight," Falcone said.

"There are regulations. I must brief Dr. Graham."

"Until you hear from me, don't brief anyone. That is a presidential order. I'm going from here directly to the President. I will recommend to him the people to be briefed. They will not yet include Dr. Graham. This information cannot be disclosed right now. Consider yourself and your two people to be absolutely silenced. The President alone will decide how to handle the information."

"Okay. But there's something else."

"My God! What now?"

"A coincidence. And I don't like coincidences. I don't trust them."

"Neither do I"

"In 1958, a hydrogen bomb was dropped near the mouth of the Savannah River."

"A bomb in the river? What the hell are you talking about?"

"Right at the beginning, I wondered, *Why Savannah?*"

Lanier said. "If you're going to knock out an American port, why not New York? Newark? Baltimore? Long Beach? Even Charleston? Back in my mind, somewhere, I had known about that 1958 bomb. So did Liz. We didn't give it credibility for this explosion. But her analysis looked like—not exactly, but *like*—the radioactivity that would have been produced by the explosion of that bomb."

"*Like*. I would think you'd have the exact signature and—"

"We *do* know what the exact signature of that kind of bomb—a Mark fifteen Mod zero, to be exact. But fissile material is unstable. In half a century, the uranium core would degrade, producing isotopes that we can deduce, but not with certainty. That type of bomb was a hybrid, a transitional design between fission—the Hiroshima atomic bomb—and thermonuclear, the hydrogen bomb. It used a uranium fission implosion to produce a secondary implosion. As a result—"

"Never mind the physics for now, Rube. How the hell did it get there?"

"The Strategic Air Command—SAC—was staging an exercise. A SAC bomber, a B-47, simulated the dropping of a bomb on a Soviet city while evading Air Force fighters simulating Soviet interceptors. The city playing the Soviet role was a place near Washington—Reston, Virginia, I think. When the pilot thought he was over the target, he pressed a button on a gadget that figured out how close he had come to hitting the target.

"Then the plane headed to its base in Florida, supposedly flying through Soviet fighters, simulated by Air Force F-86 Sabrejets. Something went wrong. A jet crashed into the B-47. In an attempt to land, the pilot of the B-47 decided to jettison the bomb and—"

"A *real* bomb?"

"Yes. One of our first hydrogen bombs. SAC demanded absolute realism."

Falcone nodded, looking stunned. "Go on," he said.

"The F-86 pilot was able to eject. He survived. The pilot of the B-47 managed to land, saving himself and his crew by jettisoning the bomb off the coast. The plane landed at Hunter—the same field I just flew from. It was a SAC base then. When news got out, the Air Force said the bomb was incapable of a nuclear explosion because it did not have its triggering mechanism.

"The Air Force searched an area around the mouth of the river for several weeks. But they didn't find anything. There was another unsuccessful search a few years ago. End of story—until now.

"It's only a matter of time before GNN or somebody digs up that story and starts speculating. There are survivors in Savannah right now who are wondering about that bomb. They haven't forgotten about it the way most of us have. It's only a matter of time—a short time— before there's talk about the bomb, *our* bomb."

"You're absolutely right, Rube. Any suggestions?"

"I'm a big guy for telling the truth."

"But what's the truth here? Some bad guys set off one of our bombs? What bad guys? How did they get it? Or did the goddamn thing finally go off on its own? If so, why? And has the Air Force been lying all these years? Questions, questions. And no answers. That's what I have to tell the President."

"There's some other news you can tell him," Lanier said. He reached into the black briefcase he had on his lap. "Preliminary report on destruction and radiation levels," he said, handing Falcone a few sheets of paper stapled together. "But there's more . . . more than a report. Sean, I don't want to go back there. No one would want to go back there. I will. I know I must. But there has never been anything like this. Sean, it's beyond reports, beyond anything that can be put on paper—or put on a TV screen.

"I read about someone in Hiroshima seeing bones stacked upon bones and bodies that were half bones, half ashes. Well, there was one place, near the river, a few hundred meters probably from where it detonated. And there was nothing there. Nothing. No bones. No bodies. Nothing.

"The temperature there, for a nanosecond, was probably about 7,000 degrees Fahrenheit. At that temperature, things simply vaporize or become ashes, and the ashes blow away. There was a slight breeze when we drove up, and we could see ashes blowing in the wind. Ashes. People as ashes.

"You know those charts we've seen at briefings about the bomb? Those concentric circles, with ground zero in the middle? Well, forget about those concentric circles. The reality is that this . . . this thing I've lived with for most of my life is not neat. It flows up a river. Or it gets stopped by a little hill. Or it runs in jagged line. It's a monster, Sean. Not neat.

"But there always has to be a report, doesn't there? Well, now you have a report. The report will tell you that things are not as bad as they first seemed—and this is not just bullshit to relieve the President.

"Let me give you a few fast facts and suppositions. Because this happened at night, most people were indoors. Kids in bed. Mom and Pop watching TV. There's a blinding flash as something explodes. We believe it went off just above the ocean surface. We aren't sure about that, but it's a good bet.

"There is an electromagnetic pulse, a surge of hellish heat. Then an enormous wave and a terrific wind rush up the river, crushing buildings, sinking ships—doing the kind of damage and killing associated with tsunamis or earthquakes.

"Radioactive particles are borne by the water and wind. The particles vary—and so do their effects. Just about all of our real and theoretical studies have been based on air bursts, some at high levels, some lower. We have to extrapolate—well, guess—about this kind of explosion. About the only data we have is from a nuclear weapon detonated during tests of effects against ships, back in the forties.

"On the basis of that data, along with our aerial photos, on-the-ground survey, and other NNSA analyses, we estimate that immediate deaths—due to drowning and being crushed to death, mostly—to be somewhere between two thousand and three thousand, with injuries running as high as thirty thousand.

"As for radiation deaths, we believe that there were few, if any, deaths due to acute radiation syndrome. Most survivors were inside, and even those who were outside are not going to drop dead.

"But we simply do not know what the long-term effects of this disaster will be. We can only watch and wait, hoping that we don't see increases in thyroid cancer or leukemia, as happened after the reactor explosion in Chernobyl and as we expect in Japan. The last estimate I've seen is that the ultimate long-term death toll for Chernobyl will be about four thousand premature deaths caused by radiation-induced cancer."

Lanier sounded like a scientist used to lecturing nonscientists. Now, he paused, and Falcone half-expected him to say, "Any questions?"

But instead, he simply said, "We live in a fucked-up world, Sean, a very fucked-up world."

51

As Lanier was flying back to Georgia, Falcone was in the Oval Office briefing President Oxley about Lanier's discovery. Oxley listened impassively, never asking a question or showing a response, even when Falcone told of the jettisoned bomb. Falcone ended the briefing by handing Oxley the NEST preliminary report in a blue folder bearing the presidential seal.

Oxley read slowly. The only sounds in the Oval Office were his sighs as he turned the pages. After reading the last page and closing the folder, he looked across his desk at Falcone and said, "What can I say? What can anyone say? Except 'why . . . why?' " His jaw tightened and his face turned grim. "And 'who?' Who in the name of God did this?"

"I have no answers, Mr. President."

"That's what I'm supposed to have, Sean. Answers." Oxley said after a pause, "And I don't have any. Not a single goddamn answer."

"Well, sir, this report contradicts Stanfield's claim about the bomb being carried on the *Regal*. If the explosion was one of ours . . . a bomb about twelve feet long and weighing seven thousand six hundred pounds—those are Lanier's figures—then it wasn't a matter of a suitcase bomb.

Whatever they carried aboard—*if* they carried anything aboard—it could not be a Mark fifteen Mod zero."

Oxley nodded, as if there were no words left.

"The report," Falcone said. "Should I—"

"The report," Oxley said softly, picking up the folder. "Yes, the estimates of the dead, the dead without names or ages or faces. The dead. We've got to find out who did this, Sean. Who did this. . . ."

He placed the folder on the desk, moving it carefully so that it lined up inside some invisible desktop grid. "Who knows about this, Sean?" Oxley asked.

"Lanier and two lab technicians," Falcone said. "Lanier agreed to keep it tightly held. Distribution is up to you."

"Good. I'm calling in Ray and Steve and Stephanie. I want to get Steve working on a statement. And I'll ask Stephanie for advice on getting this out. I'll tell them about the good news on radiation. And figure how to spread the good news. Yes. And I'll tell them about the estimates of the dead. I'll tell them all that."

Oxley was talking at an unusually slow pace. Falcone sensed that the President was a man coming out of shock, a man who was struggling to comprehend the incomprehensible.

Falcone spoke into the silence: "My advice, Mr. President, is to publish the entire report—it's only fifteen pages long. The *Times,* maybe the *Post,* will publish it and you can put it on the White House Web site. If you keep anything out, people will wonder what is being hidden. When you announce it—"

"I'm not making any announcement, Sean," Oxley said after a pause. His voice was again firm and cool. He held up the blue folder and waved it like a banner. "Sean, this has got to be absolutely secret."

Oxley put down the folder, stood, and walked around the desk. Falcone stood, knowing that the President had begun his polite ritual for bidding Falcone goodbye. Their meeting was over, and Falcone realized that no matter what the President did next, he would do it on no one's advice but his own.

Oxley draped an arm across Falcone's shoulder and said, "You go find the bastards who did this, Sean. And I'll start doing what I have to do."

Oxley returned to his chair as Falcone moved toward a door.

"Hold on, Sean," Oxley ordered, still in that firm, cool voice. "You deserve to know how I am going to handle this."

Falcone turned and listened. Oxley picked up the folder and said, "Admiral Mason, as our man on the scene, announces the NEST estimate of casualties and the low radiation readings—bad news but good news, too. He also announces that, because of the lack of radiation hazard, some restrictions on the media will be lifted. Stephanie will take that on: a media pool at first, then a tour of Army and FEMA facilities. Maybe a chance to meet the family of that girl—the Georgia Tech girl."

Politics rarely surprised Falcone. Nor did a politician's lightning-fast shifts of emotion. He searched for the words of his response, unable to blurt out his shock at Oxley's calculated musings after reading about death and destruction—and after getting that congressional invitation to his doom.

Falcone felt his own blunt style trumped by politics, by the realization that he was advising not only the President but also the Politician who dwelled within. He was unable to respond.

"Well, Sean, what do you think?" Oxley repeated.

"I think that Lanier's report completely knocks down Stanfield's claim that Iranians carried the bomb on board in their baggage."

"And so?"

"We can work on refuting Stanfield. We can divert the turncoats in Congress."

"That's my worry, Sean. As you would say, 'I'm on it.'"

"And the probability that it was one of ours? Shouldn't we tell—"

"Think about it, Sean," Oxley said. "If I released the full report, the way you suggested, we would have pandemonium. Panic. Accusations. *Our* weapon? *We* did it? My God! Questions and no answers. And all on top of Stanfield's rant. No, Sean. This report has got to be absolutely secret. *No* disclosure about the dropped bomb."

"But, Mr. President, surely someone . . . some cable commentator . . . will learn about the old bomb and draw conclusions that—"

"Right, conclusions. But not scientific credibility. If someone does recall the old bomb, so what? It's a coincidence. That's all."

Falcone found his voice, and he wondered, as he often did in the Oval Office, whether his words were being recorded. "A cover-up, Mr. President? Are you suggesting a cover-up?"

"No, Sean. Of course not. The White House—not me, but this grand old building—will simply have no comment."

"But, sir. When will you—the White House—reveal the report's conclusion that it's one of ours?"

"We reveal that, Sean, when you find out who set it off."

"And if I find that it was set off by accident? That there was no enemy?"

"I want an answer, Sean. That's all. Just get me the answer."

"Yes, Mr. President," Falcone said. He turned and walked toward the door, yearning as much for sleep as for getting the President the answer.

52

After two hours of sleep on the cot that Mae had set up, Falcone made coffee, picked up clean clothes that Mae had hung in a little closet in the anteroom, and went into the bathroom for a quick shower and shave. He went back to pick up a cup of coffee and a container of yogurt, which he carried to his desk. He looked at his watch. Seven fifteen. Then he looked through the windows at the outside world. Another tranquil morning out there.

Mae walked in, carrying a glass of water and a handful of vitamin capsules. "Just like the old days," Mae said. "Remember that last filibuster?"

Falcone certainly remembered that filibuster—when cots were set up all over the Senate—with which a single senator had paralyzed the entire institution. His stream of senseless talking blocked for a time the presidential nomination of a federal judge—and won the babbling senator a few political points. That filibuster had been just one of the incidents that had fueled Falcone's decision not to run for reelection.

He dutifully gulped down the vitamins and water, then picked up his cup of coffee and turned to the stack on his desk. Mae was still standing there, and he knew she was not through with him.

"You need to look at this," she said, placing a plain manila folder atop the stack on his desk

"Not now, Mae. I've got a—"

"Oh, yes. I know. Oh, my! Probably a meeting with President Oxley himself. Imagine that! But this"—she pointed to the manila folder—"is very important."

Mae Prentice had worked with him through his political career in Massachusetts and Washington, not only as what used to be called a secretary but also as his stalwart gatekeeper, the den mother of his office staff, and the Mary Poppins who soothed irate constituents or graciously aided confused constituents in need of help.

She had drawn upon her talents when she accompanied him to DLA Piper. She treated enormously wealthy clients with the same attention and sympathy that she had shown to the lowliest constituent appealing to Senator Falcone. And when Falcone went to the West Wing, she went with him. A slim and fit seventy-year-old with defiantly red hair, she still had an infallible knowledge of Falcone's needs even before he knew them. He nearly always accepted her suggestions about scheduling, and he always listened to her warnings.

"Mae, please," he said, moving the folder aside.

"Remember the Flanagans in Boston? The big cop family?"

"Mae, come on!" Falcone said, looking up. She glared down at him.

"All right," he said in a theatrically weary voice. "Yes, I remember the Flanagans. Two or three generations of cops. One of them was shot and—"

"Killed. They caught the guy who did it, and you put

he son of a bitch away for life. You were the cops' favorite
prosecutor."

"Mae. What are you getting at?"

"That cop's daughter became a cop. She's a sergeant
now, and she sent you this," Mae said, picking up the
folder and taking out a one-page e-mail and printouts of
a series of photographs.

"The e-mail was almost lost," Mae said. "On its
way to some West Wing e-mail limbo when Jack in
communications—he's such a nice boy—spotted *Boston*
and knew I'd want to see it. He forwarded it to me. The
attachments are JPEG digitized photos. I printed them
out."

Mae was a genius at cutting through red tape and defy-
ing bureaucratic systems. But even if she was a bit too
much of a gadfly, he had to give her heed. So, as Mae was
talking, Falcone obediently glanced at the e-mail. Suddenly, he understood what he was looking at. He looked
up from the page. His hand was shaking. "My God, Mae!"
he said. "This is tremendous!"

"Yes, I thought so," Mae said and left the office.

The sending address on the e-mail was private, not the
Boston PD's.

Dear Senator Falcone:

   I am Kelly Flanagan. I hope you remember me. I am a
sergeant in the Boston Police Department, but I am
writing you as a private citizen.

   My uncle, Dr. (dentist) Pat Flanagan and his wife,
Kathy, a teacher, were passengers on the cruise ship
Regal. Because they are childless, I have been like a
daughter to them. I guess that they are dead.

When Uncle Pat got one of those smartphones, he started sending me photos via the Internet. He got a kick out of doing that. He took the attached photos of my aunt Kathy. From the date and time on them, I think that they were taken just before the ship went down.

When you look at them, you will see a bright flash on the last one. I didn't think much about that when I first got the photos. I just looked at Aunt Kathy and cried a lot. When I heard the President's speech about a nuclear device, I thought about that flash. I was going to call the FBI or maybe a superior in the Boston PD. But I just heard Stanfield and he mentioned the Boston PD and the cruise ship, and I figured a lot of politics is popping up. But I thought this was really important and I wanted to send it to someone I knew I could trust.

I don't know if anything can come from these photos, but I know you will do what you think ought to be done.
Sincerely,
Kelly Flanagan

The first four photo prints were essentially the same: a smiling Kathy Flanagan on what looked like a ship's ladder. The fifth print was a flash of light. Nothing else. If it had not been the last in a series of these particular photos, it would have been discarded.

Over her right shoulder hung the crescent moon. He had a flash of memory about seeing that crescent himself. Realizing he was looking at the face of one of the dead, he was gripped by an intense feeling of horror and loss. He felt tears welling up.

He steeled himself to look closely. At the upper right corner of the image he saw what he thought was the bow of the *Regal* and faint lights beyond. He spread all five prints on his desk and saw that Pat Flanagan had moved slightly after taking each photo, changing the perspective so that the images of the bow and the lights also changed.

In an instant he was wide awake, for now there was little doubt that a nuclear bomb went off at sea and not aboard the *Regal*. And those lights in the background. Something about them . . .

He picked up the phone, "Mae. Find out how to get in touch with Kelly Flanagan."

"I have her home number, cell phone, and the Boston PD's nonemergency number."

"I'm not surprised," Falcone said.

"Let's try the cell phone first," Mae said. A moment later he was talking to Kelly Flanagan. He thanked her abundantly and told her to keep the information to herself until she heard from him again.

Falcone picked up the red phone and said, "Mr. President, I think I have an answer."

"You sound like you got some sleep, Sean. I wanted to call you about something, but I wanted to give you a chance for a nap. Come on in."

Falcone hurried down the hall and was admitted to the Oval Office by a Secret Service agent he did not recognize. To expand the Presidential Detail, agents had been brought in from several cities, where they had been working on counterfeit cases.

"Mr. President, we have a breakthrough" Falcone said exuberantly. Oxley pointed to a chair. But Falcone could not sit down without blurting out the story of Kelly Flanagan's photos and their significance

"That's very interesting, Sean. Now please sit down."

Interesting had about the same effect on Falcone's enthusiasm as the point of a pin would have on a balloon.

"I've decided," Oxley said, "to accept the invitation and address the joint session tonight. I want your response to what I see as my options."

"But, sir. Given this new information, can't you postpone the address?"

"I can't afford a postponement, Sean. I'm running out of time."

"Yes, sir," Falcone said. He knew when Oxley was beyond persuasion.

Oxley picked up a yellow pad with a mass of curved-over pages. He flipped back to the first page and then began, "The way I see it, I have four options. One, I can take no action until we know exactly who is responsible for the destruction of Savannah. Or I can do one of the following."

He turned to another page of the pad, then put the pad aside and continued, "Two, I can impose a naval blockade on Iran until it destroys all of its nuclear facilities and allows open and free elections with international monitors to ensure all demands are met.

"Three, I can launch a surgical strike, using conventional weapons, against their leadership, the IRGC and those facilities that contribute to their war-making capability.

"Four, I can unleash a nuclear attack against all known and suspect nuclear sites, decapitate the Iranian leadership, and demand a formal surrender.

"There may be some variations on each of these options but, Sean, as far as I'm concerned, those are the stark choices."

"Mr. President, it would irresponsible—from a sheer evidentiary basis—to attack Iran without knowing more," Falcone said. "The information I just brought you is an example of the kind of leads we'll be getting. My strongest instinct—and I'll bet yours, too—is to be careful about blaming Iran. If the United States goes to war on the basis of Stanfield's accusation, it will be even worse than when America went to war against Iraq over the allegation that Saddam had weapons of mass destruction! The international community would—"

"Would what, Sean? Call us lawbreakers and rush to the International Criminal Court? We have been attacked with a nuclear weapon. War has been declared against us. Thousands of Americans are dead. And more will be dying from this for years to come." He paused and added, "And there's the *Elkton*."

"But, sir, there's no evidence that Iran was responsible for that attack either. If anything, the evidence points to an Al Qaeda cell still operating in Iraq. We didn't go after Iran then, and the political consequences of attacking Iran now—"

"It's my job to ponder political consequences, Sean, not yours."

Falcone, stung by the presidential jab, did not reply.

"Assuming I take one of the options, Sean, I suppose you would prefer the blockade?"

"It sounds benign enough, compared to a strike," Falcone responded. "But it is fraught with danger. What if the Russian or Chinese vessels fail to stop and be searched? Do we fire warning shots across their bows? What if they ignore the warning? Do we sink their ships or just disable them? Would they respond in kind with their warships?"

"For God's sake, Sean, I don't need a Harvard dissertation. I know the perils of a blockade."

Falcone suddenly felt tired again. "Well, sir," he said, "you've been told that a conventional attack will not knock out their nuclear sites. So what is left is option four, the nuclear option."

"Yes, Sean. That seems to be what is left. But, I promise you, I am not committed," Oxley said, rising to signal that the colloquy had ended.

"Thank you, Mr. President," Falcone said. As he walked out he heard Oxley pick up the phone and tell his personal secretary, "Margie, call the Speaker of the House and tell him I accept his invitation and will attend the joint session."

The photos were still spread on Falcone's desk when he returned to his office. He opened the folder and reread the e-mail from Kelly Flanagan: . . . *you will do what you think ought to be done.*

53

A joint session of Congress always sends an electrifying jolt through Capitol Hill. All 535 members gather in the House of Representatives chamber and sit in a large semicircle in large brown leather chairs. The best known joint session is the annual occasion for the president's State of the Union address, usually, both a somber and celebratory event. Members respond to the president's declarations with cheers or, sometimes, wih a few jeers. Journalists hang precipitously over the balcony to watch the proceedings below, trying to catch every reaction to the president's words, looking for affirmation or dissent in the expressions on their faces.

Ordinarily, members of the president's cabinet, the Supreme Court justices, the Joint Chiefs of Staff, and members of the Diplomatic Corps join the lawmakers. It is one of the few moments during the year when the three branches of a divided government sit as one to hear the president of the United States speak to America in a kind of national fireside chat.

But tonight would be different.

This joint session was being convened at the behest of a presidential candidate, not the President. The leaders of the House and Senate had abandoned all allegiance to their political affiliations and agreed to the extraordinary request. The purpose was to hear President Oxley tell them what action he intended to take in the wake of the attack on America. They wanted action, and if he was not prepared to give them action, Congress was prepared to take it.

During the previous three years there had been many hearings in both houses about the threat that Iran posed to the Middle East and to America's interests there. But there had been no debate or even any serious consideration about going to war against Iran. For Congress, there had not been any classified briefings on what waging war would involve. And yet many members were prepared to declare war for the first time since Japan attacked America at Pearl Harbor in 1941.

This would also be an historic event. Among members and their staffs, among journalists and pundits, their only questions were: Will the President appear? And will the President agree to be bound by what Congress decides?

. . .

"Margie, cut the phone calls," Oxley ordered. "I've talked to all the leaders I need to for today."

"But, Mr. President, the Chinese and Russian presidents have called three times."

"They can wait. I need to be alone."

Being alone is different than being lonely. But Oxley felt as if he were the only man still alive in the nightmare world that had become his to wander.

He had read in detail how harrowing the Cuban Missile Crisis has been for President Kennedy, how close the United States had come to nuclear war with the Soviets. To outsiders, it was a simple morality tale: Handsome young prince stares down ugly bear and sends him packing back to Siberia.

Only it was not that simple. A misplayed word or step and the dogs of war could have been unleashed. Few could have calculated the outcome. But it would have been bad. Horrible.

Had Kennedy blinked or painted Nikita Khrushchev into a corner, one that didn't allow him a face-saving exit, much of the world could still be a heap of radioactive waste.

Now, radioactive waste had saturated Savannah and its people. And Oxley had to do something about it. But what? What was the right thing to do?

Oxley's penchant for pursuing the facts and acting according to the dictates of the law had not been playing well with the American people. The arguments he had heard from Sean continued to ricochet inside his mind. But he had had a meeting with Ray Quinlan and gone over the four options with him. And his words now were echoing in Oxley's mind: *"Evidence be damned.*

This is no time to be a lawyer. The American people need a warrior."

What if we were wrong and Iran had nothing to do with bombing Savannah? How could he—the leader of the free world—hold his head high in the howling winds of hate that would blow through an America turned lawless?

Love it or leave it. That was the simple chant that danced across his mind. Teasing him. Haunting him. So simple. But it was also so much more complicated. *"To love one's country, one's country had to be lovely."* Isn't that what a wise man had once said? Would it be lovely for America to strike out blindly against its known enemies? How lovely would it be for millions of people to die?

He had to choose. He could not refuse to attend the joint session and allow Congress to declare war. The Constitution gave that power to Congress. Yes, but it was the commander-in-chief who was to urge the Congress to exercise this power. Congress could not lead the nation into war. It could only support its commander's war cry and express its collective support to follow him into battle. That was clearly what the Constitution said. He could not yield this power to Congress. The Founding Fathers never contemplated having 535 commanders-in-chief.

Whatever happened tonight, he could ignore the action of Congress and try to appeal to the Supreme Court to validate his claim that only the president could declare war. But an appeal to the Supreme Court—being a lawyer instead of a warrior—would force a constitutional crisis. On a less lofty level, it would also probably give the election to Stanfield, who would hammer out a theme of vengeance against Oxley's plea for restraint.

Oxley stared out the tall windows facing the wide lawn that even in October still lay like an emerald carpet behind the Oval Office. His thoughts were flooded with doubt. But a leader was not permitted to doubt. He had to be strong, resolute, convinced that his option, his exercise of might, was right. . . .

54

Falcone was sitting at his desk, staring at the photos and wondering what to do. He looked at his watch: 9:32. In less than eleven hours, President Oxley would be addressing a joint session and America would be at war—or on the verge of war.

Out of the corner of his left eye, he saw a fluttering on the television screen. A banner reading IRAN AND THE SAVANNAH BOMB was running along the bottom of the screen while a pretty face was saying: "GNN correspondent Ned Winslow has obtained a document showing that the two Iranians removed from the doomed cruise ship *Regal* were members of the IRGC. Tonight at six Eastern Standard Time."

"Jesus!" Falcone exclaimed. Stanfield must have had that document and was timing the leaking of it as a prelude to President Oxley's speech before Congress. Falcone picked up a phone and said, "Mae. Get me J. B. Patterson."

Three minutes later Patterson was on the phone. Falcone pictured J. B. in his office. He always seemed to be in pain, the pain of striving, his long face strained and unsmiling. Yet, he looked like a poster image of an FBI agent: dark suit, white shirt, blue or crimson tie, tightly knotted.

"Sean, what can I do for you?" he said cheerily.

"It's about the Iranians taken off the *Regal*."

"We're making progress."

"What have you got? And what does Ned Winslow have?"

"Winslow? Right. DHS leak. We've got two agents at GNN's Washington office right now, determining details about the document."

"What is the document, J. B.?" Falcone asked, knowing that a conversation with J. B. was Q&A. He rarely, if ever, voluntarily proffered information. Agents were trained to testify in court, and the training included warnings to limit your answer to the exact question that was asked.

"A DHS report on the two subjects," Patterson said.

"Well, interesting, J. B. Does the document support or refute Stanfield?"

Patterson paused a few seconds to prepare a response. "I can't answer that authoritatively, Sean. Perhaps you should see it. I will send you an agent with a certified copy of the document."

"Thank you, J. B. One more thing. I need to talk to a digital photography specialist. Somebody who can get as much out of a digital image as possible."

"I'll call the lab personally, get the director, find the best man, and call you back," Patterson said, audibly glad to finally say something positive.

He called fifteen minutes later. "Found the man, Sean. Turned out I had signed a citation for him six months ago. Well, I sign a lot of citations for people in the lab. He wrote our handbook on the use of digital image processing in the criminal justice system."

"I assume he'd be at the FBI Lab in Quantico."

"That is correct."

"I'll be sending a White House helicopter for him in ten minutes. What's his name?"

"That urgent? Perhaps I—"

"Yes, urgent. Name?"

"Knox. Tony Knox."

"Get word to him, J. B., that he's wanted for a sensitive White House assignment. Then have him call me on a secure line so I can sketch what I want done. And he can figure what he needs to take with him."

"Are you talking about evidence, Savannah evidence?" Patterson said. "I am obliged to ask."

"Perhaps."

"Well, the proper way to handle—"

"The chain of evidence will be maintained, J. B. I was a prosecutor once. And handing it off to Knox makes it solidly FBI."

"Point taken, Sean."

Falcone arranged for the helicopter to fly to the FBI complex on a large swath of ground at a Marine Corps base in Quantico, Virginia, about thirty-five miles south of Washington. Knox called him ten minutes later and began a rapid flow of questions.

"You have many questions, Mr. Knox," Falcone interrupted. "And I have only the situation to present to you," Falcone said. "We have some printouts of images that were attached to an e-mail. They were taken by a smartphone that was lost in the . . . explosion in Savannah. They may contain very important information. This is an extremely sensitive matter, and speed is of the essence."

"Understood," Knox said crisply. "Please forward the e-mail to me so that—"

"Sorry, Tony. I have to hold the e-mail and attachments

tighter than a gnat's ass. Whatever work you do will be done in the White House, or, more accurately, in the adjacent Executive Office Building. You'll have access to our photography and communications facilities. But bring what you need with you. When you disembark the helicopter, you will be escorted to my office. If I am not here, you will deal with my deputy, Anna Dabrowski. All understood?"

"All understood," Knox said. He sounded youthful and eager.

Falcone spent the next ten minutes meditating how to arrange a leak. *Music Man* popped into his mind, and then *Midas,* in one of those word associations that seem inexplicable. Then he called Rachel's cell phone.

"This is Sean," he said. "I must see you. Urgent."

"Here at the Hay-Adams?"

"Not today, regretfully," Falcone said. "So glad to reach you. Providential. See you in Lafayette Park. Right in your backyard. There's a bench by the fountain."

"I'll be there in ten minutes," Rachel said. She only needed three of the minutes to check the battery on her wireless mini-recorder, slip it into a side pocket of her slacks, open her blouse, attach the lavalier microphone to her bra, and button up. She donned a black Burberry funnel-necked belted coat and put on black ankle-high boots.

"Mae, I'm stepping out," Falcone said over his shoulder as he rushed out, his black raincoat on his arm. "Be back in half an hour or so. Please track down Phil Dake and tell him to stand by for a call from me. It's going to be another long day."

October can bring spring days to Washington, and this was one of them. He felt he was escaping from prison when he passed through a guard station on Pennsylvania Avenue and crossed the broad pedestrian-only walkway to Lafayette Park. Along the sidewalk fronting the park was a clutter of cardboard and wooden signs and a stout, bewigged woman who for the last four years had stood a daily vigil protesting nuclear weapons. Falcone gave her a thumbs-up as he hurried into the park.

"Beautiful woman, beautiful day," Falcone said when, scaring off a squirrel, he reached the bench where Rachel sat. Rachel looked up and smiled warmly. "It is so good to be seeing you again," she said.

"Some day, if this is ever over, I hope we can have that drink. But—"

"Yes. Always 'but,' always duty," she said. "I assume it's about Savannah."

As Falcone sat down next to her, he recognized a Secret Service agent about to sit down on a bench about twenty feet away and say something to his right wrist.

"There's not much time, Rachel. I'm going to talk fast and carelessly. If you or an invisible colleague has a recorder going, so be it. I'm beyond caring."

"Very melodramatic. And is that man talking to his wrist recording us?"

"He's a bodyguard I didn't ask for."

Rachel nodded, "And the urgency?"

Falcone told her about the draft pages Phil Dake had given him and his belief that Dake had received the material about The Brethren from the Mossad.

"Interesting," Rachel said. "You deduced the Mossad taps and bugs? Dake did not tell you?"

"He did not give me anything more than I have told you. Dake never reveals his sources."

"I remember Dake," Rachel said. "An interesting man who knows many secrets, doesn't he? I think I would like to see him."

"Perhaps you will. I would like to make a proposition."

Rachel smiled and said, "That is a phrase I have heard many times. What do you propose?"

"Senator Stanfield has set in motion a situation that almost certainly will result in the United States attacking Iran with nuclear bombs. It could set off the Armageddon that Israel rightfully fears."

Rachel nodded, waiting for him to go on.

"I believe that you and Dake and I can stop Armageddon," Falcone said. "Let me first give you my motivation," he continued, speaking rapidly. "By getting information to the right people at the right time, we can prevent the war. And—"

"And you will leave it to Israel to stop Iran's nuclear bomb."

"I suppose that is the logical result, from your viewpoint. But I believe that the reality is that by not attacking Iran now, we—our country, your country—allow something like a normal process to take place. Stop Iran's bomb-making, yes. But not with bombs. The world does not deserve a nuclear war."

"Please, Sean," she said. "I have always trusted you, and I trust you now. What is the 'normal process' you talk about?"

"I believe, not spiritually but practically, that important parts of the world are moving toward a normal, intuitive faith in reason. The Middle East is changing before our eyes."

Rachel did not answer for more than a minute. Then, suddenly, she stood and said, "I can't talk anymore, Sean. I can't even listen. I must leave."

Surprised, Falcone started to rise and said, "But I believed, hoped to—"

"Goodbye," Rachel said. She waited a moment, then threw open her coat and unbuttoned her blouse.

The moves startled Falcone, who thought she had gone crazy. Rachel laughed, held up the lavalier microphone, and rebuttoned the blouse.

"All right," she said. "Let's talk." She sat down, closer to Falcone.

"Attractive accessory, Rachel," Falcone said, smiling back. "Here's what I want: names, times, places. What I want to do is produce, in the next few hours, evidence for the President that will save him—and make it unnecessary to attack Iran."

"So what you want me to do is give you intelligence information I am not empowered to give you," Rachel said.

"Yes, for the good of your country and mine."

"Sean, your idealism was always beyond belief. Why not let Oxley go through the motions of blaming Iran? It will not necessarily bring war. Besides, from what I know of the surveillance, you don't get a connection between The Brethren and the bomb."

"I'm counting on Dake and luck. Let him at those transcripts, those surveillance reports. License numbers. Comings and goings to Parker's house. I'm hoping to get enough to stall the process.

"I want to at least put enough doubt in the President's head to make it impossible for him to link Iran to the Savannah bomb. What we know about the bomb already shoots down Stanfield's story about the bomb being on the cruise ship. I'm going to tell you what is known only to me, the President, and a couple nuclear scientists."

After hearing Falcone tell about the Savannah River bomb and the Flanagan photos, Rachel said, "Amazing. Your own bomb. But Iran is still not exonerated. All you know is that the bomb was not on that cruise ship, as Stanfield claimed. Iranian operatives could have somehow found the bomb and set it off."

"Correct. But I have seen two documents that make me think you can help lead me to the people who did do it."

"The Dake document, yes," she said. "And?"

"And a cable that 'Velvet' sent, saying she had warned Midas about The Brethren."

She did not show surprise. "Well, interesting. We must change that code. But I can't see how my reference to Midas—"

"Rachel, who is Midas?"

She did not answer for nearly a minute. Her gaze was toward the White House, which shimmered through the arching waters of the fountain.

"It is a beautiful, solid-looking building," she said. Then, as if released from a spell, she turned to Falcone and said, "I cannot give up Midas, for reasons that are not pertinent to our talk. But the names, the surveillance on members of The Brethren, they are obtainable."

"On your authority?"

"Yes. I need only go to the embassy and take them to a secure room. We are a surprisingly loose bureaucracy at a certain level. But let us talk some more," she said, grasping his right hand. "I understand your frustration, your rage, all the emotions that I see in your eyes. Go over this for me."

"Thank you, Rachel," Falcone said, looking down at their clasped hands. "Here is what I know. Or think I know. Israel has been keeping General Parker under surveillance because Israel believes that The Brethren's yearning for Armageddon is ultimately not in Israel's interest."

"That is true," Rachel said, nodding. "One of our more emotional—and influential—officials believes that The Brethren's agenda threatens Israel. He also believes that pro-Israel does not mean pro-Jews. He does not trust fundamentalists. A substantial investment in surveillance was ordered. The principal target was the easiest, General Parker. Bugging, tapping, fairly rigorous surveillance."

"And you picked up names. And when someone found out Dake was looking at The Brethren as the subject of a book, the Mossad decided to feed him some information."

"Yes. Dake was not keeping his work secret. He couldn't. He had to talk to people, tell them what he was doing. I'm supposed to be one of the Mossad's leading experts on America. I knew enough about Dake to realize that he would be a good outlet for beginning a general erosion of The Brethren's power—and their idea of hastening Armageddon."

"So you set up the passing of some information to Dake?" Falcone asked.

Rachel nodded and mischievously waved at the Secret Service agent, who looked flustered and went back to pretending to read the *Washington Post*.

"So, don't you see the sense in revealing more now?" Sean said. "Giving him transcripts, surveillance reports?

Obviously no harm would be done to Israel. It may even be good for Israel. Eroding Brethren power, as you say."

"Very slick, Sean, making me an accessory. But it's not that simple. I'm not just going to hand you the names so you can pass them off to Dake."

"I'm not proposing that, Rachel. I want you to meet with Dake and give him the names so that he doesn't feel like he is being used."

"He is not a fool, Sean. And neither am I. He'll know he's a messenger in some kind of Israel-U.S. game."

"But he won't care, Rachel. He's a journalist. He's not worrying about geopolitical strategy. He just wants material that no one else has, material that he will put in a *Post* story and then in a book. That's the game, Rachel."

She stood, and Falcone, doing the same, said, "You'll be hearing from Dake. And things, I hope, will move fast." He told her about Oxley's decision to go to Congress.

"Thanks for that little bit of news," Rachel said. "It'll be in a Velvet cable in a few minutes." *And the Savannah River bomb,* Falcone thought.

She reached out to shake his hand, then changed her mind, embraced him, and kissed him full on the lips. "Just to give your bodyguard something to wonder about," she said, pulling back.

"Goodbye," she said and turned down the walk that cut through the park, toward the Hay-Adams. Each of them wondered when they might meet again.

55

Back in his office, Falcone had a brief handshake meeting with Tony Knox, whom Anna took off to the White House photography suite in the nearby Executive Office Building. The agent sent by J. B. had come and gone, and an envelope from the FBI was on his desk. Before opening it, he called Dake, who answered on the first ring.

"Thanks for calling back," Dake said. "I just wanted—"

"Phil. Something has come up. How soon can I see you where? I suggest where we met and had scrambled eggs."

"Fifteen minutes."

"Make it half an hour."

He opened the FBI envelope. The cover note—"Here it is. Will keep you informed"—bore the signature of J. B. Patterson, director of the FBI. Patterson always formally signed any sensitive document that circulated outside the Bureau. There was an inherent formality about the FBI and its documents, unlike the CIA, whose unsigned analyses would sometimes have a relaxed tone, as if imparting information to an interested colleague. When he read an FBI report, he could easily imagine an FBI agent speaking clearly and convincingly from the witness stand in a federal court.

He skimmed through, ignoring the numerous bracketed references that cluttered up the story that Stanfield had so darkly imparted. Two Iranians entered the United States from Canada at Detroit, using fake Iraqi passports. They bought one-way tickets for cash, which should have alerted whoever was supposed to watch for such matters, and flew to Boston.

They boarded with legitimate tickets purchased through a Venezuela travel agency. Shortly before the *Regal* sailed, they were seen entering a "crew only" area that led to a luggage storage hold. When a crewman questioned them, they "accosted" him. He and other crewmen subdued them. The ship captain called the Boston Police, who escorted them off the ship and notified the local Homeland Security office, where an unidentified official ordered them held on charges of immigration violations and possessing fraudulant passports.

No one apparently thought to take off their stowed luggage, just as nobody had spotted the fake passports and the one-way tickets. So there was nothing more sinister than that. Stanfield had stretched a security-breakdown incident into a terrorist attack. Presumably, Ned Winslow would be doing the same on GNN just before President Oxley appeared before Congress.

The report named the Homeland Security official who ordered the men held. Falcone assumed he was a member of The Brethren and had leaked the information to Stanfield, along with the passenger manifest. The FBI was questioning the Iranians and the DHS official.

Falcone called Anna Dabrowski on her cell phone and found her still in the Executive Office Building. "How is it going with Tony Fox?"

"He seems very capable and thinks he can find something more in the images."

"Good. How long? Any idea?"

"I pressed him. He says a couple of hours. It's mostly studying the image by framing out a certain section of pixels and then—"

"Okay. Keep him working. If you have to reach me, you may have to use my cell phone."

"Oh? You will be out of the office?"

"Yes. I have something working. Will tell you later."

Falcone called in Mae rather than talk to her on the phone. "Mae," he said. "I have to meet someone privately. I'm going to try to duck my security detail and go home. You can reach me by cell phone. I should be back here in about an hour."

Mae Prentice nodded, scowling. She obviously did not approve. And she had her suspicions about what was going on. *It was so unlike Sean,* she thought.

Falcone walked out of his office and headed down a flight to the White House Mess. But instead of following the smell of coffee, he went through a door that led to the tunnel between the West Wing and the Executive Office Building. He found a stairwell and climbed to the EOB ground floor. He walked the polished floor of large black and white diamond-shaped stones to the Seventeenth Street entrance, took the stairs to the street-level security post, showed his VIP White House identification badge, and strode out to the sidewalk. Too tired to walk the few blocks to his condominium, he hailed a cab.

Dake was waiting in the lobby when Falcone's cab pulled up to the entrance. He nodded to the concierge in the lobby, entered one of the elevators, and used his key to authorize a rise to the penthouse. They did not speak until they were in Falcone's kitchen, where he began making coffee.

"Phil, glad you could come. A lot is going on."

"So I've heard," Dake said, perching on a stool. He doffed his tan topcoat on another stool. He wore black slacks, a blue-and-white checkered shirt open at the collar, and a Harris tweed jacket.

"I'm going to unload a story for you," Falcone said, turning away from the coffeemaker. "Everything I tell you, unless I say otherwise, is deep background and cannot be attributed to me. I'll answer what questions I can, but, because of the press of time—which is part of the story—I'd like to get through the story uninterrupted. You can take notes or record or both. Understood?"

Dake took an oblong notebook and black Laban pen from one pocket and a silver-colored digital recorder from another. He set the recorder on the counter. "Understood," he said.

Falcone went through it all: the tsunami error, the Coast Guard helicopter discovering what turned out to be an EMP, the realization that a nuclear device caused the disaster, Lanier's revelation about the Savannah bomb, the Flanagan digital photos refuting Stanfield's allegation blaming two Iranians, the FBI report identifying them but not connecting them to the bomb, Falcone's suspicion that a DHS official leaked the manifest and the report on the Iranians, "and the leaker was probably a member of The Brethren."

Dake listened, holding back from questioning, processing the narrative, picturing it in print, thinking he was listening to a prosecutor's opening statement. Mention of The Brethren surprised him.

Falcone poured each of them a second cup of coffee, paused, and said, "Now, you come in."

Dake looked at him puzzled, but did not speak.

Falcone resumed the story, bringing in The Brethren, the papers he called the Dake Donation—inspiring a quick Dake smile—and his conversation with Rachel Yeager.

"She agreed to give you more information than you got from one of her associates, the Confidential Source—the CS—sprinkled through the Donation. I trust her. She trusts you. She is holding out on one name, apparently a Brethren bankroller with the code name Midas. Otherwise, I think she's going to give you a lot of material. Good luck. Here's her cell-phone number. You're probably going to be meeting her in a safe room in the Israeli Embassy."

"I've been there before," Dake said, with another smile. "When you began this marvelous story, you said 'the press of time' was part of the story. Meaning?"

"The President goes before Congress at eight o'clock. I hope that when he speaks he will have the answer to who did the deed and how they did it." Falcone said. "I'm convinced, on little more than a hunch, that there is a connection between Parker, The Brethren, and the Savannah bomb. I'm hoping you find it."

"That's all?" Dake asked, smiling again.

"That's all. Good hunting."

Dake looked down at his notes, then looked up and said, "You mentioned a NEST guy named Lanier and a Boston cop named Flanagan. Can I get phone numbers on them?"

Falcone hesitated before answering, "No. They're not reachable . . . except through me."

"Okay. I'm on it," Dake said, switching off the recorder and pocketing it. He flicked back to the first page of the notebook, took a cell phone out of another pocket, and, looking at the number Falcone had given him, punched the numbers of Rachel's cell phone. "Might as well get started. Time is of the essence."

56

Dake hailed a cab outside Falcone's condo and gave the address of the Israeli Embassy, which was in northern Washington, in an area designated as an international diplomatic quarter. The cab dropped him off at the squat brick gatehouse attached to the wrought-iron fence surrounding the embassy. After he identified himself to the security officer behind a high counter, he surrendered his driver's license, smartphone, and recorder, the contents of which he had sent, by his smartphone, to a secure Internet storage area. He was given a temporary badge and directed to a bench, where he awaited his escort.

In a few minutes, a short, muscular man in a black suit, white shirt, and black tie arrived and took him through the gatehouse, across a courtyard, and into the embassy, a buff-colored structure with deeply recessed windows topped by arches. He passed through the light and airy entrance atrium to another security checkpoint. He and his silent escort then ascended a staircase to a second-floor hallway. About halfway down the hallway was Rachel Yeager.

"Good morning, Philip," she said, holding out her right hand. "Good to see you again. Both older, but, I hope, wiser." She was wearing a gray, knee-length skirt and a ruffled, wine-red silk blouse.

"The years seem to have passed you by," Dake said as they shook hands. Her grip was as strong as when, some years back, he found himself working with her and Falcone to clear the name of a murdered senator. Memories tumbled into his mind. Killer Angel. Saved Falcone's life. And the .22-caliber semiautomatic Beretta once held in that lovely warm hand. . . .

They entered a small, windowless room. On a desk in the middle of the room was a laptop computer and a wire-frame rack containing file folders in several colors. Rachel directed him to a chair in front of the computer, which was open, its screen blank. She took a green folder out of the rack and sat down in the chair next to Dake's.

"Sean asked me to move fast, and that's what I'm doing," she said. "I am aware that one of my colleagues gave you some access to our intelligence service's files on The Brethren. On this desk is far more information, and what I am giving you focuses primarily on transcripts of conversations recorded in the house when General Parker conducted meetings of a special group of Brethren. I have pulled the files that I believe mostly pertain to that special group.

"Sean, as he has probably just told you, believes that this group, known as The Five, has some connection with the Savannah bomb. There are also surveillance reports and transcripts of pertinent telephone calls.

"I will go over the files with you. As I take up a folder, I will give you a file number. You will enter the number on the laptop and the file will appear. You may copy material from the file—but not the file number—to the thumb drive inserted in the computer. If I see something that I do not want you to copy, I will say so.

"In your books, you are scrupulous about indicating sources while withholding actual names. You use such phrases as 'quote from background interview unquote' or 'quote from documents reviewed by the author unquote.'

For purposes of attribution to this material, you may say, 'quote an Israeli intelligence official unquote.' All agreed?"

"Agreed," Dake said, clenching and unclenching his hands, as if he were an athlete preparing for action.

"Good," Rachel said. "Let us begin. . . ."

Four hours later, with a fifteen-minute recess for pastrami sandwiches and coffee, Dake removed a thumb drive that had accumulated hundreds of lines of names, dates, and conversations. Rachel had limited Dake to four hours so that he would have a chance to develop some research that might serve Falcone in his race against time.

"I'd like a lot more time with these jewels, Rachel," Dake said after standing up, stretching, and pocketing the thumb drive.

"Maybe . . . someday," Rachel said. "Not many people have that cell-phone number."

The remark gave Dake some encouragement. After a hasty goodbye and an escorted exit back through the gatehouse, he found a cab waiting for him. Rachel or someone was speeding him on his way.

After giving the address for his home in McLean, he took out his cell phone, quite sure that Israeli technicians had copied its data—and were disappointed when they found nothing of much value. Well aware of cell phones' vulnerability to snoopers, he tried to avoid storing sensitive information. He was also sure that the empty recorder had disappointed the snoopers.

He called his researcher in the Book Factory and told him to drop all other projects and be ready for a new one. "The deadline's seven thirty," he said. "Yeah, Mark. That's seven thirty tonight. I'll have a list of names with some

information about them. Get out the file marked BRETH-
NOTES."

"The notes you gave to Falcone?" Mark Lassen asked.

"Right. I mentioned a guy named Norman Miller, big
contributor to Stanfield's campaign. Find whatever you
can get on him, including his private phone number. I'm
pretty sure he lives in Potomac, and I'm going to want to
talk to him."

57

Dake carefully hung his topcoat in the hall closet, passed
through the center hallway to his bedroom, walked into
his closet and carefully hung his sport coat, then retraced
his steps and briskly went up two flights of stairs to the
Book Factory. Mark Lassen met him at the open door of
the room, which took up nearly the entire third floor.

Lassen, six foot three with the carriage of a soldier,
was a retired Army intelligence officer who had lost his
left leg to an improvised explosive device early in the
Iraq War. When Dake interviewed him for the research
job, he pointed to the two-story climb as a possible problem. Lassen responded by saying, "I've got the best pros-
thetic leg that a lowest-bid DOD contractor could provide.
I'll race you to the third floor." Lassen won and, unlike
Dake, was not breathing hard. Lassen became Dake's
full-time researcher, supervising two part-timers who
were called in when research on a book reached a crucial point.

"What have you got?" Lassen asked, walking over to a

table bearing a computer with two monitors. The table was next to an oak rolltop desk.

"We're going to find out pretty soon," Dake said, sitting at an oak swivel chair in front of the desk. Dake took a key ring from his pocket, unlocked the desk, and rolled up the top.

The desk and chair had belonged to Dake's father when he was the editor of a weekly newspaper in a little North Carolina town. The desk had been modernized, a computer tower fitted into what had been the desk's deep drawers, a monitor and keyboard installed on the desktop, between two sets of pigeonholes stuffed with notepads, envelopes, and scraps of paper that constituted part of Dake's private filing system.

Lassen maintained the locked filing cabinets that lined two walls. Those paper files were slowly becoming anachronisms, for much of the research that Lassen pursued and managed was arriving in the form of computer files. Lassen's research was faultless, but Dake often relied upon his instinct, which he sometimes fancied was produced by a journalist gene carried in his DNA.

He switched on the computer, inserted the thumb drive into a port, and copied its contents onto his computer's hard drive. As the material was being copied, Lassen pointed to one of his monitors, where he had drafted a short profile of Norman Miller.

As you know, Norman Miller founded and still owns True North, a private equity firm. *Fortune* lists him as among the twenty-five wealthiest men in the country.

Miller made more than $1 billion one year and yet nearly went insane with jealousy when he read that a competitor had made $3.5 billion. His jealousy led him to take bigger risks with his investor's funds, resort to more leverage, cut more corners.

The SEC accused him of securities fraud and built a strong case against him. But he was able to buy his way out of a conviction and jail sentence by agreeing to pay a $50 million fine and not admit to any wrongdoing.

He and his partners celebrated—and appeared on the front pages of the *New York Post,* in photos showing them entertaining high-cost prostitutes while sailing the Greek Isles on a 300-foot yacht. Another article followed on Page Six: Miller's wife of seventeen years had left him . . . for another woman.

Miller's life was in a tailspin. He realized he had lost his moral compass and was in great need of a spiritual anchor. Born a Jew, he remained deeply committed to his Jewish roots. His philanthropy for Jewish causes was well known. But Judaism no longer satisfied his needs.

After seeing several prominent Jewish intellectuals and financiers convert to Catholicism, he flirted with the idea of becoming a Catholic. According to his biography *Man of Many Paths* (unauthorized but accurate), he was intrigued by Catholic rituals and the intricacies of its theology. But he was disgusted by revelations of sex abuse of young boys by priests. He decided to become a nondenominational Christian. As a guest of a leader of The Brethren, he attended the National Prayer Breakfast last year, where he met General Parker.

Miller may have been drawn to The Brethren because he could continue to support the cause of Israel's security while associating with powerful people who were able to influence world events.

Incidentally, Miller's biblical namesake, Hosea, seems to have a little joke attached. Hosea, at God's command, marries a harlot, in what was to be an example of God's relationship with the unfaithful nation of Israel. Hosea's harlot wife sleeps with another man and has a child whose father is unknown. Hosea divorces his wife, then takes her back. Miller had been divorced twice and had a daughter by his first wife. The daughter, Harriet, is now twenty years old and lives in Switzerland.

"Nice job on Miller," Dake said. "I have a hunch about him. But first let me give you a rundown on what I've got and what we have to do. Basically, we have five Brethren names picked up by the Israelis, who knew the five were up to something but didn't know what." He told of Falcone's suspicions that the men were somehow connected to the Savannah disaster and gave him a fast account of how the NEST experts blamed the explosion on a U.S. nuclear bomb.

"Broken arrow," Lassen said when Dake finished, unsurprised by Lassen's lack of visible reaction. Lassen digested, absorbed, summarized, and analyzed information, but he never allowed it to migrate from his reasoning brain cells to the cells that registered emotions.

"Broken arrow?" Dake asked.

"That's what the military calls lost nukes. Just think. There're enough of them to rate an official code name."

"Well, this is one arrow that was shot. Our job is to find out who fixed it and how," Dake said, turning to his keyboard. His fingers moved as swiftly as they did when he sat at a piano and played Chopin's *Revolutionary Étude,* one of his favorite pieces. He copied what he had written over to one of Lassen's monitors and the two of them read in silence:

Norman Miller. Sounds like banker to project. Biblical name Hosea.

Parker (Amos). Leader. Gets cryptic cell-phone calls from untraceable phone. Has expensive, sophisticated bug-proof room on second floor.

Albert Morton, ex-Navy (Jonah). Was captain of nuke sub that carried SEALS for Special Operations Command. Founder of Lodestone, think tank with DOD contracts.

Ed Hudson (Malachi). Ex-Special Forces. Commercial diver. Lives in Morgan City, Louisiana.

Dr. Michael Schiller (Micah). Nuclear expert, Department of Energy. Wife ex-Stanfield staffer. About to become vice president of a lobbying outfit for nuclear power plants.

"Interesting bunch," Lassen said. "As a researcher, I'm impressed. I can see how the Israelis could get a lot of this with bugs and taps. But you said those guys used their biblical names at the meetings that the Israelis bugged. So how come we have the real names?"

"The Israelis also had outside surveillance. Got the real names from license numbers—Miller's Mercedes, Hudson's Harley, Morton's SUV, which had vanity Virginia plates: ADMIRAL."

"And Schiller?"

"Used the Metro to Capitol South station. Clandestine photos. Schiller was still wearing his DOE ID tag. I think they may have had more on him but didn't give it to me. I assume that the Israelis don't talk about keeping a very close watch on nuclear weapons scientists at DOE and elsewhere in the U.S."

"Okay," Lassen said. "What's the plan?"

"The Mossad routinely got their addresses and their landline and cell-phone numbers. Call them. Try to rattle them. See what they might drop."

"So you buy Falcone's idea that these guys somehow set off the bomb?"

"Yes, I do."

"Jesus, Phil! It just doesn't make sense. These guys may be fundamentalist nuts. But they aren't terrorists."

"Well, let's find out. You take Schiller and Morton. I'll take Miller and Hudson," Dake said, looking at his watch. "Let's see what we can get in two hours."

"Record?" Lassen asked. Spotted around the room were four cubicles containing phones and Skype Web cameras. The phones were all connected to audiovisual equipment that recorded and stored conversations and videos. Lassen and the other researchers were under strict orders to obey various privacy laws by recording only with permission.

"Record without permission this one time," Dake said, adding with a sly smile, "in the name of national security."

Dake went off to one cubicle, Lassen to another.

58

When Falcone returned to the White House, Anna told him that J. B. Patterson had taken personal command of the examination of the *Regal* digital images. "He's in the EOB with Tony Knox," she reported. "Set up what he called a crime command center in the Vice President's ceremonial office. Max gave him permission. He got a kick out of his office being commandeered by the FBI."

Falcone again took the tunnel to the EOB and found Patterson amid Victorian splendor, sitting on one of the spindly legged, gold-cushioned chairs around a long table. Illuminating the room were multibranched chandeliers that were replicas of gaudy gasoliers: gas globes on top, electric lights below. Behind Patterson was a huge black marble fireplace with a gilded mantle. Ornamental stenciling and marine symbols adorned the walls and ceiling. In the nineteenth century, the room was the office of the Secretary of the Navy. Now it was the ceremonial office of the Vice President.

Computer monitors were glowing in a room where a typewriter had once been a novelty. Next to Patterson, Tony Knox was squinting at an oversized monitor connected to a black metal case and a device that looked like a miniature sound-mixer console. Cables snaked down the highly polished table to other monitors being watched by four young men and women in blue windbreakers emblazoned with FBI in yellow.

Patterson rose and greeted Falcone. "There's something else, Sean. Somebody also gave Ned Winslow an FBI document. He gave it up when our agents questioned him. Said it came to him with the report on the Iranians. It's got to be leaked by someone in the Bureau. A Brethren bastard, I assume." He handed Falcone a sealed manila envelope marked FBI CLASSIFIED. "Seems a passenger on the *Regal* sent a message *from the ship* about seeing suspicious characters. The passenger's name was Flanagan, Patrick Flanagan."

"That's terrific, J. B.," Falcone said, holding up the envelope. "It absolutely proves that the man who took the photo was definitely aboard the *Regal*."

"Well, I'm glad it makes you happy. I'm not happy

about having to track down a leaker at the Bureau. But the good news is that we're making tremendous progress on the photos." Like a master of ceremonies, he swept his arms to take in the people at the table. "I brought in some more techs from Quantico to speed things up." He nodded toward Knox. "Tony, tell Sean Falcone what's going on."

"First of all, I asked Director Patterson to send agents from the Boston office to Sergeant Flanagan and have her retransmit the images to this computer," Knox said, pointing to the black metal box. "That way I am not working with printouts. I got much, much better images. More important, I got what is called Exif, meaning exchangeable image file format. That's the name for the nonimage information contained in the image's data. By teasing Exif, I can extract date and time, the make and model of the camera, the shutter speed, and data indicating the sensitivity of the camera's digital imaging system.

"By having several separate images, I can deduce subtle bits of data that vary with each image. In this computer I am mimicking the camera's digital imaging system and essentially adding more power. I can enlarge and enhance. I can also cordon off sections of the image so that I can concentrate on part of the overall image. Here's what I mean." Knox pulled back so that Falcone could lean in and view the monitor.

At the lower left corner of the monitor was a miniature version of the original snapshot of a smiling Kathy Flanagan. The rest of the monitor contained a greatly enlarged image of the upper right portion of the snapshot: a murky silhouette of something not quite as black as the night sky surrounding it.

"Now watch," Knox said as he moved control levers.

The silhouette grew larger and sharper. It looked like the arm of a crane with a taut cable hanging from it. Knox touched the levers again, producing the illusion of the image shifting. Now on the monitor was a dim outline of what could be the bow of a ship. Floating inside the outline were spectral white letters: *J-A-M-A*.

"What do you make of it?" Falcone asked, his eyes on the screen.

"Jeanie," Knox called out. A woman on the other side of the table looked up.

"Copy me what you've got," he said, touching a lever. On the monitor appeared an overlay on the dim silhouette.

"Jeanie has extrapolated, adding an interpretation over the true image," Knox said. The overlay looked like a sharper version of the white lines that a TV weather forecaster draws over maps. Now the image was clearly the starboard bow of a ship, the arm of a crane with its cable in the water, and something emerging. *J-A-M-A* was also sharper.

Falcone turned to Patterson and said, "We've got to talk, J. B." Falcone walked down the long room and stood in front of the second ornate fireplace. Patterson followed. "You saw that image, J. B. Would you say that it looked like a crane hauling something out of the sea?"

"Yes, looks that way, doesn't it?" Patterson said, sounding puzzled.

"J. B., I've been keeping very close some information that I received from the head of NEST in Savannah," Falcone said. He went on to tell Patterson about the U.S. nuclear bomb off Savannah.

"My God, Sean!" Patterson said. "Why didn't—? Never mind. You're Lone Rangering this. But, you're right. It *does* look like something being lifted out of the water. And, of course, Tony and Jeanie did not have prior knowledge. Still"—a note of caution cut into his voice—"still, this isn't forensic. We can't prove—"

"Forget proof, J. B. We need an active investigation, starting with *J-A-M-A*."

"Right. I'll get people on this immediately. It shouldn't take long to get the name of every ship whose name begins with those letters. And then find it and—"

"If what I assume happened," Falcone said, "that ship does not exist anymore."

"Of course. Okay. We'll throw everything we have at identifying it, tracking down the owners." He pulled a cell phone from a holster on his belt. "Director here. Get me Deutermann." After a moment's pause, Patterson added, "Meet me in my office in ten minutes."

Patterson holstered the phone, saying to Falcone, "Assistant Deputy Director Henry Deutermann is running the Savannah investigation—under my direct supervision. Luckily he came back to headquarters this morning to brief me. Ray Quinlan wants all we've got. For the President, when he—"

"Tell Deutermann what I just told you. But keep it away from Quinlan. I want the chain of command to be you-to-me-to-the-President. I'm as anxious as Ray to help the President at the joint session tonight. But I must be the only one handling the Savannah bomb information. Got it?"

"Not quite, Sean. My boss is Attorney General Roberta Williams. And I'm in law enforcement. My job is to bring in criminals so they can be put on trial. I can't follow your kind of chain of command. I will do my job. And I will keep you informed. Period."

"Okay, J. B. We play it your way. But please tell me about that ship as soon as you get anything solid. And one more thing. Very sensitive. That last image, the one that is all bright light?"

"What about it? Tony gave it a pass. Says it looks like a malfunction of some type."

"Before you head back to headquarters, tell Tony to e-mail that image to me, and tell him to give me its day and time data."

Shortly after Falcone returned to his office, the image arrived. He immediately called Lanier.

"Something has come up, Rube."

"So I see," Lanier responded. "GNN's calling it a constitutional crisis."

"Well, yes. A crisis in a crisis," Falcone said. "I've got something else. I'm sending you a digital image, a photograph taken by someone aboard the *Regal*. The last of a series of snapshots. All it shows is a brilliant light. Can you please see what you and your deployable lab can do with it?"

"Brilliant light? My God!"

"Right. Now, something else. Ever hear of a Dr. Michael Schiller?"

"Sure. Met him a few times. Didn't know him personally. Worked in DOE's Los Alamos National Laboratory. Last I heard he was transferred to DOE in Washington. What's up? I can get some more information if you want. I have general access to personnel information. But—"

"Was he involved in weapons development?"

"I believe so."

"Get me what you can—as fast as you can."

Dake decided to call Hudson first. He Googled Morgan City, Louisiana. It was about seventy miles west of New Orleans and called itself the gateway to the Gulf of Mexico in the hunt for the Gulf's shrimp and offshore oil.

"My name is Philip Dake. I'd like to talk to Ed Hudson," he said to the woman who answered the phone.

"So would I," the woman said. "I'm his wife and I'd like to know where the hell he is." She paused. "You don't sound like the guy who calls him. You from Washington?"

"Yes."

"Well, I guess you don't know where he is, either."

"That's right. When did you last see him?"

"About ten, twelve days ago. He called me every day or so, from Washington, I guess. Said he was on a diving job in Chesapeake Bay. Haven't heard from him for . . . let's see . . . four days, yeah, four days ago."

"Oh," Dake said, keeping his voice calm. "Well, I'd like to leave my number for him to call . . . when he gets back. Thank you." He gave her his number and hung up.

Michael Schiller answered the phone on the first ring.

"Good afternoon, Doctor. My name is Mark Lassen and—"

"I am very busy. I do not know you."

"This is just a routine call, Doctor."

"What is this about?" Schiller asked. Lassen thought he sounded nervous.

"I am calling for the *Washington Post*."

"Wh . . . what is this about?" Schiller repeated.

"It's about your meetings with General George Parker—who called himself Amos, I believe. You were known as Micah, interesting name. And Albert Morton, or Jonah. And a diver named Malachi, or Hudson. And—"

"Enough! Enough!" Schiller hung up.

Lassen called him back immediately, getting only a busy signal. Assuming that Schiller's phone was off the hook, Lassen called Albert Morton, who lived not far away, in Falls Church, Virginia. A male voice answered.

"I am calling for Albert Morton," Lassen said. "Captain Morton?"

"This is his son, Albert Morton, Junior. Do you have news?"

"Not exactly," Lassen said.

"I thought you were the Coast Guard," Morton Junior said. "I reported . . ."

"Oh, yes," Lassen said, taking a chance, "the report that Captain Morton is missing."

"Any news?"

"Actually, I was calling for any further information you might have. The name of the boat, for instance?"

"I'm sorry, sir. As I said when I called, I don't know the name of the boat. All he said was that he would be away on a friend's boat for a few days. That's all my mother and I know."

"Thank you, Mr. Morton," Lassen said. "Sorry to bother you."

Lassen ran to Dake's cubicle just as Dake hung up on Schiller.

"Phil, we've got to call the Coast Guard," he said, rapidly repeating the conversation with Morton's son.

"No. Better to call Falcone. He'll be able to get a faster

response," Dake said, turning back in the cubicle and dialing Falcone's cell phone.

Falcone put in a call directly to Admiral Mason aboard the *Trumbull* on the assumption that the commandant of the Coast Guard would get the information faster than a mere national security advisor.

Minutes after Falcone pocketed the cell phone, Lanier called.

"Something interesting, Sean. Schiller did work at Los Alamos in weapon development. He was transferred, rather abruptly, to Washington right after a serious incident at the Los Alamos lab. I'm sending you an e-mail over what they tell me is a secure line."

Falcone had turned his office into his version of a crime command center. Mae had found a large square table and had it set up in the middle of the office. Around them, at laptops, sat Mae, Anna Dabrowski, Jeffrey Hawkins, and James Annaheim, the analyst from the National Geospatial-Intelligence Agency who had worked with Falcone on the night of the Savannah disaster. There was also a White House communications technician at a laptop and a phone console. Periodically, Falcone dropped off a piece of paper or talked to one of the tablemates. They were gathering the ingredients for what Falcone envisioned as the narrative of discovery that would be presented to the President before he headed off to Capitol Hill.

60

Norman Miller's grand home in Potomac looked like a Venetian doge's palace that had been transported to a Maryland hill. The mansion, full of excessive splendor, looked over the Potomac River and was surrounded by five acres of the most expensive real estate in suburban Washington. A six-foot fence of wrought-iron pickets surrounded the property. A driveway curved up to the front door from the gatehouse security post at River Road, the two-lane highway that ran from Potomac to Washington.

Behind the mansion's facade of limestone handmade bricks were both a regal residence and a modern office complex, the headquarters of Miller's creation, the private equity firm that he had named True North. Its five employees parked their cars behind the mansion. Nearby was the entrance of an underground garage, where Miller tinkered over vintage cars from the collection at his Florida home.

Miller was working on the fluid-drive transmission of a green 1950 DeSoto when his cell phone rang. He, like many cell-phone users, believed that few people knew his number. He did not recognize the number on the phone's identification screen.

"Mr. Norman Miller?"

"Who is this, please?"

"My name is Philip Dake. I work for the *Washington Post*."

"Look, you've done enough coverage of True North. Whatever your question is, my answer is 'No comment.'"

"This is not about True North, Mr. Miller. It's about

your meetings with General George William Parker, also known as Amos, and Albert Morton, whom you also may know as Jonah, a commercial diver named Hudson, or Malachi, and—"

To Miller's churning mind came a memory: a poker game in his Dartmouth dorm. He had scooped up fifty-four dollars and seventy-five cents with a pair of eights. His roommate later told him that he had thrown in a hand that contained three kings. Miller always considered this the beginning of his high-risk, high-gain career.

"Look, can I call you back?"

"Yes, in fifteen minutes. Otherwise we will have to go with what we have."

"Which is?"

Dake, deciding to take a chance, replied, "What we have is that you and fellow members of The Brethren were involved in the detonation of a nuclear bomb at the mouth of the Savannah River."

After a short pause, Miller said, "Where do you live?"

"Why?"

"I want to talk to you man-to-man."

"Why? To make a deal?"

"Please give me your address. . . . I can certainly find it."

"Yes, you can. And you can send somebody with an AK-47."

"How much do you know about me, Dake?"

"The usual publicly known information. Plus a lot of knowledge about Hosea and his friends."

"Yes. I am somewhat of a public man, Dake. And whether you admit it or not, I am sure you are recording this conversation. I kill you, I am in big trouble."

"Well, yes. But, you kill me, I am dead."

"I think we should talk, Dake. Where are you?"

Dake gave his address, thought for a moment about calling Falcone, and decided to wait until he heard what Miller had to say.

Lanier's e-mail arrived about twenty minutes after Falcone spoke to him:

A couple of years ago, an enormous wildfire came dangerously close to the Los Alamos National Laboratory, which was evacuated. Afterward, officials discovered the disappearance of a hard drive that was being created for NEST. The hard drive reappeared about two weeks later. In the DOT investigation that followed, several staff members were either involuntarily retired or transferred. Schiller was transferred to DOT Washington. Nothing negative appeared on his record. He's 63 years old and about to retire. He is expected to become a vice president of a Washington-based trade organization called Nuclear Renaissance.

Falcone immediately called Lanier. "Thanks much, Rube," Falcone said. "I have only one question: What was on that hard drive?"

Lanier took a moment to answer. "All I can tell you," he said, speaking slowly, "is that one of our tools is a continually updated hard drive that contains everything known about disarming various nuclear weapons."

"Would reverse engineering be possible?"

"You said one question. My answer to your second question is, Yes, probably. Schiller has that kind of knowledge. Even saying that over the phone could put me in Leavenworth. Anything more on that will have to be in a highly secure environment. Now, about that photo with the big flash. . . ."

"Yes?"

"Liz couldn't get anything meaningful about the light spectrum in that flash. Anecdotally, it looks like what you think it is. But here's one fact for you: The time stamp is within the *minute* that we calculate it happened. Don't forget. We deal in nanoseconds and the image time stamp deals in hours and minutes. So we don't have anything definitive. There's nothing forensic here."

"Understood. Thanks," Falcone said, about to hang up.

"One thing more. Remember I told you that all we have on surface water blasts are some reports from a test back in the forties? I looked at an image from that test. In the mushroom cloud are bits of the ships that it blew sky-high. In the image you sent me I thought I could see . . . I don't know . . . something. Maybe debris."

Falcone scribbled a few lines on a yellow pad and handed that and a printout of Lanier's email to Anna Dabrowski, who had given herself the task of preparing a rough draft of what Falcone called The Narrative.

Falcone had given J. B. Patterson a deadline of 5:30. Patterson called at 5:20. "Here's what we have," he said. "Two agents assigned to putting together a time line noted that the *Regal* would need a pilot. They found the port's chief pilot, Craig Reynolds, on Tybee Island. He was on the side of the island that was not hit as hard as the part near the mouth of the river. His son Michael was the *Regal*'s pilot and is presumed lost. Reynolds says that he had noted a ship anchored off the river mouth for about a week. He worried about it maybe interfering with navigation. And—get this—he reported it to the Coast Guard. Its name was *Jamaica Star."*

"Great stuff, J. B.," Falcone said. "What do we know about the ship?"

"We're working that very hard, Sean. The Coast Guard station was wiped out, but Reynold's query produced a report that got copied to Coast Guard headquarters in DC. Essentially it says the captain of the ship, a Jamaican, had an underwater archaeology permit to search for a Civil War submarine—the *Alligator,* lost while it was being towed in 1863. The day before the explosion, the Coast Guard, suspecting some kind of drug deal, started an investigation of the ship. It seems that the *Alligator* did not go down anywhere near Savannah."

"The ship is registered in Jamaica?"

"Yes. But have you ever tried to find the owner of a merchant ship? We're in phase one of that. There are corporations within corporations, documents scattered all over the place."

"Understood. Thanks, J. B. Thanks much."

61

Dake was on the phone. "I need you to come out to my house immediately," he told Falcone. "I have something . . . someone you need to talk with . . ."

"One of The Five?"

"Maybe the biggest interview I have ever had. He knows a lot—a helluva lot—about Savannah . . . I can't say more . . . You need to talk to him."

"Jesus, Phil. You sure about this guy? I've got—"

"I don't deal with fools or flakes. You know that. He's real, Senator, and . . . he's got answers."

Falcone caught *Senator*. Dake was calling him Senator again. Meaning, as he said before, that Dake was still dealing with how Falcone was running the world, over-seeing matters of life and death. . . .

"Okay, I'll be there in twenty to twenty five minutes. But this better be good. I don't have much time."

"Come alone," Dake said. "This guy is real spooked and he doesn't want any witnesses. Not until he gets what he wants."

"Which is?"

"Just come alone, Senator. And hurry."

Falcone went to the square table in the center of his office and said to Dabrowski, "I need to talk to you, Anna. I need to slip out of here and I have to move fast."

"You've been pushing yourself awfully hard, Sean. When a man is in a hurry, the devil is happy."

"I've heard that one from you many times. But, believe me, the devil is not going to be happy if I get what I think I'm going to get. I need your car. In the secure lot?"

"Yes. Here are the keys. It's a 1996 Pontiac Firebird Convertible. You can work a six-speed stick shift?"

"Yes, Anna. And I promise to drive carefully."

Falcone called his security detail and asked for a stand-down while he dealt with a personal emergency. He found Anna's Firebird in the West Wing parking area, made his way to Constitution Avenue, crossed the Potomac on the Theodore Roosevelt Bridge, headed north to the Capital Beltway, and, enjoying the speed and ride of the Firebird, took the exit to Georgetown Pike and, relying on Dake's hurried directions, managed to find the McLean cul-de-sac where Dake lived.

Dake opened the door and brought Falcone into the living room. Norman Miller sat in a brown leather chair, a wineglass in his right hand. He looked calm and haughty—the stone face that had launched countless deals negotiated at the edge of the law. He put the wineglass down on an end table, taking care to place it on a coaster that bore a compass rose. He reached out his hand, but Falcone did not take it.

Falcone took a recorder out of a suit-coat pocket, placed it on the end table next to Miller's chair, and said, "Talk."

"Oh, not again," Miller said. "I've just poured it all out to Dake. That's why he called you. He's got a recorder, too."

"Talk," Falcone repeated.

"Very well," Miller said. He looked toward Dake, who picked up a bottle and poured another drink.

"Thank you," Miller said to Dake, then looked up to Falcone. "It was called Operation Cyrus. The plan was to pull up the '58 bomb, put it aboard the ship, and sail it through the Straits of Hormuz to Bandar Abbas, a port that is the main base of the Iranian Navy. Parker said that the Brethren higher-up directing him had Iranian connections and shipping connections, and we'd be able to dock without any trouble.

"The captain would claim that the ship had engine trouble and request aid. It was all supposed to be fixed. The captain and crew—all Jamaicans—would slip off the ship at night, along with Schiller, Morton, and Hudson. They'd be driven to Tehran. Next morning, the bomb would explode, destroying the port. The Iranians would blame either Israel or the United States—or both. And Armageddon would begin. This is very good wine."

"Did you really think this would work?" Falcone asked. He felt an urge to strangle Miller.

"You know, I had the same doubt," Miller replied. "Then I pictured Osama bin Laden planning nine-eleven and being asked the same thing."

"What went wrong?" Falcone asked.

"A lot depended upon Schiller. He was, I think, even more of a fanatic than Parker. Schiller said he had figured out how to rearm the Savannah bomb. He had been a weapons developer and—"

"Schiller stole a hard drive from Los Alamos," Falcone said. "Is that the start of it? Does he have any other plans to use his expertise?"

"I don't have any information about Schiller. I was strictly the banker, running money to finance the operation."

"Your money?"

"My God, no!" Miller smirked.

"Well, whose money then?

"I . . . I can't tell you that."

"Because you want to hold out one big negotiating point?"

"No. Because I can't. Let's table that for the moment."

" 'Table,' as in negotiations?" Falcone asked.

Miller did not respond to the question. But he talked on, telling how Morton, with his Navy and Pentagon connections, chartered the *Jamaica Star,* implying in his dealings that he was a contractor for a highly sensitive U.S. government operation. The ship, with Morton, Ed Hudson, Schiller, and the crew and captain on board, had spent a week in Chesapeake Bay, about an hour's drive from Washington. Off Solomons Island, in a secluded cove, they practiced retrieving, hitching, and raising the bomb.

"Parker made at least one visit to Solomons, I think," Miller said. "He thought that using a place named Solomons was part of God's plan."

"Did you go to Solomons Island? Did you board the ship?"

"Yes. Once. Parker had us all meet there, on the ship. About a week before . . . before—"

"Tell me about the meeting on the ship."

"Not much to tell. Schiller said that the tests had been successful. He said they were able to replicate what they would have to do in Savannah. He said that the bomb— the real bomb—was buried in silt at a depth of about forty feet. He knew an awful lot about that bomb. I got the impression that he had had access to very secret information. For the practice in the bay, for instance, they used a model built to Schiller's specifications."

"Who built the model?" Falcone asked. "Where is it?"

"I don't know the answers to either question. Don't forget, The Brethren has members and resources far beyond The Five, as Parker called us."

"So, Morton and Hudson were on the ship when it went down?"

"I assume so. Morton, Hudson, and Schiller were to transport the bomb. But Schiller, as I understand it, was about to get a lobbying job in Washington and didn't want to spend time away. And he didn't like being on the ship in Chesapeake Bay. Almost a phobia, I guess. So he was not going to board the ship until it was about to sail to Iran."

"How was he going to get to Savannah?" Falcone asked.

For the first time since the questioning began, Miller did not respond promptly. Falcone repeated the question.

"He was to fly down on my aircraft."

"The Gulfstream jet?"

"Yes."

"Where is it right now?"

"In a hangar at Manassas Regional Airport."

"Just outside the aerial exclusion zone around Washington."

"Also, a lot cheaper rental than a hangar at Dulles," Miller said, affecting a smile.

"Let's get back to Schiller. Tell me more about Schiller," Falcone said.

"Odd duck. Genius, I guess. He said he had prepared a device that replicated what he called the arming capsule. Theoretically, there was no arming capsule in the bomb when it was jettisoned."

"That's the official U.S. Air Force story," Dake said to Falcone. He sat down in a chair next to the fireplace and motioned Falcone to another. But Falcone remained standing, glaring down at Miller.

"So the plan was to haul up the bomb and insert Schiller's device?" Falcone asked.

"Yes, as I understand. As I told you—"

"Was Schiller to bring the device to Savannah on your Gulfstream?"

"No. Too risky. I assume it was loaded onto the ship at Solomons."

"We have information that the ship was off Savannah for a while, at least a week. Do you know why?" Falcone asked.

"No. Schiller was very guarded. But he did mention the detector he had put together for Hudson to use when he was looking for the bomb. Schiller claimed he knew the location within a few meters but needed a diver on the bottom to pinpoint the spot."

"Do you have any idea about what went wrong?"

"No. Except—"

"Except what?"

"All I could think of was electronics gone wrong. I tinker with cars. Imagine trying to hook up a twenty-first-century automotive computer to, say, a '58 Chevy Impala. If you didn't do it right, you might blow up the Chevy. In retrospect, that seemed to me the kind of risk that Schiller was taking."

"You never saw a drawing? Never saw anything on a piece of paper?"

"Correct," Miller said. "Now don't forget that Parker was an old hand at what he called black ops. Everything was need-to-know. I didn't need to know anything more than where to pick up and deliver the money. Lots of money. The bomb model alone cost two hundred thousand dollars. I put the money, in hundred-dollar bills, in a brown paper bag and took it to a seafood joint in Solomons. I watched a waterman pick it up and I left. I never saw the delivery of the model. Everything was compartmentalized. That's the way it worked."

"Ever hear of an archaeological cover for the operation?"

"Parker did mention that he and Morton had arranged a cover with the help of a Brethren member in archaeology. That's all I know about that."

"How about Stanfield?" Falcone asked. "How much did he know?"

"He knew nothing about the bomb. After it went off, I was told that there was a Plan B and—"

"Who told you?"

"Isaiah, the invisible head man. That was his code name."

"The name you refuse to give me."

"Correct. As usual," Miller continued, "a messenger delivered me a briefcase and a note telling me to deliver it to Parker. That was the system. A briefcase full of hundred-dollar bills delivered to me by a messenger, counted by me, and delivered by me to Parker or to a drop Parker sent me to. But this time the briefcase was locked. That seemed strange.

"The briefcase was easily opened. Inside, I saw a cell phone and two envelopes, one marked Amos—Parker's code name—and the other marked confidential. I steamed open the envelopes. The one for Amos told him to call a certain number, where someone would direct him to the person the confidential envelope was meant for. I later tried the number, which had been disconnected.

"The papers in the envelope were the *Regal*'s passenger manifest and a report on the removal of two Iranians from the ship. There was also some kind of report to the FBI about Muslims on the ship. When I saw Stanfield on television, I realized the purpose of the documents: make it appear the bomb had been on the *Regal*. He was duped into promoting Plan B."

Falcone had been taking notes. He looked down on the notes and started to speak when his cell phone rang. He pulled it out of his pocket and irritably said, "Falcone here."

"This is . . . Rachel. The Parker tap is still being monitored. I just got called about it. Apparently someone named Micah called Parker and said he had just been called by Dake. Micah said everything was coming apart and he couldn't live with what had been done. Then there was what sounded like a gunshot."

"Thanks, Rachel," Falcone said.

Stunned, Falcone gestured to Dake, who rose and joined Falcone in the hallway. "Schiller's probably dead," Falcone said. "I need to get the FBI there right away. You've got his address?"

"Mark—my researcher—has everything upstairs."

"Run up, get the address—and give it to Anna. Here's her number." Dake, never without a notebook and pen, jotted it down. "Tell her to have Patterson hit that address fast and seize every computer and communication device. Also, Miller's Gulfstream in Manassas. And, on my authority, have her tell Patterson to get a very broad, classified search warrant for Miller's house in Potomac."

Dake went up the stairs two at a time.

62

When Falcone returned to the living room, Miller was pouring himself another glass of wine. "Well, that's about it," Miller said, stretching out his legs as if to check the tassels on his Gucci loafers. "I had started making plans to permanently disappear. Then I got the call from Dake, and I realized that it was over . . . that the Oxley administration was putting pressure on me, figuring that I could be the unindicted co-conspirator. So that is why I am here."

"What exactly do you want, Mr. Miller?"

"My life—personal, professional—is falling apart," Miller said softly. "I had genuinely thought The Brethren could save me. I believed, truly believed, Mr. Falcone. Armageddon! I was ready to start Armageddon!

"About all I have, Mr. Falcone, is a lot of money and a daughter. I want to live where she is. Raise bees or something. Lay low with a new identity and never be seen in the United States again."

Falcone held up his cell phone and shook it, angrily saying, "I can get FBI agents here in ten minutes to arrest you for—"

"For what, Mr. Falcone? Conspiracy? You must know as well as I do that a conspiracy charge is very, very hard to even get an indictment for."

"You want to walk away as if you did not take part in a mass murder? How about three thousand counts of murder?"

"I have long respected you, Mr. Falcone. I'm surprised you'd engage in fantasy. All you have is whatever is in that recorder. I doubt that it will hold up in court all by itself. You are not a law-enforcement officer. I am not being formally interrogated."

Miller reached over, picked up the recorder, and switched it off. His arrogance returned as suddenly as it had momentarily disappeared.

"What I want, Mr. Falcone," Miller said, "is a document, signed by the President, allowing me to leave the country. I will have that in my pocket when I make the necessary arrangements to fly away, develop my new identity, and never return."

Falcone looked at his watch and said, "Assuming that such a document is feasible, what do I get?"

"Isaiah is very powerful. He warned me that if I ever revealed his name my daughter would be killed. I need a month to disappear. Thirty days from today you will receive Isaiah's name and whatever evidence I have to prove his guilt. What you do after that, is up to you. I will, to all intents and purposes, no longer be alive."

Falcone picked up the recorder, sat down in the chair, and did not speak for a full minute. *Morton dead. Hudson dead. Schiller dead. We pick up Parker, sweat him. The President gets his answers.*

"Okay, Miller. Here's the deal," Falcone said, looking at his watch again. "You will stay here until I tell you otherwise. I am heading from here directly to the White House. FBI agents have impounded your aircraft and are searching your home. If the President signs the document you requested, we will release your aircraft and you can carry out your plan.

"If I do *not* get Isaiah's name within thirty days, the wrath of the federal government will fall upon you. We will issue an international warrant for you on charges of masterminding the Savannah explosion. We will track down your daughter in Switzerland, and extradite and jail her for aiding a federal fugitive. We will seize every cent that you and True North possess from here to Singapore and Dubai. We will move in federal court to have you brought before a grand jury in Savannah. And you will enter that federal courthouse without the protection of U.S. marshals. That, Mr. Miller, is our side of the deal."

Dake had waited for Falcone to finish before entering the room. "I'm heading off, Phil," Falcone said, walking toward the hallway. "It's nearly time for the President to head for the Hill." He pointed to Miller. "He's staying here to wait for news from me. As for you, Phil, there's an embargo on everything that happened here today until I tell you. Agreed?"

"Agreed," Dake said as Falcone opened the door.

. . .

President Oxley was scratching out the speech he was going to deliver at the joint session. He had not summoned his speech writer. And there would be no teleprompter. This one was too personal—and, he was discovering, too hard to write. This was going to be from the heart.

The angry buzz from his telephone console jarred him out of his dark ruminations. He angrily answered with, "Damn it, Margie. I said no more—"

"It's Sean, Mr. President. He said it was urgent and I thought—"

"It's okay, Margie. Put him through."

"Mr. President, I need to see you now," Falcone said, speaking into his cell phone and speeding down the Georgetown Pike toward the Capital Beltway.

"I'm getting ready for the Hill, Sean."

"Don't leave before I speak with you. And I think I'll need the attorney general there, too. She may to have to draft a document."

"What in hell is going on, Sean? Where have you been? I tried to—"

"Answers, Mr. President. I have answers!"

"What? What answers?"

"Can't tell you on the phone. I'll be there in twenty . . . no, fifteen minutes."

"Sean, I can't wait. I have to leave. Congress—"

"Congress will wait, Mr. President. Just don't leave until I speak with you. I'll explain everything," Falcone said as he hit the Firebird's accelerator and swung into the Capital Beltway.

63

On the way to Capitol Hill, Oxley turned introspective. *How tremendous is the power of the president,* he thought in this rare moment of meditation. *How terrible as well. The power to heal or destroy. A minute might change the course of a speech or that of a missile . . .*

As the line of black, light-flashing limousines and SUVs sped up Constitution Avenue, Oxley marveled at the strange and the capricious ways that life unfolds. You think it's meaningless or you think you're driven by fate. But who said, "Control your fate or somebody else will?" And these men, these Brethren. How could men who loved this country and the doctrines of Christianity plan a mass murder? And what happened, what atoms went awry to produce catastrophe in the land they said they loved?

The phone in the car rang. It was Falcone, confirming Schiller's death—an apparent suicide—and reporting that FBI agents had surrounded the House of The Brethren.

Oxley's vehicle turned quickly off Constitution Avenue and passed through the barriers guarding the entrance to the Capitol. Oxley peeled open the small envelope Falcone had handed him just before they had walked out of the Oval Office. He was surprised that Falcone had declined his offer to ride with him to the Hill. But Falcone had begged off, saying that he had to get back to work finding more answers.

Oxley glanced quickly at the two lines Falcone had scrawled: *He may live long, he may do much. But here is the summit. He never can exceed what he does this day.*

A smile broke across Oxley's face as he contemplated

the words. He remembered reading John Kennedy's *Profiles in Courage* about Edmund Burke's eulogy to Charles James Fox. He hoped that he was worthy of the sentiment.

The limousine stopped. A Secret Service agent opened a door of military armor five inches thick. As Oxley exited, he looked up at the magnificent dome of the Capitol, one of the most beautiful and most recognizable pieces of architecture in the world. Sixty-two tons of steel, two hundred and eighty-eight feet high, topped off with the *Statue of Freedom*. He couldn't see *Freedom* in the darkness, but he had studied her so many times before, he knew her every line.

Her right hand rested on a sheathed sword while her left hand held the laurel wreath of victory and the shield of the United States. Oxley had always been fascinated by the history of her construction. Originally, Thomas Crawford, the sculptor, had planned to have *Freedom*'s head wear a liberty cap, a Roman symbol of an emancipated slave. But Mississippi Senator Jefferson Davis, an avowed slaveholder who would become president of the Confederacy, supervised the Capitol's construction. He was enraged when he saw the liberty cap and ordered it replaced with a military helmet and crest of feathers. . . .

Amazing, Oxley thought. *Old Jefferson Davis trying to erase the bloodstain of racism from our history. . . . I wonder what the old boy would say if he saw me walking into the Capitol, a free man and leader of the free world. . . .*

A Secret Service agent, seeing the President as a standing target, touched his arm gently and broke Oxley's momentary reverie. He nodded for Oxley to proceed to the center door of the Capitol. Wrapped in a tight cocoon by his heavily armed escort, Oxley moved quickly up the stairs and entered the Rotunda.

Once there, he paused again, taking in the architectural simplicity of the massive room, and then walked briskly down the corridor that led to Statuary Hall, where all of the major networks had staked out their cameras and crews so they could apprehend members of Congress eager to pass their comments on Oxley's speech.

The dark mahogany doors to the House Chamber parted and Oxley entered as the Sergeant at Arms bellowed, "Mr. Speaker, the President of the United States!"

Oxley could see that virtually every member of Congress was present. None dared to be seen on the campaign trail on such a momentous occasion. All stood and applauded as he strode toward the raised dais. There was none of the handshaking and hugs that usually marked a president's entrance and departure. Just respectful applause.

The Speaker officially greeted Oxley, which again produced an outburst of applause that was unusually brief. The traditional political battle lines had been drawn, but tonight little difference existed between those who had voted for Oxley and those who were determined to defeat him.

Sipping from a glass of water and clearing his throat, the President made a quick survey of all in the room. Members of the Supreme Court were present. So were the uniformed Joint Chiefs of Staff. Diplomats had not been invited and the visitors' galleries had been closed to the public. Security had never been as tight as it was tonight.

Because of a surge of death threats against the President, he had grimly decided to assure an orderly transition. "I want you out of the line of fire," Oxley laughingly told Max Cunningham, ordering him back to his undisclosed location. Everyone noticed that the seat next to the Speaker, where the Vice President normally sat, was empty.

"Mr. Speaker," Oxley began, thinking as he looked into all of the somber faces, *I hope to God, Falcone got this thing right.*

"I have been invited by the Congress to address you and the American people about the state of our nation. It is not about budgets or programs, but rather our nation's security, and our very survival.

"This is one of the most critical issues we have ever faced, certainly in recent history. During the past four days, ever since the terrible destruction took place in Savannah, Georgia, I have tried to keep you informed as best as possible under very difficult circumstances.

"There was great confusion at first. We received reports that a tsunami had struck our coast. As with most first reports, it proved to be in error. What destroyed much of the beautiful, historic city of Savannah, as we now know, was a nuclear bomb. . . ."

Oxley paused, casting his eyes from left to right, focusing on the faces of individual members. He easily picked out Senator Mark Stanfield's face. Stanfield stared back expressionless.

"As your commander-in-chief, charged with the duty to protect America and to vigorously respond to any attack upon our country, I have been relentless in the pursuit of the facts involved in this horrible event . . . to determine who could do such a terrible thing. And why.

"I am absolutely resolute in my determination to capture and punish those responsible. . . ." Oxley was hoping for applause, but it did not come. He still sounded like a law professor.

"Tonight, I am prepared to disclose to you, to the

American people, and those around the world, who per-petrated the attack, how they were able to do it and why.

"First, the bomb that exploded just four days ago was made in America."

Members turned to each other. Some audibly gasped.

"And those who caused the bomb to explode were Americans. Successful members of our society who oc-cupy positions of power and influence in our lives. I can only describe them as men of zeal, men who once were committed to principles, men who were once well-meaning, perhaps—men who meant no harm to their fel-low Americans. In their excessive and outrageous zeal, their blind devotion to a cause that was not rightfully theirs to pursue, they caused egregious, catastrophic harm to the very people they professed to protect."

Oxley systematically disclosed how this small band of zealots, whose religion had little to do with Christianity and everything to do with power, planned to retrieve the bomb ejected by a U.S. Air Force bomber in 1958 off the coast of Savannah, and transport it to the shores of Iran with the goal of detonating it there.

"Their plans went awry. As the bomb was being raised to the surface of the water, it suddenly exploded.

"Let me say that at this very moment, The FBI is in the process of arresting the leader of this small group of men—three of whom have died, two in the explosion they caused, and one apparently by his own hand. So as not to impede the FBI's ongoing investigation, I will not disclose any names at this time. They know who they are and they now know that we are coming for them.

"At this time, I also want to say to my friend, Senator Mark Stanfield *(my loathsome friend,* Oxley was think-ing), I know how strongly you feel about the threat that

Iran poses to us and to our allies. I share your view. I believe you were correct in suggesting that the two men who were taken off the cruise ship in Boston were no mere sightseers. They were Iranian operatives who, we believe, were making a trial run on a cruise ship to assess a serious weakness in our security system.

"You assumed that the cruise ship was carrying a nuclear weapon. It was not an unfair assumption . . . but it was a false one. This does not diminish in any way the threat that Iran poses to us and the free world. What it does do, however, is offer us a lesson that we must always remain dedicated to the pursuit of facts—and not be guided by phantom or false leads . . . leads that can cause some to take action that will harm our nation for generations to come."

The heads turning toward Stanfield made a rustling sound. Stanfield looked straight ahead, again showing no expression. But his neck and face started to flush. He knew Oxley's spear had just landed in his chest.

"There's another lesson for each of us willing to listen and learn. We must do everything in our power to rid ourselves—*responsibly* rid ourselves—of these terrible weapons. These weapons that, as Winston Churchill said, 'we must beware, lest the Stone Age return upon the gleaming wings of science.'

"For too long we have held the notion that these are just bigger, more powerful arrows that we hold in our military's quiver. It is nonsense. They are weapons that one day will lead to the total destruction of all that we cherish and hold dear.

"What happened in Savannah was just a small sample of their destructive power. Today's nuclear weapons are of such size and power that they will turn the earth into a wasteland. Where birds do not fly. Where fish do not swim. Where people do not live. . . .

"I ask all of you here, and those who are watching, to join in the effort to call upon all nations that have nuclear weapons to begin the process of eliminating them. And all nations that are pursuing nuclear weapons to abandon their goals.

"President Kennedy reminded us so many years ago, that we hold in our hands 'the power to abolish all forms of human poverty or all forms of human life.'

"Let us make the wise choice, Mr. Speaker. The right choice.

"Thank you. And God bless America."

Epilogue

It was unusually warm for a November evening, allowing Falcone to step out in shirtsleeves onto the large terrace of his apartment. His favorite libation in hand, Falcone surveyed the magnificent panorama he enjoyed from his terrace. The Washington Monument, Capitol Hill, the Justice Department . . . He was convinced that global warming was real and not a fabrication of hot-eyed environmentalists.

But just three days ago, a cold snap whipped through Washington, dumping four inches of snow onto the traffic-clogged streets. Predictably, critics of man-made weather catastrophes ridiculed the notion that the planet was heating up.

The weather didn't make much sense, but as Rachel had reminded him on leaving his office, not much did these days.

Three weeks had passed since Oxley had delivered his speech on Capitol Hill. It hit the Congress and the country like the bomb that had destroyed Savannah. Most members were stricken speechless, so much so that they avoided the cameras that lay in wait for them in Statuary Hall.

They needed time to think about the folly of their plan

to issue a declaration of war and move to impeach Oxley if he refused to attack Iran. But some were brazen enough to express total rejection of the President's account of what happened. They rushed to the microphones of friendly broadcasters who shared the belief that Oxley had lied to the American people and had engaged in a bizarre cover-up of an Iranian-sponsored attack on America.

Those expressing disbelief were a minority, but, sadly, there were millions of people who would believe them. Partisan political talk-show hosts, crazed bloggers, political misanthropes, paranoids and psychopaths, or just plain Oxley haters—all enjoyed equal access to the new social media, a force powerful enough to sweep out governments across the globe. . . .

Philip Dake had filed a blockbuster story in the *Washington Post,* under the sensational headline: U.S. DESTROYED SAVANNAH.

Falcone had smiled when he read the story online just after midnight. There was not a word about The Brethren, although Dake divulged considerable details of how the plan had been conceived and how its execution had been so horribly mangled. At the request of the Justice Department he omitted the names of the individuals involved until the men were in custody.

Falcone was not completely surprised. Dake was being true to his particular tradecraft. He was going to make a major book out of what he knew, and why take all the air out of the sails with a full disclosure in a daily paper? Maybe Falcone was being too cynical. Dake was crucial to breaking the story, and maybe he didn't want to see Oxley's campaign get swamped by storms of protest that would blow across the country. The protesters would claim that Oxley had indicted the Christian faith itself instead of the small group of zealots who perverted the Christian religion in the pursuit of absolute power.

There were hints, disconnected references buried in the bottom of the story, just enough to tease the readers and make them wonder whether there were more levels to the truth of what really happened. *Post* editors had given Dake all the room he had wanted. They knew someday soon they'd be running a six-part series once the inevitable book was published.

Overnight polling showed that Mark Stanfield's numbers had dropped after Oxley's speech. Oxley didn't gain much. The people were still angry that it all had happened on his watch, but hell, that was all part of the game. . . .

The morning after the President's address. Falcone had risen from his cot and found J. B. Patterson's signed report on his desk. On Falcone's orders, the FBI released Norman Miller's private jet. Miller, surrounded by a phalanx of bodyguards, boarded the plane and flew off. His pilot had filed a flight plan for Montreal, where he boarded a chartered airliner flying to Zurich.

An FBI Critical Incident Response Team had stormed the house when Parker refused to emerge. Fighting off arrest, he broke an agent's nose. He was put in a restraining jacket and placed under military guard at Fort Myer, near the Pentagon. A search of Parker's home produced computers and evidence that the house "had been bugged and the phones tapped by unknown parties."

Schiller apparently shot himself with a .22-caliber semiautomatic Beretta found at his side. Investigators were analyzing the contents of his computer and hard drives hidden in his home.

There were other Brethren still buried in high places. There had to be. How did Senator Mark Stanfield get word so quickly about the change in the DEFCON status after the attack on the *Elkton*? Who fed Stanfield the information about the Iranians carrying false passports aboard the *Regal* . . . ?

But what troubled Falcone the most was Midas. Who was he? Did he mastermind Operation Cyrus or just fund it? Did he have other plans, other people in place?

Falcone called Rachel, reminding her that she had promised to reveal the identity of Midas. Once again she demurred, saying that she had not heard from her superiors and would let him know as soon as possible.

The following day, the *New York Times* and *Washingon Post* published major stories about the death of billionaire Rolf Eriksen in his family's Connecticut mansion.

"Mr. Eriksen's mother found the body and called the family physician," the *Times* story said. "The physician, a family spokesman said, certified the cause of death as heart failure. The body was removed by a local funeral home and cremated before Southport police could begin a routine 'untimely death' investigation. A police spokesman said that since the physician was not in attendance at the time of death, his certification of death by heart failure was 'irregular but legal.' "

The *Post* story quoted anonymous financial observers as speculating that Eriksen had killed himself with a drug overdose after learning he was under investigation by a private investment counselor for diverting funds from his mother's company, Eriksen Inc. "Betsy Eriksen did not like trouble," one source said. "Cremation avoided it."

After reading the stories, Falcone called the Hay-Adams and learned that Rachel had checked out. He had Anna make an official call to the Israeli United Nations delegation. Anna was told that Ambassador Yeager had been recalled to Israel.

Falcone found himself wondering often about where and who Norman Miller was. The CIA and NSA had kept a tight watch on Miller until, one day, he vanished. But in some strange way, Falcone believed that Miller would keep his word and disclose the identity of the man who had conceived and funded Operation Cyrus.

Falcone knew it was Rolf Eriksen. It had to be.

He had asked for the CIA's analysis of the sudden death of a Hamas assassin in Dubai. "The drug used," the analysis said, "was probably a large dose of succinylcholine, which produces asphyxia and death due to muscular paralysis."

Falcone imagined Rachel, up to her old Killer Angel tricks, gaining easy access to Stonemill, perhaps paying a social call on Betsy Eriksen, dropping into Rolf's library to say hello . . . and rushing up to find Betsy and say that Rolf had keeled over . . . Betsy summoning a doctor, a distraught Rachel being chauffeured back to New York, then whisked away to Israel. . . .

Maybe Dake knew the answer. Maybe he was saving the secret to make sure he had another blockbuster. Maybe it was Falcone's fate to never know.

But that was no longer his concern. The people were going to the polls tomorrow to vote for their presidential candidate. The attack on Savannah had shaken confidence in Oxley and it was still possible he could lose.

Falcone hoped not.

America was in need of men like Oxley if it was ever going to deal with the challenges that were infinite in number and complexity. The only thing he absolutely knew was that he was packing his bags. He had given his last service to his country and was determined to move on to a life of personal freedom.

AUTHOR'S NOTE

This is a work of fiction and all of the characters and events are the product of the author's imagination. There is one exception, though: the bomb that is central to the story is real. On February 5, 1958, a U.S. Air Force F-86 fighter collided with a B-47 on a simulated combat mission. The pilot of the B-47 jettisoned one of America's first hydrogen bombs off Savannah's coast.

The Air Force searched for more than nine weeks but failed to find the bomb.

Responding to persistent fears of local people and an inquiry from a congressman, the Air Force in 2001 issued a thirteen-page report that reiterated what had been said in 1958: "The bomb was incapable of a nuclear explosion." The Department of Energy, according to the report, "determined that there is no current or future possibility of a nuclear explosion."

The Air Force report can be found at http://www.nukestrat.com/us/afn/AF2001_Savannah1958.pdf.

ACKNOWLEDGMENTS

I'm frequently asked how long it takes me to write a novel. The clever answer I offer is, "A lifetime." Publishers are not impressed with cleverness, and their tolerance for procrastinators is not unlimited.

I've been blessed to know Tor/Forge's Tom Doherty, who nearly two years ago, along with editor and author par excellence Bob Gleason, asked me to write a fictional account of a subject that consumed my waking days and sleepless nights at the Pentagon. Fortunately, both tolerated my extensive international travels and logistical excuses—up to a point. Once they advised me that my novel was listed in the 2011 fall catalogue of Tor/Forge publications, my ruses were up. The hammer had fallen, and I could no longer run out the clock or escape their e-mails that oh-so-gently asked, "So when did you send in the manuscript?"

I am indebted to Tom Allen, historian, author, and friend, whom I've had the pleasure to know and admire for more than thirty years. Tom has been a great mentor and constant source of sage advice and encouragement. He is a veritable fountainhead of information and wisdom—the possessor, no doubt, of a Jesuit education—and rivals Google in the speed and depth of content produced in response to any question I have, however minor or seemingly unrelated it may be to the arc of the novel's narrative or that of its characters

A salute goes to General Joseph Ralston (Ret.), the former vice chairman of the Joint Chiefs of Staff, and former Supreme Allied Commander Forces Europe, who zeroed in on the literary license I took and made sure that I was not too far off target.

Admiral Jim Loy, the former commandant of the U.S. Coast Guard, and deputy secretary of Homeland Security, helped steer me clear of some dangerous, subsurface obstacles that I had failed to anticipate.

Craig Kelly, former ambassador to Chile, a baseball aficionado, called balls and strikes (with diplomatic gusto) on key elements in the story line. I am also indebted to Nicholas Burns, former ambassador to NATO and Greece, and currently a professor at Harvard, who has a jeweler's eye for detail and factual accuracy.

My sincere thanks to Dean Graham Allison, who is a prominent expert on the threat posed by nuclear weapons. I relied heavily on his seminal work, *Nuclear Terrorism: The Ultimate Preventable Catastrophe,* and drew in particular on examples of the lapses in security contained in pages 3–6, 46–49.

In the interest of full disclosure, General Ralston, Admiral Loy, and Ambassadors Craig Kelly and Nick Burns are also colleagues of mine at The Cohen Group. Rest assured, however, that they remained loyal to their professional code of honor and pulled no verbal punches!

I benefited greatly from discussions with former colleague Frank Miller, an expert in all matters related to nuclear weaponry. Frank has spent most of his life worrying about and managing the metrics of throw weights, pay loads, and the dangerous consequences of strategic imbalances in nuclear weapons.

While time and distance frequently separate us, I remain inspired by the talent, friendship, and motivational support offered by brilliant novelist Richard North Patterson, who throughout his personal and professional career has never blinked while staring into the white light of controversial moral issues.

I have borrowed liberally from the thoughts and insights of Gabe Erem, one of the most extraordinary men I know, whose knowledge of strategic issues and the dangerous back alleys of Middle East politics is unparalleled.

Finally, the person I turn to for intellectual balance and penetrating logic is my wife, Janet Langhart Cohen, author, playwright, and force of nature who was once described as "a cupcake—with a razor blade inside." Indeed, Janet is the alter ego of the character Rachel, and the reason I dedicated the novel to Velvet, who is smooth, beautiful, and dangerous.